THE VOIDSTALKER EXTRACTION

THE VOIDSTALKER EXTRACTION

TRIPLE C REPORTS
BOOK 1

LIV EVANS

JAY THOMAS

Skip It Publishing

Ship It Publishing

The Voidstalker Extraction
First published by Ship It Publishing in 2022
ISBN 9780645611502

© 2022 Ship It Publishing

For any enquiries please visit www.shipitpublishing.com

Cover: Ivan Zanchetta (www.bookcoversart.com)

Editing: Tracy Kisgen (www.trkisgen.com)

Special thanks to Treece Stubbs, Ellen Escobido, Lolet Johnson, and Danelle
Escobido for the translation.

For the nerdy older brothers who instilled a love of all things sci-fi in their pesky younger siblings.
Xx Liv & Jay

THE OPS ROOM onboard the Latagarosh was quiet as it orbited a sleepy planet called Baldalan in an unclaimed sector of the Void. The glow of a dozen holographic projectors, dotted around the room, illuminated the faces of three tired and bored Operations staff members as the lights on their headsets blinked their steady, standby rhythms. Until the scouting team on the planet broke radio silence, there was little the Ops staff could do but monitor their own stats.

As Martin Englethorpe, one of the officers, kept an eye on his allocation of the output, he remembered the saying he had heard when first joining the renowned Triple C: "If Operations Specialists have time to get bored, it means more pilots come home alive." He had never worked on a mission with a casualty. They didn't happen often in this company. So, even though he could barely keep his eyes open, Martin was glad for the quiet.

"Okay, Scout Wing. Top three most fuckable ..." began the specialist beside Martin, as he smoothed his sleek blond hair back against his head and grinned.

"Norgard, this isn't the time," chastised Hermedilla, the man to Norgard's right. Martin had only worked with him once before, but clearly, he was the more serious of the two. "Plus, you know Sergeant Johansen will snap your neck if you talk about any of the women in her wing like that."

Norgard snorted. "Come on, it's just us on this deck. Who's gonna know?"

Martin frowned as he looked around the darkened room. "The commander will. I swear he has this area bugged to know what's going on in here."

"He was a mech pilot once. Don't let his present rank fool you, Eggles." Norgard leaned forward and changed his output display as he spoke.

"Don't call me Eggles. I hate it when people use that—"

"But it's so much easier than ... what is it, *Englethorpe*?" Norgard teased.

Martin bristled at the slight as Norgard and Hermedilla laughed. He wasn't sure if Norgard was teasing him because he was the new guy, or because Norgard was generally just a jerk to everyone. He reminded Martin of those kids he grew up with who seemed to enjoy making others uncomfortable. Usually, Martin tried to avoid people like that, but the Ops Team loved Norgard, and if he wanted to ingratiate himself with the crew, he'd have to make some sacrifices.

"Oh, like 'Norgard' and 'Hermedilla' are any easier? Yeah, those two names just roll off the tongue." Martin glanced at the men, figuring that he'd rather go along with the expected banter than let them think they'd bothered him as much as they had.

Hermedilla raised his hands in self-defense. "Why are you bringing me into this? I'm not the one acting like a dick."

"Well, you found my name so funny," Martin snapped.

Hermedilla shrugged. "You sound like some medieval duke or something."

A loud yawn broke through the space, and Norgard leaned back in his seat, kicking his heels up and crossing them over the edge of the console. "Anyway, like I was asking," he said, reclaiming the attention in the room. "Top three most fuckable scouts?"

Martin drummed his fingers against his own console loudly. The base of it was made of the same dull, burnished steel as the floor and wall panels, and carried sound far too well.

"Seriously, can we *not* do this?"

Norgard rolled his eyes. "You don't wanna play, Eggles, you don't have to. I'm sure Hermedilla will."

Hermedilla shook his head, the spikes of his dark hair wobbling slightly, and fixed his teammate with a pointed stare. "Actually, I think it's messed up for you to be asking about them like this."

"Man, fuck both you of you." Letting his feet fall from the edge of the console with a loud bang, Norgard flopped forward dramatically. "You guys are no fun at all. No wonder you're alone during our downtime." With a huff, the disgruntled man turned his attention to his screen, idly scanning the orbital sensor data.

Once again, the Ops room fell quiet, the hum of the coolant system for the electronics filling the space. Tension was never a good thing in the Ops room and the three of them knew it. However, Hermedilla had nothing to lose by pissing off Norgard, but if Martin kept making mistakes when dealing with the other guys in the team, his social awkwardness could cause them to tease him relentlessly.

After taking a deep breath, Martin admitted, "I think I

don't want to play because my number one is down there on the mission."

"Ha," Norgard jumped upright in his seat. "I knew it. I knew there was a reason you volunteered for the shift tonight. Only an idiot would swap what you had for a mission like this unless he had some ulterior motive."

Hermedilla tilted his head to the side. "Oh, right. Wasn't Specialist Kernwick supposed to be on this shift? I just figured she was sick or something."

"Nah, I swapped with her," Martin explained, ignoring the fact Norgard called him an idiot. He was content with his decision, knowing that's all that counts. "I let her have my data credits for a week so I could be here."

"You got played. Damn rookie," Norgard tutted, his voice full of pity. "Having someone offer to take a dead shift like this from you *is* the reward. You gave a week's worth of data to sit here and occasionally hear the voice of some hottie? Dude ... you need to get laid." Norgard shook his head slowly, and Martin's cheeks burned. He had never felt quite so stupid before.

The lights on the monitoring deck flickered a split second before a new voice broke into the room. "Nest? This is Starfall and Sleeves, doing our hourly check in. Do you copy?"

Norgard nudged Martin. "Hey, you take it."

"What? Why?" Martin frowned at him. "You're on the radio. I'm tracking signatures."

"How are you supposed to speak to your number one fuckable if you're on signatures, huh?" Norgard tapped the unit and assigned the mic control over to Martin. "Do you ever want her to know who you are? Or are you just going to keep creeping from the shadows?"

While there was an insult mixed into Norgard's comments, he had a point. This was the sort of opportunity

Martin had been hoping for. He smiled, glad that taking the hit to his ego had paid off.

"Please tell me you birds are still awake?" There was a groan through the radio. "Honestly, the frequency with which you Ops guys fall asleep while we're on missions is alarming. You're meant to be watching our ass-"

"Copy that, Starfall," Martin spluttered, realizing that being on mic meant that he had to actually talk, not just daydream about it. He leaned forward, resting his elbows against the console. "We're watching your ass and it's looking fine."

Silence fell on the radio, and in the Ops room. Martin frowned as he tried to figure out why, and then he replayed his comment in his own head. "Ah, Void," Martin groaned.

Norgard and Hermedilla burst into laughter.

"Right, well, hopefully you like what you see," Starfall replied, a hint of amusement in her tone.

"But not so much that you haven't been doing the right scans," Sleeves interjected, sounding a little less appreciative of the blunder.

"No, not at all. I just messed up my words earlier. You're both looking peachy from up here. We haven't had anything worth reporting. Thanks for checking in, we'll keep you updated," Martin promised.

"Peachy?" Norgard mouthed.

Martin winced, cursing himself again. *Why am I like this?*

"And with that juvenile double entendre, we're out," Sleeves announced. "Don't fall asleep, and make sure you're not too transfixed by the thought of Starfall's ass to catch any pings," Sleeves said before the lights on the comm unit flicked off.

Exhaling with relief, Martin sank back in his seat and scrubbed at his face with both hands. Norgard reached over, ruffling his dark black hair. Martin batted him away. At least, he tried to, but Norgard was too fast.

"Working with you two is like dealing with a couple of toddlers." Hermedilla suddenly sounded far more tired than before as he switched up his readouts. "I'm gonna kill Kernwick for swapping her shift."

Silence blanketed the room as the specialists conducted the required scans and monitoring to ensure the mech pilots on the planet surface were still in the clear. It was easy work for them, as there was nothing that stood out or raised any red flags. Working in operations meant accepting the monotony. It was part and parcel of their job, but it wasn't why they got paid so well. They earned their money during the real action on a mission. There was a certain level of trauma induced by having to listen to a firefight, but having so few ways to help, beyond providing technical readouts. Banter between specialists was often accepted, as it was a coping mechanism to deal with both the drudgery and the stress. Unless it was Norgard's kind of banter. Hermedilla was right about that. Locker room antics were generally frowned upon, and Johansen had a reputation for obliterating anyone who talked shit about her all-female team.

"So ... Sleeves or Starfall?" Even though he had to know Johansen would tan his hide for it, Norgard did not appear to be dissuaded.

Martin supposed it was his own fault for dangling the "number one" comment in his face like a carrot. Ignoring the bait, Martin brushed some wrinkles out of his gray uniform shirt, his fingers passing over the Triple C logo on his chest. After fourteen months with the company, he still enjoyed the symmetry of the symbol; the concentric Cs were easily read from any angle. The choice to make them look like circuit trace paths around the hexagon background helped them stand out from a distance. Martin snapped out of his trance as he heard Hermedilla's voice.

"Surely not Sleeves," Hermedilla said as he scanned through the readouts of energy signals on the planet.

"Yeah, I don't picture you as a tattoo-loving kind of guy." Norgard smirked victoriously, probably pleased he finally managed to rope Hermedilla into the conversation. "You're more the girl-next-door type. Besides, I don't think Sleeves goes for the lads."

"I'm not uptight." Martin narrowed his eyes at Norgard.

"Whatever." Norgard snorted. "Still, as a rookie, I'll have you know that Starfall's no girl-next-door."

"Seriously?" Hermedilla turned on Norgard. "How in the Void would you know?"

"When you've been around long enough, you get a radar for these kinds of things." Smug cockiness radiated off Norgard as he straightened his shoulders.

Martin realized he'd made a mistake. When he admitted that his number one was on the mission, he was hoping they could move on. He didn't want Norgard, or Hermedilla, to start saying unsavory things about Starfall. She was a skilled pilot, and one of the tamest scouts.

Despite the teasing, Martin smiled to himself as he thought of Starfall. He hadn't spoken to her beyond a casual greeting in the hallway, or when she'd walk through Operations on her way to mission briefings and debriefings. He was always struck by how beautiful she was, with her hot pink hair, and dark brown eyes he could drown in.

Like Martin, Astera was still relatively new to the company. Pilots usually covered their slick black jumpsuits in all sorts of patches and trinkets, but Astera's was always crisp and unadorned. Some people whispered that it was because she wasn't settling in well, but Martin believed she was beyond all that fussiness. She was elegant, classy, and clearly didn't have time to waste on accessorizing her clothing when she should be training. It was probably how she managed to avoid a lot of the social drama too many people in the company got roped into. He liked that about her. She was just the kind of woman he was looking for.

That thought helped Martin get a grip on himself. "I know, we could call Johansen in and see what she thinks?" he suggested sarcastically, suddenly feeling protective of his crush.

Norgard cocked an eyebrow at him. "What crawled up your ass?"

The silent tension returned to the room as Martin decided to ignore Norgard. He'd already embarrassed himself and given far too much away.

As the monotony dragged on, Norgard's foot started tapping against the ground. At first, it was irregular and light, but it got louder and more persistent, and Martin swore the guy would implode with the building energy.

"Okay, if not the scouts, how about the Infantry Wing? Everyone's got a top three for that group."

Hermedilla sighed and Martin's shoulders stiffened.

"Guys, come on—"

"Stop," Martin snapped to attention as an energy signature crossed his screen. Martin held his hand up to forestall any further protest from Norgard. "Nest to Starfall, come in, Starfall." Martin radioed, waiting, and watching the new signal warily. The other two specialists leaned in, whispering to each other as they realized what he had seen.

The comms crackled. "This is Starfall. Go ahead, Nest."

"Starfall, we are reading a new energy signature within the target zone. Can you confirm?" Martin asked as he assigned a designator to the signature.

The pregnant pause that followed was unsettling for the group. Then again, Starfall was probably relaxing in her powered down mech and had to spool it back up and turn on the passive sensor display. It was a relief when Martin heard her voice again. "Um, yup, Nest, I'm picking up an energy signal, too. Looks to be a mech powering on. Do I need to act?" Norgard leaned across Martin to take over the comms from his console. "Negative, Starfall. So long as you've been powered down and running on your passives, they shouldn't have picked you up on sensors yet. They could be cycling out their patrol mech. Hold position until further orders."

"Copy that, Nest. Starfall, out."

Martin frowned as the plume of the energy signature on his readout continued to grow. "Our surveillance didn't see anything bigger than a few infantry mechs for their perimeter patrols, right?"

"Yeah, should be one on active patrol and two more on standby. Why?" Hermedilla asked.

Martin paused the scroll and pointed at the readout. "This energy output is too high for an infantry class mech's power plant." He figured it had to be a spearhead class instead; the mechs containing the heaviest weapons. Weapons that would wipe out Starfall's and Sleeves' petite scout machines as easily as an elephant would crush an ant.

"We are running at a lower orbit than usual. We're probably reading higher flux because of our distance to target," Norgard reasoned as he flipped the channels on his display to check what Martin reported.

"Nah, I compensated for that. I think they are firing up their backup mech," Martin said, looking over at the ranking specialist in the room. The blob of energy grew until it had to be a cluster of mechs. "Or ... mechs."

"Could be." Hermedilla narrowed his eyes, his jaw

clenched as he changed the settings, most likely hoping to pull the signatures apart. "Doesn't mean they have picked up our scouts, though. You two keep an eye on the new marks. I'll radio Sleeves."

Martin turned his attention to the energy readings and it became clear the new mechs were nearly warmed up. They would be on the move soon.

His chest tightened, as he thought of Sleeves and Starfall sitting down there, while these new enemies were powering up just miles away from them. He rolled his shoulders and told himself that they still had plenty of time. Starfall would be fine. She knew how to handle herself on a mission.

Meanwhile, Martin heard Hermedilla raising Sleeves on the other channel. "Sleeves, this is Nest. Come in."

"Nest, go ahead."

"Sleeves, we have multiple energy signals detected. It appears the base is waking their mech defenders. No indication of purpose or intent. Stand ready to cover Starfall's escape path to the pickup."

Sleeves was in a Falcon, which was one of the few mechs that could dance between being a scout or infantry class depending on fitout. Sleeves' particular machine had exchanged the heavier armor plating for information gathering systems but had kept the firepower. So, it wasn't quite as light, or smart, as Starfall's Hummingbird, but it was the perfect passive data sweeper, that could sit back and cover the stealthier mech while still sweeping for intel. Martin felt that getting Sleeves to cover Starfall's extraction was a wise decision on Hermedilla's part.

"Understood, Nest. Moving to nav Delta to cover exit lane."

Norgard shook his head as he pulled up the navigation

map. "Negative, Sleeves. Remain on station. Stay in position," he advised.

Martin figured Sleeves would have to find a more creative way to get into place to cover Starfall's retreat. He had read the reports as part of his pre-mission prep. The intel from the client on this mission was clear that the base had seismic sensors to pick up mechs in motion. They only work to a certain sensitivity which was another reason why Starfall, in her Hummingbird, had gone to scout base, and Sleeves had stayed farther back.

"Maybe the energy signatures are trying to mask the signal we've been waiting for?" Martin offered, hoping he was right so that the situation would feel less dire.

"That seems like a stretch, rookie," Norgard grumbled, rubbing his chin.

"You got a better explanation?"

The three specialists all looked at each other. It was clear that no one had a better idea.

Hermedilla sat up. "Norgard, contact Command. They'll need to be down here for this. It's above our grade."

Norgard nodded and picked up the phone at his desk. Now that he was on his feet again, Martin got a better look at the yellow framing on his Ops Section patch. Mech pilots would call a pilot wearing that color "Lieutenant", but amongst the Ops Specialists, it was more an indicator of seniority, than rank or achievement. Thankfully, Norgard wasn't the most senior staff member in the room. Hermedilla held that honor. It was also why it was his call to reach out to the command staff. Everyone seemed to hold their breath as Norgard waited for the phone to connect. When it finally did, he cleared his throat and spoke. "Officer of the Watch? This is the Ops Room. We are requesting Command verification of mission critical asset ... yes, immediate Executive Class escalation ... Roger that." He hung up the phone and looked at the other two. "They're going to wake the top brass. Should be around ten minutes."

"Starfall may be under attack in ten minutes," Martin protested.

"You wanna go up there and wake the XO yourself, lover-boy?" Norgard snapped.

Martin started to drum his fingers against the console again as he looked between the door to the Ops room and his control screen. He knew better than to bust rank on a mission like this, but that didn't make it sit any easier, especially when Starfall was down on that planet. Major La Plaz's room was only a few corridors away. As Head of Intelligence and the Triple C's XO, it was important to keep him close to Ops. Martin muttered a curse as he returned his attention to the screen, making sure his breathing was slow and steady as the pulsating energy signal expanded.

"Nest to Starfall." Hermedilla leaned forward as he radioed in, glancing at Martin as the anticipation in the room reached a suffocating level. "Hold position until target deter-mination has been made."

"Copy that," Starfall replied via comms, any hint of earlier teasing, or amusement, in her tone wiped away by the new developments.

Time in the control room slowed to a crawl. As the seconds dragged by, measured by the frantic tapping of Martin's fingers on the console, the three Ops Specialists had no choice but to assume no news was good news. Even if waiting was the hardest game on a mission like this, it was preferable to the alternative.

"Signals are still growing." Norgard stated the obvious as the dots on the holographic projection warbled into a more threatening mass.

Martin turned his head to the side, hoping that looking at it from a new angle would help him take it all in. He figured it was either one big mother of a power signal, or the initialization of a full unit of hulky mechs coming online.

Neither option was good for Starfall.

The radio flared to life again. "Starfall to Nest. Did you guys go out for a cup of tea or something? Even my passives are picking up on this now."

Hermedilla leaned forward, even though it made no difference as his mic was on his headset. "Repeating orders: hold position until a determination has been made."

"Right, shall I tell that to the Harrier and two Eagles that just woke up inside of the compound?" Even through the radio, it sounded to the team like Starfall was speaking through gritted teeth.

Martin grasped Hermedilla's shoulder as he interjected. "Starfall, location scans were negative for hostile mechs."

"Of course. I'll tell them to power down because your sensors didn't pick them up, so they can't exist. Gimme a minute, I'm sure they'll gladly oblige," Starfall retorted.

Martin winced.

Before anyone could respond to Starfall, the door at the rear of the Ops room cycled to reveal Commander Durroguerre, holding a sealed thermos of coffee, and doing up the final clasp on his collar. His navy uniform jacket was wrinkle free, and the purple trim of his rank stood out against the inky fabric. Even though he must have been asleep just moments ago, his dark eyes were alert as he strode over with the kind of confidence and purpose that came with decades of experience.

The specialists glanced at each other. Being as late as it was, Major La Plaz was the one who was supposed to be on call. Seeing the owner, and commander, of the company here in the flesh was a rare occurrence in the Ops room.

"Status report," the commander ordered, looking between them. His chiseled jawline was sprinkled with salt-and-pepper stubble that he rubbed while waiting for their answer.

"Uh, multiple energy signals on the planet in the target area, sir," Martin said as he jumped up from his seat and saluted. "Unclear if the base's mechs are powering up to engage our assets on the ground, or if the mission critical asset is already on site."

"Sit down, Specialist. I need you at your console, not saluting me." The commander waved his hand at Martin, whose cheeks reddened as he sank back into his seat. "Have you performed a spectral analysis on the energy signatures?"

"Negative, sir. Initial energy levels are consistent with a mech's fusion core activating," Hermedilla answered. Being the senior specialist in the room, it was his responsibility if something wasn't done as mission protocol dictated.

"Perform one now," the commander ordered. His mouth opened to say more, when a feminine voice blared through the comms.

"Nest? Please tell me you guys haven't drifted off to dream about peaches again. I've got three hot mechs getting antsy, and I need to fucking move."

Turning to a spare console, Commander Durroguerre pointed to the headset laying on it. "Who's that on the comms?"

"Private Starfall, Scout Wing. She's our forward OP mech, running passive and powered down," Martin explained.

Even as he did, Hermedilla was trying to talk with her on the comms and encouraging her to not break cover.

"Hermedilla, I'll handle this." With a frown, the

commander picked up the headset and slipped it on. "Starfall, this is Knuckle Duster," he announced, using the callsign all the pilots would recognize.

Martin bit the inside of his cheek as he waited to hear Starfall's reaction to the commander being on the comms. It was a clear sign that an increasingly bad situation was about to get much, much worse.

CHAPTER 2

ANY SENSE of frustration and amusement Astera Ramos felt at the lack of intelligence from the Ops guys was wiped away when she heard that callsign.

Knuckle Duster.

The fucking commander was in the Ops room?

She made a mental note to bang some heads together when she got back to the ship. They should have told her they were escalating the situation to that level. She would have even made a point of keeping her sass to herself. The last thing she wanted was for the commander to hear her mouthing off.

But that was a matter for later.

Astera had more present and important matters at hand. She cleared her throat and leaned against the backrest of her mech harness as she nudged the radio trigger with her chin. "Starfall here, Knuckle Duster. What can I do for you?"

"Starfall, you can start by doing your job. Your orders are to hold position and detect the presence of a mission critical asset. Ops is aware of the situation and following standard operating procedure on this mission. Stay focused and keep your head in the game. Copy?" The commander's voice was more of a bark.

Astera scrunched up her nose at being called out over the comms.

She was going to do a bit more than bang some heads together.

The whole reason she had taken the Baldalan mission was so that she could show off her talents and make herself more valuable to Sergeant Johansen. Now, she'd gone and made an idiot of herself in front of the commander. "Copy that, Knuckle Duster." She tried to sound contrite, but was certain she had failed. It was hard to sound anything other than annoyed when she was being ordered to remain still while three bigger, uglier, mechs were far too close for comfort. Still, she knew better than to argue with the boss of her boss's boss.

Looking around, Astera tried to ignore the flock of infantry mechs in the distance. Despite all the sensors they had back on the Latagarosh, she had actual eyes on the situation. And what a situation it was turning out to be.

Baldalan was one of the more interesting planets she had been sent to in her year and a half with the Certified Cast Company or, more informally, the Triple C. It was warmed by two suns, and brighter than most as a result. The extra sunlight led to the planet being covered in dense jungle and it was humid enough to make her wonder how long it would be before her Hummingbird turned into a sauna. Still, at least if she was going to boil in her suit, she'd go out with a good view. This continent's surface was covered by a breathtaking, and contrasting, mix of lush rainforest, and deep, craggy, chasms cutting intermittently across the ground, making the place feel almost like a naturally formed maze.

The dark wooded and thick-trunked trees soared high above the top of Astera's mech. The canopies were full of rich, emerald green leaves and draping serpentine vines that were much more fun to observe than to maneuver through. Still, Hummingbirds were light and flexible enough to make relatively easy work of it. She didn't like having to leave Sleeves behind in her Falcon, but they didn't have much choice. Besides, Astera didn't mind operating alone. Sometimes it was a luxury not having to worry about other people.

A camouflaged netted, electric-wire fence surrounded the compound Astera had been sent to scout. With a bit of ingenuity and good old-fashioned sharp edges, she had cut her way through the mesh and given herself a good view of what was going on inside. But what had initially looked like a hodge-podge warehouse yard, now contained some very large, very deadly mechs that would eat her Hummingbird for breakfast. Her fingers itched to tap the controls, to get her own sensors online, but she didn't want to get back to the ship and have the commander dress her down any further.

"Head in the game. Copy that, Knuckle Duster," Astera said, using her forearm to sweep loose strands of pink hair that had fallen from her braid off her sweaty forehead. Then, she made sure her comms were off before muttering, "Come on, come on," to herself as she watched the mechs in the compound running through their startup procedures and warming up their weapons. Her stomach twisted into knots, and it took all her restraint to avoid jumping into motion. Astera was fine with sneaking around, and was even down for firefights, but she did not like the waiting. If it were her choice, she'd be on the move already, but part of being in a company like this meant sacrificing personal agency.

As the tension built in the cockpit and sweat dripped down the back of her neck, the radio crackled again. "Starfall, new orders," the commander finally said. "Engage your sensors. Field strength is too noisy for orbiting sensors.

Surface confirmation of asset presence is required. Instructions to follow."

The tightening in Astera's gut turned from unnerving to near painful. He still wanted confirmation of the asset? Even when she was staring at three big ugly mechs? She considered arguing, but closed her eyes instead and flicked the switch to wake up her Hummingbird and bring the active sensors online. "Copy that, warming Calliope up now," Astera replied using her nickname for her mech. She hoped the commander was as good as everyone made him out to be, and she wasn't just getting her mech all fired up to draw the attention of the hostiles less than two kilometers away.

With keen, practiced eyes, Astera followed the projected lines of code that rose over the mech's inner visor. As they turned back on the system stats were just what they were supposed to be, and she was once again glad that the mechanics back on Latagarosh had accounted for the increased atmospheric humidity. "Nest, sensor systems are now online."

"Roger that," one of the Ops lads replied. She wondered what the commander was doing if this one was back on comms. She cycled through the list of specialist's names that were on this briefing. She'd seen all the men around, but she had trouble matching their faces and voices. "Be advised, signal determination required from Command. Set filters to detect J-band radiation from asset vicinity. Once the outlined levels are reached, asset confirmation is complete. You can then proceed to Nav Delta under cover of Sleeves."

Astera's fingers flew over the controls to get the required processes up and running. It was all pretty routine for her, given her long history with scouting mechs. The J-band radiation measurements flitted across her screen, and she drew up the mission briefing, waiting until the data matched the targets before letting out a soft breath. "Nest, radiation targets confirmed. Leaving post on a heading for Nav Delta now. Sleeves, you copy?"

"Sleeves here. Copy that. I'll be waiting and watching your peachy ass," Sleeves chimed in over the radio.

With a snort of laughter at the reference to the Ops grunt's screw up from earlier, Astera kicked her movement functions into gear and started to wind her way back through the surrounding forest. The path she had taken must have been one used by the large, almost feline-like predator species on the planet. She hadn't run into any, but she'd read bio reports about them. Despite their natural grace, they were rather hefty, and the trampled leaves and branches on the forest floor left her a good path to follow. She hoped her luck held out and she would avoid a close encounter, because she didn't want to have to fire on one of those creatures and give away her position.

Her mech, Calliope, was a Hummingbird, and the lightest machine available. Like the Sparrows, it was a tall, slender model. To reduce the frame size, they didn't have a pilot seat like other mechs did. Instead, the Hummingbird and Sparrow had vertical harnesses that pilots strapped into with a five-point belt and extra bands that fastened around their knees and ankles. Whilst in stationary or transport mode, a small saddle post could be ejected from the rear of the back plate to rest on, and ease to tension on the legs, but that was useless when Astera was running through the underbrush. Instead, her legs took the impact of each one of Calliope's footfalls, her entire body bouncing as if she was the one doing all the running.

She had just found her stride when the same Ops guy sounded in her ear. "Starfall, those mechs are on the move.

They're heading for the compound gate. Stay away from the main road, copy?"

"Copy." Astera grasped the controls tighter. If she had to avoid the main roads and still make it back to Nav Delta before the enemy mechs did, she'd have to push it up a gear. "All right, Calliope. I know you and I have only been friends for eighteen months, but we gotta kick this escape up a notch." Astera let go of the controls just long enough to pat the dashboard of her Hummingbird.

The Certified Cast Company was rare in that pilots didn't have to share mechs. Astera figured it had something to do with the fact that Durroguerre used to be a pilot himself. Whatever the reason, she didn't care. It was nice to have something of her own.

Taking the controls firmly in hand again, Astera reduced function on some of the sensor equipment and rerouted the power into her drive, so she could move faster. With the Ops grunts and Sleeves monitoring the situation, she could sacrifice a little detection if it meant getting to Nav Delta a couple of minutes earlier.

"Starfall, where you at? My trigger fingers are getting itchy," Sleeves muttered over the radio. Astera could picture the way the lines on her forehead would be creasing together in anticipation of a firefight.

"Your trigger fingers are always itchy, Sleeves." Astera stopped, groaning as she jumped Calliope across a fallen log and took the landing harder than intended. "You should get that checked out."

Sleeves laughed. "Sure. I'll look into that right after you find a decent hairdresser to work on those shitty dark roots showing through the magenta. Or when you finally commit to something and get it properly modded."

The rhythmic footfalls and sweltering heat in Astera's mech made her heart thump against her chest so hard it hurt. Still, she appreciated the banter. "Let's find an esthetic technician together. I'll fix my hair while you ask if they can remove that shit ink on your arms. Who drew it, your kid brother?"

Sleeves' tattooed arms and Astera's bright pink hair were a constant point of discussion for teams outside of the Scout Wing. Body mods and genetic tweaks were par for the course these days, so archaic things like tattoos and hair dyes were always viewed with a measure of interest. Their relatively small contingent had come to be seen by the rest of the company as the eccentric ones. Sergeant Johansen tried to shut the gossip down, but they all knew there was truth to it. Spending long hours sneaking around dangerous places and skulking in the shadows took a certain kind of person, Astera mused. The kind who either had something to hide or who had given up trying. People often thought she was the latter, because of her easy smiles and pink hair. She didn't bother trying to dissuade them of the notion. Not when she was really the type who had something to hide.

Without thinking, Astera brought one hand up to wrap around the charm that hung from her neck. The metal of the old bullet casing was warm from her body heat, but the familiar weight and shape comforted her. Yes, she had secrets, but she would keep them in her past where they belonged.

The forest thinned out as Astera changed heading and made for the cliff running parallel to Nav Delta. Once she hit that slope, she could jump down, and Sleeves would be able to see enough to provide cover fire so she could get to the dropship. When she got close, Mother Hen could then cover Sleeves' retreat. Flicking her radar onto Calliope's HUD, Astera noticed that the mechs that were racing to meet her on the road had stopped at the side of the gorge. She frowned, but kept running.

Why would they stop?

If they had detected her, they had to know where she was going. The only option now was to slip into the dried-out gully, or double back and try to tackle the river. When they set up shop, the hostiles must have dammed the water at the source to cut off flow to the trench and filter it through the forest river instead. It turned what was probably a rather tame flow into white water rapids, and gave them convenient protection to the east and west of their encampment, with the densely forested mountains protecting them from the north. Their supply road was to the south, and they monitored it closer than parents watched a newborn.

"Starfall to Nest?"

"Nest, come in." It was Commander Durroguerre again.

Astera was panting as the heat and adrenalin of the chase set in. "The bogeys have stopped, sir. I don't like this."

"You don't have to like it. You just need to get out of there," Durroguerre replied. "You're only a kilometer out from the rendezvous."

"Copy that," Astera grunted. She nudged the drinking tube on her shoulder closer to her mouth and took a sip of mech-warmed electrolyte mix. It wasn't the refreshing cold water she was craving, but it would keep her hydrated. She had to press her lips together to keep herself from spraying her drink all over her visor as the Hummingbird's foot slipped on a rotten vine. Instead, she swallowed, coughing, and swearing as she struggled to keep the mech vertical and crested the ridge.

"Ah, Starfall, glad you could join me," Sleeves chuckled. Astera looked out of the visor and saw Sleeves' camouflage-painted Falcon model, which she affectionately called Perry, rising into view, guns whirring into readiness.

"We gotta stop meeting like this, you know I like it too much when your guns run hot," Astera teased. She crouched Calliope and gripped a sturdy tree at the edge of the gully, ready to slide down the side of the shallow section she'd found earlier that day. While it wasn't in the briefing, she had made a note of it on her way into position from the landing site. It never hurt to have options for an escape route.

"Gotta keep 'em hot to impress you and cover your retreat, babe. You know how I like watching as you—"

Sleeves' transmission was cut short as a slick missile whistled through the air and slammed into the side of Perry. The explosion shook the forest. The rock wall of the gully crumbled on both sides, and Calliope lost her footing. The world spiralled as gravity slammed Astera and her mech downwards.

With a scream of rage, Astera whipped Calliope's torso around and used the mechanical arms to grasp and claw at the wall as they fell, trying to find purchase or slow their descent.

"Nest to Ground. What's going on?" Durroguerre's voice was as calm as ever, but the demand in it was clear.

Astera tried to blurt a response, but Calliope crashed into the ground and all the wind exploded from her. She choked and gasped for air, but every part of her chest felt as though it was being stabbed by a thousand red hot knives.

"Sleeves? Starfall? Report, now."

A chunk of metal and glass slammed into Calliope's windshield, sending a network of alarming hairline fractures scattering over the glass. Astera blinked at the white, pink, and crimson chunks that were splattered over the camo paint of the debris. Looking up, lungs seizing hard enough to bring tears to her eyes and turn her vision black at the edges,

Astera's entire body stiffened. The opposite wall of the canyon was covered in scorched mech parts and the bottom half of a torn up mech suit that dripped blood and oozed eviscerated organs.

Astera tried to tear her eyes away from the grizzly sight as reality hit her just as hard as that missile had hit her friend.

"She's dead," Astera wheezed, the words numbing everything from her lungs up.

CHAPTER 3

COMMANDER HENRI DURROGUERRE lifted his head at Starfall's ominous proclamation. He swiped his hand over his console, scrubbing the data back thirty seconds. The display lit up with a powerful flicker. What could only be some sort of brutal detonation. "The hell was that?" he barked, jumping to his feet.

"Uh, looks to be an anti-mech missile. Fired from the base. Might be why the mechs stopped and held position," Eggles reported, switching up his displays to focus on the base again.

"Intelligence branch didn't say anything about anti-mech defenses, sir," Hermedilla protested immediately.

"Must have been hidden in the new construction the client was so worried about. Status of our team?" Henri sat down and pulled on his headset.

"Sleeves and the Falcon are down. Starfall is still online," Norgard reported.

"Starfall, we're gonna need more than that." Henri peered at Norgard's console.

He determined that, with the ridge down into the valley

from Nav Delta, it's possible the base's mechs wouldn't see Starfall. The aftermath of Sleeves' fusion reactor scramming might even have hidden Starfall's energy signature. If that was the case, they would only have minutes to get her out of the target area before the mechs on the ground got wise to her.

There was a slight crackle on the other line. Eggles leaned forward and flicked up the volume control on the comms.

"Sleeves ... Sleeves is down," Astera wheezed. "Calliope and I took some damage from the fall. Running my own diagnostics now."

"Starfall, negative. You have danger close. Get your mech back on its feet and proceed toward Nav Gamma. When I tell you, find cover and initiate emergency shut down. Copy?" Henri knew it was a strange order, but she needed to get somewhere safe and cut her energy signal before she was found. She'd be a sitting duck if they detected her. She was still way too far away from the dropship, Mother Hen, to assist.

"Pausing diagnostics," Starfall spluttered to the backing track of an awful metallic groan. "She's up, but she doesn't like it. Proceeding to Nav Gamma now ... probably leaving a trail of coolant behind."

On the tracking screen, the crew could see the delayed trajectory of Starfall's retreat, which seemed far slower than Henri would have liked.

"Nothing we can do about it while you're on planet, Starfall. Keep moving; you've got to put distance between you and your pursuers." Henri gave her the abridged version of his plan. Flicking his mic off, he turned to Norgard. "Give me a distance and a bearing to the mechs the instant they make any move to pursue that Hummingbird."

"Roger that," Norgard said simply, as he got to work on his

console. The flippant chit-chat was gone now that there was a real crisis. The three Ops specialists were solely focused on the job, just as any commander would expect.

Beside Henri, Eggles' fingers beat out a rhythm against the console. "Come on, Starfall. Move," he pleaded as he watched the energy signature of Astera's mech limping along the valley.

"Nothing more you can do for her from here, son. Just keep an eye on her signal and mark it the moment her fusion core goes cold," Durroguerre warned him, running a hand over his own buzz-cut hair.

"Roger that, sir." Eggles sighed, taking a deep breath, and stilling his hands.

As the commander of a successful mercenary company that traveled the Void, Henri had accepted many missions. As far as directives went, this one was supposed to be simple. Baldalan was a nothing planet in the middle of a backwash system. The Kolos Admiralty had asked them to drop in, spend some time scouting to detect some standard radiation, and then report back. The general idea was it was newly settled by people without much in the way of means. Yet. However, in his time as commander, Henri had also learned that even the simplest of missions could go ass-up without warning. This, it seemed, was one of those missions.

"Starfall to Nest. The debris around the explosion site slowed me down. Clear of that now. I've climbed back up the ravine and am in the forest again. The old girl's still limping, but I'm picking up speed," Astera panted. The heavy footfalls of the mech echoed between her words, irregular and ominous. "You mentioned pursuers? Is it the mechs from the base?"

"Don't concern yourself with that, we are keeping an eye

on them. You concentrate on getting out of there. Right now, Sleeves' core detonation is acting as cover for your signal. It should give you-"

"Commander, bogies on the move. Bearing eighty-one-point-five degrees. Range three-point-three kilometers," Norgard blurted out in the middle of the commander's radio message.

"Starfall, power off. Emergency power down," the commander ordered, waiting, and listening for her to go cold on the other end. Looking at Eggles' console, he noted the young specialist had found a sensor setting that let him see where the base mechs were located, as well as a flag on the map where Starfall would have powered down. It was clever work, which Henri would have to commend him for later.

The Ops room was dead quiet as the distance between the flag, that was supposed to be Starfall's position, and the energy signatures of the mechs, grew shorter and shorter. Everyone stared, unblinking as they seemed to be following along the same topography Starfall used.

"They must be picking up her leaking coolant ..." Hermedilla muttered.

"Just tell me how far off they are." The commander's voice was barely a whisper.

"Less than one-point-five kilometers and closing, sir," Norgard reported.

The comms channel was eerily silent. Not even the crackle of static came through the speakers. If Starfall was shut down, she wouldn't have enough power to talk to the jumpship orbiting above her. All anyone could do was wait and watch the three circling energy signatures as they drew closer and closer to the flag on the map. The tension was so complete, so engrossing, that no one dared take a big breath for fear even that noise might alert the patrolling mechs on the planet.

The energy signatures drew within five hundred meters of the flag where Starfall was supposedly shut down. They separated and circled around where the signature went dead. Walking in a slow spiral, toward the center, the mechs moved closer and closer together.

Eggles' short nails scraped against the console as he balled his hand into a fist. "They should be right on top of her. How are they not seeing her?"

None of the others in the room had a good answer for him as the three enemies seemed to be spreading out again. To everyone's horror, they then proceeded along the valley in the direction of Nav Gamma.

"Hermedilla radio Mother Hen and tell the captain we are revising their flight plan," Henri said softly without turning around. He brought up the map and scrolled out. "Tell them to program their trajectory for the backup landing site."

"That's a long way, Commander. Can a damaged Hummingbird make it that far?"

"She doesn't have a choice, Specialist. Make that call immediately," Henri ordered. They didn't have time to waste arguing. He wheeled back to the screen. It looked like two of the mechs were moving onto the open area they had labeled as Nav Gamma, but one of the mechs was lingering on station where the flag for Calliope remained. One of the opposition pilots wasn't convinced they had lost their quarry.

"Come on buddy, she's not there ... move on ..." Eggles muttered, watching the screen.

As if by willpower alone, the third mech signal started moving off to join the other two. With a sigh, the team let some of that relief wash over them.

As they did, Norgard chimed in, "Sir, I'm getting an RF signal from the planet. Very faint, but it's on our comms band."

"Task another of our antennas to pick it up. Boost it; she might be trying to talk with us," Durroguerre ordered.

Norgard did as he was told and the whirr of the dishes on the ship's exterior told them that they were turning to bear on the planet. "I got it on another antenna, but it's still pretty weak."

"Good enough, put it through."

"—est, Starfa—... Co—in, Nest. Nest, St—all... Come—t."

"Starfall, we are receiving. We read you, come back," Henri said through the comms, before calling to the specialists, "Get more antennas on that."

While the specialists scrambled to comply, Henri tinkered with the settings at the station to see what magic he could work for himself.

"Starfall here–" Henri was glad to hear her feminine voice burst through the comms, even it if was still tinny. "It's good to hear your voices. Void, that was close ... they've moved on, but they are between me and Nav Gamma. I can't get Calliope around them in time, given her state. Over."

"Starfall, not sure how you're reaching us with your power off, but I'll take it. Nav Gamma is a no go. We need you to switch to the secondary pick-up point at Nav Iota. Copy?" The commander spoke slower than normal, wanting to be sure the scout could hear him through the bad signal.

"Rerouted some battery lines to power comms," Starfall said, voice halting. "Without the diagnostics I don't know if I'll make it to Nav Iota. Gonna need to switch back on to figure that out."

"Negative Starfall, danger close. I repeat, danger close. Remain shut down. I say again, remain in power down state.

Bogies will detect you at this range. Remain powered down until further notice," Henri repeated, fighting against the bad signal they were stuck using. Still, he had to admit the trick with the battery backups was pretty smart for a fresh pilot. "Starfall, describe present location. How are you maintaining operational stealth?" he asked, curious how they couldn't have found her when she powered down.

"I'm within twenty meters of the last ping I sent when you ordered a shut down," Starfall informed him. "As for operational stealth, this magician doesn't like giving away her secrets on less secure channels. Do you need to know, or can I remain mysterious?"

"If it's working for now, keep it to yourself. With this signal quality, there's no telling who is listening. As for Nav Iota, it may be further from your present position, but lucky for you, it's all downhill. I'm sure your Hummingbird can flit down the path even on a busted leg." Henri smiled, knowing that facial expressions changed verbal inflections that were detectable over the radio. He wanted to help Starfall stay calm by keeping the mood light, even as he watched the monitors. Sure enough, the three mechs continued to congregate at Nav Gamma, though he wasn't sure why.

"Flit or slide? I guess we'll have to wait and see." Starfall's panting seemed to slow, but her voice was still rough. "Knuckle Duster, can I run something by you real quick?"

"Go ahead, Starfall." Henri smiled at the use of his handle. Part of him still identified more as a mech pilot than a commander, so it was nice to hear it from time to time, especially from some of the new staff.

Starfall cleared her throat, but it sounded like something between a laugh and a cough. "You may want to change your job advertisements if we keep picking up tickets like this. All mech pilots get free access to a sauna on mission ... this place is as hot as an old–" Starfall cut herself off. "I'll stop there. You get the idea."

Norgard and Eggles chuckled beside Henri, and he couldn't help but join them.

"Well, at least she watches her tongue around you," Hermedilla muttered.

Henri laughed quietly and turned back to the console. "Starfall, how about I give you an extra fifteen minutes in the shower? Would that make up for the inclement conditions of your cockpit when you get back?"

"Fifteen minutes?" Starfall snorted, her amusement evident. "Knuckle Duster, someone's gotta teach you how to negotiate a deal. You're supposed to start with a high offer and then let them work you down. If that's the best you've got, that's just plain insulting."

Henri grinned to himself. "Fifteen minutes, Starfall, take it or leave it. One of the advantages of being commander is that I don't have to negotiate with my pilots." His tone was serious, but there was a lilt to his words that hinted at the smile on his face as he spoke.

"Youch, Knuckle Duster ..." Starfall let out a low whistle. "Insulting, but what's a girl to do? Hopefully it'll be enough to get me smelling pretty again. I'll take the fifteen minutes happily if—when—I get back. Thanks for the offer." Starfall's worry still seeped through, even in the playful banter.

"All the more reason to make sure you get back. We'll let you know when the coast is clear to proceed, Starfall. Nest, out." Henri clicked his comms channel off, but didn't move the antennas off their points yet. They may still need them if Astera stayed on battery power. In the meantime, he got to work organizing things on the ship for Starfall's arrival. While their radio banter was light and easy, he knew it would be anything but when she got back. It was going to be a long night for all of them.

CHAPTER 4

NAV IOTA MIGHT AS WELL BE an entire galaxy away with how wretched Astera felt. Stuck in the humid cabin of her mech, over fifteen meters up in the air, she was as close to done with the mission as she could be without actually having finished it. Her arms and legs ached from holding the controls in position for so long, and there was a sharp throbbing in the back of her head as the adrenaline of the retreat started to wane.

Still, she counted her blessings, and was grateful that the enemy pilots hadn't thought to look *up*. It had been a risky and delicate move, getting her mech to climb the tree, but the trunks of the flora on this planet were special. Supersized, and strong to endure the natural trials of the climate, the trunk she had scrambled up was broad enough that Calliope's arms and legs barely managed to circle it. She wasn't thinking much as she climbed, she was too stuck in fight or flight mode, but on reflection she knew it was lucky she managed to get any grip on the trunk at all.

The comms buzzed for a moment before the commander's

voice filled the cockpit. "Nest to Starfall. You're clear to continue on your previous path."

And not a moment too soon, Astera thought. Moving slowly, not wanting to change Calliope's weight distribution too much, she started the power-up procedure. On the climb down, Astera discovered that she disliked the idea of falling for the second time that day. The high-pitched scraping of Calliope's panels against the tree made her wince, but she supposed it was better than if she'd been blown to smithereens earlier. She could deal with any panel damage if she could just get back to the jumpship. What she needed to focus on was making it down the trunk without dropping to the ground and getting crushed up in her tin can.

"Void ... me and my bright ideas," Astera muttered to herself, shaking her head as the feet of the mech slipped, and she slid down a meter, before finding purchase again.

The rest of the descent went with about as much swearing and muttering, but she made it. On the ground, she was able to stand Calliope upright and run a system diagnostic to get a better idea of what state she was in.

The answer, in short, is "not great," Astera thought to herself.

In the tumble down the chasm wall, she must have sliced a coolant line. She was losing it fast. She barely had enough to make it to Nav Iota, and that was only accounting for her movement needs. If she had to fire ... well, she'd make a good static sentry tower for future generations. Luckily, her corpse would be charred by the internal temperatures of her mech, and therefore much easier to remove for whoever found her.

Not wanting to waste any more time, Astera spooled up her navigation unit and entered the new location. She tried not to give up the moment she saw just how off-track she had gotten in her retreat. She confirmed the new destination and started to move, knowing the Latagarosh would tell her if there were any bogies incoming.

Calliope whined and clunked around a lot more than a scout mech should as Astera pushed her onward. The cockpit went from humid to utterly sweltering and as she ran, Astera's head swam. With her full power reactivated, she moved her comms system back to the secure channel.

"Starfall to Nest," she called through, "Gonna need you to tell me if there are any places that refill coolant on the way to Nav Iota. This girl's thirsty."

Astera knew there was nothing between here and Nav Iota, but she wanted them to know she was running low, and she needed the distraction to keep her mind off the increasing likelihood of her dying before getting back to Mother Hen.

"Sadly, there isn't. With the river rerouted, you can't even go for a dip. I would recommend you use the topography as much as you can. If you can find a rocky defilade on these ridges, you can coast on the unstable ground along the slope and save yourself some energy usage in moving your limbs," the commander advised. From how confident he sounded, Astera wondered if he had done such a thing himself in the past.

As Calliope ran, each step jolted through Astera's limbs like electric shocks. She ignored the pain and focused on her breathing, then split her attention between piloting and her nav computer. She managed to find the edge of the ravine she had fallen in, and could probably head back in that direction and follow it, at least part of the way, to Nav Iota.

"Knuckle Duster, I've got a pretty rock-covered ridge to the west of me, but I'm not sure whether the extra resources used to reach that path will balance the benefits of the cooling

... any hints on how to calculate whether it's worth it?" Astera asked, pulling her drinking line close and taking a small sip.

"Starfall, proceed on current path. Looking now." That was all the commander said as Calliope trundled along. It was heartbreaking to hear how the right leg was grinding against the mech chassis as it moved, but there wasn't much that could be done about it. From the sound of it, that whole panel would probably need to be replaced.

"Starfall, it is close, but you can probably save some energy if you follow the contours of the hill to your west. So long as you keep proceeding downhill, you should have enough slope left to make it worth it." Astera glanced at the nav map as the commander spoke to get an idea of what he was talking about. "It will also kick you out into a notch that keeps you from having to go back uphill towards Nav Iota. It will lead you to a chasm that will leave you with no room for evasive actions if the mechs head your way. However, it's your call."

Astera was relieved he gave her an option rather than an order. It gave her the opportunity to assess her needs on the ground. Not all mission leaders had enough confidence in their pilots to do that kind of thing. She scrunched up her nose as she followed the route as he had described it on her map. They would be able to pick her off like a fish in a barrel if she got caught in the chasm, but if she had to choose between being blasted away in an instant, or boiling alive in her cockpit, she would choose the faster option.

"Nest, I'm not reading any bogies on my screen. Are you guys reading anything?" Astera asked.

It was Eggles who answered. She remembered his voice now from a few times he had said "Hello" to her when they passed in the corridors. "Negative. The ones that were after you are slowing. They may turn, but there's no way to predict whether they will pick up on your path."

With a heavy sigh, Astera committed her computer to the new navigation route. "Right lads, looks like I'm all in. Please let me know if anyone decides to turn tail on me."

The descent in the landscape became more evident as Astera guided her injured mech through the trees. It was a rough ride, between the slippery forest floor and the constant buzzing in the back of her head, but she managed to make it to the chasm without incident. It only took a few minutes under the cool sheltered shadow of the rocky expanse to feel a slight dip in the cockpit's temperature. Astera was grateful for every bit of it. She stole a glance at Calliope's operating temperature and saw that it stabilized. It still wasn't ideal, but *stable* was better than climbing.

The floor of the chasm below rushed up toward Astera as Calliope slid down a path. Even controlling her speed, it was going to be a rough stop at the bottom of the hill. Her already damaged legs groaned in protest as the Hummingbird slammed to an abrupt halt, but she managed to keep them upright. The chasm wound a bit back and forth, but overall stretched towards Nav Iota. Visibility was next to zero inside the stone walls, but it was all in the shade so Calliope was able to limp along. Going back to active movement, rather than half stepping, half slipping, the temperature began to rise again. Astera would only have a few extra minutes of operation before crossing that dreaded thermal shutdown barrier.

"Starfall, take cover."

The message blasted through so fast Astera didn't have time to do much of anything before an explosion, somewhere above her head, drew her attention.

The aftermath of an anti-mech missile exploding against the walls of the chasm provided the backdrop to the shower of rocks and debris heading for the already pulverized Hummingbird. Even worse, her sensors detected a second incoming missile.

Astera's heart beat so hard and fast in her chest that she felt it throughout her whole body. She only had a moment to react before she pushed Calliope faster and then dove once she got some momentum. As the mech skidded across the dirt, the wall to its left crumbled where the cockpit just was.

"Void, under attack," Astera cried through comms as she checked her sensors. They were clear, but probably not for long. Somehow, she coaxed Calliope back on her feet. The mech staggered as she tried to push it harder, and Astera's vision blurred. "Got a proper limp now, Knuckle Duster ... and it's getting real hot in here. I can't see straight anymore."

"We'll worry about that when you get back up here. For now, move that narrow ass of yours before they bring the chasm down on your head." The commander's words held a sense of urgency that Astera hadn't heard before.

The sensor display lit up with incoming fire. It seemed that the base defenders knew they couldn't catch up with Starfall at this point and settled for burying her in rubble.

In that moment, with bullets and missiles flying all around her, Astera's woozy mind reminded her of the Scout Wing patch on the arm of her flight suit. It was a shield shape, with the image of a targeting reticle above the Triple C logo. Apparently, it was chosen because it represented how the scouts had their marks in their sights, but the other wings teased that it was because the scouts always wound up getting shot at. She used to be annoyed by the assertion, but she snorted to herself and thought that the smart-asses had been right all along.

Astera didn't so much get Calliope to run as she did stop her from stumbling. It felt like drunken dancing, only suited in twenty-five tons of metal, and wearing a pulsing fusion reactor instead of a fancy necklace. *Void*, Astera thought, *what I wouldn't give for a stiff drink right about now.*

But the promise of alcohol was not what kept her moving. It was the sheer will to live. Her sensors were pinging off missiles like they were a spring shower, and she wasn't sure if Calliope was moving, or if it was the ground shifting beneath their feet as she fled. Probably a combination of both.

A great rumble started behind her, and she chanced a look out the back of her cockpit.

"They're gonna bury me alive," Astera panted through comms as boulders tumbled into the chasm behind her. More missiles hit, right overhead this time, and she cried out as she rammed Calliope's speed to full.

It isn't enough.

A heavy impact right in the back of her chassis sent the Hummingbird careening forward, knocking the wind out of Astera as they hit the ground. Despite the onslaught of stabbing pain as she tried, and failed, to suck in a breath, she refused to let the agony distract her. She pushed Calliope to her feet.

She had to keep moving.

"Starfall, come in. Starfall, respond." The commander's voice sounded frantic now. Astera shook her head, she must have missed a call in the noise of the explosion.

"I'm here," she grunted, unable to string together anything more complex.

"Starfall, be advised, dropship Mother Hen is on station at Nav Iota. She's waiting for you; keep moving and you'll get home, I promise," the commander urged.

Astera clung to that vow as she put every ounce of energy she had into piloting her mech home. She could not have responded to the commander's words again if she tried. She gasped for breath as Calliope stumbled down the narrow chasm. She bounced off walls as often as she took a step, but Astera managed to flick the sticky switch on her comms, leaving it connected. She heard the commander's concern. Even if she couldn't speak, maybe he would hear her panting and be satisfied that she was still breathing.

The journey to Mother Hen seemed endless. The world around Astera continued to crumble. After what felt like an eternity, the planet base must have smartened up. Astera had to grind the Hummingbird to a halt as a missile hit up ahead and the cliffs came down in front of her instead of behind. She barely had time to flatten the mech against the wall, and cried out in shock as a shard of rock sliced straight through the edge of her cockpit. The visor, already weakened by the hair-line fractures from her fall, started to crack.

"Starfall, respond. I know you're still with us. You're nearly there, less than a kilometer from the dropship. Don't stop now. I don't know your condition, Starfall, but I know you won't quit." The commander's voice had become more conversational. It seemed he was trying to will her to push on with his words, trying to make her move with nothing more than the sound of his voice.

"Trouble ... b-breathing—" Astera wheezed, clinging to his words. She leaned the mech out from the wall and peered past the cracks in the visor. The rubble formed a nasty barrier between her and the exit, and just as she considered how to get over it, the early temperature warning started screeching in the cockpit, rattling off her dazed brain like a sonic weapon. "Way ahead ... caved in ... too hot to climb." A hacking cough surged up from her lungs, splattering the internal controls of her mech with a violent spray of crimson blood.

"Starfall, do you have access to a screwdriver or some

other multi-tool? If you do, look for a panel down by your feet marked 'Four-G'. Use your tool to take it off."

Blindly groping at the pocket in her jumpsuit, relief rushed through Astera as she felt the slight bulge of her multi-tool against her thigh. Her fingers trembled as she tugged it out, and then fumbled for the button to ease up her harness and give her more room to squeeze down in the cockpit. She grunted as her knees buckled at the loss of support, and barely had time to throw her head back before her chin hit the control panel. She curled up, panting hard as every breath made her lungs ache, as if being stabbed by a million thick needles. She blinked away the black spots in her view as she looked for the panel. "Four-G," she wheezed, forgoing radio call protocol in favor of being able to breathe, "found it."

"Once you have it open, find the wires on the right side of the circuit board. Take the bottom wire, pull the connector adapter off, and wrap the bare wire around the third pin from the top. Don't waste time putting the cover back on, you only have a few minutes, at most, before the core's hardware kicks in anyway. Once you hear the alarm shut off, get back on the stick and get out of there," the commander ordered.

Astera focused on his words and nothing else. She saw them for the life raft they were, and even in the impossibly tight confines of Calliope's footwell, she clung to them. The spots swimming in front of her eyes and the pain in her chest subsided as she narrowed her concentration to keeping her hands steady, and keeping up with the instructions. Getting the panel open was the hardest part, as even with the screw-driver attachment, her hands just didn't want to work. She let out a sigh of relief as she finally got it open, and then double checked the wires and counted the pins before doing what he said. Once she was finished, she fell back against the side of the footwell, coughing again. When the attack was over, she noted the absence of the alarm, so she wiped the blood on her lips away with her sleeve and pulled herself to her feet.

Reengaging the standing support in the cockpit helped to ease the shaking in her limbs, and Astera groaned in relief. She had no idea what she had just done to her mech, but she trusted the commander. Knowing she couldn't waste any more time, Astera put her hands on the controls. "Going now," she said, looking at the rock wall ahead and telling herself she had to make it. She knew progressing was the only way she'd get out of this alive.

As she did with many things in her life, Astera threw herself at the challenge. There was no space for thought, or doubt, as she lugged Calliope up the ever-shifting barrier of boulders. Rocks, dust, and other debris showered down on her as she ascended. Sweat poured off her, dripping into her eyes and making her blink rapidly to ease the stinging. She wasn't sure if her body was giving out, or the cockpit was getting hotter, but she would have killed for even a breath of fresh, cool, air in that moment.

In any other situation, having a wish granted might be a good thing, but not in this instance. Astera's relief came when a rock from the lip of the cliff wobbled out of place and fell, slamming into her visor before disappearing somewhere below. The crack in the side of her windshield tore apart, and the outside air whooshed in.

"Stupid-fucking-thing-to-ask-for,"Astera panted, berating herself as the crack continued to grow. She tried looking past it, but dirt filtered into the cockpit and she coughed again.

Still ... she could see the top of the wall. It was only a few meters up. A second wind surged through her, and everything felt numb except her mind. She kept climbing, and the next time Calliope's foot slipped, she let out a defiant cry and used the adrenaline to push herself harder.

When she got to the top of the pile, she didn't pause. She flipped the legs of the mech over the edge and used the momentum to slide down the other side.

"It's getting ... fucking hot ... in here ...." Astera was sure that her mech had metamorphosed into a furnace. She wanted to rip her flight suit off, or press her face to the crack to breathe in some cooler air, but she didn't have time.

The Hummingbird let out an awful whine as its feet slammed into the ground on the opposite side of the rockslide, the impact almost cracking Astera's teeth. But she didn't care. In the distance, she could see Mother Hen. Just as she launched forward, she got several pings.

More missiles coming her way.

"Intercept incoming ... Mother Hen ... Please," she begged. She knew she couldn't outrun them.

"Mother Hen's got you, Starfall." The voice was the calm cool tone of Captain Darlek, Mother Hen's pilot. Just as the missiles entered range, Mother Hen's anti-missile system kicked in. Several high velocity bursts of kinetic rounds whizzed over Calliope's head and a few dull explosions behind her told her the coast was clear. Ahead, the side panel on Mother Hen's Mech Bay opened, the gangplank lights glowing in welcoming ripples, beckoning her forward.

It felt like another hour passed before Astera limped poor Calliope aboard, but once the mech crossed the threshold, the automated mechanics on board took over. The articulated arms guided the crippled machine onto mounts in the back of the dropship and secured it for flight back to the Latagarosh. She sagged against the cockpit restraints, and phased in and out of consciousness as the mechanics on board worked to shut Calliope down, and to make it safe for Astera's extraction.

When the shutdown was complete, and with the knowledge she was in capable hands, Astera allowed herself to fully succumb to the fuzzy blackness tugging at the edges of her vision. The general, throbbing pain throughout her body faded into the background as she passed out, and she welcomed the gentle call of unconsciousness.

CHAPTER 5

HENRI SAT BACK and pulled off his headset. With a puff of breath, he glanced at Hermedilla. "Don't forget to write up the summary report for this mission, Specialist. I imagine Sergeant Johansen will want to read it when she wakes up."

With that, the commander stood up from his seat and grabbed his now drained and cold thermos. Any sense of tiredness he still felt when he had been called in to assist was long gone, replaced by uncomfortably conflicting pangs of grief and relief. It was never easy to lose a pilot, but he had to be thankful that at least one of them survived.

"Button up this mission correctly, gentlemen. I know the admin will be a nightmare, but we lost a good pilot tonight, and another one may be critically injured. We've got to do this right," he told the three Specialists before leaving the room.

Stepping into the hallway outside the door, he strode along the corridor in the command deck, heading for the elevator to the hangar. Mother Hen would be back by the time he got down there and he wanted to see Starfall's injuries with his own eyes. As the commander, he never forgot that his pilots weren't just numbers on a page. They were people, just like he was. He'd witnessed when the military used pilots, like him, as chips in a gambling bet.

Riding in the elevator, he saw the team of Command staff rotating off the night shift and heading for the barracks. No one seemed to want to say anything to the commander as he impatiently watched the numbers count down on the elevator screen. When the doors opened, everyone parted and let him out, then he made the turn for the infirmary section. It was kept near the Mech Bay to cut down on time to move wounded pilots from the dropship to the surgical suite. It was a design decision he had made after years of experience and careful consideration. Striding into the infirmary, he looked around. Surgical Doctor Lily Ross was rostered as on duty, so he was relieved to have a medical specialist waiting for Starfall when she arrived.

The field medic on Mother Hen would have called ahead to warn the infirmary of their incoming patient, so the team was already prepped for an emergency. The main room was longer than it was wide, with four beds on both sides, and tracks for curtains that could be pulled for privacy around each one. The middle of the room was kept clear and was broad enough for two gurneys to pass side-by-side without fuss. At the rear of the room, there were double swinging doors that led to an operating theatre, opposite three, private, critical care rooms.

As far as mercenary medical bays went, the one aboard the Latagarosh was exceptionally well equipped for the size of the company. Henri's old friend and colleague, the chief medical officer, Doctor Annalise Colwyn, fought him long and hard for every inch of it. Room was a premium on any spacecraft, but Annalise had presented a solid case and Henri had never really been able to say no to her.

Doctor Ross looked up from the scanner she set down on a

tray beside and empty bed, and nodded in greeting. "Looks like the team had quite the mission," she said, tone low and grim.

Ross came on board with them to hone her craft under the careful supervision of Doctor Colywn. As an ex-teammate of Henri's, and one of the original founders of the Triple C, Annalise had patched up Henri more times than he could count. Anyone who trained under that kind of expertise was bound to be good.

There was a low chime, and the intercom system in the room activated. "Infirmary, Mother Hen is docking now. One patient incoming, unconscious, stats rapidly declining."

"Copy that. Bring her in and I'll take care of her," Ross promised.

Ross turned her attention to the two nurses hovering nearby and gestured to the doors at the back. One of the nurses tinkered with a control panel and the doors opened, as did the ones leading directly into the surgery.

"Commander?" Ross called, looking at him seriously. "This may be a while. You can take a seat if you want, or I can send someone to let you know when she's in recovery."

When, Ross had said. Not *if*, *when*.

Henri glanced at the front door of the Med Bay. "I'll wait until she gets here. I need to see the state she's in for myself. Maybe once I'm sure she's in the clear I can go back to bed. You understand, right, Doc?"

The doctor's face softened for a moment, and she opened her mouth to speak when the comms exploded to life again.

"Doc, trauma team has the patient, they're on their way to you now," the Mother Hen medic announced.

Ross didn't finish her thoughts. She went over to the sink and scrubbed in, finishing just as the front doors to the infirmary opened with an electronic hiss.

The woman on the gurney was a mess of sweat-streaked dust and blood. There were tears all through her black pilot suit. The internal moisture wicking layers were slashed and the zipper down the front was already being pulled open by the trauma team. Somehow, the black-rimmed Scout Wing patch survived on her shoulder. From the skill Astera had shown on the planet, it was hard to believe she was considered a private. Looking at her face as she rolled by, Astera's vibrant magenta hair was plastered across her unnaturally pale face, and her eyes fluttered under tightly closed lids. She had pretty, delicate features that made the crusted blood around her mouth appear even more worrying. The deep red, almost black, stains down the front of her suit were a sign that the dropship medics didn't have time to clean her up. The only thing they could focus on was keeping her alive. The trauma team were working as they ran alongside her, measuring and scanning, trying to do what they could for her before handing her over.

The sleek flight suit that clung to Astera's petite frame was in tatters, with the red blush of forming bruises showing on the skin underneath. The tears and blood weren't nearly as concerning as the wheeze in every minute, rattling breath. It had been hard for Henri to hear it over comms towards the end of the mission, but now he knew why. Looking at her laid out in front of him, he had no doubt that her lungs and ribs were in trouble.

The Med Bay medics took over from the trauma team. As one lifted Astera's bloodied hand off the stretcher, Henri noticed her fingers had formed around something in a tight fist. With firm, but careful, movements, the medic pried her fingers open and frowned, plucking a small item out and setting it on the end of an empty tray nearby before putting her arm back down and peeling the suit open to start the removal process.

The doors to the main operating theatre swung shut after the doctor and her assistants, and the trauma team all seemed to deflate as they mingled in the Med Bay. One of them walked over, picking up the metal cylinder that the medic had taken from Astera. They frowned as they turned it this way and that, not able to figure out what it was. Then they looked up at Henri, offering it to him.

The commander took it. The metal casing was small, something from a decades old bullet. Judging by the caliber, he knew it must be the kind that would have been retired when Starfall was barely knee-high. What looked like a short phrase was scratched over the surface in an untidy scrawl, and there was a hole in the top that made Henri wonder if it had been on a chain, or string, around Astera's neck before she'd grasped at it.

Even if he didn't know exactly what it was, or where it came from, the commander knew from experience that pilots were a superstitious bunch. They often strung up little trinkets in their cockpits to bring them luck, or to remind them of home. If a pilot could save anything from a broken mech, it was usually their good luck charm.

Henri turned the casing over in his hand, trying to make sense of what was etched into it. It wasn't Spacer or one of the trade languages. It might have been one of the regional languages from Earth that spread as people had migrated across the galaxy. He frowned, figuring that it was probably none of his business. This object didn't belong to him. All he wanted to do was make sure he was able to give it back to Astera. If she had been clinging to it like that, even as injured as she was, it must hold meaning.

IT FELT like Henri had just fallen asleep when the piercing tone of his comms unit split through his rest. Even if he wanted to ignore the sound, covering his head with his pillow, and rolling over, he couldn't. As the commander of a company like the Triple C, his sleep was a minor priority compared to ensuring the safety of his crew.

For the second time in less than twelve hours, Henri sat up in bed, rubbing his eyes as he croaked, "Accept call."

The incoming communication connected and before he could even ask what it was, a sharp voice snapped down the line. "Have you listened to the Ops room recording?"

"I didn't need to. I was there." Henri sighed and rubbed his eyes. "And good morning to you too, Sergeant Johansen." He reached for the sealed container of water he kept on his nightstand. Taking a long sip to moisten his dry throat, Henri let Greta launch into the complaint he knew she would be making after losing one of her scouts.

"Good morning?" she scoffed.

Henri could picture her shaking with rage from those two words alone.

"There's nothing good about it. I woke up to find I've lost a pilot. Sleeves is—was—one of the best scouts we've got."

There was a slamming sound through comms that was loud enough to make the commander jump.

"I need to know how a simple mission fucked up enough to lose one of my women. So, I get up and listen to the damn mission recording, assuming that the damn Ops Team did everything they could to watch over my crew. You know—" she paused for impact before railing on "—do their actual Void-damned job. But no, instead of staying alert and keeping an eye on the monitors, they were too busy discussing their 'top three fuckables' in my wing."

Henri winced as Greta finally stopped. Even through the comms, he could hear how heavily she was breathing from all her ranting. It was a pause, and Henri knew that if he didn't intervene now, he would not be able to get a word in until she was out of breath again.

And who knows how long that might be ...

"Greta, I know how hard it is to lose a pilot," he soothed, using her name to try and personalize things and show that he did care about her pain. "You want answers, but I was there in the Ops room last night. For most of the night, the Ops Team was on overwatch. There wasn't much for them to do. When there was, they tightened up the screws. I got called in for asset verification and in my presence, the team performed as expected."

As the weight of the night settled on his shoulders, Henri leaned back against the headboard of his bed. "What happened to Sleeves is something no one wants to see. If anything, blame me because our intel branch didn't pick up on the anti-mech missile they had hidden on site. Had we known it was there, we would have had a different game plan. But don't put this on the Ops Team. The enemy is outside the ship, you know that," Henri explained, trying to both calm the Sergeant, as well as reason with her, about pursuing disciplinary action. She hadn't asked for it yet, but it had to be why she called him so early.

"It's not about what they did when you were in the room. Of course, they were textbook perfect with the commander around," she argued. "But beforehand, they could have missed critical hints because they were too busy talking shit about my pilots. I want a full investigation into the readings from the mission."

"The only ones they read were mechs powering up. When they reached anomalous levels, they called me in. What are you trying to prove here, Greta?" Henri asked, already feeling defeated.

"Did you see those early recordings for yourself? Or are you just going on the information after you got into the Ops room? Sleeves is dead, Commander. You used to be a pilot, you—"

"Whoa, stop right there, Sergeant." Henri straightened, and tension radiated in his jaw as soon as she turned the discussion in that direction. She wasn't Greta anymore, but the platoon sergeant of his Scout Wing. "You're right, I *am* a pilot, and there are two things all pilots know: one, good pilots die and two, even the best commanders can't change that. I know it sucks that Sleeves isn't here anymore; but one of your pilots *is* here because of the work done by those three men in that Ops Room last night. Be thankful for that, Sergeant." He paused, hoping that would be enough for her.

"I'm thankful Starfall came back," Johansen conceded, voice still full of fire. "Which was also due to a damn good amount of skill on her end as well as guidance from Nest. When it comes to Sleeves, we need to do things right. If a pilot doesn't come back, we ask 'why.' We investigate. Even if the Ops lads didn't miss anything, we owe it to Sleeves and her family to confirm that. And to the Ops lads to ensure that, if they did miss something, they are given the chance to skill up so it doesn't happen again."

Henri's shoulders sagged. "You are right about that, Sarge. If this signature masking technique is something they use in the future, we must figure out how to see through it or we're going to wind up with more dead pilots. I'll put Captain Owens and Chief Engineer Petrovic on this to lead our post-mission inquiry. Will that satisfy you?"

"It's a good start, but there's one more thing." Some of that energy had fled her voice, and she seemed just to be running on the steam of it now.

Of course, that isn't enough, Henri thought to himself.

"Make it fast, Sergeant."

"They were still talking shit about my pilots. That kind of chatter is unprofessional and downright disrespectful. It has no place in an Ops room. It needs to be addressed," Johansen said firmly.

Greta had a point. The three specialists were on duty and non-mission chatter was fine, but it was not acceptable for them to be objectifying their colleagues. "Agreed, I'll talk about it at the next Executive Group meeting to ensure all of the crew are given a reminder, and I will see that the Specialists are reprimanded appropriately."

There was a disgruntled sigh on the other end of the line, but Johansen said, albeit begrudgingly, "Fair enough." Then, she cleared her throat. "Starfall is out of surgery and in recovery now. I went to see her. Doc Ross said she pulled through well."

Henri closed his eyes as relief flooded through him. "Great news, Greta. I'll check on her when I can. See you at the mission debrief this afternoon." He ended the call with a simple voice command and rolled back into bed to get a few more hours of sleep.

CHAPTER 6

A SHARP KNOCKING on the door was the only warning Henri got before a young man with the red trim of a corporal on his crisply ironed uniform jacket walked into the room. In an instant, the lights were switched to low, and a mug of coffee and tray of freshly cooked breakfast was set on the table in the corner.

"Morning, Commander," the young man said in a tone far too bright for Henri. Each of the corporal's steps between the table to the display screen on the opposite wall was punctuated by the dull thunk of his cybernetic left leg hitting the floor in a slightly uneven gait. "I know you've had a long night, so I canceled your non-essential appointments to give you a bit more time to sleep, and to fit in the debriefing, and review this afternoon."

The corporal, Jason Zhang, stood by the screen. "I've got your itinerary up here. I'll wait outside while you get ready for the day."

Zhang had been working with Henri for a year, after climbing the administrative ranks, following a disastrous mission as an infantry pilot. He'd lost his leg and acquired some grounding nerve damage in the accident, but remained dedicated to the Triple C. Since becoming the commander's assistant, he had proven himself to be capable and diligent ... and not afraid of facing some of the disgruntled muttering and threats Henri had made, on occasion, when his sleep was interrupted prematurely.

"Is there anything you need from me before I step out?" Zhang asked, most likely wanting to hear a response to make sure Henri was awake before he left.

Not for the first time, Henri chastised himself for giving this kid the access code to his room. Sitting up, he leaned his head to the side with his eyes closed as the corporal moved around the room. "No, that's all. Thank you, Corporal ..."

Henri waited to hear the door cycle closed before he blinked the sleep out of his eyes to look at the wall-mounted display. True to his word, the kid had juggled some things around and given him the morning off. With a smile, Henri threw his torso forward, trying to fling himself up onto his feet. Once he was standing, his nose led him to the tray of breakfast which he devoured with great gusto. The coffee that accompanied it helped force his eyes open as he took out his datapad and brought up the mission logs from the previous night. His conversation with the Sergeant had him curious about those energy readings ... and what the specialists had said.

He scrolled back in the notes, checking the recordings of the Ops Team. He rolled his eyes as he listened to the conversations that went on before his arrival. He noted that the new specialist, Eggles, had even gone out of his way to swap his shift so he could be around to listen to Starfall's voice. It was a little creepy, but he hoped it was nothing more than the exuberance of youth and inexperience.

"Okay, Greta, maybe you have a point ..." he muttered to

himself. He kept scrolling until he saw the moment he'd walked in. He scrolled back and paused again.

"Norgard didn't perform a spectral analysis on the surface readings when they kicked on," he murmured before sipping the last of his coffee.

Rising from his seat, Henri strode to his private bathroom for a quick shower. He'd barely dried off before hauling his uniform on. He swiped his datapad from his table and tucked it under his arm before stepping out of his quarters and called out, "Zhang, is the chief engineer scheduled to be in the Mech Bay at this hour?"

Zhang was waiting in the corridor outside, as always. His black hair was spiked to perfection, and he seemed as if being awake and on top of everything at this hour was his natural state. "Affirmative, Commander. The chief engineer should be in Mech Bay One or Two at this time of the morning."

"Great, thank you," Henri said. "I'd like you to get back to the office and see about adding another half hour to the staff meeting this week; I have something to include on the agenda. I'll be in the Mech Bay for the next hour, or so, if anyone is looking for me." He turned and headed for the elevator.

Snapping off a salute, Zhang headed down the corridor in the opposite direction, toward the executive wing of the ship. Henri rode down to the Mech Bay level and paused at the junction that would take him to the infirmary. Looking down the hall, he remembered that Starfall was in recovery. Although, even if she was out of the woods, she still might have been unconscious. He resolved to check on her later in the day. For now, he had an investigation on his mind.

Striding into the Mech Bay and breathing in the familiar odor of metal parts and grease, Henri looked around for the chief engineer. As he figured, he found Vitali Petrovic standing on a platform directing the inspection of Starfall's mech, Calliope, with two of his staff.

"Hey, Chief," Henri shouted up at the group of engineers on the lift, before the husk of the Hummingbird.

At the sound of Henri's voice, the balding, barrel-chested chief engineer looked over the railing of his platform. Rather than wait for the slow hover of the platform to reach the floor, he swung himself over the ledge and landed on the ground beside him with a grunt.

"Ugh, I'm getting too old for that." Petrovic groaned as he straightened and rolled his heavy-set shoulders. Even standing at full height, he barely came up to Henri's chest. "Came to check on Calliope?"

That wasn't quite what Henri had come by for, but he was interested in the Hummingbird's condition all the same. He decided it would make a good enough segue. "What's the damage?"

"It ain't pretty, I'm afraid," Petrovic said, rubbing his short wiry beard. "I've barely managed to finish cleaning the blood out of the cockpit. There was a lot ... is Starfall going to pull through okay?"

"She's in recovery now, we'll just have to wait and see."

With a heavy sigh, the chief gave Henri a tour of the decimated Hummingbird. He started from the outside, with all the panel damage, and worked his way in. He showed a particular skill for knowing not only what each part did mechanically, but the impact it would have on the pilot's experience.

When they'd first met, Chief and the Commander had been applying for mech training together. It was back in the day when all pilots shared mechs, and Chief was rejected from the first draft because of his height. It was too expensive to tailor a mech to suit him, especially when they swapped pilots out frequently, but he loved the idea of mechs too much to leave them be, and became an engineer instead. That career path almost ended, too, when he had been distracted and tried to work on a core before it had cooled, but the mechanical arm that the medics put on, in place of his burned limb, was just as dexterous as the original.

"Starfall would've felt like Calliope's boots were made of lead," Petrovic explained, "the shock absorption is completely gone. It rattled everything else loose, which is one of the reasons the coolant line was so vulnerable when it got hit."

To make his point, the chief shoved his stubby mechanical arm through a gaping wound in Calliope's exterior and wiggled it around until, with a grunt, he managed to pull out a bit of casing that had cracked, something that should have protected the coolant line, but was evidently smashed to pieces. He held some of the cracked insulation up for the commander to see before throwing it onto a pile of scraps and wiping some grease off his hand and onto his pants.

"The bird's salvageable, Commander, but I gotta be honest ... it might be significantly more economical to consider issuing Starfall a new mech." Petrovic frowned as he patted Calliope's hull. He looked at the mech with a sense of sadness one might reserve for the loss of a friend or loved one.

Henri was shocked by just how damaged the internals on this scout mech looked. It also reminded him of just how beat up its pilot looked the night before. While he was guiding her back to safety, Henri had severely underestimated the conditions she must have been working under. A new sense of respect filled him at the realization of the ordeal Astera had gone through. She certainly deserved all the extra water allocation he had promised. Probably more.

Sadly, they weren't anywhere close to a planet that had a Mech Yard to find a replacement for her mech. On top of that, he knew that Starfall liked the chassis. He still remembered the way her dark eyes had lit up when he showed her around on her first day in the company.

"We can't go get a replacement frame, Vitali. We're stuck here; the company that hired us told us to hold. Even put down a retainer to make sure we didn't go anywhere while they looked at the mission data we were able to collect."

The news of a hold would be information to anyone outside the commander's office. It was one of the last things he saw before shutting down for the night. He didn't want to let on that the Triple C was still working for the same company that nearly cost them two mechs, but Henri had his own reasons for sticking around.

"Do what you can to get it back to fighting shape. I don't think Starfall's going to be ready to join it any time soon, so take your time. Meanwhile, I need to pick your brain about some data we got from the mission. Can we talk in your office?" Henri asked as they finished their lap around the damaged Hummingbird.

"Of course," Petrovic grumbled. He called out to some of his staff that he'd be back shortly, before gesturing for the commander to follow him. They walked through a warehouse of mechs in various stages of assembly and service, to a small, glass-walled office at the rear of the deck.

The office should have been empty, but as they approached, Henri could see the assistant, at the desk, just outside the door, shrinking further and further back in his seat as Greta Johansen bore down on him, her eyes narrowed as she jabbed a pointed finger in the poor man's direction. Henri had to hold back an audible groan.

As an ex-scout herself, Greta had an athletic but svelte frame. However, her slick black hair was pulled back off her sharply angled face in a neat bun, and the severe lines of her uniform jacket, trimmed with the orange of her station, added bulk in just the right places to make her appear more intimidating. Henri assumed it was a combination of her appearance and personality that helped the sergeant seem threatening.

"What's going on here?" Petrovic demanded as they approached.

Greta turned around, the smile on her face reminding Henri of a feline predator who had just spotted its dinner. "Ah, Chief. I was just asking this young man when he was expecting you back in your office."

Behind her, the young officer gulped and stepped back, his eyes darting to the door to his right, and the chief nodded. The lad was gone in an instant.

"You don't normally seek me out." Petrovic unclipped the belt of tools around his broad waist and threw it onto the assistant's desk with an obnoxious thunk. "What can I do for you?"

Greta looked up at Henri. "The same thing you're here to do for him, I'd wager," she said, cocking one eyebrow up in a perfect arch.

"Maybe ..." Henri figured there was no way out of it, so he gestured for both Greta and Vitali to step into the office. Vitali walked over and sank into the grease-splotched chair behind his desk, almost disappearing behind the mountain of spare parts and other bric-a-brac.

Henri waited for Greta to join him by the door and lowered his voice. "Just a reminder that while you outrank Private Benitez, he is the chief's assistant. As a sergeant in command of other pilots, I would hope you'd remember to act professionally with all departments, especially the one that puts your mechs back together."

Not waiting for Greta to reply, Henri skirted past her and

joined the chief. He pulled his datapad out from under his arm and put it on Vitali's desk to let it connect wirelessly. He didn't bother with any preface or context. He just jumped right into business. "Vitali, say I wanted to power a long range anti-mech turret. Would that take a bigger power supply than a security mech's core?"

"Not necessarily bigger, but you can get away with less shielding." Vitali reclined in his seat, and rubbed his ruddy chin, as he considered it. "Mech cores are shielded with so many redundant layers of protection because no one wants to be responsible for boiling a pilot in their cockpit, due to a stream of leaking particles while the mech is in operation. The power core for an installed defense turret can be air-cooled and is usually away from anyone, or anything, it can damage. That's why we can typically pick them up easier when someone kicks them on."

"Would we be able to pick one up from orbit?" Henri asked.

Greta observed the interaction with great interest as she remained by the door.

"It's possible. Despite what you might think though, the atmosphere and magnetoshpere are excellent at absorbing radiation of all kinds." Vitali leaned forward, his face lighting up with the novelty of a new puzzle to consider. "But you might still be able tell it's not a mech's power source by the flux density."

"Anything else that might give it away?"

"Well, the lack of shielding, or I should say, the reduced shielding, would allow some higher energy particles to escape. Not enough to be dangerous to anyone nearby, but certainly energetic enough for it to stand out."

"That's why the J-band radiation could only get picked up by a ground observer." Henri glanced at Greta as he spoke.

"So, if you had a group of mechs standing around it and they all kicked on at once, would that muddy the signal enough to mask it?"

"From a ground-based observer? No. From our orbiting ship? Probably."

"What if you were to run a spectral analysis on it from up here?"

"Maybe." Vitali rocked forward, putting his chin in his hand. This time, he chewed his answer over for several long moments before speaking. "There are windows in the absorbance spectrum of air, so typically those are the wavelengths we see. Baldalan is different; it has higher humidity, so we should see gaps in all the same places where water absorbs energy."

With that, Henri tapped the screen of his datapad, uploading the energy readings the Ops Team had recorded. "Can you scrub this signal and see if the data points to an installed power supply rather than a mech core?"

Vitali bent over the screen. "Hmmm, lots of noise in this recording." His jaw tightened and his bushy brows furrowed. "Might take me some time to run a signal analysis on it."

"Do it. I want our Ops Team to be able to figure out what our enemies are hiding in the future. I'd rather not have a wing of mechs walk into range of an anti-mech turret without knowing it's there." Henri's lips twisted into a grimace at the thought. They couldn't get Sleeves back, but they could learn from their mistakes to try and avoid losing someone else the same way.

Greta cleared her throat. "That would be ideal." She turned to the commander. "Can we speak outside, please?"

"Sure, Sergeant." Henri confirmed the files were transferred from his datapad before tucking it back under his arm and nodding to Vitali in farewell. He strode over to the door, and pulled it open to let Greta out first, before joining her.

Looking around at the noisy Mech Bay, Henri frowned. "Maybe we should move this to my office," he called over the sound of machinery.

Greta nodded in agreement and kept her lips pressed tightly together, as if stopping herself from talking. Once she agreed, Henri turned on his heel and led her out of the Mech Bay and towards the elevator. They rode up to the Command Deck together, walked past the bridge, and into his office. It was a modest size, given his position, and it was utilitarian in design and functionality. He had a desk, a chair, and a couple of seats opposite for people who came to meet with him. Beyond that, there were the standard screens he used to monitor operations, but it was a clean, uncluttered space.

Stepping behind his desk, Henri gestured to one of the visitor chairs. "Won't you sit down?"

Greta frowned at the chair, then sat and took a breath to collect herself before speaking. "You asked the Ops officers to run a spectral analysis when you walked in."

Henri sighed as he took his own seat. "I did. Specialist Hermedilla admitted he hadn't run one before my arrival. Given the nature of our mission, I'm guessing he knew as well as I did that the real information would be coming from Starfall's sensors. I asked for one to make sure there wasn't something else we were missing. As the chief said, the J-band emissions weren't going to reach our orbital sensors." Sitting back, he continued. "Our intel, and our packet from our employer, told us they didn't have anything big enough to fire into orbit, but it seemed like a lot of power all in one spot; I wanted to make sure our ship wasn't in danger," he explained, hoping that would be enough.

"So, it isn't part of standard procedure?" Unlike when

Greta was demanding repercussions for the way the specialists were talking about her pilots, her tone now seemed different. Almost deflated.

"Not in this case. Like I said, the real confirmation was going to come from the ground. Our sensors were there to provide overwatch and, in this case, an indicator for our forward scout to engage her active sensors."

Johansen leaned back in the seat, ran a hand over her smooth hair and then, letting out a deep sigh of resignation, "Did you want me to notify the families?"

Henri shook his head. "I'll write up the communication myself, but I'd like to learn more about Sleeves. We did a few missions together, but, being the commander, I rarely spent time with her. I heard things, of course, but what did I miss by not talking to her?" he asked, looking to his wing sergeant for help.

"Sleeves was the backbone of the unit, and the best corporal we could have asked for." Greta scrubbed her face in a rare concession to an emotion other than her default of righteous rage. "She treated all my pilots with as much tough love and protectiveness as she did her kid brother. She was always talking about him in their downtime. She was looking forward to our next leave so she could use some of her savings to take him to Venus."

Once Greta started speaking, it seemed she didn't want to —or couldn't—stop. She told Henri some funny stories about the tough scout who was rough around the edges but all heart inside. She spoke at great length and didn't seem to notice how much she shared with him until she looked up and saw the expression on his face. She cleared her throat, "Will that, uh, will that be enough?" She had stories for days, but realized she'd spent long enough talking.

Henri smiled, a look of warmth and appreciation on his

face "That will be more than enough. Thank you for sharing about Corporal Monique 'Sleeves' Hughes." He made sure to use her full name, too, as those often got lost in the day-to-day flow of nicknames and callsigns around a mech unit. He wouldn't let his people forget that the pilots and crew around them came from somewhere. That they all had histories that predated their time in the Triple C.

CHAPTER 7

HENRI RUBBED HIS EYES. The strain from reading, and rereading, his letter to the family of Monique Hughes was starting to get to him. It didn't help that he sat through a multi-hour post-mission review to arrive at the same conclusions he had found during his talk with Sergeant Johansen. Still, the meeting was part of the company's standard operating procedures, and it would look suspicious if they did not have a proper debriefing. Blinking his eyes open, he read the letter one final time. After recounting what others had said about her, it was hard to find his own words, especially about a pilot he rarely spoke to. Skimming it one more time, he felt safe that it was error-free and sent it off to the administrative office for a proofread.

The door chime startled him out of his seat. Henri thought Zhang had cleared his schedule, but when the door opened, Henri realized there was a private appointment he had forgotten all about. "Annalise?"

"Henri, please don't tell me you forgot about tonight," the ship's chief medical officer pouted as she brushed past him on her way into the room.

"No, I ... I had a lot on my mind today," he said, skirting around the truth as he shut the door and followed her.

"You and me both, Henri. Got anything to drink?"

"Sure." Henri walked into the seating area of his suite. He opened the cooler and grabbed two of the beers inside. Popping the tops, he brought them over, passing one to Annalise.

She smiled, clinking the necks of their bottles together before taking a dramatic pull of the drink. "Ahhh, one of the perks of Command, I guess," she mused, sitting on his couch, and slouching back. She paused, tilting her head to the side as she watched him. "Hey, are you okay? If tonight's not a good night, I can come back."

"No, no, it's all right. In fact, I'm glad you're here." He crossed the room and sank down onto the couch beside her.

Annalise turned, tucking a leg under her as she really looked at him for the first time since entering the room. "Then how about we talk for a little first? It seems like you've got a bit on your mind." She patted his thigh. "Is it about the mission yesterday?"

Henri nodded. "It was supposed to be so simple. Send in some scout mechs; watch the base for the signal we were trying to find; exfiltrate to extraction. But it went bad, really bad. One experienced pilot was killed, and a second promising pilot wound up in Med Bay." He shook his head. "Ever since, I've been asking myself if I missed something that could have saved our pilots. I suppose I'm not the first commander to wonder the same after a mission like that."

"That is the great weight of a commander's position, or so I am told," Annalise said, taking a sip of her beer. "But I know you. We've worked together for over a decade. You always do the best you can in the moment." She set her drink down on the side table and took his hand. "It is truly devastating that

Sleeves is gone, but Astera will pull through. I checked on her before coming over. She may be small, but she's built tough."

Henri smiled. "I've only spoken to her a few times, but after talking with her on the radio and knowing what she did to get off the planet, I know you're right about her. Still, she should never have wound up in that position." He paused, shaking his head. "So much I keep replaying in my head, wondering if I was too ambitious, if I maybe blinded myself to the warning signs. I know what I would do if I were down there, but that's just years of piloting talking to me. Part of me is still the pilot that took the risk of founding this company; that guy who took all those chances along the way when I should have pulled out. Maybe I'm not supposed to be a commander." He finally said what had been eating at him all day.

"Hey, look at me, Henri." Annalise took his drink from him and set it aside. She cupped his cheek, but he wasn't quite ready to meet her gaze "You need to back yourself. I don't know the details of what happened down there, but it sounds like you made some tough calls. I'd be more worried if this wasn't eating you up." She let her hand drop onto his thigh. "Want to know how I know you're meant to be commander?"

Henri finally blinked and shifted to look deep into her eyes. So many nights, back when they were trying to be a real couple, he would lie with her and look into those eyes. Something in their deep green shade reminded him of living on a planet, brimming with life. It always helped calm him down. "Tell me."

"You're a good commander because you give a shit," Annalise told him gently. "Because you're not sitting here, raging and blaming every other person in the company for what happened. You're a good commander because you are looking at your role in things as well. Which means if you made any mistakes, and that's a big if, you're going to learn from them." She took both of his hands in hers. "You lost a pilot yesterday. That will never be easy, nor should it. If it is, then you need to get out of the job. But for now? Learn what you can and let everyone know how you go about making sure it doesn't happen again. That's what you've always done, and what you will continue doing."

Henri closed his eyes for a moment and exhaled, feeling his body relax. He reached out and settled his hands on Annalise's hips. "Thanks. I tend to forget that I don't need to let thoughts run around in my head all day, picking up steam." He pulled her onto his lap, and turned to rest against the back of the couch as his arms slid around her. "I don't want to think about that anymore tonight," he confessed, desperately craving a break.

With a wicked smile, Annalise leaned in and kissed him. It was quick, but reminded him of the true purpose of her evening visits. "Good, because it's been a long day for me too, and I just want to forget it all." She wrapped her arms around his shoulders and kissed him again. This time, she lingered in it and helped the mood shift from one of reflection to anticipation.

THE MORNING ALARM roused Henri far too early following the night he spent with Annalise. As usual, she had left after they finished; neither one of them needed the gossip that would come from someone seeing her coming or going from his quarters, not when Annalise only wanted something casual, without strings attached. Checking his datapad, he found that the administrative section had sent out the post-mission report, and he was glad to see Sergeant Johansen's approval already on the document.

With a groan, Henri pushed himself out of bed and went about his usual routine. This steadied his mind more than anything: routine. He could switch off and let his muscle memory carry him through the morning. Before ducking out of his room, he retrieved the bullet casing he had taken from Astera and tucked it into his pocket. As usual, Zhang was waiting for him in the hallway beyond. When the young man went to begin his morning report, Henri raised a hand.

"Save it this morning, Corporal. I'm heading down to the Med Bay to check on our downed pilot. Whatever needs my attention can wait until after that," he said, already moving in that direction.

The step and thud of Zhang's leg echoed behind Henri as the corporal followed. "Copy that, Commander," Zhang said with a nervous look at his own datapad, and the rather packed timetable on the screen. He did not argue, though. "Would you like me to attend with you? Or should I head back to the office to take care of some of the administrative tasks for you?"

"If you could get through some of the admin, I would appreciate it." Henri was confident the corporal would be able to complete some of the basic tasks without oversight. He had proven himself to be astute and thorough and, if Henri was honest with himself, he would rather not deal with that kind of thing anyway.

"Then I will be in the office; let me know if you need me, Commander." Zhang gave him a crisp salute before walking off in the opposite direction as the commander.

"Will do, Corporal." Henri gave the young man a return salute. He smiled to himself as he turned to walk to the Med Bay. There was a time when he was an eager pilot in training and he wasn't all that different from the corporal in those days. He tried to push those thoughts away though. He didn't want to be grinning like an idiot when he reached the Med Bay. That would cast the wrong impression. When he arrived, he saw Annalise approach, her face serene.

"Good morning, Doctor," Henri said, keeping everything professional now that they were in mixed company.

"Good morning, Commander. I was just about to call you. Ms. Ramos is awake, but my staff found a couple of issues we need to go over before you see her." Dressed in dark grey scrubs with the blue trim all majors wore, Annalise looked every part the chief medical officer. She gestured to her office by the door. "Shall we?" She stepped in front of Henri before he could enter.

Henri knew better than to ignore Annalise's concerns, so he put aside his worries about the mountain of tasks he had that day and decided to give her the time she needed. "Lead the way." He walked along behind her, looking around to see that the Med Bay was relatively, and thankfully, very quiet.

The pair walked into Annalise's meticulously clean and ordered office. Annalise sat behind her desk and immediately pulled up a crewmate file on her desktop screen. Henri took the seat on the opposite side of the desk and leaned in, watching as she pinched the image of the file and turned it around. With a flick of her fingers, it opened to display Starfall's name, Astera Ramos, across the top.

"Normally I wouldn't bother you about any of this. It's something the admin staff should be following up on, but it brings up a lot of questions about our onboarding process or–" she hesitated, drumming her fingers on the screen, "–potentially, the staff member herself."

With a swipe, Annalise redirected the file to Astera's next of kin details. Company policy required three contacts for this section. There were three there. It all looked fine, but Henri knew there must be a problem if Annalise wanted to speak to him, so he waited for her to reveal her concerns.

"We tried contacting all of the people she listed and found that they were all dead ends," she tapped each one in turn to show several attempts had been made to contact each. "I asked admin to follow up, and they said they couldn't find any of these people in the current directories. Which doesn't matter so much now that she is awake, but if something had happened, we would have to go on a serious fact-finding mission to contact someone to give us medical consent. It's not something myself or my staff have the time to do in that context."

Henri leaned forward. "You're telling me every one of these names is bogus?" He scrolled through the list himself and noted all the attempts at contact from the admin team. It's not that he didn't trust them; it was just hard to believe that no one came back in the affirmative.

"Every single one of them. We even called her last work-place, and while they could find her file, and a record that they had provided us with a reference when we onboarded her, they couldn't find a single person who actually remembered working with her to ask if there were any other alternative next of kin options," she said, sounding equally as surprised as she looked over at him.

Henri's eyes narrowed. "Then who is she? Where did she come from?" he asked, rhetorically. He stood slowly, looking at his old friend, his suspicion rising. "Did you take DNA samples? We may need to run them against the Warp Corporation's criminal database." He hated himself for even suggesting it.

There were a few different ways to travel across the Void to visit the various galaxies throughout known space. The Latagarosh, like most other ships that traveled between systems, used a jump drive. The engine was capable of propelling vehicles at faster than light speed to turn what would otherwise be years of travel into mere hours. However, the Void was vast, and even the best FTL drives could not compete with the limitations of time and distance. That was where the warpships came in. Their drives were expensive marvels of modern technology that folded the distance between different parts of space to make traveling between them infinitely faster than if they had traveled faster than light. Given their expense, such ships were few and far between, and tightly controlled.

The Warp Corporation was the leading organization facilitating long range warp jumps to speed up travel times across the galaxy. They ran along predictable routes, with scheduled stops in the most important systems. Their reputation for safety was well known, as was their stand on not facilitating the spreading of unsavory characters. To avoid assisting pirates, criminals, and the like to spread their malice across the universe, they kept a thorough database of all known criminals and insisted on full, and verified, manifests before helping a ship warp between systems. Their checks provided the quickest way to learn if someone had a record, as they already had links to all the various forms of government across the Void. The Triple C made sure they ran record checks on all of their staff, but they opted for the less invasive identity searches, rather than DNA-based ones.

Annalise seemed surprised by his suggestion, but she nodded. "I'll run those now," she confirmed, already tapping away at her screen. "Are you still going to see her today?"

"I am, but don't let on about this discrepancy yet. That will come in time." He ran his hand over his uniform to smooth it. "For now, we're all relieved she is back and awake. We're going to act like there is nothing wrong." He walked towards the door, suddenly even more determined to speak to the injured pilot. It would be a challenge to keep the anger in him from simmering over onto his face when he was in the room with her. He slipped his hand into his pocket and wrapped his fingers around the bullet casing, deciding he would hold onto it for a little longer. Nothing set Henri off quite like being lied to.

CHAPTER 8

ASTERA WAS CAUGHT between wanting to take in her surroundings to reassure herself that she had survived, and wanting to pass out again. The last thing she remembered was collapsing just as the staff in Mother Hen secured Calliope for travel. It was hot, and every part of her was screaming out in agony.

Now, something had changed.

The temperature.

She had never been more grateful for the cool, sterile, recycled air of the Triple C's jumpship. Astera could have done without the full body pain, though. Especially as it had landed her in the Med Bay. Astera hoped she wouldn't be out of commission long. She wanted to avoid a lengthy stay in such a place, with too many nosey doctors poking around.

Deciding things couldn't possibly be that bad if she'd made it back to the ship safely, Astera tested the waters by tentatively wiggling her toes. Her calf muscles felt heavy and dead, but didn't protest at the movement. Braving a little more, she then tried to see if she could draw her legs up.

"Ah! Mother fuck–" she hissed, grasping the sheets at

either side of her hips. She had forgotten how much of that motion would go beyond her thighs and require movement in her core. Normally, it would be fine, but absolutely everything in her torso objected to the effort. She let her legs fall back against the mattress as each panted breath stabbed her lungs like burning knives.

Astera let go of the sheets and raised her arms, finding that much easier so long as she didn't raise them too high. She peeled off the top sheet from her chest to peer underneath. She found her body tightly wrapped in bandages from armpits to belly button, and there were already deep purple bruises on her hips. Below that, she spied a pair of unfamiliar panties, and discovered further discoloration on her legs, as well as some cuts which had begun to heal. "Damn ... must be some good pain killers," she whispered to herself.

She let the sheet drop as a yawn tugged at her lips. Maybe going back to sleep would be a better idea than staying awake. The bruises and cuts did not look good, but Astera had dealt with injuries like this before. The stabbing in her lungs, though, that was new. She figured she needed to take advantage of the painkillers before they wore off and the fuzzy edges of pain turned into something sharper. Astera settled her arms back by her sides, wishing she could curl up on her side, and let her heavy eyelids settle shut.

As her mind began to drift, the hiss of the door opening and the patter of two sets of feet roused her. She opened her eyes, having to blink once more against the harsh lights. Even through the bleariness, it was easy to recognize the commander and Doctor Colywn entering the room. Once they saw that Astera was awake, Colwyn called over her shoulder, back into the hallway and a pair of nurses came in. The nurses set to work checking Astera's vitals and the like, as the two ranking officers sat down in chairs beside the bed.

"How are you feeling?" Colywn asked in a clear, professional tone.

Astera wanted to blurt out how much better she would be if she got more sleep, but that wouldn't be fair to the doctor. She was only doing her job. It was also easier to temper her anger at the sight of the commander sitting beside her. She hadn't expected a visit from the boss.

But he wasn't the one asking her the questions.

"Like I've been trampled by my own mech." Astera's throat was so dry it was hard to get the words out. "But it looks like your team cleaned me up well. Thank you." She turned to the commander and felt a smirk forming. "Doesn't mean I'll let you wiggle out of those fifteen minutes in the shower, though, Knuckle Duster."

The commander chuckled, but his expression was a little stiff. "I don't know if fifteen minutes is going to be enough to wash off all the sweat that got ground into your pores when they pulled you off that rock. Let's add another fifteen for good measure."

The nurses did their best to apply topical analgesics to the bruises, but it was clear that it was going to be a while before they healed. For the first time, Astera took in the tubes connected to her, and she saw that they were pumping plasma and fluids into her, most likely to replace everything she'd lost in the fight and subsequent escape. "We've got the best possible medications going into you to ensure a swift recovery, but you're still going to need to stick around here for a week or so. So, you can save that shower time for one luxurious soak," Colywn explained.

Astera frowned. *A week?* The thought of being stuck in bed for that long was daunting. Her annoyance was suddenly interrupted by the image of Sleeves' mech exploding right in front of her and she winced, looking away from the doctor.

"That makes sense," she conceded. At least she was still alive. "I suppose it'll take a while to get Calliope back up to scratch. Sorry about that, Commander."

"Don't worry about it. In fact, I'm impressed you were able to get your mech back to us after everything that happened. You are right though; we'll need to rebuild the frame. We'll try to put the decals and all back on, but don't be too disappointed if you must personalize everything again when you are both up and running," the commander explained, addressing her worries in one go, showing once more that he was still a pilot at heart.

If Astera could shrug, she would have. Instead, she settled for shaking her head. It set the room spinning around her, and she made a mental note not to do it again. "It's okay. After that, she deserves a new paint job. I'll have to let the chief know not to bother trying too hard with the decals." Astera liked the chief; he was always good to her. She didn't want him work too hard if she was just going to repaint the panels anyway.

The commander shifted in his seat, his attention seemingly a million miles away, for a moment, before snapping back to the present moment. "It'll be a while before it gets to repainting stage. It's more important to make sure that everything is working. Need to be able to trust your equipment in the field. Until then, is there anything you would like brought down from your quarters? Anyone we should notify beyond the usual command structure?" he asked.

Astera's hand went to her neck. "I had a little charm on a necklace. I thought I grabbed it before I passed out. Maybe I dropped it somewhere ..." she looked down at her hands and bit her lip.

"What sort of trinket was it? I can check with the medical staff and see if it's in with your goods in storage," Colwyn offered, moving to rest at her bedside. Meanwhile, the commander sat forward, fully present in the conversation.

"It was a bullet casing. Just a tiny thing really, but it uh–" she cleared her throat "–it means a lot to me." She then returned her attention to the commander. "If I'm going to stay here, I will just need some basics, one of the other scouts may be able to get them for me. I share my room with Kitty, maybe I can talk to her," she suggested, not entirely sure the commander would want to rifle through her underwear drawers.

The commander nodded. "Of course, I'll pass a message to Kitty through Sergeant Johansen."

The doctor took a datapad from her pocket and turned it on. She tapped the screen a few times before swiping her finger up and down. "I can't see any necklace or charm listed on our intake, but the Mother Hen crew may have put it in the pocket of your pilot suit when they pulled you out of the cockpit. I can get someone to take a look and let you know tomorrow."

A sudden sense of gratitude overwhelmed Astera at the kindness and she blinked back tears. She didn't deserve it. "I ... I'm sorry I couldn't bring Sleeves back. It all happened so quickly, I wish I had told her I was okay, that I didn't need cover," Astera whispered.

The commander leaned closer. "Don't do that to yourself. She was following her orders, just like you were. You didn't pull the trigger on that missile; you didn't sneak it onto the planet either. You did more than your job just getting back to us in one piece. Celebrate that, remember that whenever you feel those thoughts creeping back in. Mourn Sleeves, share stories and laugh with your wingmates, but do not blame yourself. That won't honor her, or yourself, for the job you did."

Logically, Astera knew the commander was right, but she replayed the moment over in her head a million times, trying to think of something she could have done differently to prevent Sleeves' death. Then again, even the Latagarosh hadn't seen that missile coming, what hope did Astera have? Still, the feeling that she should have done more haunted her. Monique was her first friend when she joined the Triple C. A tear traced down Astera's cheek and she hastily wiped it away.

"What happens now that Calliope is damaged? Does it come out of my pay?" she asked, desperately needing to change the topic to something less painful. She should have known the answer, should have read the employment contract properly when she got the job, but she was just happy to be working for a reputable company. She hadn't planned on getting injured, or damaging her mech.

"Nothing comes out of your pay. The mechs are the Triple C's property, so that's why we repair, rebuild, and maintain them. We absorb those costs and the pilots always get to keep their pay for every mission completed. Speaking of, you have already been paid for yours, as well as two bonuses; one for hazard, another for getting your mech back to us so we didn't have to purchase a new one. You saved us considerable funds," the commander explained.

Relief flooded through her. If she was back with–

Astera's hand instinctively flew to her neck to clutch the bullet on the chain that was no longer there. The absence stopped that line of thinking in its tracks. She had to live in the present and right now, she was grateful to be safe from financial damages because of what happened. She let out a soft breath and winced at the pain in her ribs. "That is good to know, thank you."

"No need for thanks. You just worry about getting better.

Let me handle everything else; it's my job, after all." The commander tried his best to reassure her, but there was something he wasn't saying. Even through the haze of pain meds, it was easy to see restraint in his eyes.

Astera had gotten reasonably good at reading people over the years. Paying attention to nuance was a skill more developed than even marksmanship, or hand-to-hand combat. When she watched the commander, that sense kicked in and the worry that had been slowly ebbing away returned. "What is it?" she asked warily.

The commander waved his hand. "Nothing you need to worry about. I'm going back and forth with the customer about sticking around and doing more of their dirty work on this planet, or not. I think part of my brain is still back in the office trying to figure out how to break up this negotiation deadlock we've found for ourselves." He sighed, stretching a bit in his seat. "Like I said, you worry about getting better. Let me handle everything else."

Astera was unconvinced, but she nodded. It was not wise to push someone in charge. Instead, she turned to Doctor Colwyn. "I know this sounds stupid, but I'd do almost anything for a shower. How long until I can scrub up?" she asked, longing to feel the hot water cascading over her skin and cleaning the grime and tension away.

Colwyn frowned. "Not for a while, I'm afraid. We have your wounds sealed, but I'm worried about your nervous system. Your core temperature got pretty high; I want to keep you here for observation to make sure you don't have any brain damage," she explained. "But don't sell our sponge baths short. They do wonders, according to former patients."

Astera shifted uncomfortably at the mention of a sponge bath, but forced a smile onto her face. "Right ... I'll be sure to leave a five-star review for the sponge baths." She didn't like strangers touching her, no matter how clinical. "Thanks for everything so far, Doc. I'm sure I was a mess when I came in.

"Doctor Ross and the surgical team will probably tell you they were just doing their job. Deep down, they, like the rest of us, are glad we were able to put you back together. Given the circumstances, it could have been a lot worse. Your job now is just to rest well and do what you're told," Colwyn said with a wry smile.

It sounded terrible. "I'll do my best," Astera lied.

"Doctor Colwyn, if you can figure out how to get this one to do what she is told, feel free to let me know," the commander chimed in, grinning over at Astera.

A laugh sputtered from Astera, but then she pressed her hand against her chest as daggers of pain shot through her lungs. She gasped. "Ouch, fuck." She glanced at the commander. "Don't make me laugh, boss," she said even though she enjoyed the reprieve in his tone. "Besides, I did what you said to get off the planet. I mean, maybe I don't obey orders any other time, but as long as I do it when it counts, right?"

For the first time, Astera really looked at the man who ran the Triple C. From a distance, his build and uniform made him look older somehow. Or, maybe it was the title of "Commander" that did that. Up close, Astera was surprised to find he looked much younger than she assumed he was. She figured he was, perhaps, in his early forties. It made it all the more impressive that he was the commander of his own mercenary company, when most people were at least a decade, or two, older by the time they reached that level.

"You do listen when it matters, so that is important," the commander conceded. "So, listen to me now; lie back, relax, and worry about getting better. Those are your mission objectives. Can you do that for me, Starfall?"

She stopped herself from rolling her eyes at the pointed

use of her callsign. "I've never really had downtime before." Astera scrunched up her nose. "I'll try my best, but I may go mad stuck in this room on my own."

Doctor Colywn nodded, apparently not surprised to hear it. "Anyone would. You can be moved out to the main ward later if you will find it helps, but I want to keep you in here for a couple of days first, okay?"

"That sounds fair, thank you." Astera smiled at her. Then, she turned to the commander. "Between the half hour showers and orders to rest and relax, people might just think this is the best job this side of Earth." Astera nodded at him.

"Nah, the best job still remains 'rater of stuffed animal fluffiness'," the commander joked as he stood up. He moved to the door and waited for the doctor to join him. "I'll be back tomorrow to check on you. If I have news about what the company is doing, I'll fill you in with that as well."

"Thanks, Commander." Astera was impressed that he would commit to coming in and visiting her again. She'd assumed this visit would be his last, but maybe he really was the kind of leader everyone said he was. She watched as the commander and Doctor Colywn made their way out of the room, and then relaxed back against the bed. She looked down at her broken body and closed her eyes at the flashbacks the color of the bruises triggered. She pushed the traumatic memories aside and focused on what came after, on the survival. The hard part was over now; she had gotten off the planet alive. She just needed to heal and get back into working shape, so the commander had no reason to kick her out of the Triple C.

CHAPTER 9

THE COMMANDER STOOD in the hallway as Annalise closed the door behind her. He turned and walked with her down the hall. "In your office," he said simply, and softly, so no one overheard. He went ahead, pushing through the door, then closing it as she joined him. Sitting down, he scooted his chair over to hers.

"You won't find the item among her effects," he admitted, sliding his hand into his pocket. He withdrew the bullet casing and opened his palm. "She was gripping this in her hand so tight. One of the medics took it from her and I said I'd keep it safe. With what you have told me about her phony history, this might point us in the right direction."

Annalise's dark brows knitted together at his words. "What do you plan to do with it? Surely there's no point trying to track the round. There must be billions of them in the galaxy." She reached out and gingerly turned it over in his beefy hand, brushing her finger over the engraved letters. "Maybe this might help more than the shell itself?"

Henri pulled his fist away. "I'm thinking that the combination of caliber, language, and Astera herself, might provide answers. It's not much to go on, but there's something real and concrete about her," he explained, glancing out the window towards the doors that led to her recovery room.

"I'll bring it back tomorrow; maybe, I'll tell her that you found it and gave it to me or something. Might help her to open up about where she got it. I can't picture her being a spy; I don't think an agent would put themselves at risk like she does, but if having her here is dangerous, I need to find out."

"If the criminal history comes back clean, regardless of what else we discover, I want to keep Astera here until she is healthy and fit to go," Annalise said seriously, fixing him with a look that warned him not to waste time arguing. "I know you hate dishonesty, but I am not letting her out of here until I know she is strong enough."

Henri nodded. "I know; I'm not about to throw her in the brig while she's still recovering. I'm not that heartless. But I have a duty to the rest of the company to ensure Astera's very presence isn't putting everyone's lives in danger."

Rubbing the back of her neck, Annalise nodded. "That is fair." She laughed softly. "Nothing is ever simple in this company, is it?"

"No, but if it were *simple*, I'd sell off the company and retire somewhere. Once we iron everything out and the challenge is gone, that's the sign that it's time for something new," he said, smiling at her. "But I'm in no hurry to get to that point. I like the company and the people in it. Getting us here was no small feat and I'll be damned if I walk away from it now."

Talk of retiring had been a point of contention between them during their early days. It was also the reason Henri followed up on his own comment so quickly. He had been more than ready to let go of the lifestyle and settle down on a nice planet with her, but Annalise wasn't the settling kind. So, they had both stayed in the company and continued to live the life, and Henri had convinced himself that it was what he still wanted. There were some hard days, and some downright heartbreaking days. Losing a pilot was always the latter.

"Do you want a drink? Or is it still far too early for that?" Annalise offered, most likely knowing there was little else she could do to help.

"It's a bit early, Doc. As a medical professional, I am concerned about your cavalier attitude towards intoxicants," Henri chided, but his grin hinted that he really didn't mind so much. "Besides, the good stuff is back in my quarters anyway."

Annalise laughed and stood up, reaching over to rub Henri's shoulder. "Then sit here for as long as you like, but I must get back to work. Feel free to call, or drop by my room if you want to chat, okay? You don't have to carry this alone." She gave his shoulder a squeeze before she left the room.

"Thanks, Doc," the commander called after Annalise. He looked down at his hand, rolling the casing back and forth in his grip. It was such an odd object for a mech pilot to keep. The caliber was too small for a mech autocannon or point defense gun. It looked like a casing for an infantry weapon, or handgun. It made the etched message even more cryptic to him. Closing his fist around it again, he pushed himself up to his feet.

Luckily, the crew left him alone on his walk back to his office. He was too deep inside his own head to register the faces passing him in the hallways anyway. When he arrived, he sat down at his desk, setting the bullet atop the glass with a light clink. He nudged it over to the scanner in the corner, and let the computer do its work. Rolling it across the cylindrical side and standing it up on the sensor, he helped it take a three-dimensional scan of the casing. Within a few minutes, a digital replica of the casing spread itself across the screen on his desk, and he zoomed in on the engraving.

Hindi ako nagtagumpay pero ikaw ay kaya mong gawin.

Henri frowned at the words, not recognizing any of them. Then again, he wasn't much of a linguist. He copied the text and pasted it into the ship's knowledge base, hoping he could at least get the gist of its meaning. The result came up immediately, identifying the inscription as Tagalog, with the translation flashing across his screen.

I didn't succeed but you can do it.

Even though Henri didn't picture Astera as the kind to love inspirational quotes, she clearly held this message in high esteem. On their own, the words would have been rather innocuous. Engraved into a bullet casing, though? That was something else entirely. It held the air of a past action, or a promise, that made Henri shift uncomfortably. Who was the one who had failed? And what was *it* supposed to be?

Unfortunately, knowing what the inscription meant only made the pink-haired scout seem more of a puzzle to Henri. With his face set in hard, pensive lines, he snatched the casing back up and tucked it away in his pocket. There was no use mulling it over when there was a pending criminal record check. He'd get his answers soon enough.

THE NEXT DAY HENRI ROUSED, as usual, to Zhang's knocking as the young man brought in breakfast and the morning reports. Thankfully, it was the right mix of foods and coffee to help deal with the self-imposed, mild, hangover and the morning reports helped wake up his mind for the day to come. To get the overly eager corporal out of his room, Henri asked him to prepare the minutes, and send reminders for the meetings he had with various teams that afternoon.

Clear-eyed and sufficiently awake, Henri retrieved the casing from the pants he'd worn the day prior and left his room. He kept his hand in his pocket as he walked towards the Med Bay, fingers wrapped around the metal. The look of determination and purpose on his face parted the crowd for him. No one was brave enough to stop the commander when he looked like he was on a mission, and he was glad for it. Stepping into the Med Bay, he strode right to Doctor Colwyn's office. After last night, he was ready for his turn to talk with Astera privately. However, he wanted Annalise's approval before he did anything.

"You look like a shark that's caught a whiff of blood," Annalise observed, peering over the top of her datapad. Whatever she saw on his face made her drop her usual chastisement for him barging into her office unannounced. "Did you figure something out?"

"I've deciphered the text on the bullet, but I need to talk with her to get a read on it. Is she awake?" Henri asked, not bothering to sit down.

"She was when I checked in about twenty minutes ago." Annalise gestured to the door. "I probably don't need to say this, but I will anyway. Just take it easy on her, okay? I know you want answers, but she's high on painkillers. There is a fine line between questioning someone and taking advantage of the state they are in."

Henri nodded. "I know. I'll tread lightly. I don't intend to let her know that she is under investigation. If I push, she'll just clam up. Other than that, can I speak with her?"

Most likely sensing his eagerness to chat, Annalise sighed heavily and nodded. "Go ahead." She gestured towards the doors. "I'll tell the staff to give you both some space."

"Thanks." Henri was already walking towards the door as soon as she gave permission. Striding down the rows of beds, he pushed through the door at the back of the main room and made his way to Astera's private suite. He stopped just outside, knocking at the entrance and calling out, "Astera, may I come in?"

Through the window, Henri saw Astera look up from the datapad on the table in front of her. There were still dark circles under her eyes, but she appeared far more alert than she had the day before. She was also far cleaner, which Henri knew meant the nursing staff had provided her with a sponge bath. Her vivid magenta hair was freshly washed and neatly brushed. It cascaded over her bare shoulders, the ends brushing the top edge of the bandages wrapped around her chest. A mix of recognition and curiosity flickered in her dark eyes. "Come in, Commander."

Henri pushed through the door and walked over to the chair beside the bed. "Well don't you look better; did you sneak in your extra shower time since I saw you last?" He grinned, turning the chair, and scooting it closer the side of her bed.

Astera snorted. "I wish." She shook her head and then winced at the movement. She looked down at her own body, at the bandages she was wearing all around her torso in lieu of actual clothing. "Have you ever had a sponge bath, Commander? I haven't. Well, at least until this morning. Not quite used to the process, but ... at least I'm looking shiny, right?"

"Your hair is, at the very least. And sponge baths aren't bad; depends on who's giving you one." The words slipped out before he could stop them, but he didn't kick himself like he usually would if he misspoke in front of a staff member. He hoped it might draw out Astera a bit. If she was willing to open up, their talk might go better. The laugh she gave him reassured him that the lapse wasn't in vain. Sitting down beside her bed finally, he retrieved the casing from his pocket and held it up.

Astera's eyes widened, and she sat a little straighter.

"Oh, speaking of shiny, the Doc did find this in your effects. I guess it was in a pocket or something, so they didn't find it right away. This is what you were after yesterday, right?" he asked, extending his hand out for her to take it.

"I ... I thought it was gone for good." She took the casing from him gingerly and turned it over in her fingertips, scanning the inscription. Then, she rolled it onto her palm and closed her fist around it. "Thank you." She clutched it to her chest and smiled.

"Not a problem," Henri said, sitting back. "Interesting inscription on it. You don't see many folks using Tagalog, even back on Earth. If you don't mind me asking, what's the story behind it?" He kept his tone light, curious, as though he was just trying to make easy conversation.

Astera's shoulders stiffened at the question. She looked at him as a flash of something, panic maybe, passed over her, but the tension disappeared just as quickly as it had come. "It's just a token from a stupid bet between an old friend and I."

Henri had been in this job for long enough that his bullshit detector told him when someone was giving him a story. It was pinging insistently as Astera looked down at the casing in her hand. He kept his poker face because there wasn't enough to go on just yet.

"But ... let's back up. You know Tagalog?" she asked, sounding impressed.

As Henri figured, there was the misdirection that usually

followed a lie. If she was hiding something, it was best for her to keep his mind off it. She was good, but not scared enough for Henri to be worried.

"I had to run it through our knowledge base, but I could guess at the language." In normal circumstances, Henri wouldn't push, but this wasn't a normal circumstance. "And stupid bets are nothing to be ashamed of. Some of my best stories involve *stupid bets*. Some of the OGs can tell you a wager I made where I could only use one hand on a particular mission. Almost backfired on me," he confessed, as he tried to steer things back to her story again. He kept his eyes on her, watching for some hint about whether it was that sort of bet or something more sinister.

Astera laughed, undoubtedly familiar with similar antics. "You said it *almost* backfired on you? Does that mean you won in the end?"

"I did. They underestimated how good I am at the sticks, much as I underestimated you," Henri said with a proud grin as he sat back. "You pushed Johansen and I for that mission and we relented, figuring it would be good to get you some stick time on an easy job. What you showed me, when it all went sideways, told me you had a lot more talent and experience than I realized. I want to apologize for not having faith in you. I won't make that mistake twice."

It wasn't a line or a tactic; Henri's estimation of Astera had grown in the aftermath of the mission, despite the mess with her employee record.

After laughing along with his story, the slightly surprised, and bewildered, expression on Astera's face showed a hint of vulnerability, before it disappeared under her usual playful disposition. Only, Henri couldn't help but wonder whether it was truly her demeanor or a mask. "Thanks, boss. I ... really appreciate the compliment. Those are big words coming from someone with your track record. I'm afraid I won't be able to show you my stuff until I'm all healed up. I guess the suspense may just make me even more impressive next time you let me back in the cockpit."

"That's why you need to worry about getting healthy and nothing more. Lay back, relax, and dream of that long soak you have ahead of you. You let me handle the administration. So much more I need to tackle as a result of that mission. Who knew there'd be so much paperwork coming out of it?" he muttered, getting to his feet. Moving as nonchalantly as possible, he walked to the door while listening to hear if Astera would nibble at the hook he cast out.

"Paperwork?" Astera asked as his hand was mere millimeters away from the panel. "I suppose there is a lot of that when someone di—" she stopped, shook her head, and then sighed before continuing. "Has Sleeves' family been told?"

"I put together something nice to explain what happened. I know she kept in touch with them, so I would have hated for them to start wondering why they stopped hearing from her." Henri paused, considering his options, and then decided to try his luck. He turned back to Astera, leaning casually against the wall and tucking his hands in his pockets, keeping his body language purposefully casual. "I was more worried about you. We were looking into finding your next of kin, but I think some info got cross-populated with someone else's dossier. Now that you're awake, we can fix all that. Not today, of course. The Doc wants me to let you rest until you've recovered."

Henri pretended not to notice how her face drained of color.

"I'll check in with you again tomorrow to see how you're doing," he promised. For good measure, he gave her a smile and a wave before he left her room.

Once more, Henri made his way straight to Annalise's office. Through the glass, he could see she was tapping away at her datapad, so he didn't bother to knock.

"Astera doesn't want us to know who she is or where she's from. I let it slip that we know her paperwork is BS and she locked up like a Gen Three mech on a frost world." Henri shook his head. "It's either scary for her, or dangerous for us. Given her behavior up to now ... I really hope it's the former. She's been such a good pilot for us and Johansen loves her. If Astera can get that woman to warm to her, she's either one of the best spies ever or genuinely a good person. Something in me is leaning towards the latter."

Running a hand over his stubble roughened chin, Henri couldn't believe how much the situation was eating at him.

Annalise finally tore her attention from her work. "A genuinely good person?" She leaned back in her chair, watching him carefully. "Have you ever spoken to her before today?"

"Sort of. She was in my ear for months about getting more dangerous duty. I figured she was just another hothead that wanted to prove herself to me, but everyone that talks about her has nothing but good things to say," Henri explained.

Annalise crossed her arms over her chest. "Uh-huh ..." She stared at him until her gaze became uncomfortable. "Just be careful with this investigation, okay? I want to believe the best here, but it's becoming clear that there are more lies twisted around her than we first expected. I don't want you getting caught up in them because she's got a pretty face."

"It's not about her pretty face," Henri retorted, annoyed at the insinuation. The fight drained out of him almost instantly though, as he ignored the slight and took in Annalise's other words. "As usual, you are right about the rest. I'll be careful."

Annalise hummed somewhat smugly at the concession.

Henri stepped towards the door but didn't like leaving things between them quite like this. "Will you come by again tonight?"

"If you're not too caught up in your own head with Astera," Annalise replied, letting her words sit for a beat before adding, "and the whole situation, that is."

Henri had been friends (and more) with the chief medical officer long enough to know that her pause was entirely intentional.

"I won't be," he promised, although he wasn't sure whether he was trying to convince Annalise, or himself.

CHAPTER 10

ASTERA STARED at the closed door, lips slightly parted, brown eyes wide, for a long time after the commander left. Her heart hammered against her already aching rib cage.

They know something is wrong with my information.

The knowledge rattled around in her head, and she wondered just how much they had seen. All her details should have connected, she'd sure as hell paid enough to make sure they did. Of course, if they tried to track down her next of kin, there would not have been any replies, but that happened sometimes. People moved. People got busy and didn't reply right away. She looked down at her broken body, trying to figure out how much effort it would take to rip out the monitors and tubes, and all the junk keeping her on the bed, to follow the commander. To ask what he meant.

Although that would make her look more suspicious. Maybe she had imagined that ominous hint in his tone. Perhaps she was just more worried than she should be because of her state. Either way, she knew she couldn't chase him. She had to play it cool, and she had to figure out what to tell him if there were cracks in her story.

As Astera lay there, wondering what could be going on outside her recovery room, she heard voices in the corridor. Then, the footfalls started. There were a lot. More than when it was just the commander or the medical staff. The steps sounded hard, like combat boots. The kind the ship security wore. Panic flared in her, and she looked around to try and find a way to disconnect and disappear.

The door flew open.

"Starfall!" a chorus of voices cried out as four women burst into the room.

Astera was so filled with anxiety that it took a moment to realize it was the other pilots of the Scout Wing, not the onboard security.

Kitty, Astera's blonde-haired, blue-eyed roommate, sprang up next to the bed with a wide grin on her lips. Behind her, Glacier walked in less energetically. She peered around the room with her deep brown eyes and pushed a black lock off her high cheekbones.

"Starfall, sweetheart, we come bearing gifts," Mama Bear announced, her cheeks pink with delight as she walked in, carrying a box with both hands, with a bag hanging off her elbow.

Coming in last, Viper held up a datapad, no doubt filming their arrival. "Sorry if we woke you," she called, peering around her device. "But these three were dying to see you."

"Actually, we were *dying for cake*," Kitty chimed in, smirking at Astera. Then, the amusement drained off her face as she saw Astera was still staring at them, shocked. Kitty cupped her cheek, pressing the heel of her hand against Astera's pulse. "Void, your heart is pounding ... Mama, maybe this isn't the best time." She looked over at the red-haired elder member of the wing.

Astera took a deep breath as she plastered a smile on her

face. The racing thoughts in her mind slowed to something more manageable, and she reached up to pat Kitty's hand. "If you brought cake, then it is definitely the best time."

"See, told you our girl's always up for cake," Viper said from behind her device, walking closer. "Even if you do look like you've taken a good beating."

"Nice." Glacier rolled her eyes at Viper's comment. "I mean, you could have led with something a little more considerate. How about, 'we're glad you're safe, Starfall,' or 'you did an incredible job on that mission'?"

"Or," Mama Bear suggested, shaking her head, and walking to sit down on the end of the bed. A warm smile tugged at the corners of her lips. "We could stop bickering and ask how Starfall's holding up." Mama Bear settled her clear blue eyes on Astera expectantly.

"Well, I'll be out of action for a while. At least a week," Astera said, scratching the back of her neck and not meeting Mama Bear's gaze. "And even breathing hurts sometimes. But, I'm alive, so that's something." She stopped, sighed, and then looked up at her wingmates. At the four incredible women she had spent every day and night with since joining the Triple C. "I ... I'm sorry. Sleeves — it was all so fast — I didn't even have a chance to—" Her voice caught in her throat and tears burned her eyes.

Glacier walked over and settled a hand on her shoulder. "Now, now ... none of that. Sleeves knew the job; we all do. If she hadn't eaten that missile, it could have blown you out of your cockpit. That's how these things break sometimes. We all miss her, but don't you ever apologize or think this is your fault. You did what you had to and survived. You succeeded as far as we're concerned. Mourn Sleeves, but don't blame yourself."

Mama Bear rubbed her foot. "We'll celebrate her life

properly when you're out of here," she promised, smiling that motherly smile of hers.

"Screw future celebrations, I want my cake now," Kitty exclaimed. As usual, she kept the mood in the room from getting too heavy.

Viper took the hint and opened the box so Astera could see. "Mama snuck into the galley and baked it for you. Even made the frosting." It looked like something out of a bakery stand based in the travel hubs between here and the Core Worlds. "Get Well Soon" was written in red icing across it, complete with a cartoon version of Astera's head wrapped in a bandage.

Laughter bubbled unbidden from Astera's lips at the picture on the cake. She scrubbed at her eyes as her aching heart warmed at the sentiment. When she first joined the Triple C, she tried so hard to avoid forming any real connections, but the second she'd been assigned to the Scout Wing, all hope was lost. The crazy, intense, and often overwhelming women she worked with had wormed their way into her heart with their antics and genuine concern. It was moments like these that made her think she actually stood a chance on the Latagarosh. At least, until the commander mentioned her records. Astera's eyes flicked towards the door and she bit her lip. She didn't know what to do about that, but she had to enjoy what she had with her wing while she could.

"Mama, you're an absolute genius," Astera said, pulling herself back into the moment and beaming at the middle-aged red-headed woman at the end of the bed. "Thank you so much."

Mama shrugged as if it was no big deal to bake and decorate an entire cake with the limited luxury supplies on a ship like this.

"Can we just cut the damn thing? I skipped breakfast so I

could have enough wiggle-room in my calorie budget. I'm starving." Viper upended the bag Mama Bear had been carrying on the foot of the bed. Plates and forks tumbled out, and she started sorting them while Glacier wheeled the tray table over so Mama could settle the cake box down onto it.

With a frown, Mama leaned over and looked at the utensils from Viper's bag. "Oh, dangit. I forgot the knife. I'll be back," she said, straightening up.

"Don't bother." Kitty put a hand on Mama's shoulder and then reached down the front of her tank top, tugging a multitool from her bra. She flipped through the various options until she found the knife. "Aha. This should do."

Whilst Glacier rolled her eyes at the offer, no one protested as Mama took the knife and started sectioning the cake into extremely generous pieces. "I saw the commander in Doctor Colwyn's office as we walked in. Should we invite him in for cake? He looks like the type to appreciate a home-baked slice," Mama said as she worked.

Viper snickered at the comment. "Yeah, I'm sure that's the only reason you want him in here, Mama."

"Oh, come now. I can't help if it I like watching handsome men enjoy things I've spent time baking," she said with a grin as she served out the pieces onto the waiting plates in Glacier's hands.

Laughter bounced through the space and Kitty sidled up beside Astera again. "Don't go scaring us again, okay?"

Astera rested her head on Kitty's shoulder. "I don't intend to," Astera agreed, happy to talk about anything other than the commander.

"Now, I know the admin staff probably did their usual thing, but do you want us to get a device in here so you can call someone who isn't on your emergency contact list?" Glacier asked before taking a delicate forkful of cake.

Anything but that, Astera thought to herself.

She shook her head. "No, it's all good. Nothing I can't handle once I'm out of here," she lied.

Glacier nodded as she chewed, but that glint in her eyes didn't disappear. Astera's cover story never seemed to satisfy her sharpest wingmate. Glacier was always subtle about it, of course, but it was clear that she didn't believe the simple "bored outer rim girl seeks adventure across the galaxy" thing. There were plenty of mech pilots in the Triple C with such backgrounds, but the Scout Wing seemed to draw in those with a bit more nuance, or darkness, in their pasts.

"I heard through the grapevine that there'll be a follow-up mission to Baldalan," Kitty said, changing topics, much to Astera's relief.

"By 'grapevine,' do you mean Helen from Ops?" Astera teased.

Kitty shrugged as she poked a piece of cake with her fork. "A good reporter never reveals their sources."

"Then spill, because you're not a damn reporter," Viper said.

"Maybe I will be in the future. Don't want to mess up my career prospects before they begin, you know?" Kitty pushed the cake around on her plate. "Point is, we're not done here yet."

"Well, it won't be us." Mama Bear frowned over her cake. "They're going to send the heavies down to hit that place. Now that we know whatever you and Sleeves were looking for is down there, the client will want it salvaged or destroyed. That's how these things go." She sounded sad about the prospect of a further mission at a site that cost them a pilot and a dear friend.

Glacier looked over. "Yeah, but thanks to Astera's efforts,

they won't be going in blind. They will be better off this time. They can handle things."

Viper poked at her slice. "I wonder how heavy they are going to go in? Seems like overkill for the old man and the OGs to level that site. They don't get out of bed for less than a-hundred-k. Or so I've been told."

As everyone talked about the potential for another mission planetside, they finished up the cake.

"If you like, I can bring some things down from your locker. It's so impersonal in here," Mama Bear offered.

Astera jumped, having tuned out the conversation. She just kept thinking about her escape from that planet. Kept seeing Sleeves and her mech, Perry, being blown to a million pieces. "Oh, um ... it's fine, but thanks for the offer," Astera said with a grateful smile. The last thing she needed was for the others to realize just how sparse her wardrobe really was.

Most of the pilots and staff on the ship decorated their small shared cabins with pictures and artifacts from home. Kitty had constantly bemoaned how clinical and bare Astera's side of the room looked. Astera insisted that she hated clutter and changed the subject. The truth was, she didn't really have anything, nor could she afford to get attached to bits and pieces. She had learned the hard way that loving things only made them more painful to leave behind when the time came.

"Right, well, if anything changes just give me a buzz," Mama said, not seeming bothered by her refusal.

After that, the group fell into a somewhat awkward silence. The gaping hole left by Sleeves' death was painfully obvious in that moment, because the rough-and-tumble woman wasn't there to fill the silence with one of her irreverent observations or goading remarks. Astera was sure she would have had something to say about how much of a mess she was, or ask who had given her a sponge bath and if they had provided a happy ending.

A small, sad, smile trembled onto Astera's lips at the thought of her friend, and she concentrated on the sweetness of the cake to distract herself from the emotions welling up inside of her.

The silence of the room was broken as the door opened again. Astera looked up and through the glass door to see Operations Officer Englethorpe. Popping his head into the room, he paused as he saw all the women around Astera on the bed. "Oh, you have visitors already ... I, um, I can come back later." He started to back away.

Kitty beamed, setting her plate down on the side table. "Oh no, please don't go. Astera would love to have some more company." She prowled over to him and pulled him back into the room.

Eggles swallowed as Kitty dragged him into the space, clutching a small wrapped present in his hand. "No, it's all right. I don't want to interrupt her time with her wingmates," he said, shifting the small box behind his back.

"What have you got there?" Viper grinned to herself as the poor young man was clearly overwhelmed by all the ladies around Astera. It was so clear that he was just trying to get out of there while remaining polite.

"Just something for Astera, but I can give it to her later." Eggles tried again to get out of this awkward situation.

"Nonsense, no time like the present." Kitty grasped his shoulder and steered him over. Poor Eggles looked everywhere else except at Astera.

Astera sighed. "Guys, seriously?"

Hearing Englethorpe's voice just threw her straight back to the mission. He had been part of it too, and she could only imagine how the tragedy had impacted him and the other Ops guys. While he wasn't down there on the planet, she didn't envy anyone who had to listen to what she went through.

"Here, have some cake." Mama took Viper's near empty plate and scraped the last mouthful into an empty corner of the box. She dished one of the final two slices onto the same plate and shoved it into Eggles' hands, as Kitty parked him at the foot of the bed.

"Oh, uh, thanks," Eggles spluttered as he tried to figure out how to balance the gift and plate at the same time.

Astera's wingmates watched him with obvious amusement. He gave them all an uncertain smile and just stood there, looking as though he would rather be anywhere else.

"You know, you're supposed to eat cake, right? Not just hold it," Glacier supplied, making Kitty snort out a laugh.

"Of course." Eggles tucked the present under his arm and then quickly took a bite of the cake.

"How is it?" Mama asked, sitting a bit straighter and watching him closely.

Eggles chewed a little more before mumbling, "Umf — sweet," around the portion still in his mouth.

"You know, Starfall tastes even sweeter," Viper said in a low, suggestive tone that made poor Eggles choke on his cake.

"Void, that's it," Astera snapped. "Piss off. All of you." She glared at her wingmates for making the poor guy so uncomfortable. Her gaze only softened when she looked at Mama, and she gave her a grateful smile.

"Ladies, I believe Starfall has spoken." Mama snapped the cake box shut and wheeled the table away from the end of the bed. Then, she stood up and started mustering her wingmates towards the door. "I'll be back later, love. You behave." Then, with a final wink and some amused laughs from the other ladies, they were gone.

Astera groaned and slumped against the back of her bed.

She rubbed her neck nervously and took a tissue off her bedside table. She offered it to Eggles, to wipe off some of the frosting that spluttered all over his hands at Viper's last comment. "Sorry about that lot. They can be a little intense at times."

Eggles carefully scooped up the cake crumbs from his uniform, folding them into the offered tissue. Once he'd checked his clothes, he swiped his face and hands with the crumpled tissue. "It's okay. I've learned to avoid pilot hang-outs since I started here. I should have just left and come back later." He tossed the tissue in the bin by the bed. "I'm glad to see you looking so well. It felt touch and go there for a while." He fidgeted a little.

"Please, take a seat." Astera gestured to one of the chairs her wingmates had completely ignored.

Eggles sank into the chair, but squirmed, appearing unsure of what to do with his legs, or his hands, or his present, or his gaze. He wound up settling on resting his one ankle on the opposite knee and cradling the gift in in his lap. "I hope we didn't embarrass you," he said out of the blue.

His apology seemed out of place. Was he talking about the mission? *Embarrass* was a strange word to use.

Astera's dark eyebrows furrowed in confusion. "What do you mean?"

Eggles fidgeted with the box in his hands. "Oh, um, nothing, just ... I wanted to apologize about Sleeves. She was a real credit to the scouts." He smiled, but from the expression on his face it was clear that he was still torn up about losing a pilot.

"She was," Astera agreed, unable to say more.

"Oh, uh, I, uh, got you a little 'get well soon' present," Eggles said, placing the small gift box into her hands. "Sorry it's not pretty, I just had solar wind shielding; proper wrapping paper isn't really a thing onboard the ship."

Biting her lip, Astera looked at the parcel he had given her. "You didn't have to do that," she said gently, offering it back to him.

He shook his head and tucked his hands under his thighs. "I know, but it sucks laying around in a hospital bed. I thought you might want something to look at while you're here."

Still hesitant, Astera started to pluck at the "paper." Apart from the sweet treats or bottles of alcohol from her wingmates on her fake birthday, it had been a very long time since she had received a genuine gift from anyone. In the years before she joined the Triple C, all presents had come with strings attached. Astera had to stop herself from asking Eggles what he wanted in return. But as she looked at his smiling face, she knew he was just trying to be thoughtful.

"Thank you," Astera said.

Somehow, Eggles had found a small plastic box. It looked like the modular stuff the Engineering Team used, but cut and repurposed to make a case. Inside it, there was a small furry figurine of a Saint Bernard dog, carrying a medical kit in its mouth.

"That was the mascot of the Search and Rescue team my folks used to work for. I guess it's a tribute to some old myth about big dogs in the mountains. I thought you'd like a little companion to help you get better," Eggles explained.

The figurine made Astera smile immediately. It was the cutest, but also one of the most ridiculous, things she had seen in the longest time. She gently stroked the silky brown and white fur, then looked back up at Eggles. "This is so sweet. I'll give him back to you once I get better. If it belonged to your folks, I can't keep it."

Eggles shook his head. "They gave it to me when I was

sick; it's only fair it goes to someone else who is in hospital. I want you to keep it. It will make me feel better to know you have it, and use it to remember me by."

His words immediately made Astera wary. Her stomach pitched, but she reminded herself where she was. She made a resolution to accept the gift, and find some way to return it to him later. She didn't want to fight with him. "Does it have a name yet?" she asked instead.

Eggles chuckled. "No, I never figured it needed one. He was always just my hospital buddy. Do you think he should have a name?"

Astera held up the figurine. "Look at this face. Of course, he needs a name," she said with a laugh. "Give me some ideas."

"Well, I always called him 'Buddy,' so why not formalize it? Or, I think those dogs are called Saint Bernards so, he could also be a 'Bernie'?" he offered, blushing.

Turning the dog to get a better look at its face, Astera tossed over both options in her mind. "I think 'Bernie' is cute," she said with a decisive nod. She set Bernie down on her lap, absent-mindedly stroking the soft fur as she looked back up at Eggles. "So, how are you holding up? That couldn't have been easy on you and the other Ops guys."

Eggles' face blanched. "You don't need to worry about me; you were the one that was in real danger during all that. I'm just amazed you're still with us. That's what matters to me." Eggles froze upon realizing what he'd said.

Once again catching a hint of something *more*, Astera cast her eyes down at her lap. She took in her condition. It didn't seem to matter when her wingmates were in the room, but with Eggles, she became acutely aware of the fact she was wearing bandages rather than a real top, and that even though her body was clean, she was covered in bruises. "What a mess," she said, blushing. "Sorry, I look terrible."

Eggles waved a hand dismissively. "I don't mind; this is temporary. You'll be back to yourself soon enough. But don't think you look 'terrible' to me."

Aware of the growing tension, Astera struggled for find something to say. "I'm sure I'll look better after the extra shower time the commander offered me. I managed to weasel fifteen minutes more out of him. A whole half hour in the water; that's gotta count for something, right?" Astera said, keeping her tone light.

"That's impressive; I didn't think he'd move on those fifteen minutes after how hard he negotiated with you. Man, thirty minutes in a shower. You could almost soak yourself in a bath with that kind of time."

The idea of a real bath made Astera groan with longing. "Oh, you're a genius. That would be amazing," she said dreamily, leaning back against her pillow. "Maybe I need to speak to someone in engineering, or supply. Surely there's something tub-like around the place that I can borrow. I could ration the extra half hour and have *a couple* of baths."

"A bath does sound nice. Just being able to let go and suspend myself in water for a while," he said. "Here's hoping for some R&R on a planet like Lorentia I, or Pacifica. A few days on a beach would be a welcome break."

"It's been years since I went swimming for fun," Astera confessed, then her eyes widened as she calculated it. "Damn ... over a decade." Then, she closed her mouth to stop herself from saying more. Eggles didn't need to know that her last non-recreational swim had been across choppy waters, after she ejected herself from the escape pod she was in before it crashed into a jagged cliffside. Nor did Eggles need to know that she had almost drowned in the process. Her hand grasped at the charm she normally wore around her neck, but it wasn't there. It rested on her bedside table. Astera shook her head to dislodge the onslaught of uncomfortable memories and looked up, focusing on Eggles once more. "What else would you do with R&R time?"

Eggles sighed. "Probably sit and read, soak up some sun somewhere, eat real food at a real café, with good company. I miss being in a city." He spoke so wistfully that Astera wondered if he thought about it a lot.

"You sound like you're overdue for a break," Astera observed, looking at him a little closer. She had seen him around the ship and in the Rec Deck, but had never spent much time talking to him. He'd always been very polite, and he came across as one of the sweeter kinds of recruits that teams like Ops or Engineering would eventually grind to a pulp unless he stood up for himself. She hoped the others were being good to him. The Void needed more kind people to balance the nasty ones.

"I've only been here fourteen months. It's so much more nerve-wracking than I thought it would be. It just takes a lot out of you to sit and listen without being able to do anything." He looked down at his hands.

Astera frowned. "It must be difficult," she agreed, leaning closer but wincing as her ribs smarted. The sheet fell down a little to reveal that, while she had nothing covering her neck and shoulders, she wore clean bandages resembling a tube top. "I hope you guys got a good debriefing and have someone to chat with."

Eggles' eyes widened as he looked up. His gaze lingered on the flash of skin. "Uh, yeah, though it felt like they wanted to blame us for what happened. No one's really talked to us to see if we are okay. Don't know if they don't care or what ..." he admitted, but his eyes darted from her face to her body and back again. It was clear he didn't mind the bruises as much as Astera did.

That didn't sound right. The commander had been surprisingly kind to her, so she couldn't believe he'd just let the Ops guys languish. Astera reached out, putting her hand on Eggles'. "Are you okay?" she asked, genuinely concerned.

Eggles swallowed hard and met her gaze. "I am now that I see you're alive and on the mend. I thought ... I thought we were going to lose you, too, for a while there. I-I just sat there, watching the screen, wishing you could just get out of there. I'm so glad the commander was there to take over; I don't know if I could have kept it together for you like he did."

"Hey, you did your best. That's why the protocol is there. You did exactly what you needed to, at the right time." She squeezed his hand. "I wasn't sure if I would make it back either, but knowing you guys and the commander were up here watching me helped. I didn't feel so alone." She bit her lip as she thought of the commander and the cool confidence he had exuded over the comms. How he refused to let her spiral or get distracted. The Ops lads had done the right thing by getting the boss when they had.

"But ... I didn't help you when you needed me the most." Eggles stood, hands on his hips as his head dropped. "I should have been there for you. It should have been *me* helping you get out of there. That's what you do when you like—" He clapped a hand over his mouth and stopped his rambling.

"I gotta go. My shift starts soon." Eggles grabbed the small, empty plastic box and jumped out of his seat, turning towards the door.

Astera was left dizzy by the admission in his words. A big part of her knew she should let him go, that it was safer that way, but he was so kind, and she was so vulnerable. "Wait," she called out, sitting forward and letting out a soft cry as she moved too fast. She held her hand against the knife-like pain in her ribs. "Englethorpe, wait," she rasped.

Her voice was either too weak from her injuries, or he was hellbent on leaving. Either way, the sounds of the ward filtered in once he'd opened the door. Eggles kept his head down as he walked along the corridor. Within a few steps, he was through the doors and out of sight.

Astera sighed and sank back down against her bed. She frowned as she reached for Bernie. She turned the small figurine around in her hand, looking at the silky brown and white fur as she took several deep breaths. She wished Eggles would have stopped, but maybe it was for the best that he left. There was something about him that drew her in, and he was too good for her. He needed someone simple. Uncomplicated. Someone who was utterly *not* her. She squeezed the dog in her palm and closed her eyes to reduce their sting.

CHAPTER 11

HENRI SCROLLED through the contract which brought them to Baldalan for the fourth time since sitting down. Somewhere deep in his mind, part of him wondered if maybe the language had changed since the last time he looked at it, but it was still laid out as firmly as it had been each previous time: "Under no circumstances will the Triple C be allowed to assault the target without authorization from the client."

"I should have known when they made such a point of including that in the negotiations. There should have been no reason if we were being asked to scout it ..." he muttered, kicking himself again for not thinking ahead when they accepted the contract in the first place.

Now, the Triple C was stuck in orbit, waiting to hear back from the Kolos Admiralty. They had sent the Admiralty the mission data, then sent a revised report when they requested more information, and then sent through yet another revision when the previous one wasn't good enough. It was infuriating because Henri didn't know what they were playing at, and after losing a pilot, he wanted nothing more than to ditch this planet and finish up with the ill-fated contract.

Getting up, Henri paced the deckplates of his office, rolling the various options he had around in his head. He could ask for activation of the termination clause. Sure, the company would stop getting paid a per diem fee while they worked on getting a new contract, but at least he would be back in control. He could see if there was another contract available, on the network in the sector, so they had something to do while they waited. That didn't seem viable given how far it was from everything else. Also, it was so sparsely populated that the camp below was probably the only thing worth hitting.

Henri stopped as he contemplated an option he didn't want to take, but figured he should try rather than continue to float out here. Turning to the holocaller on his desk, he slid in the identification disk that would connect him with the client. While he was only supposed to use it to signal completion of tasks, he figured they would want him to go to work, rather than continue to collect the orbital standby rate. The console indicated the connection was underway and he waited, glass in hand, for that uncooperative rep from the Kolos Admiralty to get on the line.

It took longer than Henri expected for the Admiralty to answer, but when they did, it was the representative that had given him the official contract staring back at him, his disembodied head and shoulders hovering over the holocaller. He already looked annoyed, which Henri had come to believe was just his natural state. "Durroguerre. I assume the mission has been completed to our satisfaction?" the rep asked.

As Henri figured, no one in the Admiralty's merc office had passed anything on to the rep. Either that or he was being completely unprofessional on the call. "You've had several satisfactory mission reports over the past forty-eight hours. They have all had the information you need, but your people keep rejecting them. They also seem to keep missing the request for stipend for repairs," Henri said, voice firm and perhaps bordering on terse. "So, we're stuck here in orbit waiting for you to do your part and close up the contract. Now, I'm happy to keep cashing per diem checks, but I'm guessing your accounting department wants me off your books. I'm calling to help that happen," Henri said before sitting back, drink in hand.

The rep, Mel, sighed and shook his head. "You make it sound like the hold up is on our end. You have a job to complete, and if you do not complete it, we will have no other choice but to take legal action. The orders have not changed. I do not know what you are waiting on."

Henri sat forward, brows crinkling with a mix of confusion and annoyance. "What are you talking about? We scouted the base; we confirmed the presence of the signal you wanted to see. What have we left out here?"

"A short, one-off reading is not confirmed presence. For example, if someone took a sixty second recording of you at a bar in Grendina, that does not confirm your continued presence at said bar," Mel said, sounding bored.

"We have the data of the signal. We have the recordings of the sensor data. We even have the wreckage of a Falcon blown apart by the anti-mech missile turret they installed on site. What other proof do you want?" Henri asked, his tone rising, despite his best efforts to stay professional.

Mel cocked an eyebrow at the change in his tone. "Well, in short, we want more. More proof, more recordings, more readouts," he said, as if it was obvious, "and perhaps next time you run recon, you can remind your scouts that photos are one of the most basic, and necessary, forms of evidence."

If Mel had been physically in the room, Henri would have punched him. Instead, all he could do was shake his head in disbelief. "There are no pictures because the mech facing the turret was obliterated and the other one was facing the other way, running for its life." Then, he let the words Mel chose roll around in his head a second time. Looking at the holodisplay again, Henri sat up. "So, you'll pay for another scout drop with all the after-mission stipends?" It was an idea that infuriated him a little less.

"You want us to pay you to do the same job that you did not complete properly the first time?" Mel almost scoffed, but he shook his head as his mirth settled. "I can send you a contract for a second scouting run, but you are going to have to absorb some of the costs yourself, as the first run was mismanaged. We'll give you the same rate as the first mission, but no post-mission stipends."

Henri's eye twitched at the word "mismanaged." After all, it was the lack of intel from Mel and the Kolos Admiralty that led to them walking into this mission without any idea that an anti-mech turret was going to be on site. Still, he had to play it cool or risk the contract being terminated.

"Fine, but all other points of the original umbrella contract remain in place. This concession is to be a one time only change in our terms. I want that clearly delineated in the paperwork for this second drop." Henri laid it out, figuring that Mel wouldn't kick up a fuss. From the way he was acting, it felt like there weren't going to be any contracts after this one. After all, they'd been waiting for three days on an assault mission contract; the lack of urgency from Mel regarding that had the commander suspicious.

"I'll have it drawn up and sent over within the hour. Good day, Henri."

Before Henri could reply, Mel cut the transmission. The holographic rendering of his face looked as though it trickled back into the projector and then dissipated. Slowly, Henri's residual frown morphed into a grimace as he pulled the connection disk from the comms unit.

"Well, I suppose I better get my 'scout' mechs ready for their drop," he said to himself, standing from the desk and heading for the Mech Bay. Already the plans were tumbling into place as he strode through the ship. As usual, the others on the ship knew not to interrupt the commander when he looked stern. He didn't even stop when he got to the Mech Bay. It took an automated part mover to nearly run him over for him to snap out of his zone.

Looking around, Henri watched the repair work continuing on Astera's Hummingbird. The damaged torso had been made whole again. Based on how bad it looked when she brought it in, it was a wonder they had salvaged the chassis. The internals and engine were another matter. He was admiring the work Vitali and his crew had done when he felt a mechanical hand on his shoulder.

"You shouldn't hang around here, staring into space, Boss. That's how you wind up with a spark in the eye or a wrench up your ass," Vitali joked behind him.

"A wrench in the—" Henri stopped before he could finish that question. Some things were better left unaddressed. "Sorry, I was just happy to see you managed to save at least one mech from that scout run for me, but I dropped by because I was wondering if you might get a few more scout mechs ready for me."

Vitali shrugged. "I mean, the rest of the Scout Wing is ready to go at a moment's notice. You don't need to check with me about that." He gestured to the four other mechs standing in a row beside Calliope.

"Oh, I know that, but I think that we're not using all the tools at our disposal. How long has it been since we fielded Pestle's Infantry Wing?" Henri asked, walking down the bay until they reached the row that had two Harriers, a Kite, and a squat looking Eagle mech beside Sergeant Pestle's Falcon.

Vitali furrowed his brow. "Um, three months? Last time was that defense contract on Ostylia ... but I thought you said this was a scout run. You don't use a wing like Pestle's for scouting. It's an Infantry Wing, like you said."

"Did I say it was an 'Infantry Wing'? I'm pretty sure they are in our systems as a Scout Wing. I mean, sure, as they are equipped now, I could see how someone might think they are infantry mechs ..." Henri trailed off, grinning at Vitali.

Vitali peered down the row of mechs as understanding dawned on him. "Oh. Yeah, right. I think we classified them as 'infantry' for that job. Boy, I've been so busy, I forgot to get them back to their original designation and loadout. I'll get on that right away, Boss." He chuckled to himself as he pulled his datapad from his belt and started scheduling the jobs.

"Oh, and Vitali, be sure you put back those anti-missile systems they always run. Can't have them going out there without the vital, standard equipment they always use," Henri added.

"I wouldn't dream of sending them out there without their usual complement of gear," Vitali promised.

"I knew you'd get around to it eventually, Chief. Thank you. We should have the contract in hand within the hour, so time is of the essence on this retrofit." Henri tucked his hand in his pockets before turning to leave.

"I'll have everyone on it before then. Best I can quote you is ... forty hours for all members of Pestle's Wing," Vitali said as he turned to take the ladder down to the work floor.

"Do it in thirty and I'll bump your bonus by fifty percent," Henri challenged, knowing that the engineers thrived on a good deadline.

"I can do thirty-six hours for thirty-five percent," Vitali countered as he stood at the top of the ladder.

"Done." Henri left the engineer to his work, turning to leave the Mech Bay. They needed to be better prepared for this new mission than they were for the last. He would speak to the Ops Team and fill them in with the parameters so they could get to planning, and then, he intended to go to the Med Bay. Their best source of intel from Baldalan was currently convalescing there.

CHAPTER 12

ASTERA SOON LEARNED that keeping Bernie on her bedside table was a bad idea. His cute, black, puppy dog eyes seemed to watch her as she tried to lay back and relax after her visitors. She spent the entire afternoon squirming, trying to avoid his gaze and all the thoughts in her mind. Her injury-addled brain was still spinning from her company that day. She had been expecting to see her fellow wingmates, and they never failed to impress with their consistent level of intensity. They were exhausting at the best of times but, for once, they weren't the ones who had sapped her energy.

She knew it was stupid, dangerous even, but Astera couldn't shake the warmth that had suffused her broken body when she spoke with Eggles. She had been careful to avoid getting close to her crewmates since joining the Triple C, but it had been so long, and she'd forgotten how nice some non-sleazy flirting and playfulness felt. It reminded her of the something her father used to say when he spoke about his undeniable love for her mother; humans weren't meant to orbit with one another, they were designed to collide. While Astera's previous collisions had led to catastrophe, perhaps it was time to try again, to see her own interest as a hopeful spark rather than an ominous warning.

"You're cute, but don't think for one second I won't chuck you in that drawer so you stop staring at me." Astera rolled her head to the side and took in the sweet Saint Bernard figurine again. Bernie just stared back at her blankly, like any inanimate object would.

As tempted as Astera was to follow up on her threat, lifting her arm to move him would just bring a whole new world of pain. So, she closed her eyes instead, and every time she thought of the commander's piercing stare and pointed questions, she pushed it away with that feeling of warmth brought about by her other visitors. There was no evidence that the commander had figured out who she was, or where she came from. Worrying about it was just wasted energy.

Maybe, after she recovered, she could focus on building some relationships on board the Latagarosh. The brass would have a harder time kicking her off the ship if she was well liked, she reasoned. Finally falling back asleep, she allowed herself to believe that was the truth of the matter, and that it had nothing at all to do with her growing need to feel connected again, to something bigger than herself.

The next day, Astera was awoken by the now familiar sound of Doctor Colwyn's steady, assertive footsteps. She peeled her eyes open reluctantly to see the doctor walking across the room. "Ah, Astera, nice to see you're awake," she said in a warm, professional tone as she tapped the monitor beside Astera's bed and scanned over the readouts. "How are you feeling?"

Astera let out a dry chuckle. "Like I've been trampled by a mech."

"Ah, so just as we would expect," Colwyn retorted without missing a beat, offering Astera an amused smile.

"Your stats are looking good. If your pain is too much, I can give you something for it. Unfortunately, it will just be part of life while you recover." She closed the health monitoring software and turned to face Astera. "Now, I know yesterday was a big one, with at least half of the company stopping by to visit, but I've got another visitor for you. I know you're probably tired, but Commander Durroguerre is famously difficult to deny." She patted Astera's hand before heading to the door, just as the commander opened it.

"Oh." Astera gulped as she looked at Durroguerre's rather well built, but somewhat imposing, figure in the doorway. She forced her lips into a smile and smoothed down her hair, wishing that she could look a little more put together for a visit from the brass.

The commander was not smiling as he entered. Neither was the Head of Intelligence, Major La Plaz. When the commander spoke, his tone was all business. "Sorry for disturbing you Starfall, but the client is sending us in again and we want to make sure we're prepared. The major and I have the wireframe of the terrain and base, but we'd like you to add anything you think we are missing about either."

La Plaz took the projector bases out of his pocket and set them up around the room. Astera just blinked, her brain overloaded. The commander today seemed like a different man to the one who had spoken with her just the day before. She tried to shake off the weird feeling, and the fact he was asking about Baldalan rather than her past. "Oh, okay ... I'm not sure how much use I will be," Astera spoke slowly, trying to buy herself some time to process. "I guess it depends on what you've got already." She gestured to the projectors.

"Well, a lot of what you will see won't be different from your pre-mission briefing, Starfall," La Plaz explained. He had put together the mission and briefed Astera and Sleeves before they dropped. He was a clever, if icy, person, but perhaps that was a façade that went away when he wasn't working on a job. It was hard to know, as nearly no one saw the second-in-command in his downtime. Most Triple C employees figured that was by design.

La Plaz switched the holographic projectors on as the commander brought the lights down in Astera's recovery room. At first, the hologram was just a series of points, then a wireframe, before filling in to look like the planet's terrain. Even the trees she passed were rendered in remarkable detail.

As she saw in the mission room, the topography of ridges and valleys hovered into view before Astera. It looked very much like the old briefing with some new additions from the data they gathered from the last mission. Astera noticed the buildings of the base were better developed, for one. She thought maybe being in orbit for so many days, the Ops Team must have gotten pictures of the base from every angle at this point.

The commander came over and sat on the edge of the bed without asking, his back mostly to Astera. "Now, I know it's hard to think back to it, but we need your help reconstructing some things," he began as he used gesture controls to zoom in on the map. As the view narrowed, the pair of mechs added to her retreat path became clearer. The one in the center of the view was obviously Astera's Hummingbird. The other one was ...

"Sleeves ..." the name came unbidden to her lips as her fists clenched the sheet on both sides of her. Astera's heart pounded and her head swam as the wireframe threw her back into those last few moments before her friend was killed.

Astera closed her eyes and checked her own breathing, before making a conscious effort to slow it down, and to let the muscles in her hands relax. When she opened her eyes again, she looked at the sheet covering her legs, and the way the material tented between her feet.

"The ground was slippery there," Astera said slowly so that her voice would not shake. "It's a forest floor in a hot, humid biome, but ... it was worse than I expected. The rotting vines on the ground have this kind of gooey sap. When you step on them, they burst and the mech feet go for a slide. It makes it hard when you're running." She watched the commander and the major as she spoke, wondering if that was the kind of thing they needed.

La Plaz tapped at the tablet he had taken from his pocket after setting up the projectors. "That's a useful detail. It will help us moving forward in planning our approach ..."

Then the commander explained, "That's not exactly what we came here to get, however. Since we couldn't recover Sleeves' Falcon and examine the damage, we can't reconstruct the impact point. We need your help working backwards so we can extrapolate the missile's flight path." His voice cracked ever so slightly, showing a touch more emotion than Major La Plaz.

Astera almost choked on her next breath, as she gaped at the commander.

"We're right here, in the Med Bay. We're with you so take the time you need to walk through it." The commander spoke more gently and covered one of her hands with his.

Astera jumped at the sudden contact but turned her attention to the wireframe. She looked at the point where she had started, idling on back-up, and then at the bright blip in the frame, near the canyon wall. The one that had to be where Sleeves' mech sent the final emergency pulse reading.

"There was a well-worn path around there," Astera pointed to a location on the map just near where she had idled. "From one of the big, predator cats, I think. I veered off that way and followed it up there." She trailed her finger in a jagged line towards Nav Delta.

A sense of danger sizzled through her at a familiar bend in the trail. "I was around there when I got the warning from Nest about the mechs in pursuit." She figured the details along the way would help them work out timing and distances. "I pulled most aux power and rerouted it into speed."

Starfall, where you at? My trigger fingers are getting itchy.

Sleeves' voice echoed through Astera's mind and tore at that deep, dark hole in her heart. She swallowed and forced herself to continue, while she squeezed her eyes shut, to ward away the tears that threatened to arise. "The forest thinned out as I went, and I came out along that cliff."

The bluff had run parallel to Nav Delta, and she remembered thinking it would be a perfect way for Sleeves to watch her ass. If only she'd known there was a fucking turret waiting for them to come out into the open. If she would have found a different path, a better way—

"Okay, so this is the best reconstruction we have of the moment," the commander said, his voice soft. It was so unlike any other time he'd spoken in front of her. His hand gently squeezed hers. "When you're ready, I'd like you to open your eyes and help the major guide his flight line," he said, trying to coax her into looking at the two mech models now on the display.

When Astera opened her eyes, the point of view was from inside the Hummingbird, looking at the Falcon. Running out from the side, a red line was superimposed on the display.

Astera could have sworn her heart stopped beating when she re-experienced that view.

"Was it more up, or down?" the commander asked, trying to keep the questions to simple binary choices.

She couldn't find the words. "It was ...I—" Astera stopped, her hands shaking.

Ah, Starfall, glad you could join me.

We gotta stop meeting like this, you know I like it too much when you have your guns on hot.

Gotta keep 'em hot to cover your retreat, babe. You know how I like watching as you—

"Up," Astera almost yelled, trying to make her voice louder than the flashback bouncing around in her mind. "It was more up."

The words brought her back to the room and the commander's hand on hers. "Higher angle, or higher on the mech's body?" When she didn't answer, he leaned in closer and whispered, "You're not back there; you're here with us. You're safe."

But Sleeves isn't, Astera thought. She could still feel the way her stomach dropped when she saw the missile. The way the world seemed to slow as she saw the unstoppable, lethal pathway it was on. "It was like"—with a twinge of protest from her ribs, Astera lifted her arm and used it to simulate the angle of entry— "It hit right above Perry's reactor shield plating."

Saying that it hit Perry was easier than acknowledging that Sleeves was the real victim. Although, as Astera focused on the facts, it also became clear why the debris had rained down over her when she hit the floor of the chasm. The memory of the burning tatters of a flight suit, laying across the rocks of the ravine, came back to mind with startling clarity.

"I don't even think she saw it coming," Astera whispered, "It all happened so fast."

The commander nodded. "Not sure if it will help any, but I don't think she had time to feel it, either. One grace she was given before she was taken from us," he said, his hand leaving hers to gently squeeze her shoulder as he glanced at La Plaz.

The major manipulated the track of the missile on the display. Doing his best to mimic Astera's arm position, he adjusted it through the three trajectory axes and watched as the red trace danced around on the display. Zooming out from the two mechs, the major tracked it back toward the base. Tapping the tablet a few times, the red trace morphed to follow more classic missile launch profiles. None seemed to give him the path he wanted until he got to the last few. Clicking through them, they landed close to a few of the buildings until finally one intersected a large shed near the power plant in the base. "That's probably it, Commander. Not a very smart missile; it must fly pretty close and parallel to the ground to maintain lock on the laser designator the turret uses," the major explained to the commander.

"Mark it in the sit rep and briefing, and head back to let Ops know," the commander ordered La Plaz. As the major started to pack up, the commander added, "I'll stay here a little while longer."

La Plaz said something in reply and the commander spoke again, but Astera didn't really hear the rest of that conversation. The only thing she could see was the simulated line the major had locked in, the red trace burned into her retinas. She tried to blink it away, but as she did, a red-hot tear slid down her cheek. Without even thinking, she sniffed and wiped it away, turning to look at the side of her bed as she composed herself. She couldn't afford to be vulnerable. Not here, not now. Not with the commander sitting on the edge of the bed, with his strong hand on her shoulder.

"It's okay to let it out. No one is going to think less of you for weeping over a fallen wingmate," the commander whispered. She sensed him looking at her, but she did not meet his gaze. The silence drew out between them as they each seemed to wait to see what the other would say, or do, next.

It was a sign of how comfortable Astera had become on the Latagarosh that she had let a single tear fall. The work, the crew, all of it had begun to slip past the shields she had built around herself. "Are you ... are you sending in the scouts again?" she asked, thinking of her teammates, knowing that it would hurt even more if they lost another one.

The commander shook his head. "Don't worry about that; you just focus on healing. I've got the mission well handled," he said before pausing a beat and offering the next bit of news. "I'll be leading the second drop to the site."

"You what?" she spluttered, eyes wide.

"I won't put anyone else at risk of the client's ire. If I go down and act as the wing officer, the only person that gets in trouble if something happens is me. After all, we've only been contracted to scout." His phrasing seemed odd to Astera. Then again, being the commander, she assumed there was a lot he couldn't share with her, given her rank.

Still, it didn't make any sense. "But ... your mech isn't a scout class," she said, thinking of the expensive, well-tuned beast of a Condor that was kept in the bay, with "Back Breaker" painted meticulously on its panel.

The commander chuckled. "Well, you are right, but thankfully Pestle's Wing is being retrofitted as we speak. We must be prepared for that turret after all. Corporal Liang has come down with a cold, so they need a new pilot for his Eagle."

The expression the commander wore was enough to make Astera swear under her breath. This wasn't another scouting mission. If they wanted more information, they'd send down the right kind of mechs, with the right kind of sensors. Like hers, or one of the other scouts. The commander was going down there himself, most likely armed to the teeth, expecting shit to hit the fan. *This isn't a recon gig*, Astera thought to herself, *this is revenge*.

"Let me help." Astera sat up far too quickly as the offer fell from her lips. She winced in pain at the sudden movement, but did not back down.

The commander shook his head. "You're still grounded. Doctor's orders," he reminded her, but still gave her shoulder a gentle squeeze. "Believe me, I'd love for you to join us, but you're in here because we weren't careful and I can't have you getting worse by rushing back into active duty."

The commander slowly guided her to lay back down in the recovery bed. Leaning over her as he pulled the covers up, he looked down into her eyes. "Now, lay here and worry about getting better," he said, before adding, "That's an order."

Astera was about to tell him where to shove his order, but she bit the comment back, knowing it would only make him less likely to agree to what she asked for next. "Then let me sit in the Ops room. That's not active duty."

The commander pursed his lips and Astera could tell he was weighing the options behind those handsome, weathered eyes of his. "I can have someone from Ops come down here and tie you into the operational channel. Deal?"

It wouldn't be easy to put herself back into that headspace, or to sit on the sidelines, but she had to do it. Sleeves was the first person in the company who had welcomed her in, with that unique mix of shameless flirting and teasing that was her trademark. She couldn't go back in time and destroy the missile that killed her friend, but she could sure as hell help the people on the mission bring those bastards down ... and get back safely.

"Deal."

"Good, I'll talk with Major La Plaz and see who we can

spare to come down here and work with you. Until then, you have your orders, Starfall." The commander got to his feet and strode for the door, stopping and looking back at her over his shoulder as it opened. "I know it was tough to go back to that moment, but it helps more than you know. Thank you, Astera."

The genuine gratitude, and gentleness, in the commander's tone took Astera's breath away. She nodded, swallowing a ball of emotion. "You're welcome, Commander."

She watched him leave the room, and when the door closed behind him, Astera relaxed back into her bed and tried to recover from the headspin of the past twenty minutes. She reached out, picking up the little figure of the Saint Bernard from her tray table. She ran her fingertips over the silky brown fur, and hoped she was up for the task. The last thing she wanted was to fail to do Sleeves justice and disappoint the commander in the process.

CHAPTER 13

HENRI SAT in one of the larger briefing rooms, listening to Sergeant Liam Pestle talk with his team. They all seemed antsy as they waited for Major La Plaz to join them. As with most missions, it was the intelligence officer that led the meeting, so even the commander had to wait around for him to arrive. That didn't mean Henri was wasting his time. He took it as an opportunity to assess Liam's unit; yearly reviews and infrequent usage on missions didn't paint a picture of who they were as people. Doing his best to be a fly on the wall, Henri watched how the group interacted and let that tell him who he would be joining on the drop.

First, Corporal Ian Kildare sat in the back on a table, rather than the chair. Having his spine pressed to the corner, he kept an eye on everyone and everything. Even after three years with the company, Henri noticed he never seemed to be comfortable around people. He kept his eyes moving, and his back to the wall, so no one could get behind him; his natural suspicion, coupled with his capability, left no mystery as to how Kildare had earned his callsign of Mercenary.

In front of the corporal sat his mech mate, private Iroha

Kawamura. While with the company for just two years, she was as good as any pilot in the room. At least, Henri heard she would be if she could slow down and pick her positions better. She bought a little too much into the idea of her ancestral deity Hachiman protecting her at times, even if she used that as her callsign.

Corporal Liang sat with his boots on the table with his head hung back. Henri had heard that Shang-yu had a bad habit of sleeping during any spare minute.

The only one missing was the new pilot, Semtex. While she was a capable pilot, no one in the company could figure out why she took a demotion from her executive position to join Liam's Wing. She had a pretty good record in the Ops division but threw that away to become a private in the Infantry Wing. Equally surprising had been her scores in the simulators. While raw, she managed to succeed in the last few missions their Infantry Wing had been called on to complete. Maybe Private Patricia Langston was in the right place after all, but only time would tell.

Henri was snapped out of his assessments as the door slid back and Major La Plaz stepped in. Seeing the chair of the meeting finally arriving, Liam cut off his chat with Ian and Iroha to call the room to attention.

Kildare and Kawamura sprung to their feet. The noise woke Liang before he pushed himself out of his chair to stand at attention as well. As usual, the commander rolled his eyes. "Liam, we're not military; we're mercenaries. We don't stand on protocols this much."

"Sorry, sir. Force of habit, sir," Liam apologized.

"And you can ease up on the 'sirs,' Pestle. We're not at war. Well, not yet. Please, everybody, sit down," the commander waved his hand to get everyone into their seats.

Meanwhile, the major was fiddling with the mission

console. The mapped surface of the planet projected above the unit, narrowing down to the base the scout pilots would have seen before. While the scouts may have gone down first, all the pilots looked at the mission parameters, knowing that they often followed the information-gatherers down. It was almost always just a matter of time before heavier mechs would hit the ground and no pilot liked being unprepared.

Just as the major took his seat, the door to the briefing room slid open to reveal a harried, and out of breath, Semtex. She froze as all eyes turned to her, and she cleared her throat. "Ah, sorry for being late. I, uh–" she appeared to be caught up, trying to find a viable excuse, but her shoulders fell when Iroha just shook her head. Semtex sighed and rubbed her face. "Sorry."

Pestle started to sigh but bit it back. "We just started. Please come in and shut the door so we don't waste anymore time."

"Oh, right." Semtex stepped into the room properly and closed the door, then walked over to sit beside Liang.

With Patricia finally in the room, Major La Plaz cleared his throat and began. "Now, you all may be aware of the target assigned to us by our client. Surely over the past few days of being in geostationary orbit over the site, you've all gotten your chance to review the sensor and scout data. Apparently, this is not enough for our client," the major explained.

As expected, a great groan filled the room as the pilots lamented the reason why they have been stuck in orbit around this fringe world for so long. "Settle, people," Sergeant Pestle piped up, trying to bring order back to the room. He let the murmurs die before looking back at the major. "Please proceed, sir."

La Plaz resumed his briefing. "Our current mission plan is a Recon in Force mission. That's why we've selected your wing to take another pass at the base, and gather all the data that you can, so we may satisfy our client and finish our time here."

"I've already got Engineering refitting your mechs as we speak, to cut wait and respec for something more suitable for a scouting mission," Henri interjected, letting them know right away that he was aware their mechs weren't usually equipped for this sort of thing. It was going to take a shift in tactics, by them, to make the mission a success, so their buy-in was critical.

The more experienced pilots all paused, furrowing their brows as they glanced at one another. Even Liang appeared awake and alert at the news. Kildare swung his legs off the table and sat forward.

"Beg pardon, Commander, but is that wise? We'll lose a lot of our ability to fire back if the base defenses detect us. And, no offense, I'd like every weapon at my disposal if the stories about an anti-mech turret on the surface are true," Ian said, the nervous energy making him sit a little straighter in his seat.

Henri turned and looked to Major La Plaz. "You may as well tell them."

"The turret is present on the surface," the major reported with his usual cool tone.

"Void damn it, I knew it. Boss, you can't let them give us this mission," Ian argued, looking to his sergeant. They might have had the tougher mechs, but there wasn't a single machine that wouldn't be severely impacted by artillery of that nature.

"Stand down, Mercenary. The commander chose us for a reason. Let's hear him out before we start jumping to conclusions," Liam snapped, and then gave La Plaz an apologetic glance. "Please, let's hear the rest of the briefing."

Henri didn't say anything; it wouldn't do for him to undermine the authority of the major. Liam had said his piece and all Henri had to do was turn his attention back to the major. Taking the hint, Major La Plaz turned back to the board. "Since you will still be piloting larger frames than our previous scouting missions, we will be taking a different approach."

The wireframe map on the display swept over the terrain until it arrived at a new landing zone. "Mother Hen will drop you here; it is in the shadow of the mountain so you should be able to approach and remain off sensors. You will follow this contour to keep to the sensor shadow of the terrain." The red line crawled across the display, showing the contour in question.

Semtex spoke up as it seemed to switch back at one point. "Won't we be exposed right there?" she asked, pointing at a spot on the map.

"Only briefly, but you will also have a window to visually inspect the target site. You can use it to verify the status of the base defense, as well as the operational status of the turret," the major explained.

Iroha's wrinkled brow deepened before she leaned forward. "Surely our scans could tell us that."

Henri had to interject after that observation. Again, he was to throw another wrinkle at this team, but now he was about to find out whether they were up for the job. "Can't risk the signals. If they pick up our active scans, they can fix our approach. We are going in radio silent, passive sensors only."

The wing paused and all looked at one another. "We?" Liang asked. Everyone shifted as they noted his word choice.

Henri suppressed a smile; it was a little funny to him that it was Liang who picked up on that word. Perhaps the sleepy pilot observed more than everyone else assumed. "I'll be joining you on this mission. It is necessary, given one of your wingmates is down with a flu," he explained.

"Nobody's sick. In fact, the CMO signed off on their physical reviews earlier this month," Sergeant Pestle said.

"That is true, but she just told me about how bad Liang's fever is. She might need to hold him in the Med Bay until it breaks," Henri explained, turning, and looking down the table. He locked eyes with the corporal and smiled slightly, knowing he would pick up on what was going on.

Liang was about to protest, but then he met the commander's gaze. "Oh... oh yeah, I meant to tell you, Sarge, but I've been feeling like hammered shit lately." Liang added a few fake coughs for emphasis

Kildare leaned forward, his face wrinkled with suspicion. "What in the Void is going on here?" He narrowed his eyes as he glanced back and forth between the faking Liang and the commander.

"You need to read our contracts closer, Kildare. A commander cannot partake in a mission unless mission critical numbers necessitate his involvement. Now, with your wing short a man, and the other mechs in the Mech Bay out of service due to their calibration schedule, I have no other option but to join your team on this mission," Henri explained.

Kildare frowned. "I don't like it. We have a working relationship; we know how to play off each other and now he's coming in here and upsetting our balance just because he's the commander."

"If you don't like it, I'm sure I can find another bored Infantry Wing pilot to take your place. Of course, they would be the one paid for their time and risk ... Mercenary." Henri let that pause draw out so he could really land on the pilot's callsign when he said it. He knew Ian's motivators all too well.

Ian's stout indignation wavered when his callsign was thrown back at him. "Fine." He slumped back into his seat.

"Don't worry about him; he'll be fine once he's out there with sticks in his hands," Iroha added, reaching back, and patting her wingmate on the leg.

"Amazing how that worry goes away in the seat, isn't it, Private?" Henri responded with a grin toward the younger pilot across from him.

Semtex was frowning at the wireframe as she took it in. "Sir, no disrespect ... but why are we going in? Why not the scouts? I know they," she hesitated, "I know they're down a pilot for real, so you could go in with them, and have all the right equipment for the job. If you're just looking for readouts, why do you need our heavy weapons?"

Henri switched his attention to the newest member of the wing. Having an Ops background, he should have known that Patricia would put two and two together faster than the others. "A fair question. I made an erroneous assumption on the scouting mission. That assumption cost us a pilot. I'm not going to be caught unaware this time. Also, the base has at least three defense mechs on site. I'd rather not wind up outnumbered if it comes to that."

The major filled the gap in Henri's explanation by bringing up a photo on the console. It didn't match the scout data. In fact, it looked like it was something from a military supplier's inventory list. "In any event, the main worry is the turret they may have on site. While dangerous, many ground-mounted anti-mech turrets have a design flaw: the anchor."

"It should be sunk into the ground far enough to support the weight of the turret, but also tall enough for the ball mount for the turret's gimbal. From the best we can figure, they haven't had the time to fortify the installation. If they did, it would be a dead giveaway on our satellite imagery. That is our best way to take it out," Henri explained.

"But if we do that, we're the aggressors. We're not going to be on a scouting mission anymore, and anyone that does a postmortem on the mission will be able to tell that," Kildare interrupted.

"That's right. Unless one of you gets too close and *accidentally* draws fire from the base. In that case, we are within our right to defend ourselves," the commander retorted.

"Pfft, as if one of us is going to want to get shot at," Kildare sneered.

"I'll do it," Sergeant Pestle replied. "If someone must get their attention, it'll be me. My Falcon is fast enough to run circles around the defenders."

Henri smiled. He knew Liam's service record well and had been counting on him to volunteer as a decoy. Even in his Falcon, he was faster than some scouts while still loaded out like an infantry mech. Henri never bothered to ask how he did it; all he needed to know was that he could do it every time. "I hoped you'd say that, Sergeant. Never ask your pilots to do something you wouldn't do yourself. Leadership one-oh-one."

Sergeant Pestle nodded. "Exactly. So, once I get their attention, then what?"

Henri looked down the table. "Liang, do you think your Eagle could mount an EMF Accelerator Cannon?"

The tired corporal looked more awake than Henri had ever seen him. "I wouldn't be confident running with one attached, but I have a feeling you'll keep my bird safe with an EMF. You're probably the only pilot I'd trust with that fitout."

"Thank you, Corporal," Henri said, a slight smile on his face. "I'll do my best to bring it back in one piece," he added, earning a chuckle from the room.

Henri noticed everyone laughed but the sulking Kildare

in the corner. "Still think this is the wrong approach. We should send the Scout Wing in again before we do this," Kildare protested.

"Your input is noted, Mercenary, but this is the commander's call. He's going down there with us and putting himself in harm's way. Your mind should be on that," Liam reminded him.

"Thank you, Pestle," Henri said, standing up. "You'll be receiving your loadouts tonight so you can train in the simulators before we head down. Like I said, be prepared for your mechs to feel lighter and faster. The firepower was chosen so the team could complement each other, so I'd advise you to do team drills tonight. Any questions?" he asked, looking around the room.

Everyone in Pestle's wing turned and looked at Kildare, seemingly daring him to say something. Ian took the hint and clammed up. With that, everyone in the room started to get up from their seats and file towards the door, except for Pestle, who held up a hand to keep Semtex back.

She seemed paler than normal. Henri had picked up on it, but this was something for the sergeant to handle. It was his wing; it was his call. He tried to ignore it as he took a moment to speak with the major.

"I'm going to be down there, so I want you in the Ops room. Things must be tight as a drum, but don't be unreasonable, understand? If those knuckleheads want to bullshit while we are on the move, let them, so long as it remains respectful. They know where the line is, especially now," Henri explained.

"Understood, sir. I'll loosen the reins a bit, but you know my preferences," Major La Plaz countered.

"Understood. We'll make do as we go, I guess. Also, I need you to pull a remote command console from storage."

"Will do." The major's brows furrowed in confusion, but he trusted Henri all the same.

As he finished talking with the major, Henri turned around to see Liam waiting for him to finish.

"I just want you to know that my wing and I will do whatever it takes to be successful out there," Liam began.

Henri raised his hand. "Don't kiss my ass, Pestle, you're no good at it. I chose your wing because you're the one leading it and I know how desperate you are to get out there, open your Falcon up, and rip across a planet's surface at full speed. I also know your wing has the right assemblage of talent for this mission. Do what you and your wing always do and we'll be fine. Got it?"

"Yes, sir. Sorry, sir," Liam answered as they stepped outside. As they did, Ops officer Englethorpe was standing there, leaning against the wall. Henri smiled, glad to see that the young man was already waiting for him. It seemed he'd gotten his message after all.

"Ah, Englethorpe, just the man I was looking for." The commander clapped a hand on his shoulder. "Come with me, I've got a job for you down in the Med Bay."

CHAPTER 14

IN HIS TIME with the Triple C, Martin had learned that there were three things the entire crew agreed upon. The first was that it was a good place to work. Getting a job with the mercenary outfit was difficult, as their attrition rate was so low. The people who joined the company, and stayed with company, did so because they respected the company. The second was that the Triple C was a great place to work because the commander was an excellent leader. He didn't waste time with politics. He had plenty of experience surviving the Void, and he was firm, but always fair. The third? Getting called up by the commander was rarely a good thing.

Martin stood outside the briefing room, mulling over that third point. Given the events of the past week, he figured the personal summons to visit the commander was a bad omen. After losing a pilot on a mission he was running ops on, it was probably time for the ass-kicking he, Hermedilla, and Norgard, were waiting for. Of course, when Martin had arrived outside the briefing room, the door was shut and the "Do Not Disturb" light was on, glowing a faint red. It gave him more than enough time to pace back and forth, fretting over how in the Void he'd find another job if the Triple C kicked him out. Only the roughest backwash crews would be interested in someone the famous Henri Durroguerre ousted.

When the door finally opened, Martin's racing heart jumped right up into his throat. He half-stumbled, half-fell, against the wall as a full wing of infantry pilots filtered out. He tried to play it cool as they walked by, but they were too introspective to notice him. Then again, pilots generally failed to notice Ops staff at the best of times. He figured it was just as well, as he was probably wearing his worry on his face.

Martin was just watching after the pilots when the commander's familiar voice roused him from his thoughts and a heavy hand clapped his shoulder.

After blinking away his surprise, Martin said, "A job for me? In the infirmary?" It didn't make sense to him.

"Yes, that's what I just said." The commander let his hand drop. He continued down the hall into the main corridor through the ship. He didn't stop to see if Martin was following him. "We need you to run an Ops console down there. We need input from Starfall which may be vital to the mission. Since we can't bring her up to Ops, we need Ops to go down to her," he explained as they walked. Martin had to scramble to keep up.

To say Martin was shocked was an understatement. He had been expecting what he thought would be a well-deserved punishment, but instead he was being given a unique assignment. His mind whirred as he struggled to keep up with the commander. He wasn't sure why he was chosen to work with Starfall. He thought, maybe it was just because he wouldn't be as missed in the Ops room as the other specialists. He was also wondering why the commander himself was the one giving him the assignment.

Martin usually answered to his own supervisors. Either way, he wasn't about to ask the commander for answers, especially because he was worried it might cause him change his mind.

The familiar halls of the ship passed in a blur as the two men walked, and it wasn't until they stepped into the Med Bay, and walked down the corridor to the left, that Martin's stomach twisted and he realized that this wasn't just a job. It was a chance to spend more time with Astera.

The commander opened the door to Astera's private room with a sense of confidence that Martin admired. Already, there was a technician in the room, setting up a console beside the bed she was laying in.

"Gee, Commander, all of this fuss is making me feel really fancy," Astera said. The smile on her face lit up her eyes, too, and Martin couldn't help but stare. She looked much better today than she had when he last saw her. The bags beneath her eyes were lighter, and her scrapes and bruises were healing well. When her eyes slipped off the commander and fell onto Martin, her smile softened. Her hand tensed around something as she added, "Oh, and you've brought me a guest?"

"Uh, hi," Martin blurted, immediately wanting to disappear at how lame he sounded. The only saving grace was the fact that he could see some brown and white fur peaking out from a gap between Astera's fingers. His cheeks warmed at the knowledge that she was holding the beloved figurine he gave her.

"Sorry to cut into the conversation," the commander said, glancing between them, "but we're here to get set up for the mission. Starfall, this is Specialist Martin Englethorpe, he was in Ops when you were on Baldalan. Englethorpe, this is Starfall."

They had already met, but Martin wasn't about to correct the commander.

"Oh, we've run into each other before," Astera said. Apparently, *she* didn't mind correcting him.

The commander just nodded his acknowledgement. "Englethorpe will be in here with you when the team and I go down. He'll make sure all the equipment runs smoothly, and fill you in on some of the things that might be useful from an Ops perspective. For now, though, I need him to help test the calibration on the machines. I know I didn't give you any warning, but we're on a tight schedule. Is that okay?"

Astera gestured lazily towards the console and the woman who was setting it up. "The more the merrier. It's getting boring here on my own."

Martin held back a chuckle. "Might be worth selling tickets, you'll make a fortune," he said, so mesmerized by how her pink hair shone in the bright lights that he forgot the commander was right next to him. The same commander who gave them both a look that made Martin clear his throat and straighten up. "Er, sorry, sir."

The commander returned his attention to Astera. "I need to sort some things out, so I may not have time to stop by before the mission. Starfall, if you think of anything else, please be sure to let me know right away. Just send a direct message through the comms system."

"Copy that, Knuckle Duster. Stay safe down there," Astera said, the second half of her comment radiating genuine concern. The sweet expression on her face faltered into a frown that made Martin want to hug her.

The commander turned and left, and when the door shut behind him, Martin turned back to Astera. Swallowing at his suddenly dry throat, he croaked out a question. "So, um, did they tell you why they needed you specifically involved? I thought they had all your data already." He moved over and checked the height on the console. Most times people set theirs too high for his comfort so he sat in the chair in the room and wheeled it over as the tech gave him the side eye as she worked.

"Yeah, I'm listening in to give them any pointers on dealing with the terrain and stuff like that." Astera shrugged as she sat up a little in the bed. The action made her wince as she sucked in a breath.

Martin instinctively stepped closer and reached out to help, resting his hand on her arm. "Are you okay?"

She glanced down at his hand on her arm and she smiled. "I'm fine."

"So, this is all set up if you want to take a look at it, Specialist Englethorpe."

Martin flinched at the technician's voice. He'd forgotten all about her. He did his best to square his shoulders and resume some semblance of professionalism. "Yes, of course. Thank you." He stepped around the bed as Astera hid a snort of laughter behind a cough. His cheeks burned, but he liked knowing that he had amused her, even if it was at his own expense.

Having an operations console set up in a hospital room felt odd, but he had to check for the same things no matter where he was. If he were operating down here, this might count as a field technician shift. Maybe he could add it to his resume as practice if the commander did decide to kick him out of the company. He went about the checks and tests, falling into professional mode as he worked. Even though the commander didn't reprimand him, he didn't want to be unprofessional and give anyone a reason to get rid of him.

Half an hour later, Martin and the technician had

finished all their installation checks. "All clear. Thank you very much for setting it up."

"Just doing my job," the woman said dismissively, as she gave him a mock salute. "I'll be on call tomorrow. If there are any problems, let me know."

Martin returned the gesture. "Copy that, thanks."

The woman turned to Astera. "Hope you get well soon. See you 'round."

Astera said goodbye as the technician gathered up her toolkit and exited the room, leaving them alone together.

"Well, this is all set up." Martin patted the top of the unit for emphasis as he lingered.

Amusement danced in Astera's dark eyes. "It certainly looks that way. You did a mighty fine job, Eggles."

Martin puffed up at the compliment, even though she used the nickname he hated. "Call me Martin, please. Everyone in Ops calls me Eggles, no matter how often I protest."

"Martin," Astera amended with a warm smile.

The sound of his name on her lips made his body tense with excitement. Already, he pictured that word from her mouth in more intimate surroundings. He cleared his throat and looked around for something else to talk about before his desire got out of hand. "Bernie looks comfortable with you." He jutted his chin towards the figurine on her lap.

"Yeah, we've become quite close since you left him with me. He's telling me all of your secrets." She picked the dog up and wiggled it about.

Martin snorted. "That would have been a short conversation. There aren't that many to tell," he confessed. He always wished he had a cool backstory like some of the other people on board. Some of them came from prestigious families, or had dangerous job histories, or had traveled the Void ten times over. But Martin? Well, he was just "Eggles." "I'm an open book really."

Astera patted the bed beside her hip. "Will you stay a while? I could do with a friendly conversation," she said, suddenly sounding a little tired.

It took every ounce of restraint Martin possessed not to bound over and park himself at her side like the personification of the Saint Bernard in her lap. Instead, he did what he thought was a rather suave job of stepping over and sinking down onto the bed casually. "My shift is over and I have some time."

The way Astera's whole face lit up at his words made his heart beat a little faster.

"You sure your girlfriend won't get mad if I steal you away?" Astera asked.

Martin lost any suave energy he gathered at that question. "Come on, don't tease me like that. Everyone knows I'm single ... well, the Ops Team does." He frowned, as Astera's expression wavered. "Sorry, maybe you didn't know that."

"I didn't know, and I didn't mean to tease ... I suppose I was just curious." Astera gave him an apologetic look.

"Because you want the job?" Eggles asked, hope springing anew on his face. He wasn't usually this bold, but they were alone. None of the other Ops officers could overhear and taunt him relentlessly about it. Plus, he had to know. However, he hadn't thought of how abrupt he was by asking until it was out.

"It depends," Astera said, leaning back against the raised head of the bed as she watched him. "What are the conditions like? Does it pay well?" From the look on her face, it appeared she was considering it.

Martin chuckled, blasting air through his nose as he smiled. "If I had to pay you, you wouldn't be my girlfriend."

His smile waned, though, as he thought about how many jokes and one-liners had been made about his need to "pay for it." He quickly looked to Astera, trying to think of anything to say to move on from that awkward thought.

"I don't suppose you ever had trouble finding a boyfriend, though. Guys must like how you look and how good you are on the field. All that ..." He rambled a bit, trying to get the spotlight off himself. Sweat beaded on the back of his neck as he fumbled through his encounter with his crush, but wouldn't trade it for anything. Spending time with Astera was all he'd wanted since he met her.

"You're being too kind. Guys aren't exactly throwing themselves at me." Astera fidgeted with Bernie. "Not nice guys, at least. Finding a boyfriend hasn't been a priority for me for a long time, either. I've had to be—" She stopped and shook her head "I've been focusing on my career, but maybe it's time to consider reshuffling my priorities a little."

Martin's eyes widened. "I think that a career is important, but it doesn't keep you warm at night."

That might have just been his best line ever, and it wasn't even his. It was something his dad told him when he'd announced taking the job with Triple C. While they didn't see eye to eye on this sort of work, Martin knew he'd never see the galaxy sitting in a manufacturing depot for the rest of his life. It might have been stable, but it would have crushed his soul inside of five years. He had to join a mercenary company, or he'd never forgive himself. Sitting in the Med Bay with Astera, he knew he'd made the right decision.

"That's true ..." Astera's voice was light, but her expression sank a little as she looked away and fidgeted with the toy dog, seemingly lost in her own thoughts.

Martin bit his lip and let the silence stretch out. He didn't want to speak first; he'd obviously hit a sore spot. He felt it best to give her the space to jump back in when she felt ready. Turning to the console in the room, he sat down and tapped the screens. Moving from window to window, he saw that the data feed from the Ops Center was exactly what he would expect for his own console, if he were up there. He busied himself with work, setting up the displays the way he liked, but kept glancing at Astera. She seemed to have retreated into herself again, undoing some of the work they'd done to become more friendly.

Eventually, the rustling of sheets sounded over from the bed, followed by a soft groan as Astera reclined against the raised bedhead and shifted slightly onto her side. "I'm glad it was you they sent down."

Pausing his work, Martin answered, "I'm happy to be here. I was hoping to get the chance to talk with you more. I'm just sorry it took such dramatic circumstances for it to happen."

His mind reeled back to the mission, and to the conversation he had with Norgard and Hermedilla. He was so angry that he let himself get caught up in that. Astera didn't deserve to be the subject of that kind of banter. "I guess you heard the recordings of our mission chatter by now?"

Astera's nose crinkled in the most endearing expression. "No, I haven't. I don't want to relive that yet. Speaking to the commander was hard enough, hearing the actual mission recording would be so much worse."

Martin wasn't sure how to feel about her answer. If she didn't know what he said, then it was surely a good thing she wanted him down here. However, part of him wondered if it might have been better if she did know what he'd said about her. "I don't blame you. Plus, it's better to focus on what's ahead; you got out of there in one piece. Focus on that," he said, knowing this had become his mantra ever since.

"It has really made me think about what I was doing, and the things I was missing out on." Astera's lips curled into a small smile as she looked into his eyes for longer than strictly necessary. "Do you think we could catch up for dinner, or drinks, when I am out of here?"

Martin's pulse raced at her question. It was something he'd thought about for much longer than he probably should have. It felt like something out of his fantasies brought to life.

"Yes," he blurted out. All his excitement pushed the word from his lungs. "Uh, I mean, yeah, I'd really like that. Maybe something a bit more private? I'd rather not have to deal with Norgard if he saw us sitting together."

There was a spark of interest in Astera's eyes when Martin accepted her offer, but it quickly turned to confusion "Norgard? Why would he have an issue with it?"

Martin sighed. "Not so much an issue, but he's ... he's just an asshole," he grumbled. "Sorry, he's great in the Ops Center, but he gives me shit all the time," he admitted, falling into cursing a little too easily when it came to talking about his coworker. There really was no better language when it came to talking about the smug jerk.

"The guy is a grade-A asshat," Astera scoffed. "Please don't let him get to you. He and the others can be total bio-refuse. It's how they've weeded out all the genuinely good guys and left us with arrogant playboys instead." She waved a hand dismissively. "Besides, I've heard most of their exploits are just projected fantasies. If they want to have a dig, let them, because when it's all over, they'll be the ones left in the dust." There was a certain anger in Astera's tone that made it sound like she had personal experience with the matter.

Martin's mood lifted. "I think I'll manage if you're around. I just worry that he'll hang around and try to horn in on our date. It would be a date, right?" he asked, hoping he wasn't being too presumptuous. It was always tricky to categorize relationships in the company. Some people were looking for the real thing; some just needed a fuck buddy. In his fourteen months with the company so far, it sounded important to be clear with his intentions from the start.

"I would like it to be a date." Astera set Bernie back on her lap, her fingers idly stroking his fur. "And you're right. I think privacy is better. I didn't really think it through, but if my wingmates see us they may carry on like they did last time." Astera's lips curled into a grimace and her tone turned apologetic. "Sorry about that, by the way. They can be a little intense."

Martin acknowledged her apology with a smile. "Why do people get like that at the prospect of two people getting together? Like it's somehow wrong or something, to have feelings for someone," he protested, feeling like he was back in school with how his teammates and Astera's wingmates had behaved.

"I think they're just living vicariously through others. Plus, there isn't much entertainment around." She gestured to the boring medical suite, but the whole ship itself was very insulated. "As for the scouts, they just want me to 'lighten up.' Somehow, sex is seen as the cure for all ailments in this place."

She sighed as if she was tired of the sentiment.

"It seems like that's the view." Martin scratched the back of his neck. "I'm not sure how true it is, though. I've been out of the game since I got here. Everyone keeps saying I should just go to bed with someone to help loosen me up, too. They make it sound so easy." He drummed his fingers on the edge of the console as he sat, that frequent frustration weighing on him. He was very much keen to have sex, of course, but he hated the pressure he got from the others about it.

"And so inconsequential," Astera added.

"Right?" That made the tension in Martin's shoulders ease. "I want it to mean something. It's not frivolous to me. Especially with someone I like so much."

The smooth, tanned beige of her cheeks bloomed pink at his words. She opened her mouth to say something, but closed it again, clearly not sure how to respond.

That small blush made Martin happy. She was cute when she was flustered.

"But we can get into that once you get out of here. For now, we need to focus on getting you better and preparing for the mission," he said, more to remind himself that neither of them could afford to get caught up on the extra-curriculars.

"Right," Astera perked up, shaking off her inaction. Her cheeks still held that flowery shade of pink. "So, what time do you think you'll be back tomorrow? The Doc and nurses may need to do some observations and change bandages, which you probably don't want to be around for."

"Because you don't want me seeing under your bandages?" he asked, grinning at her.

"Not when it looks like this." She gestured to her wrapped torso. The purple edges of a bruise peeked out of the edge of the bandage on the top right swell of her breast. "I don't imagine this is your kind of gig."

"No, it isn't my preference." Guilt rippled through him at the reminder of her injuries. He reached over, taking her hand. "I don't mind waiting."

The skin on the back of Astera's hand was smooth and soft, but the underside held the small bumps of callouses that so many pilots had. He understood that when their hands are wrapped around the controls for hours at a time, it was bound to happen. Still, her skin was warm, and as she laced her fingers with his, it felt good.

"You know, I quite like you," she whispered decisively.

"You don't know how happy it makes me to hear you say that." He held her hand a little tighter. "Now, you really have to get better so we can have our time together."

"Luckily I have Bernie to help me with that," Astera said, letting go of his hand to retrieve the small figurine and hold it up between them. "He's been good company. Thank you."

The small gift had been even more successful than Martin had dared hope. "Then, I'm glad I remembered I had him. Feel free to hang onto him as long as you need down here. You can drop him off at my cabin whenever you like," he offered, testing the waters and the limits of his own courage.

"I'll be sure to remember that." Astera set the puppy back in her lap. She winced a little as her arm moved, and she took a sharp breath before shifting so her back was against the bed. Her skin seemed to pale at the movement and her breath caught. She closed her eyes for a few seconds and her upper body visibly relaxed. "I hope they stay safe down there tomorrow."

"They will, with your help. You can keep them out of the crosshairs of that turret," he reminded her. "That's why they want you working the mission."

"I want to be down there with them for this one, but I can't be." She frowned and shifted again, but let out a low sigh as she rested her head back against her pillow, seemingly unable to get comfortable. "I think it's time to beg the Doc for more painkillers." She gestured to the clock on the screen beside the door. "And it looks like the dinner service will wrap up before long. I don't want you missing a meal on my account."

"It's been a busy day. You should rest, so you're ready for tomorrow." He stood and brushed the creases out of his uniform shirt. "If you want, I can swing back after dinner, or hop on a video pad, to chat later? If you're not too tired, that is." He rubbed the back of his neck, hoping he wasn't being too clingy already. He just wasn't ready for his time with her to be over.

"Kitty's coming by after dinner with some things," Astera told him. "After dealing with her, I'll probably be exhausted." The small laugh she gave him showed she wasn't particularly keen about any of that. "But I'm looking forward to seeing you tomorrow."

Martin sighed. "Yeah, she's a bit ... much." The blonde-haired and blue-eyed scout was startlingly gorgeous and had a killer body, but there was so much intensity in her personality that he found her intimidating. "I'll see you tomorrow. Good night." He walked to the door. She softly echoed the farewell as the door shut between them.

CHAPTER 15

KITTY BREEZED INTO the medical suite with all the calmness and consideration of a hurricane. The bag she clutched in her hand swung wildly with the speed of her stride. Her entrance alone was enough to tell Astera that she had been right about what she said to Martin. She was already exhausted, and her roommate had only just arrived.

"Well, you only look about half as bad as you did the other day," Kitty said matter-of-factly as she swept across the room and flopped onto the end of Astera's bed without asking. Astera winced at the sudden shifting of her mattress. "I mean, your bruises have gotten nastier, but the rest of you looks better."

"I'm going to choose to take that as a compliment." Astera's voice was wry. She knew better than to be offended by Kitty's brusque delivery. The razor-sharp woman often did it to throw people off. Much easier to butter them up for information, or favors, when they were off-kilter.

"It was meant as one." Kitty flicked the tail of her blonde braid over her shoulder. She was wearing her jumpsuit, so she had probably come straight up after training in the simulator with the others. A pang of jealousy surged through Astera. Being stuck in the hospital bed was starting to grate on her, as the monotony sucked her into spirals of self-pity and worry. Kitty watched Astera closely, her head tilted to the side as if she were trying to read her thoughts.

Not wanting to give Kitty the chance to psychoanalyze her, Astera said, "So, you brought me some clothes?"

Kitty pushed the bag across the sheets. "Yep. Figured they would be better than the avant-garde bandage look you've got going."

"Thanks." Pushing through the pain of shifting and jostling her ribs, Astera hooked her finger through the handle of the bag to pull it closer, to see what Kitty had packed.

"And, just so you know, you've got the most boring underwear drawer of anyone in the wing."

"You make it a habit to know what's in everyone's underwear drawer?" Astera didn't even bother looking at her roommate as she pulled out some fresh clothes for changing into later. Her style was simple, neat, and cheap. When she joined the company, she didn't have enough money to waste on fancy stuff, nor could she risk drawing attention to herself by dressing too well.

"You betcha. Yours is boring as hell. You've literally got nothing in there besides your plain ass bras and panties. No lace, no satin, and no battery-powered sex aids to even help take the edge off. Then again, I shouldn't have expected much. 'Boring' and 'plain' pretty much describes your whole half of the room. Did you really leave everything behind when you joined? Or were you always so spartan?"

Kitty shuffled so her back was against the footboard and kicked her legs up to rest along the side of Astera's. Like most of the pilots in the scouts, Kitty was short. Smaller pilots fit more easily into the cockpits of the light, trim scout class mechs. It also made it easier for Kitty to fit onto the bed without Astera needing to shift. "You really get to know a person when you see what they keep amongst their unmentionables. You should have seen some of the stuff Viper was hiding. She likes to act as though she is all cool and nonchalant, but she's a total freak. You should see her collection of—"

"How was training?" Astera blurted, not wanting to know what Viper was collecting.

"Not the same without Sleeves."

The words crashed between them like a meteor.

"Johansen said that the commander contacted her family. They want us to get her stuff together and send it to them next time we hit a space port." Kitty's voice softened. "We were wondering if you wanted to help us with the packing."

"I'm not sure." Astera looked down at her lap. The thought of going through Sleeves' things, of packing them up, it all felt so *final*. She knew Sleeves was gone, but sending her things off would remove all traces of her, and Astera wasn't ready to give that up just yet.

"Well, we won't be going to port for a while, so you've got time to think about it." Kitty shrugged. "Glacier isn't sleeping in their room at the moment anyway, says she feels like Sleeves will walk back in at any moment. She's been bunking with her lady-friend from Engineering instead. I think the arrangement is working out nicely for the two of them. Glacier is certainly less frosty. Human contact suits her."

All Astera could do was nod. She didn't know what to say, or what to think.

"Speaking of human contact. That poor guy from Ops who came to visit you has it bad. What's his name again? Egan? Nuggles?" Kitty's voice dropped to a conspiratorial whisper.

Astera knew better than to tell Kitty what Martin's name was.

Kitty continued, unperturbed by Astera's non-answer. She had to have been used to it by this point. "He was like a little puppy dog the other day. Super sweet. Not my type, but maybe you like that wide-eyed innocent kinda thing."

Without even thinking, Astera's eyes flicked to the small Saint Bernard figurine on her bedside table. Kitty followed her gaze, then launched forward and snatched up the pup before Astera could stop her. She held it up, her face contorting in amusement. "What's this?"

Nothing, Astera wanted to snap. Although, that would make her look like she had something to hide. "It's a dog figurine."

"Duh. I'm not an idiot."

"What was I supposed to say? A potato?"

"Fine." Kitty's eyes narrowed at her. "My bad. I asked the wrong question. Where did you get it from?"

It took a great deal of restraint for Astera to resist acting on the desire to swipe the figurine from Kitty and tell her to piss off. "One of the staff here gave it to me to cheer me up." It wasn't a complete lie.

"One of the staff here"—Kitty gestured around the room—"or the ship in general?"

Astera kept her lips pressed together.

"For the love of—" Kitty cut off partway through her own rant and shook her head, annoyance contorting her perfectly plucked brows into a deep "V." "What's the big deal? Why won't you tell me where you got it? It's not like I'm going to tell everyone, or use the information to blackmail you into telling me all your dirty secrets."

Really? Astera thought. *I bet that's exactly what you'd do.* Astera liked Kitty. She did. But that didn't mean she was blind to how the wily woman used every snippet of information she hoarded.

"Starfall, you need to stop being so closed off. We all love you, and we all trust you with our lives, but we don't *know* you." Kitty sounded more frustrated than manipulative, and it made Astera pause as guilt started to seep through her. "Void! We're willing to go out and fight alongside you. Sleeves took a Void-damn shell for you and yet you won't even say where you got a stupid toy dog."

Kitty slammed the figurine down on the table and flopped onto the bed with a huff of indignation. Astera watched silently, not moving, unwilling to unintentionally spur Kitty into a deeper rant.

"Look, we all know you're running from something. No normal person shows up at a new job with three changes of clothes and nothing else to their name." Kitty sighed, throwing her hands into the air. "We've tried giving you time, letting you get comfortable, but you don't even give an inch. What's the point of running from whatever you left behind if you aren't going to try and live a new life?" Kitty leaned forward and took Astera's clenched fists in her own two warm hands. "We don't give a shit about your past, okay? Just ... let us be your friends now. Not just your wingmates."

Kitty watched her expectantly, blue eyes big, pleading, and shiny with a sheen of threatening tears. Astera's stomach lurched and bile rose in her throat.

A different pair of blue eyes swam in Astera's vision. Darker, like sapphires reflecting moonlight, and more dangerous.

Astera jerked her hands out of Kitty's and instinctively reached for the shell that usually hung around her neck. Her fists clutched nothing, and her nails dug into her palm.

"Look at these people you called friends, my Little Star,"

his deep, honeyed voice slithered through her mind as her heart pounded. *"Every single one of them betrayed you, sold you out ... now, let me show you what happens when you dare try to cross me."*

The memory of blinding agony and soul-destroying shame surged through Astera as she tried to claw her way back from the past. Kitty's hands settled on her leg, an anchor, a call through the maelstrom of her flashback to return to her body.

"Astera?"

Kitty was in front of her again. Her roommate was right, of course. She ran away so she could actually live a life, but ... her freedom still felt precarious. Fragile. She could understand why the others wanted to get to know her, but it was too risky. She couldn't give them that, but she had to give Kitty something. She couldn't risk alienating herself from the crew of the Latagarosh.

"Eggles," Astera blurted.

Kitty tilted her head to the side, brows arched in question.

"This." Astera snatched up the toy dog. "Eggles gave it to me, okay?"

Kitty's entire demeanor flipped from one of concern to one of absolute delight, a knowing smirk tugging at the corner of her lips. "I knew it. He's totally pulling the moves, isn't he? Are you going to go for it?"

Astera set the dog back down and shrugged. "I'm not sure," she admitted. She found him likeable, and kind, and she had agreed to a date, but she only did that knowing she'd have time to reconsider.

"Do you think he's attractive?"

Martin's kind brown eyes and tentative smiles came to Astera's mind. "He's cute."

"Cute?" Kitty scoffed. "Hardly sounds like you're enthused about him."

"It's not that." Astera waved her hand dismissively. "He is really kind, and thoughtful, and respectful, and sweet ... and a little bit goofy, which is endearing. I just—"

"Shit, Starfall." Kitty rolled her eyes. "You don't have to marry the dude. Just get out there, have a bit of fun, loosen up a little."

Kitty had a point. Astera had never really dated anyone before. Maybe she was giving the kindling relationship too much gravity. People in the Triple C dated and split up all the time. It was pretty normal where she was from, too. At least, for other people.

"Maybe you're right," she conceded, earning an excited squeak from Kitty. "But he seems really bashful. I'm not going to bother to ask you to keep this to yourself; I know you'll tell the others, but please go easy on him. He's nice. He doesn't deserve any taunting, no matter how playful."

With a hand over her heart, Kitty promised, "Don't worry, babe. I'm not gonna scare your new boy toy away." She jumped off the bed and gave Astera a mock salute. "Now, off to tell the ladies. They'll be delighted."

Before Astera could say another word, Kitty bounced from the room. Astera collapsed back against her bed with an *oof* and a soft curse. She sincerely hoped telling Kitty wasn't a mistake, and that trusting Martin wouldn't get her into trouble.

THE NEXT MORNING, Astera woke to the now familiar sounds of Doctor Colwyn bustling into her room for the morning observations. Astera wasn't sure why the leader of the medical unit hadn't passed her care back to a less-busy-and-important doctor, but she wasn't about to question it.

"How are we feeling this morning?" Colywn asked, as she skirted around the bulky Ops console and tapped the screen on the wall to check the medical readings.

"Body is getting better, but I'm just utterly exhausted," Astera admitted, trying and failing to suppress a yawn.

With an annoyed wave of her hand towards the Ops console, Colwyn said, "If all of this is too much—"

"No," Astera yelped a little too quickly. "No, it's fine. I just had a bit of trouble sleeping last night. Besides, if I don't do something, I worry my brain will turn to sludge and start leaking out of my ears."

"Not medically possible." Colwyn narrowed her eyes at one of the zig-zaggy charts for a moment. "Especially when you're recovering quite smoothly." She closed the charts and then pressed Astera's favorite button on the screen. The one that delivered a surge of pain relief medication straight into her veins. "If today, or your constant stream of visitors, becomes too much, just buzz one of the staff in and they'll get them out quick smart."

"Thanks, Doc," Astera said with a genuine smile of appreciation. It was hard to make polite excuses to get rid of people. Having someone run interference would be helpful, especially as she was a captive audience.

"I'll get one of the nurses to come in and help you clean up. I heard that one of your wingmates brought you some clothes. If you want something over the bandages, I'd suggest a jacket, or something with a full-length torso fastener, so we can get it on and off you easily." Colwyn stepped back from the bed and visually appraised Astera's condition. At first, her penetrating gaze had unnerved Astera, but she had grown used to it.

"That sounds like a plan, thank you."

Astera's reply seemed to be all the doctor needed as she

turned and walked out of the room. The next part Astera hated. She knew some of the people on the ship would have loved a sponge bath from any of the nursing staff, but it was an uncomfortable experience for her. She was well aware of how bruised and battered her body was, and the scars from her past were still visible, even beneath the flourish of new colors her injuries had caused. She was grateful that the staff had enough bedside manner not to ask about them, or where she got them, but it was a timely reminder of why she had spent so long avoiding any sort of physical intimacy.

When the sponge bath was over, the nurse helped her into one of her favorite jackets. The fabric was a deep marled gray, and the insides of it were soft and warm in all the best ways. It was the ultimate in comfort-wear for her, and it helped her to feel more like herself again.

It wasn't long after she was cleaned and dressed that the door opened, and a nurse appeared with a tray of breakfast, with a sweet, but nervous looking, Martin at her side.

"Good morning," Astera said, perking up even more.

The nurse glanced between the tray in her hands and the man at her side. "I wish all my patients were this happy to see their breakfast," she joked, walking over, and setting the food down on the adjustable table for Astera. She excused herself from the room, then shut the door behind her.

Martin shifted to the console table right away and plugged in some sort of data device. "I guess I got down here a little early. I thought you'd be done with breakfast by now." He tapped away at the screens and the keyboard in front of him. "If you like, I can step out and let you finish up and relax a bit."

With a shake of her head, Astera said, "No, please stay."

The conversation with Kitty the previous night had confirmed things for Astera; she was going to give Martin a chance. She pulled the tray table closer and peeled the foil off the dishes the nurse had set down. "Honestly, I'm so used to eating in the Mess Hall that eating by myself feels weird."

The Mess Hall was, at all times of the day and night, the key hub of socialization and gossip on the Latagarosh. The promise of food always had a way of luring people in, and the good company often kept them there. The scouts had taken to using it as their main hangout, and Astera couldn't think of the last time she ate a meal there without the raucous antics of her wingmates.

Martin nodded. He didn't say much as he got the table displays set up the way he liked. As the silence grew, he finally spoke. "You look a bit better today; surely, you won't be staying here much longer?"

It was true. Doctor Colwyn had been giving her some powerful, and most likely extremely expensive, drugs to help her heal and manage the pain. If her body had been left to recover on its own accord, it would probably take weeks or months, but the medical technology she had been given had helped Astera feel better with each passing day. Still, Astera knew better than to assume she would be fine to go, just because she wasn't in quite as much pain as the day before.

"It's up to the Doc," Astera replied between bites of her rather bland breakfast porridge. "When I first came to, she said 'maybe a week'."

"So, you're almost halfway through, then?" Martin paused. "I better start preparing to help you figure out how you can take your bath." He smiled to himself as he tapped a few things on the screen.

Hoping to stop herself from blurting out something stupid in response to his comment about the bath, Astera jammed a spoonful of porridge in her mouth and just smiled, the corners of her lips framed by the rosy flush of her cheeks. She kept eating as he worked, eager to get through the meal.

After a few minutes, Astera was finished. She pushed her tray table aside and glanced at the operations specialist. "So, I suppose we should be all official with callsigns and stuff, with the mission starting soon."

"Correct. Gotta keep the lines secure, and our names protected. I'll talk with the Ops Desk and figure out what my designation will be. Anything you share will be attributed to your callsign and the pilots should be ready to go with theirs," he explained.

"Am I close enough for the unit to pick up my voice, or should I ask the Doc for a chair?"

Astera raised the head of the bed and got herself into a more upright position to test it out. She winced as her body weight adjusted and put pressure on her ribs, but it was not unbearable.

"One sec." Martin picked up a headset attached to the side of the unit and plugged it in before settling it over his ears. He tapped twice on the left ear, activating it. "Nest, this is the remote station requesting authentication and designation ... Command phrase reply is Lambda Pharaoh ... Roger that, switching to designation Remote. Remote requesting radio check of adjunct personnel. Stand by for input from adjunct pilot Starfall." He nodded towards Astera.

Astera cleared her throat and put on her best neutral tone. "This is Starfall. How are you receiving, over?"

Martin pressed his headphone tighter to his ears, listening to the reply. "Copy that, Nest. Adjusting tech now." He reached into the storage beside him. Moving some things around, he found a wireless earpiece and mic. Scooting across the floor on his chair, he paused to activate it and leaned in close to settle it over her ears. His fingertips were warm and gentle as they brushed over her skin, and he smiled before he activated it for her and wheeled his chair back to the console.

The chime of the earpiece connecting sounded in Astera's ears. The ever-present hum of the open comm channel filled the silence before she spoke again. "Nest, Starfall. Can I have a retest on my comms? Over."

"Roger that, Starfall. We have you five by five on comms. Welcome back, pilot. Wing Leader, how are you receiving the new audio on channel?" the voice came, and Astera was certain it was Hermedilla. Whoever else might be up there was a mystery though.

"Nest, Knuckle Duster, we are receiving. Glad to hear your voice again, Starfall. Welcome back. Over," the commander said.

An unbidden warmth spread to Astera at the welcomes that greeted her through comms. It had only been a few days since her mission, but she was missing the whole process and feel of it. She may not have been down there on the ground, but the commander's acknowledgement, and the lengths he went to in order to let her listen in on this mission, made her feel good. Made her feel like her work was valuable and appreciated.

"Roger that, Knuckle Duster. And thanks—it's good to be here." Astera looked over at Martin and gave him an enthusiastic thumbs up that drew a soft chuckle of amusement from him before he returned his attention to the screens in front of him.

"Starfall, Boss." It seemed it was the sergeant's turn to welcome her to the channel. "Any operational intelligence you can share that we will need before touchdown?"

"That place is hot as all hell, stay hydrated," Astera said, trying not to let the sensory memories return with her words. "Once you're in the forest, the floor will be slippery. Make sure you keep your mech feet grips on tight. The predator tracks make good roads through the underbrush, but we did not see any of the large creatures, so I don't know what will happen if you startle one. Also, the tree trunks were strong enough to hold my Hummingbird without trouble, so if you need to stay quiet, and out of sight for whatever reason, make like a monkey and take to the trees."

Ever since returning, the debriefings had focused on the missile that took out Sleeves. Astera's evasion of the planet-based mechs and her escape had fallen to the background. As a result, she was yet to share how she managed to hide in plain sight when those mechs were coming in hot behind her.

"Starfall, even with our weight reductions, I don't think we can really put that to use." As usual, Kildare was the wet blanket on the mission. They hadn't even landed and he was grousing already. Astera should have expected as much, she'd never worked with him but she had heard plenty of stories.

"Whatever works for you and your crew, Mercenary. That's all I've got for now. Hope your guns stay cool," Astera said, using the customary equivalent of saying 'Good luck and stay safe.' Even the engineers and technicians used it, with it being so ubiquitous amongst the pilots.

"Roger that. We are entering orbital insertion. We will break radio silence once we land and disembark. Knuckle Duster, out," the commander sent as the channel went dead.

Letting out a sigh as she leaned back against the bed, Astera closed her eyes. She remembered her own trip to the planet so vividly, while the return was all a painful blur. She was glad that the commander was allowing her to listen in, but she could only hope that they had more success than she and Sleeves.

CHAPTER 16

INSERTION into the planet went as smoothly as possible, and the team disembarked without issue. Their mechs were on the ground for less than a minute before Henri realized Astera was not lying about the heat. It was like stepping out of a perfectly climate-controlled room and into a sauna with a broken temperature sensor ... and that was with a perfectly functional mech. He couldn't imagine how sweltering it must have been in Calliope's cockpit without the environmental systems, and with all the equipment running hot.

Henri glanced at his nav display. They had about twenty kilometers from Mother Hen's landing zone to the base, along the route that he worked out with the major. It was a bit different from the route the scout team had used as they tried to keep as much of the terrain between them, and base, as they could. While the jungle was helpful in obscuring vision of the Hummingbird Astera piloted, the Hummingbird had the advantage of a small radar profile and other countermeasures to the usual radar, infrared, and tremor sensors used to pick up moving mechs. The infantry mechs that supported him were a little too tall and heavy to follow the same strategy.

Then again, they weren't *infantry* mechs. They were *scout* mechs according to the paperwork he was going to file in his mission reports. To allow that distinction, they had to cut a lot of equipment from each machine before launching on this *scouting* mission. The other pilots grumbled about the lack of armor and reduction in their weapons, but even with the retrofit, the five mechs in this wing were more than enough to deal with the complement of base defenders they had scanned on the last mission.

As they made the turn at Nav Alpha, Sergeant Pestle got on the comms. "Still nothing on the scope, not even radar pings from the base. Are you sure they're even there?"

"That's a roger. We haven't caught any craft leaving the planet and I doubt they would abandon such a pricey piece of hardware that they snuck down so carefully," Henri reassured him.

"Surely a single turret can't be that valuable? Even mining companies can afford to outfit their plants with turrets," cut in Kildare, always the skeptic.

"Those turrets mount weapons in the same class as missile racks you'd find on any mech. This turret mounts cruise missile scale deployment systems with a design philosophy of one missile, one dead mech," Henri explained.

"You mean, it's a portable version of a dropship missile system?" Kildare's voice found a new register that made Henri wince.

"Seems to be. Let's not find out the hard way, shall we?" Henri cautioned.

"Don't worry, I'm sure Mercenary won't put himself in any danger when it comes to that turret," Kawamura interjected, making sure to remind everyone what Kildare's handle was, and the fact it was well-suited to him, despite his current objections.

"Not if I can help it, Hachiman," Kildare retorted to his wingmate. The pair both piloted the same mech class but couldn't be more different in personality. Kildare was cautious and opportunistic while Kawamura was decisive and aggressive, making themselves a complimentary pair. Their balance was part of the reason they worked so well together.

"We'll see if he gets to make that call when we approach the base. Speaking of which, we will be entering radio silence from this point forward. While we may be shielded by the terrain, we're still close enough that they may pick up our chatter," Henri warned.

"Copy that. You heard the man, time for radio silence," Pestle said. The rest of the trip to Nav Beta was quiet save the rhythmic booms of marching mech feet. Even with the sealed cockpits, the sound of several tons of walking metal was hard to drown out.

As the wing made the turn at Nav Beta, they got their first glimpse of the base in the valley below. Even with the jungle cover, it looked like the occupants had cleared away quite a bit of native foliage to improve their sight lines, pushing the base's outer cordon back by another eight hundred meters since Astera had scouted several days earlier. The recent run-ins between whoever was on the base and Henri's people must have made them a little more paranoid. As the Wing followed a run-off channel down the mountain, they once again entered the shadow of the hill.

"Semtex to Knuckle Duster."

Henri nudged his chin against the microphone activator. "This is KD. Semtex, we're on radio silence," he snapped at the poor private for breaking radio silence.

"Sorry, Knuckle Duster, but I had to relay that I didn't see any of their mechs idle in the base. Are you sure they didn't pick up Mother Hen on our drop?"

Henri frowned. He had not been able to see any idle mechs either, but didn't want to change the mission at the last minute. "Noted, Semtex, but mission parameters are unchanged. Proceed to Nav Delta and prepare for orders."

"Understood, sir. Apologies, sir."

For her first mission in the Infantry Wing, Semtex wasn't off to a great start. After finding out how much of Starfall's bio was bogus, he was starting to wonder if Semtex had faked her past mission history. She took the demotion from her cushy jobs in Ops to join the open spot in the Infantry Wing a little too quickly, but he didn't think anything of it at the time. Now, he wasn't so sure about how many hours she had on the stick. It didn't feel like a lot with her breaking radio silence so easily.

Arriving at Nav Delta, the wing formed up around Pestle in the shelter of the ridge that rose between their column and the base. As they did, Henri walked his borrowed mech along the side to fall in just behind the sergeant's shoulder. Once he was in position, he clicked his laser designator on twice. The spot flashed on the tree in front of Pestle and he took off at the commander's signal.

The Falcon sprinted forward and the sergeant's years of work piloting the smallest frame in the infantry class were on display. Using Astera's advice, he avoided swaths of the underbrush that might have caused his mech to slip as he trekked the perimeter. As he ran, he turned his mech at the torso and fired sensor pings at all the buildings. He became very noisy in the electromagnetic spectrum, to the point that none of their sensors could have missed him.

All the while, Henri proceeded up the ridge, watching the map display out of the corner of his eye. "Come on, he's mapping your base. Engage him," he muttered to himself as he pushed the Eagle mech to the top of the hill. While it was an Eagle in name, it was a bit squatter than the normal chassis. Liang preferred the extra bracing the change allowed as it put less torque on the body to fire the larger caliber autocannons he liked so much. That was exactly why Henri had chosen this mech to commandeer. The usual fitout had the added benefit of being able to balance the long-barreled magneto-dynamic accelerator cannon it was packing this time. Henri took care to keep the torso angled back to keep the tip of its barrel from digging into the dirt as he pushed the Eagle to the top of the hill. Clearing the top of the ridge, he powered on his passive sensors as he watched the base.

Sure enough, one of the buildings to the rear of the base unfolded like a blossoming flower. Green, brown, and deep dusty red camouflage netting split apart, birthing a turret the size of two transport trucks attached side by side. The barrels swung to aim at Pestle's Falcon as he cased the joint. Henri flipped down his targeting visor and leaned his face into it, blocking out light from the highly sensitive camera display. His fingers were delicate on his control stick as he clicked the zoom a few more times to tighten on the turret that filled his vision.

"They have me locked, Knuckle Duster," Pestle's voice came loud and clear over the comms.

"Firing," Henri announced. With a click of the trigger on his control stick, the magnetic rings, just a few meters beside his head, drew nearly all the power from his mech's core. The computer timing ensured the energy flux down the line of rings changed at just the right pace to accelerate the ninety-kilogram cobalt slug down the length of the oversized barrel. Reaching nearly the speed of light in velocity, the round moved so fast as to leave a trail of ions and sparks in the air behind it. With all that kinetic energy, the projectile vaporized the hinge at the base of the turret, causing it to topple over and lay uselessly on the ground.

"Scout Wing Beta, advance," Henri called over the comms, purposefully using the term "Scout Wing" just in case the Kolos Admiralty wanted their mission recording. All the mechs below rounded the corner and moved at full speed towards the base. Pestle wheeled around and made for the base as well, free of the imminent threat of the anti-mech turret.

As the rest of the converted Infantry Wing rounded the ridge to engage the base, Henri watched as the same three mechs that pursued Astera, days ago, moved to defend the instalment in the valley below him. At first glance, they appeared like normal mech chassis, but the targeting visor showed that they had been heavily modified. First off, they appeared to be mounting weapons that were far too heavy for their frames. As a result, it looked like a lot of the armor was missing to make up for that. Obviously, the leader of this force opted for firepower above all else. It wasn't the worst idea to Henri. He thought, *if you can end a fight in a few shots, you don't have to worry about receiving any damage.* But watching how they tried to track Sergeant Pestle's Falcon, it was clear they didn't have the training to make up for that.

Liam was circling the mechs, side-stepping their incoming mech-mounted missiles as they fired. It was a good thing, too, as that level of escalation was just what the Triple C needed to enact their self-defense clause in the contract. With the mechs distracted by Liam, Mercenary, and Hachiman in their Harriers marched forward, firing off laser weapons and auto-cannons. The team tactics training from last night was paying off as Ian's weapon cycled fast enough to cover Iroha as she closed and used her lasers at close range. Henri smiled at the skill on display from his team.

His position on the ridge allowed him to cover the other four. In particular, the third and heaviest mech defending the base tried to stay at range to cover the other two. A steady hand, and soft squeeze of his controls, let Henri send another slug at relativistic speeds at the large mech. It crumpled slightly as its arm fell to the ground as the slug obliterated its shoulder joint. That window allowed Semtex to pick it off with a full volley from the missile systems on her Kite.

The heavy mech had no answer as smoke from the popcorn-like explosions of the missiles covered its body. The exuberant rookie couldn't help a little cheer as the mech fell out of the cloud with a heavy thud on the turf. Everyone in the vicinity could feel so many tons of metal hit the ground and the two remaining base defenders tried to retreat. Liam's Falcon moved perfectly to cut off their escape routes and Ian and his Harrier always seemed to be firing into the thinner armor on the backside of the two mechs. In less than fifteen minutes, all three defending mechs were smoking on the ground outside the base.

"That's for you, Sleeves," Henri muttered to himself.

CHAPTER 17

HENRI HAD BARELY GOTTEN out of his mech when he heard Vitali shouting up at him. He peered over the edge of the walkway to the floor of the Mech Bay below to see the balding Earther pointing at the comm pad. He rolled his eyes and sighed as he walked over and activated the screen. "What is it, old man?"

"Commander, I think you need to see something on the feed from my salvage crews. I've got it up in my office," Vitali said, gesturing over his shoulder.

"Vitali, I just got back from the surface, I got swamp ass worse than a Nuborian summer. I'm going to shower up and sleep. Surely it can wait," Henri answered, hating the thought of interrupting his usual post-mission routine.

"Sorry, boss, but it can't. You may have to make a decision about this," Vitali replied rather gravely.

That caught Henri's attention.

"I'll be right down," Henri answered, his tone changing immediately. Everyone would just have to put up with his stench while he dealt with whatever had spooked Vitali.

Henri stepped over to the ladder and slid down, from

landing to landing, to reach the floor of the Mech Bay as quick as he could. Vitali stood waiting for him and the pair walked to the chief engineer's office. Stepping inside, he saw the feed from the monitoring truck as the camera panned while sitting amid the base they had just cleared. "What am I looking at here, Vitali?" he asked, not seeing anything that would warrant Command.

"Right there," came the reply with Vitali jabbing his mechanical finger at one of the mechs the salvage team was cutting apart.

"Right where?"

"Void, Henri! Right there." Vitali tapped at his console and zoomed the feed in even more.

It was a roughed-up logo on the side of the turret tower. The salvage crew had been checking the artillery around it to see if any of it would be worthwhile to them. As one of the crates of slugs shifted, the logo became clearer. It was a stylized letter "K", with three oval, planetary style rings around it.

The Kolos Admirality.

It wasn't like Henri to gawk, but if one of his crew members looked at him as he took that logo in, they would have seen him come close. Ice cold fury zapped through him like an electrical shock, and all the puzzle pieces he had been trying to assemble suddenly fit together perfectly.

"Those Void-damned bastards," Henri muttered to himself, reaching out to scrub the video back a little so he could watch the reveal again. "They must have known it was here the whole time."

"It gets worse." Vitali sighed as he fast-forwarded the recordings from the salvage trolley and pointed out nearly two dozen different logos and shipping labels still on the equipment. Henri recognized most of them; the Corvon Talons, Luna Prime, Qasar Shipping, Geltar Fleet ...

"Pirates." Henri and Vitali spat the word at the same time.

The arms and equipment in the small outpost of a base appeared to have been stolen from all the larger organizations across the Void. If it were the inventory of a mercenary company, like the Triple C, they would have relabelled it all and given it proper company labels. Pirates rarely bothered with that kind of thing, and the complete and utter lack of cohesive, or repeated, insignia meant that this had to be a crew that had been pillaging for a long while. Henri could think of a few possible contenders, but without proof he didn't want to make any assumptions.

"It doesn't make sense, though." Henri shook his head. "Pirates don't build bases. They capture them, strip them down to the studs and move on. That's how they have operated since the days of the Strays."

Vitali shrugged. "Unless they have loftier aspirations?"

That, Henri thought, was alarming. Between all the valuable items that had been on the base, and the fact that these pirates managed to steal one of the largest, and most expensive, turrets available from one of the most powerful political groups in the galaxy said something. If they were angling to set up a permanent base on Baldalan, all the nearby systems would have to go on high alert. This patch of the Void was relatively quiet, but that was only because someone had yet to claim it ... and nobody would want pirates to dig their flag in the dirt.

"You've gone quiet, boss. I don't like it when you go quiet." Vitali eyed Henri warily and leaned against the console that had the video feet on it, crossing his arms over his chest.

"We were set up, Chief." Henri rubbed a hand over his chin as he realized just how badly the Kolos Admirality had fucked them over. "They said they wanted us to confirm presence of the signals ... really, they wanted us to confirm the presence of the turret using our mechs to scan the base. Now they know it's here for sure, I bet they were going to have us babysit this shithole of a planet until they had a crew ready to claim the site and the turret back. We sure as shit wouldn't have been able to salvage the whole thing in one serviceable piece, and they would have known that. Our stipend is not even close to what they would have to pay to replace the damn thing. Looks like they decided to throw us to the vipers, rather than cutting their losses."

If there was ever a time Henri wanted to smash some heads together, it was now. But he knew better than that. The Kolos Admirality needed to be dealt with more delicately. He would get back at them, but for now, he needed to focus on figuring out who they were dealing with on the planet.

"I must talk with La Plaz, see what his crew can find out about the base. Then, we can start to piece this together. Tell your boys to hustle. I want a twenty-four-hour rotation to clear the site. Who knows when the pirates will be sending fresh people around to check on it."

Vitali nodded. "I'll make sure the other two shifts are so advised. You and Pestle's Wing came back pretty clean, so we won't need so much of the crew in the bay. I can shift some manpower to the salvage team."

"Good, let me know what they find in the wreckage," Henri said over his shoulder as he turned and left the office. He walked through the bay and out into the main corridors on autopilot, weaving around people as he made his way back to his quarters. One of the benefits of being a mech pilot was using muscle memory to move on the battlefield as you assess combat scenarios. It translated well to working his way through the ship. He could unpack this new information and get cleaned, and dressed, without conscious thought.

By the time Henri had cleaned up and reached the Operations section, he already had a list of questions prepped for his intelligence officer. Luckily, the man was right where Henri hoped he'd be: in the Ops Room with the team that had just handled the mission. "La Plaz, what have your intelligence officers found for us on the planet?"

The major was used to the commander skipping the pleasantries after a mission. He barely lifted his head from his console as he answered. "It's odd. We were expecting to see branding, or signs of the base's previous residents, but everything we're finding points to an organized defense force with no previous occupants."

"That's impossible. These are pirates; they had to take over this place from someone."

"Doesn't look like it. The construction is new, and not just the turret installation. Looking at this objectively, I think they built this base for themselves," La Plaz said incredulously.

"Pirates, building a base?" It was a rhetorical question, but Henri couldn't keep his puzzlement to himself.

"From what we can see, they operated it almost like an under-resourced military base. There is little evidence of people, or deliveries, going in and out. They don't even seem to have anything beyond basic dropships down there, which explains why they haven't tried to launch an air-based defense against us. Based on the size, and the lack of agricultural considerations, they had to be getting supplies from somewhere, so I had my team investigate it," La Plaz said. There was a hint of interest in his tone that told Henri he was enjoying the puzzle-solving aspect of this mission.

"So, there are more rats hiding on that planet somewhere?" Henri said, finishing the implication in La Plaz's comment. He stood, staring at the rendering of the base displayed on the screen. It had the usual things: power supply, barracks, Mech Bay, dropship landing pad, and a deep space antenna dish. The latter seemed highly suspicious considering this news. "Did we ever do a spectrum sweep on the antenna?"

"No, it was always pointed at the horizon, not up. The pencil beam never intersected with our monitors," Hermedilla answered from a console somewhere behind La Plaz. Hermedilla had a deep background in electromagnetic communications which was why he started in comms when he joined the Ops Team. Having done so well that he rose to team lead, Henri considered him an expert on all things EM.

"And it never occurred to any of you that they had a deep space antenna that they never pointed up?" Henri countered, looking at them annoyed. The two Ops officers stared at each other; their faces pulled taut with shame.

"Tracing possible paths of the signal now," Hermedilla said, sitting up in his seat and starting to work his magic on his console.

That was one of the things Henri liked about the experienced operations specialist. He didn't waste time with excuses or apologies; he just focused on making things right. Somewhat mollified by the correction, Henri muttered, "Do that and tell me where the receiver might be. La Plaz, feed me that info. I need to tell the flight deck that we're changing our orbit."

CHAPTER 18

ONCE AGAIN, Henri sat in his office, watching the connection progress bar fill. No telling how many Pulsar Probes were being used to connect back to civilized space. All it did was give him time to make sure his evidence was arranged and plugged into the holocaller for use later. He sat and waited to see Mel's face fill his display.

As with the previous time, it took a while for the call to pick up on the other side. It made sense given the time difference, but Henri had a feeling it probably also had a bit to do with the fact that Mel always seemed to be annoyed when he called. When the call did finally connect, it was clear this round of communication would be no exception.

"Durroguerre, I take it you have an update for me?" Mel asked, not even bothering with the pleasantries.

Henri put on his best compliance face, knowing that Mel was expecting a report about the base on the planet below. He did his best to look annoyed about sending out another scout to recon the base, rather than let on to the truth about what happened. At least, that was his plan to open the conversation. "Yeah ... I do. It was a pain in my ass to get, but we reconned the base as you requested. It's all in the report I am forwarding to you now."

Henri tapped the data pack plugged into his console, sending the assembled data about the base, as well as pictures of his salvage crew, tearing the base apart. He made sure the last picture was one where his team was loading the main assembly of the turret onto their salvage vehicles. He sat and waited for Mel's reaction.

Mel's focus seemed to drift off to the side, and after a moment his expression changed to one of concentration. He must have been flipping through the report. However, his narrowed eyes soon widened and he snapped back to face the holocaller input. "So, you did a subpar job of scouting, and when I told you to go back and get more information, you instead went in and destroyed their base?"

Henri had to suppress a smile as he could have sworn he also heard steam whistling out of Mel's ears.

"Correct me if you can, but your orders were for us to scout the base a second time because you were unsatisfied with data. Also, do I need to remind you of the opening line of Section Two, Paragraph One of our contract: 'The Commander of the aforementioned Company will determine the assets brought to bear to achieve the mission objectives assigned by the client.'?"

Face contorting as his mouth opened and closed, Mel finally snapped. "Yes. You pick the assets, but not the mission descriptor." There was a bang as Mel slammed his palms against the console. "I thought the Triple C had a good enough reputation, and history, to know the difference between a scouting mission and a salvage opportunity. You know, *scouting*, where you go in quietly, gather intel, and then leave as subtly as possible? What the Void do you call that?" He gestured wildly to what must have been the screen, off to the side, he used to read the mission report.

Henri spoke as coolly and calmly as he ever had in his career. Mel walked right into what he had set up. "Correct, we did deploy for a 'recon in force' mission. Given the presence of the turret thanks to our first mission, I wasn't about to send in a scout without support again. I'll also remind you of the Triple C Standing Orders, which you agreed to when you hired our company. Number three on the list is 'The pilots, in the absence of orders from Mission Control, have the authority to determine their level of response when engaged by the enemy based on mission parameters and the level of the threat.' Since that turret had already killed one pilot, we were not about to let it fire on another. Finally, Section Five, Paragraph Four of the contract you drew up for this enterprise states 'The Company is entitled to any and all salvage gained in the course of the fulfilment of this contract.' This is an unclaimed planet and you are in no position to enforce salvage rights. Now, do you want to fight this and waste more money, or will you close the contract, pay us what we are owed, and end this charade?"

It was a somewhat petty move, taking the ruins of the destroyed turret from the base ... but Void, it felt good when Henri saw the charred, ruined, carcass sitting on the deck of his cargo bay a few hours ago.

Mel's expression and posture hardened, and that steamy countenance turned to something much colder. He glared at Henri through the holocaller, but his lips were pursed in thought. "Consider this contract complete. We will finalize things as agreed upon on our end, and we will ensure that the Kolos Admirality, and our allies, do not contract the services of the Triple C ever again. We thought that you would be more professional than half of the Void-thrashing mercenaries out there, but it seems you are all one and the same."

Then, without further opportunity for questions or comebacks, the call ended and Mel's head and torso dissolved into a nondescript beam of holo particles.

Henri sighed. He knew this was going to cost him future business, but this whole mess had shown him that it wasn't worth it to work with the Admiralty anymore. The time and people wasted on this stunt by them showed how little regard they had for mercenaries like those in his company. Pushing up from the table, he walked over to the "In Memoriam" board and hung the name bar of Corporal Monique "Sleeves" Hughes. Henri's board was a copy of the one in the common room, but he kept it hung right over his mission negotiation console to remind him of what was at stake with every job he took.

He scanned the other names on the board, still stung by the memory of each one. It had been a while since they had to add a name to it, but it didn't make him feel any better about it. With a click, the console powered down and Henri hit the lights on his way out the door. It was just a few dozen meters to get back to his quarters, but it felt longer. With a sigh, he retrieved his favorite bottle of Core Worlds whiskey from storage and poured a few glugs into a tumbler on his way to the chair. He sat and sipped, staring at the space beyond the window in his room. He let his breathing slow after dealing with Mel, heart following suit as he relaxed.

With the mission over and wrapped, he was now free to consider what to do about the green and red tinged planet in the distance. Baldalan had presented more trouble than he could have imagined, but the scans the Intelligence Team turned over had hinted at communication darting back and forth all over the damn planet. The base they hit wasn't the only one there, and he shuddered to think over just what the pirates were building. He had his guys working on finding out more now, but it was proving to be a slow process, based on the atmosphere and what must have been some cleverly shielded buildings. Sure, Henri could turn the ship around and leave this armpit segment of space to deal with its own issues, but there were systems nearby that were home to billions of good, honest, hardworking people. He might have been pissed off with the Kolos Admiralty, but leaving the people on those planets with no idea of who their new neighbors were did not sit well with him.

Groaning and rubbing his eyes, Henri wrestled with what to do. He had a whole company of his own to worry about, and he would need to get them a new job soon if he had any hope of continuing to pay them. He turned away from the view of the planet that had now become a thorn in his side, and his eyes brushed over the small icon in the corner of his screen. As usual, it was lit, indicating that he had more messages waiting for him to answer than he cared to read in that moment. Although, another icon, this one with a picture of Annalise's face, hovered just above the incoming mail, with a little notification blinking in the corner.

The other messages could wait, but Henri was almost always happy to see what Annalise had to say. Using gesture controls, he waved his hand to open the message from her. The words obscured the view of the Void beyond his window as he read.

Hey, I haven't seen you since you got back from the mission. Just checking in to see how you are. I assume the fact that I don't have any of the pilots in my neck of the woods meant things went well. Here if you need to talk.

- A -

Henri smiled. Annalise was always thoughtful when it came to looking after him. In another life, they would have been married by now, but that wasn't something Annalise was interested in. Gesturing, he brought up the speech-to-text writer and dictated his answer. "You're right. Things have wrapped up, mission-wise. I'm back in my quarters and would appreciate the opportunity to chat if you want to come by. Door's open, as always. Hope to see you soon."

He watched the cursor finish and spell-check itself before he sent the message. Getting up, he refilled his tumbler and walked over to the bed. It squeaked a little as he sunk onto it. Groaning with age and post-mission exhaustion, he lifted one foot up onto the opposite knee to unlatch and peel off his boots. Each one landed with a satisfying thunk in the closet before he got up and paced his room, letting the knots uncurl in the soles of his feet.

Five minutes later, the electronic hiss of his door opening and closing heralded Annalise's arrival. She walked in, hair silky and freshly washed, wearing one of her favorite pairs of tights and an oversized t-shirt. She always took great care to clean off after work. In the early days, when Henri had asked why she wouldn't even let him pat her shoulder before she slipped into the shower, she regaled some horror stories she had heard in med school, and from her colleagues, about people who had embraced a loved one before cleaning off, and passed on horrible ailments to them by mistake. Working in the Medical Bay quite often meant carrying all sorts of biological contagions on her hair and clothing, and the last thing she wanted to do was make someone else sick because she hugged them before cleaning off.

"You look exhausted," she said, leaning against the wall as she watched him pace.

Henri stopped and turned to face her, taking another sip of his whiskey. "Our contract with the Kolos Admiralty is complete. We are on our own recognizance now," he answered, but knew she could read his face. He sighed and dropped what was coming next. "But we are no longer eligible for contracts with them, or their satellite entities, or allies." Henri frowned and cast his eyes to the floor, pausing to take one more sip at the bad news.

"You burned that bridge, huh?" Annalise crossed her arms. "I'm sure you had a good reason for it."

Henri shook his head. "I'm not certain I did. Sure, they screwed us over, but I don't know if getting revenge the way I did was the smart play. They were way too content to pay us to hang around in orbit. They were unhappy with our scout data, despite checking all the boxes of their mission parameters ... now, we come to find out that pirates are on the planet below. Not only that, the base we hit was theirs. And I don't mean they took it over from someone else, they built it, and there are more down there," Henri reported. "It bothers me. They probably had some way of tracking their turret here, but they were more concerned with having us scout the base and confirm signals than taking out the pirates that stole from them. Why didn't they want us just to go in there and flush them out? I would have taken that contract if they had been honest about it."

Henri shook his head, turning and sitting in his chair again. "I feel like we're stumbling into something bigger here and I can't figure out what," he concluded, tipping his drink back.

"Maybe they didn't want them taken out? Maybe they just wanted to know what they had." Annalise shrugged as she straightened up and walked over to sit down on the corner of his neatly made bed. "But whatever it is, it sounds like they threw us in the deep end. That cost us one crewmate, and has significantly injured another. I know that keeping our options open is good business wise, but maybe you needed to make a stand to show that we're not ones to mess around with."

Henri shook his head. "They never asked for the pilot's name ..." It was an artifact of how little they cared in his mind.

A soft sigh slipped from Annalise. "Bastards." She looked over at him, but her eyebrows furrowed in confusion. "I would come over there and hug you, but ... I can smell you from here."

Henri chuckled. "Sorry, it's been a busy day and I've probably had too much to drink. Relax, I'll be back." He stood, drained his tumbler, and set it down by his makeshift bar on his way to the shower.

Taking a few extra minutes to scrub off the accumulated stress, Henri let his body finally relax. Walking back out, he pulled on a robe on his way over to his bed, and Annalise.

While Henri was washing, Annalise had helped herself to a vodka soda. She didn't drink all that often, but when she turned back to see him in his robe as he approached, her lips curled into a smile, and she set the glass aside. "Are you just going straight to sleep?"

Henri and Annalise had been lovers long enough for him to catch the subtext, to know the real question she was asking. He stepped closer. "I could go for something to eat first, maybe another drink. But I wouldn't be opposed to turning in early." He picked up his tumbler and refilled it, leaving the invitation open so she could do what she wanted. It would tell him how she was feeling tonight and what sort of fun they might have.

She looked him up and down. "You've done enough

running around today. I'll get someone to bring some food here. In the meantime, let's just relax and unwind." Annalise slipped off the end of the bed and walked over to Henri's bedside table. She opened the drawer and pulled out some massage oil she kept there for days like today. "Lay down on the end of the bed. It's been ages since you've been on a mission. Your muscles must be feeling it. Let me help with that."

Henri smiled. "As you insist, Doc," he teased, walking over. He pulled his arms out of his robe and tied the sleeves around his waist before laying down. Tucking a pillow under his head, he looked back over his shoulder as he waited for her to start.

"That's awfully modest of you," Annalise said, a hint of laughter in her tone as she set the bottle down beside him and walked over to the comm screen, most likely to request food. She returned a moment later and Henri heard the click of the bottle cap, and oil squirt as she spilled some onto her hands. She rubbed her palms together before kneeling on the bed, straddling his upper thighs. She set her palms on his shoulders and started to knead them.

"Mmmm, you have a marvellous bedside manner, Doctor Colwyn," Henri teased, his eyes drifting closed. Only after feeling her first pass did he realize how much the drama had masked how sore he actually was.

"Really?" Annalise asked. "Most doctors don't sit on their patient's legs, Commander." She worked her hands in larger circles over his shoulders and upper back, but after the playful comment came a concerned hum. "Did you have enough of a throwback on that mission? Please tell me you're not thinking of going back into such an active role."

Henri sighed, knowing he'd have to explain why he went back out there to someone from his original crew, to whom he referred to as the OGs. It made sense that Annalise would be the one to ask. "It was my plan. To give everyone the necessary cover, I had to go down there with them. Now we know what kind of people run the base, so I have to figure out what this is all about. I can't put someone else in harm's way for my pet theories."

Her hands stilled for just a moment in their otherwise steady circles. "You have to figure out what it is all about? Does that mean you're going down again?"

"If I need to." Henri drew in a long, slow breath. "Like I said, I don't want to put anyone else at risk."

Moving down to his mid-back, Annalise said, "I know we lost Corporal Hughes, but that doesn't mean any of this is our business. It's bad enough we got involved with something to do with pirates. Surely we can leave it to the Admiralty to sort out. I know it's hard leaving without knowing why we had to lose someone, but abandoning his patch of the Void to clean up its own mess is probably safer for everyone involved."

"I know. We can leave and get more work elsewhere. Work that pays ... that's the smart play," he agreed, sinking into the pillow a little more.

Annalise shifted off his back and put her oiled hand on his right hip. She tugged on his side and rolled him over, looking down into his eyes so he couldn't hide from her as she straddled him, settling onto his barely covered lap. Her expression was so full of concern that it made his chest ache. "And why aren't you making the smart play, Henri?" she whispered, resting her hands on his chest.

Henri's eyebrows furrowed, confronted by the effect his decision was having on someone else. Someone he loved. "If pirates are starting to organize and build for themselves, how long before they get their hands on a jumpship? Or a warship? How long before they start taking over territory of their own? What's happening here is a game changer for people in the surrounding systems, and for people in our line of work. I have to know how isolated this is, or if other pirate bands are doing this, too."

A soft, almost mournful laugh spilled from Annalise as she leaned down and caught his lips in a gentle kiss. When it ended, she shook her head. "You're not designed to be the owner of a mercenary company, Henri. You care too much about others to really do what you need to do. You are the kind of person who should be leading a system."

Her hands resumed their purposeful circles on his chest, but this time she moved her hips too, and she reclaimed his lips before he could argue. He relaxed into her kiss, let it consume him. He could feel it soak up his worries. His body sagged back against the bed as he wrapped his arms around her. She pulled her face back from his, just enough so that her lips brushed over his, as she whispered, "Just promise me you'll be careful. I don't want to have to patch you up again. My fingers might shake too much next time."

Henri's eyes opened, surprised at her words. "I wouldn't want to break your heart, Doc. I promise I'll be careful." He lifted his head, kissing her again. As he laid down, he whispered back to her. "Does this mean we need to talk once our business is done on this planet?" he asked, her words making him curious.

She tilted her head to the side at his question, seemingly perplexed by it. "What do you mean?"

"Do we need to talk about us again? I can't imagine your fingers ever shaking as you work on me. Does that mean you've changed your mind about what you want?" Henri asked, that candle flame of hope sparking to life again. She'd snuffed it out so many times and he thought their fire had burned out a long time ago. Maybe it had enough life left after all.

She sat back on him a little, the press of her hips against his was a movement of convenience rather than eroticism. "I love what we've got, Henri. You know how I am; this flexibility, the freedom, it's perfect for me. You know I love you, too, you're my best friend, but ... the rest? I haven't changed my mind."

Henri sighed, the blast from his nose blowing out his candle of hope again. Maybe this time for good. "Okay, I had to ask. The thought of you with unsteady hands made me wonder ..." he trailed off, not wanting to voice the disappointment. The heartache. He should have known better than to give in to that wish. Annalise had never wavered from her resolve.

She reached out, cupping his cheek and drawing in to kiss him gently. "I may not want commitment, or a family, but that doesn't mean that it would be any easier for me to see you hurt. As I said, I do love you." Then she kissed him again, and it was clear she was done talking.

Henri kissed her back, understanding the passion he felt in her lips. He cradled her cheek in one hand and slid his other up from her hip. His calloused hands caught her oversized top and started pushing it up her body. Tonight wasn't about chatting, which was why he groaned in protest as the door chimed.

Breaking the kiss, Henri grizzled, "That will be a rookie with the food you ordered."

"They'll leave it there. Let it get cold, I want you now." To prove her point, Annalise captured his lips and held them hostage as she rocked her hips in a way that was indisputably sensual. He had been with her enough times to know that she wasn't kidding. She would not let him go until they had both had their fill.

"Yes, ma'am," he replied playfully. His hands resumed their work, easing her loose top up her body. His hips rocked, moving against hers to accentuate her grinding. A low rumbling growl slipped from his lips as he could feel her body responding to his.

Annalise moved back just enough for him to be able to peel her top off to reveal the plain black bra she was wearing underneath. As he cast it aside, she slid her hands down over his bare chest, dragging the remainder of the oil on her palms over his skin. She settled them on the knot of his robe, untying it with all the dexterity her surgeries required, then raised her hips so she could push it open and get to what she was really after.

Henri smiled up at her, but once he was out of his robe, he rolled her over onto her back. Even at his age, he could still catch her by surprise. It was just as easy as it was when he had met her nearly two decades ago, when he was in his mid twenties. His robe lay where it was left behind as they moved up the bed. He knelt beside her, leaning over, and kissing her as his hand slid under the waistband of her tights. Pulling down along the length of her lithe shapely legs, he peeled them off her so he could remove the hindrance to what tonight was about.

The moment her tights were gone, Annalise hooked her thumbs under her panties and tugged them down. He met her halfway and pulled them off completely. Then, her hands were on his shoulders, tugging him back up so that he could kiss her, and she could wrap her legs around his hips.

As soon as Henri moved over her and her legs looped around his hips, the pair moved like a practiced team. So many nights had been spent in each other's arms. Time had never dampened the pleasure, or excitement of being with Annalise. They moved in concert, knowing just what to do to heighten the other's pleasure.

Annalise was right; there was no way the food brought to them would still be warm. By the time the trays had been brought in, the steam on the lids had condensed to thick drops which were vaporized again by the microwave in the commander's room.

CHAPTER 19

"I BELIEVE that one person is more than sufficient to help Ms. Ramos carry her belongings back to her room," Doctor Colwyn said, her pretty lips pressed together in an amused, but wry expression as she gestured to the small bag of clothes at the end of Astera's bed.

Astera agreed, of course, but the entire Scout Wing who stood crowded around her bed clearly did not. After at least a week in the medical bay, she was finally being released.

Following the commander's mission to Baldalan, the company had remained in orbit around the planet and every-one, Astera included, seemed to be in a holding pattern. Luckily for Astera, it meant that she had plenty of visitors to chase away any boredom. The people she had by her bedside alternated between her teammates and Martin. She would never admit it to the other scouts, but the thoughtful Ops specialist was her favorite visitor.

Every time Martin came to visit, he would bring something sweet from the dessert selection in the cafeteria, knowing that Doctor Colwyn kept the food in the Med Bay to strict nutritional needs only. They would share whatever he brought while talking about anything and everything. At least, Martin spoke about anything and everything. He had a rather endearing habit of rambling when he was nervous, which always seemed to be the case around her. Not that Astera minded. It saved her having to come up with lies about where she came from, and who she was. It also meant that, for a short time, she could pretend to be someone other than herself. It was very different from time spent with her wingmates, especially Kitty, who would make offhand comments about her zoning out in conversations, or not really connecting with anyone outside of the team. Things were much easier with him, and every now and again he would look at her in a way that made her want to truly connect with someone again.

"You'll have to forgive my wingmates, Doc," Astera teased as she threw back the covers and turned to the side, letting her legs slide off the bed. "They have an awful habit of being over-protective and overbearing." She took her time to stand, knowing she still needed a little bit more time to get her strength and stability back after being mostly bed-bound for so long.

"Overbearing?" Mama Bear scoffed, throwing her long red braid over her shoulder as she shook her head. "We're all just excited that you're getting out of here, and that you'll be back on the team. We've missed you."

"You've missed her." Viper sighed. "I, for one, haven't minded the lack of sarcastic banter in the comms during training."

"Oh, please. I'd much rather listen to Astera being sassy than you bitching about our skills." Kitty waved her hand dismissively. She walked over and looped her arm through Astera's elbow without asking.

"We've all been locked up in the ship for too long. Firing at training projections isn't as good as the real thing," Glacier interjected, trying to calm the growing tension. "Once we get back on mission and blow some stuff up, I'm sure you ladies will get on all nice again."

Kitty snorted. "Right, because that's totally gonna happen sometime soon, when all we've been doing is orbiting this shit-hole of a planet for months."

It was a sign of how long they had all been working together that nobody bothered to correct Kitty's obvious exaggeration of their time in orbit.

"Right," Doctor Colwyn interrupted, "Astera, if you need anything, please use the comms unit in your room. You are cleared to return to the gym, but I have asked our physiotherapist to program some workouts tailored to your recovery needs. There'll be vitals tracking running while you're exercising, and if I see you going too hard, you'll be right back here quick smart."

Astera gave the doctor a crisp salute. "Wouldn't dream of going against your orders, Doc," she replied without an ounce of sarcasm. She would do almost anything to stay out of the Med Bay. Especially when she had her first "date" scheduled for that night.

After days spent talking about it, Astera had finally convinced Martin it would be okay to share a meal in the cafeteria. He was still clearly nervous about what his fellow Operations Specialists would say, but Astera promised him they would get there early enough to avoid the rush. She looked down at the time on the screen, beside her bed, and realized how late it had gotten.

"Come on, let's get out of Doctor Colwyn's hair," Astera announced. There was a general murmur of agreement as the ladies crowded around her, then parted to make way for Kitty and Astera to walk though. Mama Bear snatched the meager bag of belongings off the end of the bed and fell in behind them.

The walk back to the room she shared with Kitty took longer than Astera expected. Not only was she hoping for some alone time before getting ready for her date, but she hated how slow she had to move, and how her lungs still seemed to ache with every breath she took. The Doc told her it would be like that for a while, and not to worry, but it was still annoying enough that Astera was oblivious to the chatter all around her as they went along.

"Starfall? Helloooo? Come in, Starfall." Viper's smooth voice broke through Astera's internal frustration.

"Uh, sorry. What?" Astera looked back at the woman over her shoulder, and the dark brows above her almond shaped eyes were creased together in concern.

"I asked if you want to join us after dinner? We're heading to the rec-room to watch a new film from the Core Worlds. We can save you a seat, if you like," Viper said, sounding annoyed at having to repeat herself.

Astera went to answer, but Kitty cut in. "Are you kidding? Girl's got her first date in what ... two centuries or whatever? She won't want to watch a movie with us tonight."

Even though Kitty, for once, had the decency to leave out the rest of a comment about what Astera would rather be doing after her date, the implication was still there. Normally, Astera would be annoyed at any such connotation, but she found that the idea was not at all unappealing this time. She knew that Martin was certainly interested, but the subject was not something she needed to discuss with her team. "Kitty, you said earlier we were 'stuck in a holding pattern.' Is that true?"

From the amused expressions on her wingmate's faces, Astera could tell they caught her completely clumsy subject change, but Kitty allowed it. "I was using it as a euphemism. It just feels like a holding pattern. No one really knows why the heck we're still here. The brass is remaining tight-lipped. All I know is I am going to need to see some real action sometime soon, otherwise I may just have to eject myself into the Void. I'm sooooo bored."

Astera laughed with the others. Well, it was more of a wheeze than a laugh, but the intent was the same. They turned the corner that led to the pilot's dorms, and the irregular rhythm of the group's footsteps came to a halt.

"As much as we have enjoyed escorting you home we do need to get some training in before dinner," Mama Bear announced with an air of authority. She gestured to Kitty. "You get Starfall settled, then come join us, okay?"

"Roger that." Kitty gave her a playful salute. Mama Bear handed the bag she was carrying to Kitty, before she, Glacier, and Viper turned back towards the direction they came from. Kitty slipped the handle of the bag onto her arm and resumed their plodding journey. "So, let's get you home, huh? Have you got something picked out to wear to dinner?"

"I don't have much, you've seen my wardrobe," Astera muttered, frowning.

"You can borrow something from me, if you like."

It took a fair deal of restraint for Astera to hold back a snort. She was well acquainted with Kitty's colorful, rather daring, fashion sense. It was not something she wished to replicate.

"I appreciate the offer, but I'll make do. Martin is so used to seeing me in bandages, or athleisure, that I'm sure even my casual outfits will be an upgrade."

"Martin?" Kitty cast her a confused, sidelong glance. "Who the fuck is Martin?"

Astera shook her head, even though she should not have

been surprised that no one knew Martin's real name. Not when the Ops Team went to such pains to make the nickname stick for him. "Martin is Eggles' first name."

"Oh. Should've figured he'd have a dweeby name like Martin. Might as well stick to Eggles if you ask me." Kitty paused outside their door as she looked over at Astera, her eyes narrowed in a calculating gaze as she dragged them up and down the plain black tights and gray tank Astera was wearing. "You're right. Even nothing would be an improvement."

Astera rolled her eyes as Kitty pressed her hand against the palm reader outside their room to open the door. The familiar grating hiss made Astera sigh with relief, and when she looked inside, excited to see her bed, and the bare, but neat, space she had made her own. Instead, her eyes widened with surprise as she saw—

"Martin?" she spluttered, looking between the Operations specialist, and her roommate. Kitty just grinned back at her.

Martin straightened as he heard his name. He smiled at Astera as he turned to face the door.

The room Astera and Kitty shared was compact. There was a walkway in the middle, wide enough for Astera to stretch her arms from side to side and not quite be able to touch the bunks against each wall. Each bed was set, raised above a built-in desk and storage unit. At the far end was the door to their small, shared bathroom that held a toilet, a sink, a shower, and just enough floor space to dry themselves.

Normally, it was a clear walk from the front door to the bathroom, but not today. As he spoke, Martin stood just beside Kitty's nook, with a long, narrow tub in front of him. The air above it was obscured with curly wisps of rising steam. The tub itself looked like a repurposed cargo crate that was almost as long, and almost as wide, as the space it was set in. There was a clean, fluffy bath towel and robe, laying over the rungs of the ladders to Astera's bunk, and some fresh soap, shampoo, and conditioner, in a small bathroom caddy, hooked over the side of the improvised tub.

"Welcome back. I figured with you on the mend and your wounds healed, you'd finally want to enjoy your bath." He gestured to the tub, his eyes dancing between Kitty and Astera.

"Martin, this is—" Astera trailed off, not sure what to say about the hassle it must have been to get everything sorted, and how much the smell of the steam made her entire body tingle with anticipation.

A suggestive chuckle sounded beside her. "So, I guess I'll leave you two alone," Kitty said, winking at Martin in Astera's dumfounded silence.

Martin walked over, gently taking Astera's free arm. "I've got her from here," he said with more confidence than Astera was used to hearing from him. He smiled as Kitty stepped back and headed for the door.

"Don't be too long; dinner service ends in a few hours and my girl needs her food," Kitty teased. The titters of her giggle bounced back to them as she walked down the hall before the door cycled shut.

"Turns out the time you negotiated was enough water to fill a tub." Martin guided her over to the steamy container. "Do you need help, or should I leave you to it?"

Astera waved her hand through the steam above the water and smiled, her heart just about as warm as the air. She rested the same hand on the side of the tub and frowned. It reached her hip, so she wasn't entirely sure that she could get in, and out, safely on her own. That meant that she needed him there. It should have made her worry. Two weeks earlier, she would have quietly thanked him for the gesture but asked that the tub be emptied. Instead, she found that the idea of him being there while she undressed, and helping her in, was not at all unappealing.

"I don't think I'll be able to get in on my own," she finally admitted, returning her gaze to his. "I would appreciate some help, if you don't mind?"

Martin's cheeks colored at her admission. "I don't mind at all." Swallowing hard, he looked down at her outfit. "Do you need any help getting out of your clothes?"

Astera had a feeling that he wanted to help her, even if she could do it herself.

Before discharging her, Doctor Colwyn had made sure Astera could take care of her own basic needs, including getting dressed. She had even shown her how to get her clothing on, and off, with minimal pain. It involved a change to how she was used to dressing herself, and it was a bit clumsy, but she could do it.

But when Astera looked into Martin's eyes, she realized that maybe, just maybe, she didn't want to be capable of getting herself undressed in that moment. "I can do it, but help wouldn't go astray." Her voice dropped to a whisper as she reached up and tentatively cupped his cheek, eyes dipping to his lips.

Martin smiled wide, tracking her eyes as her gaze lowered. He shifted his hand on Astera's hip, moving to stand in front of her. "I'd love to help."

Being bolder than he ever was in the Med Bay, Martin leaned in slowly, almost as though he was expecting Astera to retreat, as he attempted to kiss her for the first time.

She didn't pull away. Instead, she closed the gap between them. The kiss was short, but not unpracticed. They were both clearly nervous, but it was sweet, and appealing, and still very promising.

When the brief kiss ended, Astera rested her forehead against Martin's as their warm breath mingled together. The silence between them was a tangible thing, and she had a feeling Martin was waiting for the axe to fall, for her to change her mind. *He has such little confidence in himself, and in his interactions with women, but it's only because he's comparing himself to jerks.* "I liked that," Astera admitted, the way that her chest rose and fell faster and her lips tingled was proof enough of that. "Can I ... can I kiss you again?"

Martin nodded. "As much as you want."

Kissing Martin—Void, being around Martin—was so unlike anything Astera had experienced before. As she joined him for another kiss, she knew he was different. She didn't feel him clawing at her clothes, even though she had asked for help getting undressed. One of his hands was still gently on her hip, the other balled into a fist at his side. She reached down, guiding his free hand to her hip as well. Once there, he didn't hold her closer, or grasp her too hard. He just let her guide their movements. He let her lead.

The newness of that feeling, of a sense of control, rushed to Astera's head and made her dizzy as the humidity in the room seemed to climb exponentially. She pulled back from the kiss. This time, when she took his hands, she helped guide them underneath the hem of her fitted tank top, the look in her eyes telling him that she wanted—no, needed—his help.

Martin's eyes filled with deep appreciation and desire as he pushed her plain black tank up her body. He didn't shy away from the marks that still lingered; his hands seemed keen to explore every inch of her as he pulled the fabric over her head. Swallowing as his eyes found hers again, he walked his fingers down to the drawstring tied at the front of her loose pants. Without asking, he opened the knot and helped the slack pants over her hips. They fell to the floor in a puddle of cloth.

Standing in just her white sports bra and panties, Astera gently rested her hand on Martin's shoulder, to keep her steady, as she stepped out of the black sweatpants that had pooled around her feet. She kicked them aside, and smiled at him as she leaned in again, kissing him as she lined the front of her body against his, relishing the way that the starched fabric of his uniform shirt crinkled against her skin. She let out a soft moan into their kiss at the feel of his warmth radiating against her recovering body.

Martin held her a little tighter as she stepped in close. His hands flattened on her back, holding her chest to his. Then, with surprising deftness and skill, he opened the clasp of her bra. Tracing his fingers along the straps, he eased them from her shoulders, but didn't move back yet. He was too committed to the kiss to stop.

The release of the tension in her bra would have allowed Astera to breathe a little easier if their chests weren't pressed together. She moved her lips from his, to trail kisses over his cheek and towards his ear. "Keep going, please," she urged him.

Martin leaned back to let her bra fall to the ground. The air between them was cooler than his body, and the change in temperature made Astera's nipples ache for his warmth once more. Martin groaned as he looked down between them and then moved his hands lower, pushing his his fingertips under the waistband of her panties. Easing them over her hips, he gazed into her eyes as he helped slide them to the floor. Guiding her feet to step out of them, he stood back up, brushing against her completely naked body, and making her tremble. "Are you ready to get in?" Martin asked, voice huskier than she had ever heard it.

With the heat of the bath in the room, and the blood rushing through her body at the situation with Martin, Astera wasn't cold, even though she was completely naked. She nodded, reaching out to take his hand. "I think this is the nicest thing anyone has ever done for me." Her cheeks flushed as she stepped back and turned to look at the tub.

Carefully, she got to her toes and sat on the edge. She grasped his hand harder as she used her core to help maintain her balance as she lifted one leg, then the other, into the water. "Oh stars, this feels good," she groaned, as her feet touched the bottom of the tub and she slipped off the edge and into the water.

She turned back to him as the hot water made her body sing with relief. It made her feel content, and even a little reckless. "You know, this tub is pretty big, and you went to an awful lot of effort to get it set up ... would you like to join me?"

"If that's what you want." Martin moved the caddy of toiletries a bit closer to her side of the tub. He walked to the other end and started to remove his daily uniform. It took a bit more effort than undressing Astera, as there were more zippers and buttons for him to open.

As his clothes fell, Astera saw that he took his job seriously, including his physical fitness. Whilst he probably was not as built as some of the other officers in the Ops Team, it was clear that he didn't slack off in his downtime.

Martin took a long, lurid look at Astera's naked body before he climbed over the edge of the tub. "Oh wow, this is nice," he admitted as he stepped into the tub.

"It really is." Astera smiled over at Martin as he settled into the water. She was a firm believer that it didn't matter who was sinking into a bath, the feeling of relief was completely universal. It was nice seeing him relaxing, as he tended towards being quite jumpy. Astera kept her legs hugged to her chest, but now that he was in, she knew for certain there was enough room for them both without the tub overflowing.

"Would you mind if I stretched my legs out?" Astera asked, telling herself the blush on her cheeks was caused by the heat of the water, not the situation she was in. What they were doing was perfectly fine. It was natural, and they were both clearly consenting.

Martin swallowed, lifting his head to look across as Astera. "Uh, no, I don't mind. Why would I mind?" He chuckled nervously, shifting his legs to one side to give her room along the other. "There, plenty of room."

"Great, thanks." Astera shifted to the side he had freed up, and laid her legs along the bottom of the tub, her thigh brushing up against his calf, her foot pressed against his hip. The release of pressure from against her ribs made her sigh in relief and she leaned back, closing her eyes. "Oh, wow."

The water level was such that the swell of her breasts hovered on the surface, and even though the water was evaporating off them fast, the bath had warmed up the room enough that it did little more than raise some tiny goosebumps along her skin.

"Must be nice to be out of the Med Bay, finally," Martin chimed sheepishly as he looked across at her. "How are your legs feeling then? Were they sore when you had them bent up against your chest like that?"

"It was more so the pressure of having my body curled up. The less against my ribs, the better," she explained, tentatively rubbing her fingers along the skin of her torso under the water, something she'd been afraid to do in the Med Bay in case she messed something up and made her stay longer.

For Astera, it was hard to ignore the scarring. Even after the doctor's exemplary work, there were some remnants of the burns around where the artificial skin was grafted. Doctor Colwyn explained that it was organic material and that her skin cells would replace them in time, but combined with some evidence of old injuries, she hated the fact that her body was a constant reminder of what she had been through.

Martin must have clued into the look on her face as he cleared his throat. "Ummm, would it help if I massaged them? You've been laying in that bed so long that it might help wake them up some more."

The offer sounded genuine, and it was very sweet, but the idea of anything but her own hands moving over her still-mottled flesh made her cringe. Still, she liked the idea of him touching her. "Not my ribs, they're still a little too sore, but I am sure my shoulders have a few knots?" she suggested tentatively.

Martin's eyes widened. "Oh, um ... I figured that I could do your—I mean, rub your—I mean, massage your thighs—er, legs for you. Since they are down by me."

"Oh," Astera cursed herself for getting it so wrong. "Uh, sure. That would be nice, too."

"If, uh, if you want, I can work my way up there—to your shoulders, that is," Martin fumbled, cheeks getting redder by the word. Still, it did not stop him from sitting forward in the tub to slide his hands under her legs. Astera sucked in a breath at the gentle, intimate touch.

Martin ran his hands up and down the undersides of her legs a couple of times, seeming to get a feel for the shape of her, before he started massaging the long muscles of her thighs and calves. He kept his eyes on Astera as he touched her, seeming to want to gauge her reaction, and avoiding any spots that made her wince.

Apart from a few small bruises and nearly healed scrapes, it felt good to Astera. Her legs were probably the least injured part of her body. A contented sigh slipped from her lips as she relaxed back against the end of the tub.

Hearing those sighs of relief, Martin applied a little more pressure as he continued. As he did, he gently moved her calves, helping her bend and flex like she did in her physical therapy sessions. "I bet you can't wait to get back into a Hummingbird again. To feel that speed and power under you," he murmured.

The talk of her mech sent Astera's mind in the opposite direction of where she was hoping it would go. "It will be good to get some action again," she admitted, his touch feeling less intimate and more clinical now, given the change in topic. "I'll need to check on Calliope at some point, too. The commander said she is salvageable, but she was busted up pretty bad."

"I heard the engineering crews are taking bets on whether its core will fire up again or not," Martin shared. "If it can't, there's really no reason for them to even try to rebuild it."

The thought of having to get another mech was not something Astera enjoyed. She had always viewed mechs as non-sentient family members. Pilots had to become so in-sync with their machines that there was often a sentimental bond that formed with them. Astera had already lost a friend, she didn't want to lose her mech, too.

Astera was so distracted by those thoughts that she didn't notice Martin gently repositioning her legs, so that she had one foot on either side of his hips. His own legs were bent to allow for the change in position, and he gently brought one of her feet up to rest against his chest. He used that placement to help stretch to tops of her thighs as he ran his hands up and down her skin.

Shaking back into herself, and alarmed at how she had been too distracted by her grief to notice the change, Astera cleared her throat. She needed to keep her mind in the present. On where Martin's hands were. "You're so good at this. Were you a physiotherapist before becoming an engineer?"

"No, remember how my folks worked in search and rescue? They would be out hiking in wilderness terrain for hours. When my mom got home, my dad would massage her feet for her," Martin explained. As he continued, his eyes found Astera's again. "Ummm, is this okay?" he asked, as his hands got closer and closer to something even more intimate.

Astera's smile was gentle as she nodded. "It feels good," she said, "As long as you're okay with it, I am too." It was an excellent distraction from her own mind.

Martin nodded, but the color in his cheeks deepened. "I just ... in this position, I could—" He swallowed, brushing his fingers higher along her thighs. "Would you, er, would you like that?"

Biting her lip, she nodded. He traced his fingertips over her most sensitive skin, and she let out a soft gasp at the tentative touch. Seemingly encouraged by her reaction, he continued to explore, and Astera's heart-rate quickened.

Just as she started to enjoy it, Martin whispered, "Would you like more?"

"Please," Astera breathed.

Martin swallowed again; his eyes locked on Astera's. He slid his hand from her and she bit back a groan of disappointment. She had said she wanted more, so why was he stopping?

Astera soon understood what he had meant when he moved his hands under her ass and pulled her hips closer to his. Beneath the water, she could feel his hardness pressing against her as he settled her on his lap. "What about this?" he asked, wide-eyed.

It wasn't what Astera initially had in mind, but it did

make sense, and she also knew it meant that he would be able to enjoy something, too, instead of her focusing selfishly on her own pleasure. "Yes." The word slipped from Astera's lips and, just as quickly, Martin slipped into her.

Martin leaned forward, catching her gasp with a kiss. He started to move inside her, and her gasp turned into a moan. It was nice being filled by him. It had been so long since she was with anyone and, even then, any pleasure she might have felt came with the shame of knowing she didn't really want to be with them. It complicated things in her mind, but this? This was all pleasure. All her choice.

"How is it?" Martin asked as she shifted against him to get a better angle. He sounded concerned. Was he worried he had hurt her? Or that it wasn't feeling good?

"It feels nice," she confessed, looking into his eyes. "It feels so nice." She pecked his lips.

Her admission seemed to be all Martin needed to continue. He caught her lips in a deep kiss as he wrapped his arms around her and kept moving. She wasn't quite able to get into a position to enhance her own pleasure, but she decided to be patient, that could come later.

The water sloshed around them as Martin moved, but the resistance of thrusting in the bath meant that his hips never pressed against hers too hard, or too suddenly. When he found his rhythm, she let out a grateful moan, resting her head back against the edge of the tub as she dragged her eyes over his body. She shifted to settle higher on his lap, her breasts rising above the water line.

Martin saw his moment and slid a hand over her breast. His movements were unpracticed, but he seemed earnest in his attempt to make it feel good for her. "Astera, this is better than I imagined," he said between grunts, his hips moving faster with each passing moment. "Void, it's all I want to do."

Her cheeks flushed at his admission, at the confirmation that this was more than just a recent fantasy for him. Astera wanted to tell him that there had to be more to life than being inside her, and that they had only just begun to get to know each other, but she kept her mouth shut. It felt too good having someone caring inside her, someone who seemed to view their joining as a privilege rather than a right.

Banishing the thoughts that threatened to intrude, Astera covered the hand that Martin had on her breast, and used it to encourage him to keep touching her. With her guidance, Martin moved his hand to help heighten her pleasure. The small grinds of his hips bumped against her clit, and they made Astera moan in earnest. She concentrated on trying to make the most out of each movement, but they were not quite regular enough to be able to build towards the release she so desperately needed.

Meanwhile, from the sounds Martin was making, it was clear that he was having no trouble building up to his own climax. He panted and groaned, his hand gripping her breast harder. He leaned in and his kiss was uncoordinated and over-eager.

From the way they had flirted, and how sweet he had been, Astera told herself that sleeping with Martin would be different. That it wouldn't be just about him getting off. As he seemed to race towards the finish line, the hope she'd been holding onto dwindled, and each thrust sent her another step back towards a place she didn't want to be. He was a different man, of course, far kinder, and sweeter, but it was impossible for her to detangle her experience now with Martin from the many times with *him*. She shifted her hips, trying to give him the right angle so he could just finish.

The moment came quickly.

Kissing her in the afterglow, Martin slowly came back to

his senses. As he did, he looked into her eyes again. "Is everything okay? I ... it didn't feel like you ..." he trailed off, apparently dreading actually asking the question.

"What?" Astera winced. "It was fine. Perfect. Great." The words tumbled out of her mouth as she tried to reassure him that things were okay.

Martin frowned. "I mean, it didn't feel like you *joined* me. Was it too fast? It was too fast. I can help you finish, too," He rambled quickly, pulling back from Astera.

"It's okay, it's my fault." Astera looked away. "I ... don't worry, you needn't go out of your way. I'm fine." She wrapped her arms around herself as she smiled at him, trying to convince him it was okay, when her mind and body were still scattered to the stars.

Martin frowned and put his hands on her shoulders. "It's not a problem. This isn't just for me; it's meant for both of us," he said leaning in for a deep, sensual kiss.

Astera sighed into the kiss, sagging against him at what he said. Her body was still wound tight with that aching need. *Maybe*, she thought to herself, *it isn't him using me. Maybe this is just how things are. I should have known better than to believe all the locker-room stories and romance movies; two people can't have amazing sex right away. It probably takes practice to learn each other's bodies.*

Astera's body sagged against Martin's, and it seemed to be the signal he was looking for. He gently shifted to the side, lifting her legs up into his lap as he leaned in to keep the kiss. Sliding a hand along her inner thigh, he worked his way higher and higher. He broke the kiss to look at her, seemingly waiting for her to tell him to stop. When she didn't, his fingers found her mound. Again, his touch was clumsy, but sincere, using her reactions to tell him where best to touch her.

This time, as Martin watched her, Astera knew that he

was trying to sense how she was feeling and what she needed. She nodded and shifted so that his fingers were in the right place and let out a groan of relief at the contact she so desperately craved.

Martin smiled at that groan and kept up the pressure there. His fingers slid in a slow circle, teasing, and searching, while he watched her face. He kept this up for a while before moving his fingers down. As he neared her entrance again, he watched her eyes, silently asking if that's what she wanted or to keep doing what he had been doing.

Astera shook her head, gently guiding his fingers back to where they were before. She helped him find the right movement and let out a soft moan as her vision swam. She held onto his shoulder as he kept that motion going, and the pleasure of it was enough to pull her away from her memories and her worries. There was something in the way that he watched her, too. A kind of interest, or curiosity, as he used his fingers on her. He was focused solely on her, and it was such a headrush to feel that concern, even if it still felt like an afterthought.

"That's it," Astera panted as Martin kept going and going. "Don't stop, please don't stop," she begged. It had been so long since someone else had given her pleasure, and the more he touched her, the more intoxicating it became. The need was so overwhelming, so consuming. When she finally came, it was like her world shattered into pieces.

Thankfully, he knew to slow his fingers after, and she collapsed forward against him, wheezing as her ribs burned. Without the distraction of the sexual pleasure, her body was reminding her that she wasn't fully healed yet.

As she recovered in the aftermath, Martin lifted her chin and kissed her again. Slowly, he eased her to rest against him. "I'm glad you got to enjoy it too," he whispered as he held her.

Astera rested her head against his shoulder, letting out a slow, shaking breath. "I'm glad, too," she whispered, "thank you so much. You have no idea how much that means to me." She closed her eyes to wall off the emotions threatening to overwhelm her, and she just concentrated on how nice it felt to be held by him in the warm water.

The two stayed in the bath until the water cooled too much for it to be comfortable anymore. Martin got out first, drying himself off quickly and wrapping a towel around his waist before he held a hand up to help Astera out. The moment she emerged, he draped a towel around her. They took their time getting dressed, and when they were done, they had to rush to get to the cafeteria before the dinner service stopped.

CHAPTER 20

THE LATAGAROSH WAS CLOSING in on a month in orbit around Baldalan. By now, most of the crew had grown restless. Astera was not as bothered by it, though. Between giving her body time to heal, and spending her spare time with Martin, she felt like the extended hold was actually a blessing in disguise. Of course, she hated looking out of the window to see Baldalan floating in space, like an ever-present reminder of what she had lost, but she was slowly growing around her grief and her pain and learning to live with it. She knew it would be a long journey; losing a friend was never easy, but she would get there. She had no other choice.

After her first encounter with Martin, Astera's old worries had resurfaced. Thinking back on the experience, she felt like she wasn't really there. She wasn't part of it. After that, they took it slower. They spent their mealtimes together, and Martin told her more about his past. She found him even more endearing than before and was always pleased to see the cute smile on his face when she walked towards him. When they had sex for the second time, it was marginally better than the first. Her confidence to share what she needed with him was growing slowly, but he was still so easily distracted by his own pleasure.

Astera sat in the Mess Hall, pushing her food around but not eating it. Already, she was wrestling with worries about her and Martin and their communication. She could tell he was trying, but he wasn't really the best at listening. In some ways, he reminded her of an eager Saint Bernard puppy, just like the figurine he had given her. The enthusiasm was all there, but the coordination? Well ... it wasn't.

"Void, Starfall. Are you going to eat that food or turn it into a stew?"

Viper's snappy comment pulled Astera from her reverie. She looked up and noticed that all her wingmates were watching her.

"Is this how you've been eating since you got out of the Med Bay?" Mama bear asked, brows creasing with concern.

Astera had never been one to skimp on her meals. She never ate a lot, but she did eat whatever she took. She knew the importance of getting good, consistent nutrition, and she never took it for granted.

Kitty leaned forward, resting her elbows on the table with her chin in her hands. "Or are you just disappointed that we're your company for dinner, and not Loverboy?"

"Hey." Mama Bear whacked Kitty's elbows off the table with the back of her hand. "We may be mercenaries, but that doesn't mean we're heathens who put elbows on the table."

"Are you really with that kid from the Ops Team?" Johansen asked, her lips pursed and eyes narrowed.

"He's not a kid," Astera said defensively, frowning.

Glacier laughed. "You sure? I don't think he's shaved a day in his life."

Shaking her head, Astera ignored the jibes. Responding only prolonged the stupidity. Looking around, Astera wondered when Martin would be getting in. He told her earlier that day that he would be late, and that he would catch her in the Mess Hall if he had a chance. Listening to the gossipy wingmates around her, she hoped he would show up so she could move to a different table, and away from the scrutiny of her peers.

"He won't be showing up," Johansen said, leaning back in her seat and taking a sip of one of the horrid green shakes she preferred to actual food.

"Pardon?" Astera frowned up at her commanding officer before taking a forkful of mash.

Johansen shifted in her seat and glanced over her shoulder, towards where the commander was sitting with some of the other members of the OGs. "He's on a discipline shift. The major assigned him his usual brand of 'Corrective Action Training' or whatever he calls it."

Astera almost choked on her food. She took a moment to swallow, before echoing, "A discipline shift?"

That didn't make sense. Martin was one of the sweetest people on board. What in the Void could he have done that was bad enough to earn him one of the horrid Engineering Support shifts, cleaning out the hottest, or filthiest, parts of the ship?

"So, did you guys hear about Semtex's latest training run? She's really on a roll," Mama Bear said to the others, leaning between Astera and the rest of their wingmates.

Viper said, in a tone far too enthusiastic to be genuine, "Oh, yeah. Cool, right?"

Suspicion coursed through Astera and she put her fork down with a huff. What, now the others were suddenly interested in something else? She turned to Johansen to ask what the Void was going on, and saw the sergeant watching her carefully.

"He didn't tell you that he was on discipline shifts?" Johansen asked.

Astera shook her head.

"Then I'm guessing you don't know why he is on them, either?"

She could only think of one thing that had happened recently that Martin might have been written up over. Peering over at the tables that the Ops Team favored, Astera noted that Norgard and Hermedilla were not in the room either. "I hope it doesn't have anything to do with the mission. I know the Ops guys did their best to help. They shouldn't be punished for what happened."

Johansen put her cup down on the table. "It has to do with part of the mission, but not the outcome." She glanced back at the commander again, and this time, Astera followed her gaze.

Seeming to sense that he was being watched, the commander looked over at them both and gave them a polite smile as he spoke to his colleagues. The expression looked good on him, and Astera couldn't help but smile back. Since being released from the Med Bay, she hadn't seen much of the leader of the Triple C. He had, apparently, been in frequent meetings with the Ops and Intelligence Teams. Everyone seemed to think there was something going on, some secret and exciting reason they were still holding, even though their contract was reportedly over.

"Commander Durroguerre wouldn't like me telling you this," Johansen said as she turned back to Astera, her voice dropping lower before continuing. "But if you're going to be seeing Eggles, you have a right to know. He and the other Ops lads are being disciplined because of their downtime chatter. It was completely unacceptable and unprofessional."

Astera's nose wrinkled. "That doesn't sound like Martin."

"Maybe not." Johansen shrugged, not seeming convinced. "He seems like a nice enough lad, but that didn't stop him from getting drawn into a game of 'top three fuckables' in the Scout Wing."

If Astera hadn't already set her fork down, it would have clattered to her plate. Her stomach dropped, and she looked at the woman who she had been working with since she joined the Triple C. Johansen had always watched out for the scouts, and Astera knew her well enough to see that the twitch of rage on her face was entirely genuine.

"Oooh, tell me who they voted for," Kitty said, dropping all pretense she was engaged in the conversation about Semtex, and leaning towards Johansen.

Johansen rolled her eyes in disapproval, but when she returned her focus to Astera, her silence was enough to confirm what Astera feared.

"It was Starfall, wasn't it? Oh, I knew he had been gunning for you for a while." Kitty's smirk split her face.

Johansen ignored her. "They tried to palm it off as something to pass their downtime, but I will not have anyone objectifying any of you like that," she said firmly, in a tone that let Astera known that she was still furious.

Astera didn't know what to say. She didn't know what was worse; that Martin had hidden it all from her, or that she was made to look like a fool in front of her commanding officer because she didn't know about it. She wanted to tell Johansen she was wrong, that Martin would never speak about her like that. Void, he had never even said the word "fuck" around her, and he stuttered over anything related to sex ...

But there was no doubt in Johansen's expression. She would have had to listen to the mission recordings, given what happened to Sleeves. There is no way she would have made it up.

Eyes stinging, Astera looked down at her plate. Any thoughts she might have had around finally finishing her dinner were charred away by the searing sense of embarrassment in her gut.

"So, if Starfall was his number one, who were the other two? I don't picture him as a foursome kinda guy, but I'd be down," Kitty said, irreverent as ever.

Astera didn't see the look Johansen fixed Kitty with, but she knew there had to be one from the way Kitty gulped and slunk back in her seat. The conversation between her other wingmates seemed to get louder and more enthusiastic, and Astera just sank back into her own thoughts.

While the others chatted the night away, Astera lost track of time. They didn't bother her again, and she was glad that she didn't have to be alone, even if she wasn't up to joining in on the conversation. It was getting late when the talking slammed to a halt around her and jolted Astera from her thoughts.

"Hey, 'Stera."

Wincing as she turned around, Astera saw Martin standing behind her, freshly showered and in some well-fitted casual cargo pants and a black t-shirt. The smile he always wore when he saw her faltered as he took in the narrow-eyed glares of her wingmates.

"Did I, uh ... did I interrupt something?" He backed up a step. "I can go wait somewhere else if you like?"

Despite what she had learned, Astera felt for him. He was clearly terrified of the way her friends were watching him. She looked up into his now-familiar eyes. Even if he had hidden it from her, she owed it to the budding relationship between them to give him a chance to explain himself.

"Yeah, you did." Mama Bear sat taller in her seat. Any semblance of a warm, caring, middle-aged woman was gone, replaced with the visage of her namesake. "There's no point waiting. We can see Astera back to her room. Good night, Martin."

Martin gaped at Mama Bear and stumbled back.

"Mama," Astera snapped. Whilst she appreciated the protectiveness, she could handle herself. She stood and picked up her tray as she gave Martin a reassuring smile. "You're not interrupting anything. You haven't eaten yet, have you?"

Muted, Martin shook his head.

"Then let's go find a table." Astera gripped her tray with one hand, and slipped her other through the crook of Martin's elbow. She guided him away from her beloved group of vengeful harpies and towards a table that had just become vacant in the corner of the room. She set her tray down and took a seat. "You go get your food; I'll wait here."

Without a word of argument, Martin turned and made his way to the food line. It was near the end of meal service, so he wouldn't get any of the good stuff, but it would do. As she watched him progress through the queue, Astera chewed over her situation, and how to approach what she had learned about his actions, with him.

By the time Martin returned to the table, Astera had decided that an outright accusation would not be fair. He was a sweet guy. She had no doubt he had been caught up in the banter, probably feeling like he needed to engage to get in Norgard's good books. Surely, if she probed, he would come clean. She had to give him the chance to be honest with her.

"So, how was your shift?" she asked as he started to shovel food in his mouth, probably to avoid talking about the awkwardness with her wingmates. "I noticed on the roster that you were meant to finish four hours ago. Did you go into overtime? Or ..." she trailed off, hoping he would fill in the blanks.

Martin gulped down his food, his eyes darting between her and where the other scouts still sat. "I, uh ... no." He shook his head, cheeks turning a deep shade of red. "I was on a discipline shift."

Astera had to hold back a smile. That was something, at least. He hadn't tried to keep that lie going. "What for?" she asked. After years of hiding her past, it was easy to make the question sound innocent.

With a new, intense interest in his meal, Martin took another bite of food and chewed slowly.

Stalling for time.

"I, er, messed something up the other day. It ... it's kinda embarrassing. I'd rather not go into it, if it's okay?"

When he glanced up at her, the shame and regret were as clear as the blush on his face. Astera was tempted to push, to ask why it was okay to say those things to his coworkers, but not to the person they were about ... but she didn't want to make him mad. She didn't want to give him a reason to walk away.

Even though things with Martin weren't perfect, Astera knew that it would be a long time before she met someone like him again. He was awkward, and sweet, and the bundle of nerves he always seemed to be fumbling with meant that he was so focused on doing things right, that he sometimes forgot about her. When they talked, he was comfortable speaking at length about his home, his family, his past. He rarely thought to ask her questions, and that worked for her. The only thing he did ask her about was what it was like to be a pilot. He seemed to hold her and the other pilots in quite high esteem, and the glimmer of wonder in his eyes when she spoke about work, told her that he was one of the Ops guys that wished they could get a shot in the cockpit.

So, yes, Astera knew things weren't perfect ... but what relationship ever was? If he was happy to live with the version of her that he had built in his head, who was she to shatter it? She couldn't imagine his reaction if he learned the truth about her past and, given how gentle and affectionate he was with her, she wasn't sure she wanted to find out.

CHAPTER 21

THE PAST WEEK had been rough for Henri. Baldalan had turned out to be a more convoluted puzzle than he first thought. It had taken days for them to get a proper scan of the secluded, well-shielded bases, and the more he learned, the more concerned he had become.

Every waking hour had been filled with technical meetings and intelligence coordination efforts. Every night, he had fallen into bed, exhausted. Each new piece of uncovered evidence convinced him that they couldn't leave without addressing the infestation on the planet below. However, the crew was growing restless, and he wasn't quite ready to let them know what was going on. He had hired his staff members, of course. Personally vetted each one. But he didn't know them, not really. Starfall had been proof enough of that. He wasn't sure who he could trust, and who he couldn't. What if someone had links to the pirates below? If they tried to tip them off? It wasn't something he could risk.

Still, they had gathered enough information that he had finally put together a mission plan. He had decided that they were just wasting time circling the planet. Now they knew where the busiest bases were, they needed to get down on the surface to see what they could find. After that, they would have enough information to share with the surrounding systems, and they could be on their way. The problem was, Henri could only think of one person who may have a reason to go down with him, but he wasn't sure if he could trust her. It was the last obstacle between him and getting the work done, so he could get his people away from Baldalan for good.

Henri's withdrawal at the dinner table he shared with his friends and colleagues had, apparently, been noted. As lost in thought as he was, he couldn't ignore some off-colored word play that Vitali wove into a story about the repairs he had been working on.

Henri laughed at the terrible joke despite himself. Deep down, he was still that pilot that didn't have time for procedure or protocol. Vitali knew it; that's why he kept trying to lure Henri out of his own mind with those jibes.

There was one voice that didn't join in with their laughter, however. Henri didn't have to look to know who was unimpressed; he could feel the tension in Annalise beside him as she rolled her eyes.

"You're doing those on purpose. You think I don't notice, but I do," Henri warned his chief engineer.

"Of course, I do. Why do you think I keep doing them?" he countered with a toothy grin before he asked Major Diane Tomlinson to pass over the salt in front of her.

Diane was always the quiet one of the OGs. She never missed anything. Not a birthday or holiday went by without a package arriving from the major. She was thoughtful in a way that lent herself well to running the administrative section for Henri. As she handed over the salt, she spoke quietly. "Before Vitali went on his tangent, you mentioned doing something for the pilots, Henri?" she asked, gently steering the conversation back to something more appropriate.

"Ah, right, thanks, Di." Henri nodded, smiling across at his old friend. "I figure so many of them have been stuck in training without dropping to the planet that they are getting a little stir-crazy up here. Why not have a boxing tournament, or something to burn some of that energy off?" Henri suggested, picking up the thread that had reminded him of just how tough the week had been.

"Do you really mean to say that you want my people to spend their downtime fixing up purposefully earned injuries?" Annalise asked, sounding just as annoyed as Henri imagined she would at the prospect.

Vitali laughed and waved his hand dismissively. "Oh, a few bruises, some scrapes. A broken bone at worst. Is that really going to be too much work?"

"Would you like me to come to Mech Bay and beat on some of your machines for the heck of it? Maybe take a blow torch or a wrench to some visors? Would that really be too much work?" Annalise snapped.

Vitali stiffened as it was put in terms he would understand.

"I agree with Henri, the staff need something to keep themselves occupied while we're stuck in orbit," Diane interjected, before things could escalate further between Vitali and Annalise. "Perhaps a suite of sports, rather than a boxing match? It'll appeal to more people, and hopefully reduce the number of broken bones and concussions Annalise's team need to deal with?"

Henri nodded. "Thank you, Di. I was just throwing out boxing as it was the first thing that came to mind," he added, glancing at Annalise, and hoping he hadn't blown his chance at having her come visit his room later that night. "Not sure what that says about me, but sitting all day in simulators doesn't cut it anymore. Something with competition, with stakes. That's what motivates the crew. We've got a big enough ship that we can have some races and other events. What do you all think?"

Vitali didn't speak right away, having already been put in his place by Annalise. Instead, he looked to her for her reaction. Diane wouldn't really share an opinion of her own, she would just organize whatever was asked of her.

"A bit of real exercise could be good for them. The gym and sim are fine, but something a little more competitive will certainly get the motivation up," Annalise said without looking at Vitali.

The chief engineer grinned. "But, comin' back to what you said before, Henri ... are you wanting to do a bit of real boxing again?"

Vitali's question had everyone at the table turn towards Henri.

"Not while we're on mission; I can't be nursing a concussion, or an injury, if I need to attend to an emergency. Like I said, that was just the first thing that came to mind," he reiterated, watching Annalise as he spoke. He knew that she was unhappy about him returning to missions, and now with the mention of boxing, she was sure to think there was something wrong.

Clearing his throat with a sip of his beverage, Henri continued. "Di, can you start working on arrangements for a company-wide competition like that, please? Maybe collaborate with some of the wing officers to figure out events and participants?"

Di nodded, pulling out her datapad to get started. Her fingers paused, however, before she looked up. "Commander, that file you've been anticipating is finished." She tapped at her screen, and Henri's datapad buzzed in his pocket.

Henri retrieved the device and opened the package she had sent through to him. It appeared that both Administration and Intelligence had combined their efforts to dig into the past of one pilot: Astera Ramos.

Scrolling through the information, Henri frowned. To say he was disappointed was somewhat of an understatement. Not so much in his team, he knew they had done their best. No, he was more disappointed in what felt like a rather unremarkable, and unconvincing, set of findings. Apart from the job history his staff had initially investigated, there were some mundane records about growing up on a fringe planet known for poor record keeping, and a narrow family history full of contacts who were deceased or otherwise completely off the grid. There were no criminal records, not even a simple fine. It seemed Starfall went straight from her home planet and into some suspect mercenary companies. None of which had any complaints or medical records beyond her basic employment.

Astera did not strike Henri as the type who could slide through life without anything on record, not when she was such a skilled pilot. Mech operators with her level of skill always had records spotted with injuries or requests for leave to attend funerals. There was not even one on Astera's file at any of her companies.

"Henri?" Annalise's voice broke him from his scrolling, and he looked up. "Everything okay?"

"Everything's okay," Henri said, giving Annalise a firm nod. "I've just a few things to follow up with tonight before I get to bed. I think it'll be a late one."

Henri pressed his lips together as he scanned the room. Normally, the Scout Wing had a table right in the middle reserved for them. He had seen Astera there, chatting candidly to Johansen not too long ago. She wasn't there now, though. He hoped she hadn't disappeared with that Englethorpe lad. He had seen the two of them at dinner together almost every night since she had been discharged. If they had already left the Mess Hall, he would need to interrupt her while she was with Eggles, doing whatever it was they did in their downtime.

Frowning, Henri tried to put that thought out of his mind. Given the way Eggles had thrown her name down in that blasted mission recording, he couldn't help but think the young lad wasn't mature enough for her. Despite the fact she had hidden her identity from him, Henri still thought she deserved someone more ... well, more.

A second, purposeful search of the faces in the room revealed the pink-haired pilot sitting at a small round booth in the far corner. She was, as he had guessed, separated from her colleagues, and sitting with Eggles. He spied a new tension there between them that had Henri rise from his seat immediately.

Before he could step away, a warm hand settled on Henri's forearm. "Make sure you're not up working too late, Henri," Annalise said gently, a hint of teasing in her tone. "You are not as young as you used to be. You need your rest, old man."

"I'm not dead yet." Henri smiled as he tucked his datapad back into his pocket. "I'll catch up with you all later."

Henri strode through the packed Mess Hall, his gaze levelled at Starfall. When he arrived at the table, he barely registered Eggles snapping up to salute him.

"Good evening, sir," the eager officer barked.

Henri waved a lacklustre salute back at the young man. "At ease, Englethorpe, you'll put an eye out with that thumb. Take your seat, I just need a moment," he told the young man without looking at him. He kept his attention on Astera.

"Starfall, I need to see you in my office after dinner. We need to have a discussion," he said, tone firm and professional. Then, he added, "That's an order."

"Oh." Astera's expression shifted from one of surprise to wariness. "Of course, Commander. What time would be best for you?"

"You have twenty minutes," he said flatly before turning and walking to the door.

He didn't give her a chance to ask what it was about, or a choice in whether she came to see him. He needed her to be nervous about the encounter, so she might slip up and give away what her profile was hiding. He strode with purpose back through the ship and made his way to his office. There, he pulled up Astera's profile and her former employer's MercNet listing on his computer. He wanted them both ready for when she arrived.

There was a knock at Henri's office door precisely nineteen minutes later. When it opened, he noted that Astera was wearing some comfortable looking black tights and a deep gray tank. Quite utilitarian choices for her time off, especially given that the gym was closed for the night. Some faded bruising still showed on the skin that her clothing wasn't covering, and the slump in her posture was enough to tell him she was probably ready for bed. Still, her vibrant pink hair was freshly washed, and her eyes seemed alert as she looked over at him.

"Have a seat, pilot." Henri gestured to one of the seats in his office.

In another situation, he might have kept her on her feet. However, he was aware that it was late at night, and that she was still healing. Making her stand would just be cruel in these circumstances.

Once she was set on the hard plastic chair across from his, he leaned forward in his seat. Resting his hands on the desk, he found her eyes and held her gaze a moment without saying a word. He watched her body language, checked to see if she recoiled from him, defending herself unconsciously. He needed to see if she walked into this office with any assumptions about why he wanted to see her.

After a silent, uncomfortable moment of her watching him warily, he tapped the datapad on the desk in front of him. "You'll be pleased to know your full file has been verified by our in-house research team."

Astera's expression and posture didn't change at all as Henri left a pause between his statements. All he got in response was a blink. "It all looks benign enough. What can you tell me about your previous employer? Why would you leave such a seemingly innocuous, routine company like that?" he asked, sitting back.

"I guess it's like you said." Astera's tone was even as she shrugged. "They are an innocuous, routine company. The Triple C has an amazing name. It felt like a good career move."

Henri listened, but he didn't nod, didn't shake his head to give away his thoughts. "That seems to be the impression one gets by looking at their listing on MercNet. Nothing detailing any combat actions, mostly escort missions in secure parts of the galaxy. Helping companies that can pay to have a mercenary company all to themselves if they want." As Henri spoke, he tabbed through the mission reports of the company. Each one had maybe a sentence or two explaining what happened. Each one listed a string of names that occasionally had Astera's among them.

"Funny thing about MercNet, it doesn't take much to put a company listing up there. Even less to add a report to it. But little things can tell you about a company's health and their real reputation. What bothers me about your previous employer is that they stopped filing reports not long after you joined the Triple C," Henri said, scrolling to the end of the mission list. He left the display there as he brought up her personnel file with her start date highlighted on the screen. He sat forward, folding his hands on the desk. "I ask you again, why did you leave your previous employer?"

Astera's breathing appeared to remain even as she listened to Henri, perhaps too even for the situation. "Because the Triple C is a better company to work for," she replied, her tone edged with worry. "I'm sorry, Commander, but ... what is this all about?"

"It's about honesty," Henri said quickly, almost before she had even finished her question. "Because I doubt that a company with a long-standing contract would up and fold suddenly because one pilot left their organization."

He jabbed his fingers against the screen to emphasize his point. Astera jumped at the sudden banging sound his action caused. "I want you to look me in the eye and tell me what I'll find if I reach out to this company's president directly. I want you to tell me what I'll hear if I call some of the other people listed on your missions and ask them if they know who in the Void you are," Henri challenged her. He sat back, crossing his arms over his chest and fixing her with an unyielding stare. It wasn't easy when she was looking back at him with those lovely, dark eyes, but he had to know the truth. "This is your chance to come clean because if I have to make those calls and I find out you lied to me, I'll dump your ass on this planet, so help me."

When he finished speaking, Henri noted the worry

growing behind Astera's eyes. That steady breathing of hers quickened, but ... if he wasn't watching, he would have missed it all. She was hiding something; he had no doubt. She was also clearly damn good at hiding, too.

Abruptly, Astera got out of her seat, the feet of the chair scraping against the metal floor. Her hands opened and closed in a clear sign of anxiety as she walked over to the external viewing window that ran along the side wall of Henri's office.

"Commander, I ... I'm sorry, I know I shouldn't have lied, I just—I had to—" she stammered, voice cracking. She pressed both palms and her forehead against the window as she tried to get her breathing under control.

Henri had gotten his reaction, but it was not what he was expecting.

In fact, her response to his brutal tone made him feel like a complete and utter prick.

The way her shoulders shook told him that he hadn't uncovered a spy, or a criminal ... he had torn apart the shell of someone who was terrified.

Henri rolled his chair back, stood, and walked toward Astera. He reached out and placed a hand on her shoulder. "How bad is it?" he asked softly, not wanting to do any more damage than he had already done. "If you're running from something, we can help, but we can't do much without knowing what's going on."

He only hoped he hadn't fucked things up badly enough that she would lie to him again.

CHAPTER 22

ASTERA WINCED INSTINCTIVELY at the feel of a heavy hand falling on her shoulder. She had to make a conscious effort to quell the panic rising in her chest, and to listen to what the commander was saying, rather than her own racing thoughts.

Letting her gaze wander out of the window, to the planet rotating in the Void beyond, Astera knew she had to give him something. She knew what she had to tell him, but the truth was razor sharp as it clawed its way up her aching throat. "I was in a bad relationship," she said, so quietly that she wasn't sure if he would hear her. "It was ... well, not just a relationship. A marriage. It was a bad marriage."

Henri stepped up beside her, letting his hand fall from her shoulder as he leaned against the viewport. "And you needed a resume that would get you a job here," he said softly, finishing the reason he had asked for.

"One that *he* wouldn't be able to track. He can't find me." Astera finally turned to face him. "Commander, please. I'd rather be stranded on Baldalan than let him find me. I know I fucked up—that I lied—and it's never okay, but I had to get out of there, I—"

"You were doing all you could to get out of that situation." The commander raised his hand to stall her verbal panic. "You didn't think of the consequences down the road. You were just trying to survive. I wish you had told me this from the start. Once I saw your skills, I made up my mind to keep you on as a pilot. Now that I know, I can help to keep you safe. Do we need to worry about some politician putting the word out about you, or another company hunting us? Anything you can share to keep you safe would be helpful at this point."

Heart thundering, eyes stinging with tears, Astera watched the commander closely. She hadn't been expecting him to say that. The most she had dared hope for was safe harbor to the nearest space port. She wanted to be grateful for it, but his questions had her fears roaring in her ears. Her hand instinctively moved to clasp the casing she normally wore around her neck, but it wasn't there. She wanted to tell him the truth, but she worried that if he had all the details, he wouldn't even take her to Baldalan. He'd probably just jettison her into the Void.

"I took care of all of that when I left," she said, voice shaking. "It's the reason for the backstory. I've changed my name, my hair, and I made sure he couldn't track me. It shouldn't be a problem. I haven't told anyone about it. Well," she let out a soft sigh, "anyone but you, that is."

The commander nodded. "If you're sure, then. The less said about it, the better. If you wish, I can keep this discussion among the senior staff. As far as the rest of the pilots will know, your profile is legit. What do you think?"

"The senior staff?" Astera blurted. The last thing she wanted was for more people to know.

"It's your decision. If you wish, it can stay just between you and I. However, I would only share the most necessary details with the senior staff so they can understand why I'm no longer looking into your history. If they know what's going on, they may want to help and make sure your trail is as cold as you profess it to be," the commander explained, tone cool and calm.

The senior staff already knew that the commander was looking into her? Void, Astera felt like a fool for thinking that the way he interacted with her in the Med Bay had meant he was not suspicious of her at all. She wondered how many of them knew, and if it would be worse if she asked him not to give them any details. Tension radiated in her jaw from how hard she was grinding her teeth while she mulled it over. The commander was already being far kinder than he needed to be. She didn't want to take that for granted or push him too far.

"Can you tell them it was just a relationship?" she asked softly. "They'll probably think I'm stupid for marrying him if I knew it was a bad thing, but I didn't have a choice. I didn't want any of it. I escaped as soon as I could."

"If that is what makes you comfortable, that is all I will tell them," he promised with a warm, reassuring smile.

Relief flooded through her, and Astera gave the commander a weak smile in return. The certainty that he would avoid her if he knew the full truth still tugged at her, but this was something. It was progress. Even though she was still carrying the darkest burden, she felt a little lighter for not having to hold all of her secrets so tightly anymore. She looked up at him. "Thank you," she whispered, voice full of genuine gratitude.

"You're welcome." He looked as though he was about to

dismiss her, before a new sense of resolve settled over him. "Now, please take a seat; there is more I needed to go over."

He waited for her to move first before walking over to sit at his desk. "I'm going on a mission tomorrow night, and I need someone to go with me. This whole thing started with you, so I figure I should give you the chance to help end our time here on Baldalan."

Astera was still frustrated that she had not been able to join the team that went with him a week and a half earlier. She was eager to get back down there, to get back at whoever the bastards were that had killed Sleeves. "I'm up for it."

Henri smiled. "I knew you would be. We discovered that the post you scouted was part of a wider network, and we've found the main base. It took the better part of a week scanning the planet, but all signs point to one location. Still, knowing where they are doesn't tell us who they are. I want you and your Hummingbird for close range scouting and pictures. Then, I'll join you in a support mech since I don't want to put anyone else at risk for one of my schemes. I'd do this solo if I was any good at the lower weight class frames, but," he gestured down to his significantly taller and more muscular frame by way of explanation. "Besides, I figure you are keen to get back behind the sticks, so it's your job if you want it."

The thought of getting back into a mech made Astera let out a breath of relief. She missed every part of being in control of one of the powerful fighting machines. "That sounds amazing," she admitted, but her eyes widened. "Void, I was supposed to check on Calliope this afternoon, but I totally forgot."

"No time like the present then. Don't let on to Vitali though; I want to keep the news of our drop quiet, until the day of the mission. With what we found at the perimeter base,

I am worried they might be more prepared than we know down there."

Astera frowned. "But it's just after dinner. The engineers would have clocked off by now. Isn't it too late to head to engineering?"

"One of the benefits of being the commander is that the Mech Bay is always open to me. Also, you're not giving the night shift enough credit." The commander rose from his seat and gestured to his door with a smile. "Shall we?"

The smile felt like an offering of sorts, one Astera was eager to accept. She nodded and rose to follow the commander. As they walked through the corridors together, she realized just how tall he was. The last few times she had seen him, one, or both, had been seated. Now, walking by his side, it took every ounce of energy she had to keep pace with his long strides. If she wasn't so fit before her stint in the Med Bay, she might not have had any hope. As it was, she was power-walking to keep up with him.

The Mech Bay was always the farthest walk from anywhere important in the ship. It sat near the rear of the Latagarosh, by the jump drive engines. It was the strongest part of the ship, structurally speaking, and the clearance required between living quarters and the engine rooms meant that there was a lot of space for them to play with to keep the mechs in.

The true scale of the mechs always hit Astera when she walked into the bay. Seeing the mechs standing in their slots, surrounded by scaffolding and with night crew engineers hanging around them, it was a reminder of how big some of the machines got. Calliope was barely waist height on some of the taller models, and far lighter.

"I think your dock is still the same. Calliope is exactly where you left her, though, she may need a new name after all the repairs Vitali and his guys gave the poor girl," the commander explained as they turned the corner that led to where Calliope was standing.

Astera stumbled her last step, and it was only the pain in her ribs that stopped her from doubling over after what felt like a sprint to get there. She looked up at Calliope, a rather spritely looking Hummingbird class when compared to Johansen's Falcon, or Kitty's Sparrow, on either side. There was very little about the machine that looked familiar to her, save for the outer shell, and even then, the paintwork was marred where the panels had been mended. She stepped closer, wincing as she reached up to brush her finger over the smooth metal of one such repair.

"Thank you for having her fixed," Astera said quietly, taking in all the damage that must have been done, and running the numbers through her head. She couldn't help but think it must have cost almost as much to repair Calliope as it would have to sell her for scrap and buy a new machine altogether.

The extent of the damage was also a stark reminder of that day, and Astera found her fingers shaking as her mind tried to drag her back to that fatal retreat on Baldalan. The pain, and the noise, and the searing heat, and the knowledge that one of her friends was gone forever, threatened to drown her. Instead of letting herself get swept away, she cleared her throat and turned back to the commander, her palm still resting on Calliope's panel.

"So ... in your office you alluded to something you found at the base. What are we walking into here?" she asked, needing to talk about something to distract herself.

The commander peered around before stepping in closer. He placed a hand on the leg of the Hummingbird class mech and leaned on it to bring his head closer to hers. "Pirates ... organized pirates."

Astera's heart skipped a beat and her head spun.

"They aren't planetside to pillage someone else's base; it was their base. They built it and it turns out, they have a network of them below on Baldalan. As best as La Plaz and I can figure, the place I want to drop is their HQ. With them losing the base we hit, we think we opened a blindspot for us to get Mother Hen within a few miles of it for us to take our mechs in," he explained. "So far you're the only one that knows what's going on, outside of the mission critical personnel."

Astera's mind was still spinning from the mention of pirates, but she was cognizant enough to know that what he was suggesting wasn't possible. "No, there are a lot of pirate bands out there, but none of them build bases," she said, sounding unconvinced. "It's not what they do. Are you sure it's pirates? Not just some kind of rough-edged upstarts looking to claim a planet?"

The commander shook his head. "I know what I saw. When we get down there, you'll see it, too."

Standing back up, he craned his neck to look up at the patched Calliope towering over their heads. It might be the lightest mech in the bay, but it still lorded over anyone. "Before then, you might want to get your bird looking like her old self ... or figure out what her new look will be." Stepping into the bay, he slid a container full of paint cans and sprayer hoses out for her.

"I think she needs a different look, but I'll keep her name," Astera said, pleased by the range of paint cans on offer. She wished it was as easy to repaint herself, but she was grateful to at least have the chance to do that for her mech.

Henri nodded. "Just don't fall out of the painter's rig.

Mission walkthrough starts at fourteen-hundred-hours tomorrow. Drop at oh-one-hundred the following morning," the commander rattled off as he turned for the door. "And remember to reset your control preferences in the cockpit."

"Copy that, Commander." Astera accompanied the acknowledgement with a quick salute and a genuine smile. It was only minutes ago that she had been ready for bed, but the promise of a makeover and a mission had her reenergized.

For the first time since joining the Triple C, Astera painted something other than her callsign and Calliope's name on the panel. Any attempt at decorating with camouflage patterns were useless for mercenary birds, as they operated in too many different environments to make any one palette work. If the paintjob was overly gaudy, she would be spotted kilometers off, which is not a good thing for a scout class mech. So, Astera kept her colour scheme simple, giving the Hummingbird matte black panels with some abstract splatters of white paint to resemble a galaxy. She made sure that "Calliope" and "Starfall" were written on the right arm of her mech, and then added a small star with three streaming trails to symbolize her callsign over the fusion core cover.

When she finally finished painting, Astera climbed up and slid into the cockpit as the commander had suggested. The settings were all still default following the replacements and repairs. With dried paint smeared over her cheek, hands, and uniform, she worked for the better part of an hour to get it back to something that felt natural. A lot of that was spent dialling in the targeting reticle. It had to be right on target this time. It had to be ready for the drop with the commander.

CHAPTER 23

HENRI LEFT THE MECH BAY, already hearing the telltale hiss of the spray hose behind him. Smiling, he thought back to the first time he painted up his own mech early on in his career. It was one of the last things a pilot did to signify a mech was completely theirs. It was important for Astera to have that chance again. Returning to his quarters for the night, he found Annalise waiting for him. Maybe his playful banter with Vitali over dinner hadn't turner her off as much as he thought.

Waking alone the next morning, Henri was left to prepare things for the mission. While it was later that afternoon, he had plenty on his plate and Jason Zhang wouldn't let him forget any of it. Even though they were off mission and circling a planet for weeks, the day-to-day business of the company still fell into Henri's lap and he had to do some creative things to keep the lights on after ending their contract. The daily per diem the Admiralty were previously paying helped with that more than he cared to admit.

Swallowing breakfast on the move, Henri tried to wrap up all his business as early in the day as possible. He wanted to see to his mech before the mission briefing; it had been too long and he needed to warm it up again. If there was something wrong, he'd need to know beforehand. It also gave him something to think about other than his conversation with Astera the night before.

Henri had his share of bad relationships. The Triple C had seen some terrible breakups, some that required the law to get involved, but he'd never seen someone react with such genuine fear at the mention of an ex as he'd seen from Astera. If her ex was so bad, he wondered if the man would come after the Triple C if he found out she was with them. Henri pushed those thoughts away as there wasn't much use in dwelling on it. He would roll with it if it happened, like always.

As he entered the Mech Bay, he looked around to find it relatively quiet, especially when he reached the area reserved for the Spearhead Wing. It took a lot of experience, and trust, to get to pilot such big, powerful, and infamously expensive mechs. Henri was thankful for that, as it meant he had some peace and quiet. Standing on the pilot's catwalk and looking at the pilot's viewport from the outside, he walked his eyes over the chassis of his Condor, Back Breaker.

Year after year, he had spent dialling in its specs, and year after year, his mental catalog of every scuff, ding, dent, and scorch mark grew a few more lines long. Vitali had offered to clean up the body of the towering mech, but Henri wouldn't let him. Each one of those marks had taught him a lesson. He hoped he would remember those lessons for the mission he had planned.

Opening a zippered pouch on his pilot suit, Henri found his old, red bandana right where he'd left it. Rolling and folding it, he covered his scalp with it and tied it tight behind his head before climbing up and into the cockpit. Once seated, he brought the battered Back Breaker to life. The hum of its massive cooling system could probably be heard in all parts of the Mech Bay, but most of the techs knew to keep away. Only the most experienced engineers were allowed to work on the Spearhead Wing. They also knew when to leave the pilots to their business.

"All right, Double B," Henri muttered to his mech, reintroducing himself after such a long layoff. "We're going to play nice tonight; all we want to do is snoop on our neighbors downstairs. We're not going to kick in their doors. Understand me?" He rubbed his hands on the control sticks on either side of his knees. Back Breaker voiced her displeasure by cycling her pneumatics.

"Hey, none of that now. Don't you get pouty on me. I told you I was just borrowing that Eagle from Pestle's Wing. Void, you're like a jealous girlfriend sometimes, you know that?" he scolded the multi-ton vehicle. Reaching above his head, he activated the slip around his mech to enter testing mode. The large lift system hoisted the machine off the floor, allowing him to run the joints and weapon gimbals through their paces without going anywhere.

From the stride cycle timing to the range of motion on his arms, each setting was checked and adjusted. Henri didn't like the bounce he felt with every step, so he dialled the center of gravity lower in the stride. When the sway in his fine targeting controls was off, he changed the pressure in the hydraulics. Piece by piece, Henri worked his way through Back Breaker's settings to get her feeling right. It had been so long since he took out his mech that he had to make sure it felt right for his physiology.

Henri must have been at it for a while, because when Major La Plaz's face filled the screen on Back Breaker's visor he sighed exasperatedly. "Ah, I should have known the only reason you would be late is because you lost track of time in Back Breaker," La Plaz said. "The mission briefing started at fourteen-hundred ... which was fifteen minutes ago, Commander."

"Shit, sorry. I'll be there shortly," Henri promised before he ended the call and took the mech out of testing mode. He scrambled out of the cockpit and moved through the ship a bit quicker than usual, feeling rather chastened by the fact he would be late for his own meeting.

When he finally stood outside the briefing room, Henri muttered, "Hope this isn't a bad sign." He brushed the wrinkles out of his flight suit to try and look, at least somewhat, presentable before he squared his shoulders and opened the door.

Inside, the crew for Mother Hen, La Plaz, and Astera all looked up at him from their seats around the mission briefing console. "Sorry I'm late. I hope I haven't missed much," he said as he took the seat beside Astera. His words to her the previous night about not being late played back in his mind and made him feel even more foolish.

There was a waver of amusement in Astera's expression, but she kept her mouth shut. Instead, it was La Plaz who spoke first.

"Thanks to everyone who came on time for their patience." La Plaz returned his attention to the crew gathered, who were all very comfortably situated in their chairs, and probably had been for at least twenty minutes. "As you can tell from how few of you are gathered, this is a small team. We are keeping numbers low for a reason; we don't want word getting out on this mission. We found some ... interesting things on Baldalan that we need to investigate before heading off. That will be Knuckle Duster's and Starfall's job. They will have their own confidential briefing following this one, but for now, we need to talk practicalities."

La Plaz turned, hitting the switch on the console table, and bringing up a holographic projection of the planet they had been orbiting for quite some time. "Now, given the stealthy nature of this mission, we're looking at a different, but more challenging, drop site. It is foolish to assume that whoever is on the planet won't be on the lookout for us, so we need to take some risks to make sure we're approaching from angles they won't expect."

The intelligence officer continued to share information with the pilot team of Mother Hen about the site they had chosen. It would be a tight fit for the ship, but with their skill, they should be able to handle it. The drop site was nestled in a crater, the surrounding rock infused with various metal traces that would interfere with any land-based tracking or detection equipment.

When Henri had asked La Plaz to find a good drop site, he knew his old friend would come through. Still, the man managed to exceed his expectations. The site would protect Mother Hen while he and Astera were out on the mission, and make it hard for the pirates on the planet to get any concerning tech in close enough to harm them. The only problem was that there were a limited number of passes and chasms that he and his mission partner could take to get into, or out of, the site. He did not envisage any issues when they set out, but the return could prove a fair bit more difficult depending on how things went. Henri was not going to question La Plaz's choice, though. If this was what he had chosen, it had to be the best plan.

The crew of Mother Hen had some questions and issues to iron out regarding the mission, but they were dealt with easily enough. It was all business as usual until the briefing turned to the mission abort parameters.

"We already know that the comms systems can get spotty on Baldalan," Mother Hen's captain, Nala Darlek, said as she sat forward in her seat, dark eyebrows furrowed with concern. "What happens if you go radio silent, Knuckle Duster? What's the protocol for that?"

Henri knew what she was really asking: *How long do you expect us to stick around if we think both of you have been blown to smithereens?*

Henri gestured to the topographical map of the area currently on display. "I have a feeling that you're going to be in the shadow of the crater, and all these mountains in the area, so we can try bouncing our signals up to the Latagarosh, and back down to you. The problem with that is the amount of power it will take, and how obvious it will be. If we put out a comm signal with that intensity, everyone in the area will be able to hear it. Plus, as the major showed, this hub is talking with all the other bases on the planet with dish antennas. That means we would need a very low intensity for us to stay below their noise threshold. Astera and I might get away with talking to each other, but radioing Mother Hen? We might not get to do that until we are well on our way back to you, Captain," he explained, not sounding too enthused about it. When he mentioned Starfall, La Plaz looked at him with a raised brow. Henri wasn't sure what that was about, but he had more important things to focus on.

"You should be safe in that crater surrounded by ferrite formations. The Ops Team will have us on sensors so if something goes south, they can radio you to get out of there. If we can't come right back to you, use the lake at the bottom of the gorge as our secondary extraction site. You'll have plenty of space to see anyone approaching to verify if it's us or not," Henri advised.

"Copy that, Commander," Nala said with a firm nod. She glanced at the rest of her team who appeared to be content with his plan.

"Any further questions?" La Plaz shut down the projection he was standing beside and straightened his shoulders as he looked at those gathered. There was a general hum of satisfaction as Mother Hen's crew all shook their heads. "Very well. You lot, head to the hangar and make sure you've restocked your weapons and have your checks sorted, and then hit your bunks. You'll be departing at exactly oh-one-hundred hours. I want you all bright eyed and bushy tailed so you can focus on the mission when it starts. From what we've experienced on Baldalan so far, you can't afford to get sloppy."

The dropship crew got up and made their way out of the room, each one giving Henri a small salute, or nod of respect, as they passed. Once the door was closed behind them, La Plaz leaned back against the console and crossed his arms over his chest, apparently feeling comfortable enough to appear less formal with only Henri and Astera in the room.

"Commander, how much have you already explained to *Starfall*? No use me repeating what she already knows," La Plaz asked, glancing between Henri and Astera. There was an odd inflection in his tone when he used Astera's callsign that made Henri frown.

"I told her about who built the base we hit, and who has built this network of bases on the planet. It was as hard for her to wrap her head around as it was for us," Henri confessed, looking across at Astera. As he did, he realized why the major sounded like that and his shoulders slumped. "I used Astera's name in the briefing, didn't I?"

"You did." La Plaz's lips set in a familiar pressed line that

Henri knew meant he wouldn't let it go. His expression softened before he turned his attention to Astera. "Luckily, the Mother Hen crew are pretty familiar with you being on missions lately, so they aren't likely to forget your call-sign. Now, do you have any questions before I show you some of the images and intel we have?"

Astera, whose cheeks tinged ever so slightly with a blush at becoming the focus of both Henri and La Plaz, nodded. "Yes. The commander mentioned that the group were pirates. Do you have specific information on that? Do we know exactly who we're dealing with? Saying 'pirates' is almost as vague as saying 'mercenaries' these days. There is a lot of variation in how they operate."

"Unfortunately not," La Plaz conceded. He turned the console back on and brought up some images taken in the base that Henri had raided on Baldalan. It showed a warehouse full of equipment with so many different maker's marks and ownership stamps that it could only have been stolen, or purchased, on the black market. Only pirates had stashes like that; everyone else relied on their loyalties to one sect, or another, to make sure they had all their gear.

Leaning forward in her seat, Astera frowned. "That's quite the stockpile." She turned to Henri. "I can see why you're concerned. That's not normal."

"It also tells us how long they've been at this. Not only did they populate this planet with bases, they've been stockpiling who knows what, and even stole an anti-mech turret from the Kolos Admirality," Henri observed. "That is the part that bugs me; the fact that they stole something so large and managed to get it shipped without anyone intervening."

"That's not too unusual." Astera's tone was authentically casual enough that it revealed a surprising sense of confidence and knowledge that Henri hadn't banked on.

"What do you mean?" Henri asked, keeping his own voice even in hopes he wouldn't startle her, so he could learn more.

Astera shrugged. "Only that there are plenty of shipping companies willing to work with pirates with the right incentive. They wouldn't have to own one. They'd just need to have a strong enough hold over a trade route the shipping company used—" Astera stopped, eyes wide, as though she was a rabbit caught in a trap.

"Enough of a hold over a trade route the shipping company desired to ... what?" La Plaz urged, glancing at Henri to make sure he caught how unusual this was too. Henri gave him a subtle nod.

"To make it worth their while." Astera sat back in her seat, looking somewhat more uncomfortable than she did only moments ago.

"I wouldn't even call this a trade route. Trade implies that something is going out as well. From those labels, it looks like everything is coming in and being added to their stockpile. Plus, there's no one out here to trade with; these pirates are the only thing around for two systems," Henri explained.

"That's not what I meant," Astera said, shaking her head.

Before Henri could ask her to clarify, La Plaz asked for him. "Then what did you mean?" he snapped.

Astera's lips parted, as if she wanted to say more, but she just pressed her lips together and sank further back in her seat. "Sorry, I was up late last night getting Calliope back up to spec. I'm not thinking straight. Please, continue."

Henri's eyebrows furrowed at the change in his mission partner. She knew more than she was letting on, but La Plaz's barking question only made her withdraw. Henri noted that for later and let out a sigh to break the tension. "This is why we need to go down there, it's all very confusing," he said, bringing the conversation back around to the mission. "Thank you, Major, for putting this together. We should get to bed so we have plenty of rest tonight for an oh-one-hundred drop."

Henri got out what he wanted to say and turned to Astera, giving her another chance to speak up. "So long as everyone has said their piece and we've covered everything?"

La Plaz stayed quiet. Astera just shook her head. "I'm good. See you at oh-one-hundred, Commander." She stood up, her chair scraping against the metal deck as she gave them both a casual salute and left the room.

It wasn't until the door hissed shut and locked into place again that La Plaz fixed Henri with a no-bullshit stare. "I wasn't aware you were on a first name basis with any of the current pilots."

Henri stood and faced the major. "Don't start. Don't make this into a thing, okay? We got to talking while she was in the infirmary. That's where I learned that she might have a bogus mech record. If you'll recall, I had your team dig into it. I've spent so much time looking at her records and trying to learn about her past that I've seen her name more than I've used her callsign. That's all that's happening here," Henri replied more defensively than he might have in the past.

La Plaz cocked an eyebrow at him. "Please don't get short with me, Henri." La Plaz reverted to first names, most likely to ease the tension. "You know I'm doing my job. If there is anything going on that may interfere with this mission, I need to know." His tone was less accusatory, but still firm, despite Henri's warning. It was, begrudgingly, one of the reasons Henri liked La Plaz in his role. He did not compromise on the important things.

"We'll be fine, Rodrigo. There's nothing going on between us. She's already in a relationship if that's what you're worried about. Between her experience as a scout pilot, her desire to make sure that Sleeves didn't die for nothing, and her background, she's the perfect choice for this mission. I trust you know that is the only thing I consider when I make a choice for my wing pilot," Henri reminded him.

La Plaz raised both hands. "I know that now. Thanks for clarifying. Is there anything else I need to be aware of, or that you need from me?"

Henri sighed. "Sorry, I know you're doing your job. But there are some things I've learned that I can't tell you. You just have to trust me when it comes to her." Henri clapped him on the shoulder. "You've done great work on getting us to this point. I can take it from here," he said, trying to reassure him.

CHAPTER 24

"THAT WAS AMAZING."

Martin stole a final kiss from Astera before he collapsed back onto the mattress beside her, and let out a satisfied groan. He slipped an arm under her, pulling her against the flushed skin of his chest.

Astera turned on her side. Her bunk was small, so being pressed against him was easier than balancing precariously over the edge of it. "It certainly was," she agreed, even if that wasn't entirely true. Ever since learning about what he had said in the mission recording, Astera wasn't sure how to act or feel around him, and it had filtered through to their intimacy.

Although, it didn't seem like Martin noticed the difference.

"Are we heading to dinner together again tonight?" he asked.

"No, I'm going to have a quick bite to eat soon and go to bed early. I have to be up super early in the morning. Or ... late in the night." Astera pressed her lips together as she mentally calculated how few hours she actually had to eat, shower, and prep for her mission.

"Do you and the scouts have some kind of thing planned?" Martin's voice slowed in the afterglow of their coupling. He sounded almost like he was ready for a nap.

"No, I've got something else to do. I'm not really allowed to speak about it."

That seemed to wake him up. The crisp sheets rustled as Martin quickly rolled onto his side. Astera's arm fell against the warm space on the mattress between them. "A secret mission?" His eyes widened with excitement. "Oh, that's so cool."

Astera chuckled softly as she shook her head. "Well, it isn't much of a secret anymore."

"I won't tell anyone, I swear," Martin promised earnestly, taking her hands and holding them to his chest. "Will it be dangerous?"

"Most likely."

Martin's eyes grew wider and flashed with arousal.

Astera frowned, her stomach twisting at his response. *Why does he look so pleased at the thought of me going into danger? Shouldn't he be concerned?*

Martin leaned in and kissed her, his lips surprisingly passionate. He draped an arm over her hips and then pulled back with a smirk. "My girlfriend, the kick-ass mech pilot." He shook his head. "How did I get so lucky?" Then, he kissed her again.

That second kiss tasted bitter to Astera, and she broke it almost as quickly as it begun. She slipped off the mattress and got to her feet, clutching her sheet to her chest, and letting the blanket fall on the man in her bed.

"A kick-ass mech pilot who needs to get enough sleep so she won't make a mistake that will get her blown to smithereens," Astera said, her tone light and teasing, even though she just wanted him gone.

Martin didn't seem to pick up on her discomfort. He just looked at her with the same expression he had an hour earlier. Back then, it was a mix of desire and adoration ... now, though, it made Astera's skin crawl.

"Right. Well, I wouldn't want to keep you up." Martin stood, letting the blanket fall to the bed as he reached for his clothes and started to dress. "What time should I look for you tomorrow?"

"I'm not sure," Astera confessed, wrapping herself more tightly in her sheet so that it would not fall off if she let go. "I'll check in with you once I've gotten back, cleaned up, and had some rest."

Now wearing his pants and pulling his shirt over his head, Martin hummed in acknowledgement. "Sounds good." He pecked her cheek and gave her a smile before getting his jacket on and zipped. "I'll see you then." With a playful mock-salute, he strode out of the room with an extra bounce in his step that wasn't there earlier.

Standing in her empty room, Astera tried to shake off the ickiness that had come with the whole encounter. She didn't have much time to think on it though, as she knew she had to have a wash and get something to eat before it got too late. She unwrapped the sheet from around her body and went straight to the bathroom to enjoy a hot, but brisk, shower.

Five minutes later, when Astera stepped out of the bathroom wrapped in nothing but a towel, a soft voice floated down to her. "So, you and Loverboy went for round two, huh?"

Astera glanced at Kitty's bunk to see the woman lying there, reading something on her datapad. "When did you get in?"

"I ran into Loverboy—"

"Stop calling him that."

"—in the hallway and figured it was safe to return," Kitty finished without so much of an ounce of concern for Astera's rebuke. "He didn't stick around for long. I didn't pick you as the fuck and release kinda gal. I'm happy to stay at Helen's tonight if you want to get some snuggle time in."

Astera snorted. "If you want to stay at Helen's, just stay at Helen's. Don't use me as your excuse."

"I don't need an excuse." Kitty waved her hand dismissively and leaned over the edge of her bunk to look at Astera. "I'm just trying to give you some private time. It's what a considerate roommate would do."

"Is that a hint that I haven't been considerate because I don't offer you the same?" Astera asked, pulling on her underwear, and hooking the back of her bra.

Kitty rolled her eyes. "This is why I never do anything nice. Everyone just assumes I'm trying to get something in return."

"Are you?"

"No," Kitty snapped. "Although, some alone time in my own room *would* be nice."

Astera sighed and rubbed her face. "Well, you'll have the whole night to yourself once I leave."

Eyes widening, Kitty asked, "What? Where are you going?"

"Not allowed to say, but I'll be back." Astera turned and retrieved a casual pair of sweatpants and a tank top from her closet.

"Oh man, you just got cleared for the cockpit and you're already getting a special mission?" Kitty flopped back on her bed, crossing her arms over her chest as she pouted. "Maybe I need to get injured enough to get the commander's attention."

"I wouldn't advise that," Astera replied, and suddenly the

playful mood in the room deflated, and the very real weight of Sleeves' death was with them again.

"Just stay safe, okay?" Kitty said in a rare moment of seriousness, which she then proceeded to spoil by adding, "There is no way I'm cleaning out your side of the room. Even if it is barren as fuck."

Astera just smiled and shook her head. "Copy that, Kitty. I'll make sure I come back alive to spare you the horror of actually having to clean something."

Having pulled her sweatpants and tank on while they were talking, Astera put her shoes on and then headed for the door.

"Where are you going?"

"To catch an early dinner, then straight back here to sleep. I have to be in the hangar by one in the morning." Astera glanced over her shoulder at Kitty, who was now laying on her stomach, facing the door, her head in her hands.

"Right. I'll tell Helen she can come over any time after one. Hope your guns stay cool, Starfall." Kitty's smile was warm with affection.

SEVERAL HOURS LATER, Astera was dressed in her black jumpsuit, standing in the hangar, and taking in the hive of activity around Mother Hen. The Engineering Team was running final checks on Calliope and Back Breaker before they were loaded into the dropship. It wasn't all that long ago that it was Calliope and Perry being loaded into the same ship, and she and Sleeves were sharing some inane banter about who was going to get the most useful intel.

"Are you sure you're feeling up to this?"

Astera's heart leapt into her throat at the sudden voice

behind her, and she turned to see Sergeant Johansen watching her. There was so much noise in the hangar that it was no wonder the woman got the drop on her.

"I was until you almost scared me out of my skin," Astera replied, turning to face her commanding officer. Johansen's face set into an expression that made it clear she was not impressed with the deflection, so Astera added, "Yes. I'm grateful to have the opportunity to go back down there and get some closure."

"Good." Johansen's face softened, appeased. "Tell me, did you wind up rescuing that casing of yours?" She jutted her chin towards Astera's chest, where the charm usually hung.

Taking a moment to dig the metal casing from her pocket, Astera held it up for Johansen to see. "The chain broke, so I'm just keeping it in my pocket for now. I'll try and get another chain for it when we get back to civilization."

Johansen waved a hand dismissively. "Look, the ladies wanted to wait until your birthday to give this to you, but none of us figured you'd go on a mission before then. I'm sure they won't mind me busting it out early."

Johansen reached into her own pocket and drew out a pretty, plaited cord made of whisker thin copper, steel, and fibre optic strands. "We had the chief keep some of these aside from Calliope's repairs. We all know you love that strange good luck charm of yours."

Astera blinked, her heart swelling with gratitude at the thoughtfulness of the gift. She reached for it and choked out a "thank you." Johansen smiled as Astera threaded the cord through the hole on the casing and tied the ends in a firm knot before pulling it over her head. She tucked it under the neckline of her flight suit and felt the warm weight of the metal settle between her breasts.

The door to the hangar opened, and the commander

walked over with a thermos in one hand and a coffee cup in the other. He gave Astera and Johansen a grim smile as he approached, and offered the thermos to Astera. "Coffee? I figure you didn't get the recommended sleep and I can't have you nodding off on me down there."

"Coffee sounds great, thanks Commander," Astera said, accepting the cup.

The commander turned to Johansen. "Come to see Starfall off?" He drained the rest of his own coffee, crushed the cup, and tossed it in the trash bin by the door.

Johansen glanced at Astera and nodded.

"Don't worry, I'll make sure she comes back safe," he said. The tone of his voice indicated that it was more than some glib platitude. It was a promise.

"Make sure you do, too." Johansen patted Astera's back. "I hope your guns stay cool, both of you."

With that final phrase, Johansen turned around and walked out of the bay, leaving Astera and the commander standing next to each other as the mechs were loaded onto Mother Hen. It would only be a matter of minutes before they were called over to get strapped into the cockpits for the flight to Baldalan, so they'd be ready for the drop the moment the bay ramp was lowered.

After the night when Astera told the commander some of what she was running from, she wasn't sure how to behave around him. He certainly didn't seem to be acting differently around her. At least, not in a bad way. If anything, some of the tension he always carried in his shoulders and neck seemed to have eased as he stood beside her.

She stole a glance at him, taking in the strong profile of his freshly shaven face. Now that she'd spent more time up close with the commander, she couldn't help but notice that he was rather handsome. Even if his hairline seemed prematurely salt-and-peppered, and his eyes were warier than most, there was something about his rare smiles that made him look young again. Astera thought he looked his best then.

As the commander watched the crew working, Astera searched for something to say. Since she was about to spend an entire mission with the man, it would be far easier if they could share some light conversation along the way.

"Back Breaker's one heck of a machine. I've never seen it up this close before. Quite a beast. I can see a lot of time and love went into that mech," she said, falling back on the best generic topic of conversation for a pilot: the craft they poured so much time and energy into.

The commander chuckled "You don't need to butter me up, Ramos. I meant what I told you when we had our talk; your secret is safe with me ... and that's not why I picked you for this mission, either."

Astera wanted to tell him that she wasn't "buttering him up," but stopped when he mentioned the mission.

He leaned forward until his head was beside hers and whispered right into her ear. "This mission isn't a perk or a promotion. I need your best today. We're going right into the nest of the pirates that took Sleeves from us. Leave any urge for revenge in your holster; I need you squared away and ice cold until it's time to pull it out. Can you promise me that?" he asked, his tone level and firm.

With the commander so close, Astera caught a whiff of his aftershave. It was a deep, heady scent that had just the right kind of maturity and mystery to make it appealing. It almost made her forget what he had just whispered. "Uh, of course," she said, her confidence returning to her only once she started speaking. "Getting intel, and making sure we know what is going on, is far more important than revenge. We need to ensure no one else gets caught up in this mess.

That would be the best legacy for Sleeves, not some hotshot firefight."

Straightening up, and towering over her once more, the commander nodded. "Very good. I'll hold you to that." He turned towards Mother Hen and started walking towards it, gesturing for her to follow. "Come on, let's get aboard. We need to be in our cockpits, ready to exit as soon as Mother Hen touches down. La Plaz may be right about the metallic compounds in the crater walls, but I don't want to be hanging around in it if he's wrong."

"Copy that, Knuckle Duster." Astera switched to mission address as they made their way to the dropship together so that they were at the right level of formality ... and to remind herself to forget about his handsome profile and aromatic aftershave.

The commander and Astera were, it seemed, the last to board. When they made their way up the ramp, it started to raise shut behind them. The commander gave her a somewhat playful salute before he pulled a red bandanna out of his flight suit pocket and tied it around his head. He approached Back Breaker, did a full walk around, and then started scaling the ladder in the wall behind the machine.

Calliope was far smaller than Back Breaker, coming in around waist high on the heavy mech. There was a ladder behind the dock, but as usual, Astera chose not to use it. Even with the time off and still feeling the dull ache of her healing injuries, it was easy for her to climb up the side of her mech and into the cockpit. She was of the philosophy that if you couldn't get in your mech without assistance, then you probably shouldn't be piloting it, because you would be screwed in an emergency.

Getting back into the cockpit for a mission, rather than the recalibrations from the night before, felt like coming home. Astera had known how to pilot a mech since her early teens, and it was the only place she had ever felt a sense of total power and control in her life. She loved the hum of the powerful fusion engines under her command, waiting for her to bring them to life.

Standing in the cockpit, Astera leaned against the lightly cushioned backrest as she strapped herself into the harness, starting with her calves and working her way up. She tested each of the straps as she buckled them up, and then extended the saddle so she could take the weight off her legs while they traveled. She decided to leave Calliope's sternum plate open for a little while to keep the airflow, and peered over to watch the commander as he settled into Back Breaker, fascinated by how different it was to get into a different class of mech.

With the top hatch of the Condor closed, it was easy to make out the commander in his seat as he went through his pre-flight checks on Back Breaker. It was odd seeing the commander in the cockpit, wearing a standard issue black flight suit and a red bandana, such a change from his well-kept professional image around the ship. Despite its size, Back Breaker was surprisingly quiet as it hung in its loading frame. That image was broken when its dual fusion cores flared to life. It seemed to stand taller as the commander woke it from its slumber. The hands, arms, and legs all bent and twisted as he ran his checks, making sure the linkages were enabled before switching to standby mode. Looking up, he caught Astera's gaze and reached to the side, grabbing his headset, and settling it into place. He nudged the microphone with his chin.

"You waiting on something, Starfall? Button up your bird and let's prep for takeoff." He watched her through the faceted panels of his front facing view port. "Better to find out that a hinge is seized up here than when we get to the planet."

Astera jumped, realizing she had been staring. She loved seeing other pilots work in their mechs, as everyone had different styles ... but the commander was right. She had a job to do.

"Copy that." She hit the button on the right side of her seat and the hydraulic levers hissed as the sternum plate closed shut in front of her. She fired up Calliope. With all the noise and hum of Back Breaker, she could barely feel her own mech flare to life. She wouldn't even know it was running if it weren't for the increase of subtle vibrations all around her.

"Looks like the hinge is fine and the bird buttons up nice," Astera said through her comms, making sure that they were still fine with everything locked and ready to go. She ran through her own pre-flight checks and tested Calliope's appendages to make sure everything was limber and her step ratio was right. Once that was done, she settled the Hummingbird back into her flight frame and Astera set her onto standby mode. "Preflight check complete, everything's smooth over here, Knuckle Duster," Astera confirmed, looking out of her windshield and at the mech that towered over her own.

"Copy that. Mother Hen, this is Knuckle Duster. Mechs are squared away and secured for transport. Mech pod clear for liftoff," he radioed the cockpit. "Check check, you on the pilot line, Starfall?" he asked, looking back to see if she had done the same.

"You're coming through loud and clear, Knuckle Duster. Are you receiving me?" she replied, fiddling with her sound settings to get them to the volume she preferred.

"You're five by five, Starfall. Set your channel selector to sequence C; there's no telling how much intel they have on our procedures. We did take out their satellite base, but you never know," the commander ordered. His tone was uncharacteristically unsettled and only stood out because of how foreign it was to his usually even expression.

Astera's nose scrunched with concern. "Everything okay, Knuckle Duster?" she asked through their channel.

"Just a nagging thought, Starfall. We need to keep the mission in mind, copy?" he replied, seeming to snap out of it as Mother Hen cleared the docking port and changed course for the planet below. The change in gravity was always the giveaway when riding on the dropship. It would be a short while before they entered the planet's atmosphere and landed at their chosen site.

An eerie quiet hung on the radio channel as Mother Hen and the flight team were using their dedicated channel to talk with the Ops Team on the Latagarosh.

"I've got the mission in mind, Knuckle Duster," Astera said with a frown, not liking how the nagging thought had him checking in on her again. "Anything about that nagging thought you'd like to share? If I can allay any concerns about me being the right person to be on this mission, I'd rather do it now than with the enemies bearing down on us."

The commander stared back across at Astera. "Don't worry. It's not you I'm worried about," he began, "But now that we're underway, I can tell you that I'm still trying to figure out why the Kolos Admiralty bothered to lie to us. A mission is a mission; I would have accepted it if they had told me the truth. What were they trying to hide, and why?" the commander asked rhetorically.

Astera let out a breath of relief as she realized the heat wasn't on her. If she was completely honest, she had a few ideas as to why the Kolos Admiralty would be hiding things, but she knew she had to keep some of them to herself. "It's possible they knew about the pirates moving in ... maybe they just don't like the idea of having them in the neigbourhood?" she suggested, figuring it was the most obvious answer.

"Without a warship servicing them, what threat could these pirates be to them?" he said, not sounding convinced. "We'll figure that out in time, though. We have something in front of us to figure out first."

As he spoke, the ship began to vibrate around them. "Entering the atmosphere; hang on," the laconic Captain Darlek broke in on their conversation.

"Roger that," the commander responded, voice uneven.

Even with the motion dampeners mounted on the loading frame, Astera felt as if she was being shaken. The entry on her first Baldalan mission hadn't been so rough, and she figured there must be something going on outside of the ship that made it even choppier. Perhaps inclement weather was brewing? That could work in their favor.

Regardless of the reason for the shaking, the movement made the pressure of the saddle post painful between her legs, so she hit the button to retract it again, and leaned into the harness straps instead, letting them take care of some of the suspension to ease the vibrations rocketing through her spine. The commander, in his larger Condor class mech, would be able to sink into a seat and let the padding and the position of his body take some of the brunt, but scout mechs were built differently, and the saddles were only good if the frame wasn't moving too much.

"Five minutes until landing. Site looks clear from here. I'll open the bay door when we touch down," Captain Darlek confirmed.

Astera's limbs lightened with the rush of adrenaline that came at the start of any mission. She checked her instruments again for good measure and smiled as she saw everything running perfectly. "Gotta hand it to you, Knuckle Duster, I think you found the best engineers in the Void," Astera said, genuinely impressed with how they managed to get her utterly broken bird up and running like new again.

"Don't let the chief hear you say that; it's not healthy for his head to get much bigger," the commander joked.

Astera was about to reply, but Captain Darlek cut in again. "Touch down in three minutes."

Pushing all thoughts of jokes and banter aside, Astera put on her game face. She caressed Calliope's controls and took a long, deep breath, sending out a silent plea to the Void that both she and the commander returned from this mission safely.

CHAPTER 25

THE RUDDY EARTH compacted and spilled around the feet of Back Breaker as Henri made his way out of the crater. The red-brown color in the soil, and layers of rock around them, hinted at the high ferrous content of whatever meteorite slammed into Baldalan ages ago. It was also what made this place the perfect landing zone for an approach on the base. The impact site had layers upon layers of ripples in the crust from the power of the event. It was a bonus, as it would also give them visual cover as they climbed toward their target, which sat on one of the cliffs nearly thirty kilometers to the north. It was going to be a long trip, but they had little choice in the matter. The pirates had picked a fantastic place to build their base, as it was impossible to land any closer without running a near complete chance of being detected.

"Nest, Knuckle Duster, do you have us on the scope?" Henri radioed the Ops Room, possibly for the last time. Beyond this point, there was too much risk of their comm signal being picked up locally.

"We read you loud and clear, Knuckle Duster, and have you on our screens," answered La Plaz. Given the way the two previous missions turned out, Henri wanted the major running the Ops Room for him. There couldn't be any lapses on this one.

"Roger that, Nest. We are breaking the horizon and heading north for Nav Beta. We will be radio silent until back onboard Mother Hen or mission parameters dictate otherwise. Over and out," Henri answered. His chin lingered by the switch as he waited for the major's answer.

"Understood, Knuckle Duster. Good luck and happy hunting. Out," the major responded. Henri smiled at his words before switching off his long-range system and turning over to the pilot-to-pilot channel.

"All right, Starfall, we're on our own from here. Like we talked about, use the terrain to your advantage. Keep the walls between us and them. We'll be running on passives so visual recognition will be paramount. Don't go running off without me, copy?" Henri reiterated the plan one more time as he neared the lip of the crater. The large legs of the Condor frame under him tilted and shifted, adjusting to ensure the center of mass didn't sway too much.

"Copy that, Knuckle Duster. Following your lead," Astera answered.

Henri was relieved that she sounded on the job and dialed in. Part of him missed the sass in her voice, but that sort of thing wasn't needed on a mission like this. Or at least, not during the important parts. Maybe he would get to hear more if they had any downtime.

Stepping over the lip, the two mechs proceeded down into the valley beyond it. A few hundred meters ahead, the first ridge rose, angling over their heads, a gargantuan shard of stone, forever displaced and pointing to the heavens, thanks to the same meteor that caused the crater.

In another life, Henri may have wanted to study the

formation, but not today. The moody gray clouds at the edge of the mission area were already moving faster than Henri figured, reminding him that time was of the essence. "Well, that might help after all," he muttered, looking into the face of the prevailing wind.

"What was that, Knuckle Duster?" Astera's voice cut into his private thoughts as he realized he had his chin resting against the switch out of habit.

"The storm system is moving into the area faster than we figured. It might not be so bad, though, if we can stay off their sensors. We might get to use it for cover in a pinch, Starfall." Henri refocused his attention on the path before Back Breaker.

"So long as my seals are intact, I'm fine with that," Astera replied as she moved her Hummingbird into position at his eleven o'clock.

As the pair of mechs moved, it was eerily quiet, outside of the sounds of their footfalls echoing off the stone walls around them. There was the occasional rumble of thunder from the encroaching storm, but not much else beyond that. Thanks to the cloud cover, they also had to contend with an added level of humidity that took the cockpit of Henri's mech from sauna, to the sunken gates of some underwater hell. If they were doing more than maneuvering their mechs around the terrain, Henri might have been able to ignore it. He knew that over eighty percent of most missions involved moving into position for a few moments of high stakes action, and then returning to the pick-up point. Something felt different about this mission, though.

The comms stayed silent as Henri focused on avoiding those sludgy vines Astera had warned him about, and keeping his mech upright. He didn't mind the silence, as it allowed him to get into a nice flow as he piloted his mech. However, before long, it was clear his mission partner was not as comfortable with the quiet.

"So, after we get to this base, then what? I know we're trying to find out who the pirates are, but once we do, what's the plan?" Astera's question had been weighing on everyone associated with this mission. La Plaz had asked him the same thing, and when he told Annalise his plans, she had asked whether it was worth the risk if all they were doing was going to have a nosey around and see who was there.

To be honest, Henri hadn't found a definitive answer. He could try to land the full company to assault the main base, but he was not convinced they had found all the outlying sites, yet. There was no way to know the full complement of mechs they would be facing. Also, a protracted campaign to truly eradicate the pirates would take months. Months during which they were no longer getting paid. It was hard to keep the lights on doing pro bono revenge work like that.

"We pass the word. Everyone will want to know that there's a pirate group that's this well funded, well organized, and well stocked, operating in this system. We still need to figure out how the Admiralty is involved and why they care so much, but I'll dig into that when we get off-world," Henri promised.

As he spoke, the pair made the turn at the next nav point. It was an elegant, silent ballet of repositioning multi-ton mechanical war machines that pilots did without a second thought. It gave them a path beyond the ridge wall that surrounded the crater and into the next layer of rocky terrain to use to their benefit. As Henri was about to add onto his promise, the long-range radio crackled to life.

"Nest to Knuckle Duster, broadcasting in the dark. Be advised we are tracking two energy signals, vicinity Nav Gamma. Current path tracks south-southwest at one hundred and ninety-five, speed twenty kilometres per hour," reported the Ops Team. From the tone of the voice, it sounded like Hermedilla on the line. With the major as the ranking officer in the room, he was probably put on sensors for this operation.

Henri flicked his HUD to show the wireframe overlay. Tapping the holographic display, he input the data as it was described. Frowning, he saw the path took them down the same one he planned to use. "Starfall, proceed forward two hundred meters and change course due east. We need to take the long way around to Nav Gamma," he intoned on the pilot channel. He started shifting Back Breaker a bit to put Calliope to his right so they could make the turn.

"Copy that, Knuckle Duster," Astera answered.

Henri watched as she slowed Calliope and took an arcing turn toward the gap ahead. Even though it took them back south slightly as they followed the concentric circles of the valleys around the crater, it would keep them out of line of sight from the patrolling mechs.

As they walked in the shadow of the rocky ledges above them, there was another roll of thunder from the clouds overhead.

Astera cut in as soon as it subsided. "That storm is getting closer, Knuckle Duster. Will that make confirmation harder?"

"It just means we need to beat the rain, Starfall. Keep on this heading. Next turn is six-hundred and thirty meters ahead," he answered, pushing his Condor to make up for the time lost with this course change.

The extra speed in the steps of the larger mech caused Henri to start bouncing his seat. Henri always imagined that the rise and fall must have been what it was like to ride horses into war in ancient times. It was the disadvantage of moving with any sort of speed in a mech of the Condor class, and one of the greatest challenges for a fledgling pilot was keeping your aim true when the world was shaking around you.

As they were about to make the turn, the long-range comms flared. "This is Nest. Be advised the mechs on our screens have changed course. New heading, east at heading ninety-five. Speed increased to thirty kph. Mother Hen, new course violates standing order cordon. Proceed with alternate orders and remain on station."

Henri groaned at that last comment from the major as sweat rolled down the back of his neck. "Starfall, our ride is lifting off, so bear that in mind when engaging the enemy," he relayed. With Mother Hen moving to the secondary site, they would have to be extra careful to avoid engaging the enemies. "Make the turn and proceed north. We have a bit of time before they get here so we need to use that window to reach the base."

"Copy that, should I increase speed?"

"Negative. I can't cover you if you disappear into the distance. Keep an eye on your passives, though. We need to know if their sensors pick us up as we move past these notches in the terrain."

The further they got from the crater, the lower the ridges were and the more porous their boundaries seemed to be. As they moved, they saw more notches and windows in the rock walls caused by wind and water erosion. After following their current track for twenty minutes or more, the terrain was more broken and inconsistent than the narrow chasm walls closer to the crater.

"Copy that, Knuckle Duster," Astera responded as she twisted her body to face west. It was a smart move on her part. It turned her primary sensors toward their pursuers and her Hummingbird could walk in that position faster than his Condor could.

After a few more kilometers of progress, Henri piped up, "Okay, head west. We need to get back on track to Nav Gamma. It will also get us off this line if they follow our path, since that notch was the only place to turn north for nearly a kilometer in either direction."

Once again, the small course correction moved them into the shadow of the destroyed landscape. The new path wasn't quite as narrow, but the footing beneath them was more broken. Astera's Hummingbird traversed it with ease, but the heavier Condor had to proceed on more cautious footing. It was tricky to move over as Henri couldn't look out the bottom of his cockpit to see where he was putting Back Breaker's feet. He had to rely on the feedback from his controls and the sound of the terrain shifting beneath him.

"Gravel underfoot, boss. Come left three meters and forward ten," Astera guided, offering what she could see from her shorter mech with the wider pilot view window.

"Copy that, thanks." Henri was pleased she had taken the initiative to direct him, it showed a broad sense of awareness and knowledge about the differences between their mechs that impressed him. Henri's fingers were feather light on the sticks as he maneuvered back onto solid ground.

Pushing up and over a rock formation, he proceeded forward until he heard Astera again. "Don't trust that lip, boss. It's a cornice on the back side. Won't support your weight. Shift back right nine meters then come forward. Prepare for a big step down."

"Copy that." Henri made his large frame dance along the rocky terrain until he could proceed forward. "This is the problem with satellite mapping. The whole area looked stable from orbit," Henri complained as they had to slow to a crawl to keep his Condor upright. Still, the teamwork made things go much smoother.

With a sigh, Henri finally stepped down the incline, allowing them to turn north to head for Nav Gamma once more. As if annoyed at their progress, the brewing storm cleared its throat with a violent roll of thunder. Henri felt the sound waves shudder through his mech from left to right, and he had no doubt this would be one impressive downpour.

"Rage all you want, storm. We're getting this done," Henri challenged as lightning flashed in the corner of his peripheral vision.

"This is Nest broadcasting in the dark. Be advised, signals turning north and increasing speed. Destination appears to be Nav Gamma," the major cut in as the structure of the base came into view through the early morning haze.

"They didn't waste any time. How are they right on our ass? They haven't painted us yet," Henri mused, turning on his passive sensor display. As he figured, it was still blank. If any targeting system was locked on them, they would have detected it.

Ahead, he saw that Calliope had come to a halt. Henri reasoned Astera had reached Nav Gamma and was waiting on station for him to catch up. He pushed the throttle and closed the distance between them.

There wasn't even a twitch, or word of recognition, as he approached.

"Starfall?"

He came up to position Back Breaker beside Calliope and twisted in the cockpit. Astera was frozen in her harness, looking dead in the water. She didn't even turn towards him when he arrived. Instead, her face was angled up, the graceful curve of her neck strained as her attention was locked on the base structure on the cliff ahead of them, the dark walls painted by the first yawning strains of sunlight.

"Astera, what's going—" Henri started to ask her as the major interjected on the radio.

"Knuckle Duster, be advised that bogies are closing on Nav Gamma. They will have visual confirmation in less than ten minutes," the major reported, sounding a touch frantic for a change.

Henri frowned at the pilot in the mech alongside his. He chose her for this mission because he had faith in her, but if she stood there much longer, the pair of them would be spotted. Once that happened, there was no telling what sort of base defenses could start raining fire down on them with a sensor lock from the pursuing mechs. With Mother Hen lifted off, they had no easy exit from the planet.

"Starfall, what's the problem? We need to retreat," Henri pleaded, trying to snap her out of whatever had shut her down.

CHAPTER 26

THE COMMANDER'S voice came through the comms again, more urgent this time. Astera could hear the concern in his tone, but her heart was pounding so hard in her chest that it echoed in her head. She couldn't tear her eyes away from the insignia on the wall of the compound on the ridge ahead of them. The sharp, asymmetrical "V" bursting through a stylised star, confirmed that the group setting up permanent shop on this planet were indeed pirates. That they were Voidstalkers: the most dangerous pirates in the Void.

They were also the reason Astera was on the run.

"Starfall, report."

"Sorry," Astera spluttered, naturally responding to the tone of unbending command in the commander's latest transmission. "It ... it's the Voidstalkers."

"Understood. Designation identified. Starfall, continue on this path and follow the contour of the elevation to Nav Delta. We can't be here in the open or they'll mark us for the in-base defenses," the commander ordered as Astera shook in her cockpit, the barriers she had built in her mind barely holding back the tsunami of memories threatening to unleash themselves.

When she didn't move right away, the commander punctured her thoughts with a sharp, "Move your ass, pilot."

Once more, his tone had her responding without her own thought. Her trembling hands nudged Calliope into action with a rough shove. "Copy that." She turned the Hummingbird in the direction of Nav Delta and kicked her into full speed. The commander was right. If they didn't get moving, the Voidstalkers could lock onto their mechs with who knows what stationed in the base above them. From her own experience, she knew they wouldn't show the company who destroyed their satellite base any mercy.

The Hummingbird's max speed, by virtue of its size and design, was far faster than that of the commander's Condor. The underbrush in the giant forest didn't help, either. Astera could navigate Calliope around it with ease, but it was a tighter, and more delicate, squeeze for Back Breaker. If Astera's brain wasn't fixated on escape, she would have taken it into consideration, but all she could think about was getting away from that base as quickly as possible.

Behind her, she could barely register the sound of the Condor scattering the smaller plants that clung to the ridges around the crater. As the Hummingbird raced ahead, the commander came through again. "Starfall, maintain visual contact. Use the terrain to block sensor contact with the enemy, but stay out where I can see you." It sounded like he was speaking through gritted, chattering teeth. At the speed they were moving, his mech had to be bucking like an angry bull. Still, it was a good reminder that even he didn't have her ping on his sensor.

Part of Astera wanted to scream that they didn't have time for that, that they needed to get to Mother Hen, now. She wanted to tell the commander that she hadn't come this far just to be captured by them again ... and that she'd much rather get blown up in Calliope than taken back to the relationship she had escaped from.

The commander's words, though, served as a reminder that she was not alone. If the Voidstalkers found her, they would also find the commander, and he did not deserve whatever they would do to him. Astera had to listen; he knew what he was doing.

"Copy that, Knuckle Duster," Astera said, body vibrating with excess energy as she slowed Calliope to a speed Back Breaker could match. She kept looking between her instruments and pivoting her head in the cockpit to see if she was in visual range so she could start moving properly again. Each second felt like an eternity. "Come on, come on ..." she muttered to herself.

The Condor carrying the commander rounded a forested corner of a ridge as he made the turn at Nav Gamma. "Visual contact reestablished, Starfall. Now, proceed at this elevation to Nav Delta. Maintain previous sensor and comms emission levels," he reminded her. While the ridges blocked the sensors of their pursuers, it sounded like the commander was not looking to turn and fire on them if he could help it.

With just Astera and the commander on the mission, a firefight would be suicide. There was no way they could survive when the Voidstalkers had a base here. Astera knew for a fact that they had a sizeable contingent of well-armed mechs. The Voidstalkers had more infrastructure at their disposal than most pirate outfits. They wouldn't have their full mech complement here on Baldalan, but if they were setting up shop, they would have enough to protect their base against intruders. For a moment, Astera wondered which officer was assigned to the base, and which pilots they would have with them; there was a chance she knew some of them. She shook off that thought. It didn't really matter, and she couldn't afford to go back there.

Instead of letting her mind race, she focused on her orders. Follow elevation and maintain comms emission levels. That was all she had to do.

Astera fell silent and let some of that terrified energy flow out of her as she guided Calliope through the ridges and into a more thickly forested terrain. Every few steps, a new memory or worry would try to push into her mind, but she let them go.

"Knuckle Duster, keeping to this elevation is the long way around. It could take hours," Astera informed him as she consulted at her map. The little dot that showed her position relative to where Mother Hen should be, looked as though it was barely moving. She superimposed the topical elevation map over her navigation layout and her jaw ached from how hard she was grinding her teeth.

"That's correct, Starfall, but it will keep the topography between us and the mechs they sent out to investigate their perimeter," he countered. There was a pregnant pause before the commander added. "Which they are doing because they have seismic sensors. It's the reason we had to send you and Calliope to the satellite base. They must have them all through this area, too. Halt your mech, Starfall. Standby for new navs."

Halt? Astera wanted to scream as she received the order. She did as she was told, even though every part of her protested against it. "Stationary now, Knuckle Duster," Astera spluttered.

Without the airflow around the mech helping to cool the cockpit, the humidity increased significantly and the sweat that had been prickling her skin beaded fully and started running down her neck and back. She measured the time with the crawl of each droplet.

The worst part of all the ridges and cliffs around them was their high ferrite composition, making them excellent sound conductors. Even though they were beyond the brim of the terrain, Astera could still hear the footfalls of the multi-ton mech frames pursuing them. As the sound reverberated up through her feet, it felt like they were right on top of her and the commander. Every part of her body screamed for them to move, to flee, but if the commander was right, that would only give them away.

"New Nav Epsilon uploaded to your map data," the commander whispered suddenly as Astera's HUD chimed. "Move directly to your right, slide step, dead slow speed," he added. It seemed that all the time since the base was discovered allowed La Plaz and his intel team to take several passes with the ship's sensors over the area. The value was apparent now as Nav Epsilon pointed to the mouth of an open cave below them along this valley. Whether it was an old lava tube or dried up underground river, didn't matter right now. It was cover they desperately needed to regroup and come up with a new escape plan.

Somewhere behind her, Astera heard the Condor shifting its weight to one leg while sliding the other along the ground as far the commander could safely reach, before transferring the weight over. After a few times, it was clear what he was doing. Moving that way minimized vibrations and hid their movement as best as they could. It seemed the seismic sensors, if they were there, were the only way their pursuers might find them. If this worked, the pair of them would disappear from their tactical view. If not, they'd be trapped in a cave with one way out.

The plan felt as experimental as it was frustrating, but

Astera followed it anyway. Keeping Calliope's movements as slow and smooth as possible, despite the abject terror flooding through her, took every ounce of her concentration. The noise of the Voidstalker's mechs crashing around in the distance didn't help but, eventually, those sounds faded. A rush of hope surged through her, which she quickly stamped down. It didn't mean anything ... yet. They could still turn around and march right back to her and the commander, and it was only a matter of time before they realized where the sensors lost them and came to investigate. She and the commander had to be gone well before they did that. A loud crack of lightning and boom of thunder sizzled through the atmosphere, and jolted Astera to action, just as the skies opened and rain started pelting down.

An eternity later, Calliope and Back Breaker were pulled to a gradual halt outside the yawning mouth of the cave. The instant that her mech finally fell still, Astera let out a groan and sagged against the weight of her harness straps, making her even more aware of how sweat-dampened her flight suit was as it tightened around her. She closed her eyes and just focused on getting her breathing steady, before taking a long draw from her drinking tube, to stave off the pounding that was growing in her temples.

When some sense of coherent thought finally returned to Astera, she peeled her eyes open and looked around, frowning. "We might have fooled their sensors, but we're just sitting ducks out here, Knuckle Duster. There is no way they are going to stop looking now they know we're out here."

"Exactly. That's why we're not *staying* out here." He twisted Back Breaker's upper torso to cover her Humming-bird. "Now, use your controls to put Calliope down on all fours. I know this goes against all your training, but trust me. You're going to need to do that in order to crawl into the cave."

"Crawl into the—" Astera stopped, mid-sentence as she was tempted to tell the commander he was nuts. Instead, she slowly turned Calliope to face the mouth of the cave. It was fairly large, which made sense given the scale of everything else on this planet. It wasn't impossible to believe that Calliope could fit into the tight space, but Back Breaker? "Void ... this is what got you your crazy reputation, isn't it, Knuckle Duster?"

Despite her reluctance, Astera realized this was their best option. With the rain thickening all around them and covering their path through the trees, this cave may be just what they needed to lay low for a while. She pressed the buttons to tighten her harness and hit the controls to purposefully lower Calliope towards the ground. The angle of moving the mech onto all fours had her suspended in her harness, with the straps cutting into her skin painfully, making it harder for her to remain light on the controls. Once more, all other thoughts were expunged as she concentrated only on getting her mech down, and then slowly crawling into the cavern.

The instant Calliope was fully concealed by the cave, the darkness helped bring the cockpit temperature down. It was a welcome relief as the sweat had started sliding down Astera's nose, and was dripping onto Calliope's windshield with a repetitive ping that was driving her mad.

"How much farther do you want me to go?" Astera asked through the comms, figuring that it was probably better to avoid getting too far into the cave network if they didn't need to.

"A little more. I'll try to fit in around you." The commander sounded like he was already moving to lower Back Breaker onto its chunky arms.

Positioned as she was, Astera was unable to see what the commander was doing, but she imagined it looked as though

Back Breaker was army crawling into the cave behind her. The coordination to move the four extremities as needed to shuffle the mech forward, was no small feat, but it wasn't long before Astera heard the near deafening roar of Back Breaker's engines as the commander slid its frame around Calliope's, hunching over her mech in the tight passage. "Okay, scoot back; I think you can fit under me now."

Carefully shuffling Calliope's frame back under the shadow of the commander's hunched over mech was probably the strangest thing she had ever done as a pilot, but also probably the most brilliant. The smaller they could make their combined profile, the more likely they were to evade detection of any kind. The cave alone should be enough to do most of the work, but if the Voidstalkers did manage to find their tracks through the rain, there was no way they would assume the mechs were hiding in a cave. Keeping your mech upright was training one-oh-one for any pilot learning to control the heavy machines. Getting two mechs down on their hands and knees would effectively make it impossible for them to make a quick escape, but ... that wasn't what Astera and the commander needed. They needed to get enough heat off them so the Voidstalkers would return to their base. Then, with enough of a lead time between them getting out of the cave and setting off the seismic sensors again, there was little hope pirates would catch up with them. If they got it right, they would be able to make it to Mother Hen safely.

"Knuckle Duster, I hope you don't mind me speaking freely here," Astera begun, clearing her throat. "This plan is crazy ... but it's also fucking brilliant." Her tone was laced with respect.

"It's only brilliant if it works," he retorted. "Step one is complete. Now, commence with full system shut down. We can't leave the cores running; they might send recon mechs out once they lose us, and even standby power will kick enough heat up for them to detect. This is Knuckle Duster, going dark."

Instead of replying, Astera went about shutting Calliope down, too. It was a familiar process that would have been enough to help her wind down herself if she wasn't still hanging in her harness. For the first time, she envied the cockpit that other mechs had, with their seats and footwells. The commander would be relying on his harness to stay in place, too, but the pressure would only be on his chest and shoulders, thanks to his seating position, not on his whole body like Astera's was.

Once Astera was satisfied that Calliope was properly shut down, she popped the hatch and took in a deep breath of the dank cave air. It smelled better than her cockpit, at least. She started unlocking her harness straps from the feet upwards, letting her body hang until she was confident that it would only be a short drop to the ground. Getting back in would be more difficult, but that was a problem for future her.

The impact of Astera's feet hitting the dirt floor jarred her shaking limbs, but it was a relief to be standing under her own agency. She took a moment to get reoriented with her ups and downs, and then walked forward to get a better view of how the commander had positioned his mech.

To say the two machines were squeezed in tightly was an understatement. Back Breaker was curled over Calliope, the open hatch hovering just above Astera's mech's back. Initially, Astera was concerned about the height the commander would need to drop from to reach the ground, but the pose he had chosen meant that he would be able to drop onto Calliope's back first, and then scale down the limbs to get to the ground safely.

"Need a hand?" she called, already looking around to see

what the best way to scale the machines would be so she could help him out.

"Uh, yeah. Catch." A large duffle bag sailed out the hatch. "One of the perks of a mech in this class: you can pack for any emergency." The commander pulled himself through the hatch at the crown of the Condor's head, making his way down just as she predicted.

"Now, all we can do is hope that the rain persists. It'll encourage them to keep their infantry at home, rather than send them out here looking for us," he explained, as he took the bag from her and opened it on the ground. Inside, he pulled out a pair of sleeping bags, a huge flask of water, and some meal packets. "Might as well settle in for a long night ... er, day," he corrected, as there was still enough sunlight filtering down through the rain clouds outside.

Astera watched the commander set up camp with a sense of incredulity. She couldn't even imagine sleeping. She knew that she would crash once the adrenalin wore off, but right now she still had too much energy to burn.

"I doubt they'll send out infantry," Astera replied, knowing that that the Voidstalkers hated being away from their more powerful toys and weapons. "They'll most likely swap their mechs over so they get fresh pilots, and have them stationed to react the moment they get wind of us again." She started to pace the span of their camp.

Pausing in his preparations, the commander turned to look at her. When Astera met his gaze, she could see the question behind his eyes. "All the more reason for us to get some rest. Can't be draggin' ass when we set out. To that point, we may want to wait for the next dusk. Not only will it give us more time to rest, but having the cover of darkness will help us with getting back out of here, considering we'll have to move without setting off their seismic sensors."

The commander returned to his work, and Astera to her pacing, but she could feel his eyes on her when she wasn't looking.

Between her reaction to seeing the insignia earlier and having just blurted out her thoughts like they were facts, Astera realized she had given too much away. The commander's keen gaze was proof of that. "Do you mind if I take a walk? Just to the mouth of the cave. I need some fresh air," she asked, avoiding his stare.

It was a few drawn-out moments before the commander answered. "All right, but stay out of sight. No telling how close they are. They might be on their way back to double check, so don't go sticking your neck out. You blow our cover and I'm docking your pay," he said with a grin, adding some levity to the situation.

"Copy that, Commander." The laugh that spilled from Astera's lips was amused, but somewhat hollow. "Don't worry, I'll stay out of sight. There are a few things I'm saving for, and I've got no hope of affording them if you get all greedy on my pay." She gave him a casual salute and started walking. She kept her strides long and swift to stretch her cramped muscles, and relished the feeling of her body becoming looser again.

It was a little difficult for Astera to maneuver around the limbs and chassis of the mechs, but once she did, it was a clear shot to the mouth of the cave. The metallic tang of rain in the air became more evident with each new breath as Astera walked towards the exit. Just as she reached the border of the external light pouring in, she moved closer to the cave walls, and stuck to them as she crept towards the entrance.

Outside, everything looked like an old earth watercolour painting. The wind and rain blurred her view, and made everything seem somewhat more surreal. It was a beautiful view, blessedly empty of the telltale mongrel mechs the pirates favored. Astera let out a sigh of relief as she leaned against the wall and tried to get her head straight. Now that the danger of their escape was on pause, the Voidstalker logo flashed through her mind again, and her lips trembled. She rested her head in her hands as her eyes stung with tears. She blinked them back rapidly, refusing to cry.

The Void was large, infinite really, but she should have known she couldn't avoid her past forever. It was inevitable that it would come back to haunt her in some way. She could only hope that she and the commander were able to get back to the Latagarosh and leave all the drama behind.

For the first time in many years, Astera sank down onto the ground and sat with her legs folded. She remembered the way that her father had taught her to focus on her breathing and calm her racing thoughts. Normally, she would close her eyes during the process, but this time she needed to remain alert, just in case someone came looking for them.

Still, time slipped by as Astera brought herself back to some sense of equilibrium. As she did, a loud rumble of thunder split the atmosphere and the ferocity of the rain increased. The torrential downpour funnelled the water into small waterfalls along the entrance of the cave. Rising, Astera moved towards one. She unzipped her jumpsuit, tied the arms around her waist so they would not get muddy, and used some of the water to wash away the tackiness and odor of sweat and rebreathed air from her skin. It was lukewarm, but still refreshing, and helped to further push away the panic she felt earlier. She was thirsty, but she didn't dare drink the water, not sure if it was safe for consumption, or if the earth it trailed over to reach her had tainted it in some way.

Just as Astera raised her cupped hands above her head to pour some of that cleansing water over her hair, her own name broke through her near meditative state.

"Astera?" Peering back into the cave, she watched the commander walking along the cave wall, trying to stay out of sight. "You'd been gone so long; I had to see if something, or someone, grabbed you," he explained, genuine worry written on his face before it relaxed at the sight of her. His gaze lowered to the wet tank she had been wearing beneath her flight suit, and the water cupped in her hands. "Oh, sorry. I'll leave you to it. Food's ready when you're done and we should get to bed before the suns get much higher." He turned around quickly, the dirt beneath his heels squeaking in protest.

"It's okay," Astera called out after him. "I'm just weather watching at this point. The water's lovely if you want to refresh a bit." She stepped back into the shadows of the cave and gave him a gentle smile as she let the water in her cupped hands trickle out.

"Nah, I'll just stew in my suit of filth until we get back," the commander said back, cracking a grin. Even so, it appeared he'd slid his bandana off since Astera had stepped away. It was easy to see that his short hair was damp in the low light of the cave. "See you when you wrap up here." He retreated into the tunnel, towards the camp in the shadow of the paired mechs.

"I'm not coming anywhere near you if you insist on stewing in your filth," Astera called out after him. "I prefer the fresh air."

Still, several minutes later, she found herself turning and making her way back to camp too. When she arrived, she looked down to see that the sleeping bags and food were set up quite nicely, with a camp light off to the side so that the shadows of the cave did not feel too oppressive. "I think that storm couldn't have come at a better time. Just hope we don't get flooded in down here," she said as she walked over and sat down on the dirt floor opposite of the commander.

"We're ever so slightly uphill from the mouth. I could feel it walking back." A plume of steam rose into the commander's face as he peeled the plastic cover off his meal pack. "Your food should be ready," he explained, as he tossed Astera a spork from the utensils he had brought along.

"Thanks." Astera caught the spork and peeled back the plastic on her own bowl. She mixed it around, her stomach growling at the aroma, even if it only smelled of bland preserved food.

Silence fell between them as they ate, but Astera could tell there was something going on behind the commander's eyes. After a few minutes of quiet, he finally spoke. "How do you know them? You identified the symbol in a heartbeat, without checking the database, which tells me you have first-hand knowledge."

It was a question, not an accusation, but Astera had been running from her past for so long that she found it hard to tell the difference.

"They're the most notorious pirate gang in the Void, everyone knows them." Astera shrugged. She was about to take another bite to eat so she didn't have to say any more, but the commander's stern expression told her that her answer would not be enough. She dug her spork back into the mound of mush in her disposable bowl and looked towards the entrance of the cave, not willing to meet his gaze. "Yes. I have first-hand knowledge."

The commander nodded as he stirred his bowl of food. "Based on our conversation on the ship, I'm guessing he was one of them?"

Astera stiffened. His words on the Latagarosh, before she told him who she was, came back to her and dread dripped over her skin, sending a shiver of worry down her spine. "Please don't strand me here. Just help me get back to whatever spacestation you're restocking at next, and I'll get out of your hair, I promise," she pleaded, knowing that her involvement with pirates had to be a deal breaker.

Brow furrowed, the commander set his meal aside. "Why would I leave you here? You think a past with a pirate gang is somehow disqualifying for members of the Triple C? Astera, you'd have to do a lot worse to get kicked out of this company. Everyone, especially the OGs, have parts of their past that they'd rather not mention. You think squeaky clean people wind up in this life? No, they live boring lives on the Core Worlds."

Astera's own food remained forgotten in her hands as she listened to the commander. She shifted uncomfortably as she took in his words. She understood what he was getting at, she knew that this life drew certain people ... but surely some things were unforgiveable. "You're okay with me sticking around?"

"Of course. I was looking into you because I was worried that you were a plant from the Admiralty or one of the other major factions we've dealt with in the past," he explained. "When someone's background has holes in it, or is imperfect somehow, it can point to a cover put together by one of the intelligence services. You came clean about the truth the other night; I was satisfied with that. Then, I saw your reaction to the symbol, and ... well, you wouldn't have had that reaction if it was something you wanted in your life. So, to me, that's that."

Astera let out a low, shaking breath and nodded. His words were reassuring, to say the least. "I certainly have no ties to any of the factions. Most of them can be just as bad as the pirates. And the Voidstalkers? This is the first time I've run into them since I left. Back on the Latagarosh I know we were talking about pirates, but I just refused to believe it would be them."

"It's not ideal for you, obviously. Now, first and foremost, our mission is to get off this planet. But, once we get out of here, and when you're ready, I'm going to need your help. I don't believe that taking over a planet and building it up for themselves is the end goal," he counseled, watching her as he spoke.

Astera already had a few ideas about the goal for the Voidstalkers on Baldalan, but she needed time to figure out how to share them, and what to say if the commander questioned her knowledge. So, instead of speaking right away, she nodded and returned her focus to her meal. She took a few bites before finally looking up into his searching gaze. "Thank you," she whispered.

"Thank me when we get out of here," he countered, digging out one more forkful of food before crumpling up his plastic bowl and throwing it into the bag. "What sort of mechs should we expect out there? I don't imagine they can afford spearhead mechs, but infantry class are easy enough to scavenge ..." he trailed off, letting her fill in the blanks.

Astera let out a soft, bitter laugh. "Between their own resources, and what they can access via blackmail and extortion, they've got more than enough to rival most of the major factions. As a matter of fact, the Latagarosh might be in danger. If the Voidstalkers are here, they probably have a jumpship nearby," she said, turning more pensive as she took another bite. She chewed it over as she considered the resources the Voidstalkers had at their disposal, and who was most likely put in charge of their base. "The ones that were hunting me on my first mission were probably infantry class. They were too fast to be any of the heavier models," she said.

"The weapons will be more powerful than you'd expect. They favor heavier loadouts over pilot comfort and decent cockpit temperatures."

Astera settled her half-finished meal on her lap and leaned back, resting her hands on the ground just behind her hips. "They would have more than that, though. For a base this size, and given they have at least a couple of satellite sites, they'd have at least several of the bigger guys; bastardised mechs made of Condor and Vulture parts. They'd have some Sparrows, too. They prefer those as scout mechs." Astera fell silent after that. She knew the last part for a fact; she had piloted more than a few of them herself.

Henri looked thoughtful as he listened and didn't interrupt. He let the pause linger as she finished, as he seemed to be rolling an idea around in his head. "They wind up going heavy on their frames and run them hot as a result. They also mash up frames of the heavier classes," he repeated, leaning back against the wall of the cave. Folding his arms, he lifted one hand to his chin in thought. "That might give us the window we need if they wind up on our tails on our way back to Mother Hen."

"Yes. The pilot's effectiveness and efficiency will start to waver after a few hours as a result. Probably even less on a sauna like this. It's just too damn hot to think rationally for long in mechs like that," she explained, watching the commander as he took all of this in.

"And I'm guessing they switch shifts at sunrise?"

"That'll depend on who is in charge," Astera said evenly. "For regular security they'll have some sort of rotation, but I imagine they've got everyone on call, ready to go if they pick up our signatures again."

"And the smallest frame they use is a Sparrow?" he asked,

his hand idly rubbing at his jaw as he looked off over Astera's head.

"It was at the time I left ... but that was a while ago now, and they've clearly changed up their MO," she confessed with a concerned frown.

"We'll just have to take that risk," he mused. "I've got part of a plan, but I need to sleep on it. You should, too. It looked like you hadn't gotten a lot of sleep before our drop."

Astera couldn't stop the slight flush on her cheeks. She sat forward and finished the last few bites of her meal before setting the container aside and stretching. She slipped into the sleeping bag the commander had laid out for her. She made herself comfortable on her back, closed her eyes, and tried to get her mind to slow, but there were too many thoughts racing through her head to feel even remotely sleepy.

"Being part of the Voidstalkers was not my decision," she murmured, needing to let the commander know that. Even if he accepted she had a past, she had to let him know that she wasn't the kind of person he might be imagining.

The commander sat forward, arms on his knees. "Captured? Or ..." he paused, clearly imagining the alternatives to his question. "Actually, you don't have to tell me what happened. All that matters is that you're with us, in the Scout Wing. I'm happy to have you in the company." With that, the commander slid into his own sleeping bag and laid back, closing his eyes.

It was kind of the commander to take that step back, to let her know that her place with the company wasn't contingent on her explaining every part of her past. The only problem was, this was the first time Astera had spoken to anyone outside of the Voidstalkers about her past, and she found it was hard to keep it in now that she had started to open up. Still, she couldn't afford to push the limits with him.

"Thanks, Commander." She let out a soft breath and tucked her sleeping bag tighter around herself, but her feet kept tapping against the dirt in time with her racing thoughts. Try as she might, she couldn't clear her mind

As she wrestled with the bag and the sleep it was supposed to bring, the commander's voice filled the space, even though he didn't move. "Astera, your beat is too fast; it's screwing up the pace of my breathing." He groaned, rolling onto his side to look at her. "All the bad memories are back now that you're here, aren't they?"

Astera forced her feet to stop tapping, but she didn't turn around. "They're never far away. I just got good at ignoring them. I'm having a harder time doing that right now," she admitted. If they weren't in a cave, the softness of her voice may not have reached him, but the echo helped.

"No one is going to get to you, Astera. Not if I have anything to say about it. You're not alone out here with them. If nothing else, Calliope is here this time, watching over you as you sleep," he reminded her, pointing up at the "mech shelter" they folded around themselves.

The promise made her feel warmer and fuzzier than she cared to admit. The part about the commander having something to say about it; not the part about Calliope. "I'd put more faith in you than my mech. She's a good machine, but she's a bit useless without my input."

The commander chuckled. "Okay, that's fair, but I guarantee you she'll get you off this planet and back home, just like she did last time. Science and engineering may tell us they are inanimate objects with no soul, but I swear, they love us just as much as we love them. That's the only explanation I have for how you got back to us last time," he admitted, rolling his head to look at her. "But, I'd much rather you get home without relying on another miracle," he added, smiling at her.

"Yeah, I think I'm fresh out of miracles anyway," she agreed, thinking that he was right about how she managed to beat the odds on her last mission. "Although, I don't think getting back had as much to do with miracles as it had to do with having you in my ear. When I first heard your voice, I wanted to clobber the Ops crew, but I'm grateful you came, because I wouldn't have made it back without you.'

"I couldn't leave you out there. Not after what happened to Sleeves. I couldn't let two of my pilots fall because someone lied to me," the commander said gently. "No one in my company is expendable."

"That's why I wanted to work for the Triple C, you know," Astera told him, loosening her hold on her sleeping bag and letting go of some of the tension in her upper body. "I figured most mercenary companies were just as bad as pirates, but your company isn't, and now I know *you're* not."

He smiled. "I'm glad I could change your mind."

Astera stared at the mechs above her. Calliope's fresh paint had held up well, even with the scratchy underbrush of the forest outside. Above Calliope, Back Breaker loomed, a much larger and more dangerous machine in many ways. "How did you get Knuckle Duster and Back Breaker?" she asked, the question spilling from her before she could stop it. She had shared so much about herself, and she wanted to know more about him. "They sound like the callsigns for someone who just throws down. After working with you, you're way more tactical than all that."

Henri chuckled. "I figured it was only a matter of time before that question came around. I earned those when I was a very different man, at a very different time in my life." He said this simply as he looked at her. After a beat, he sighed. "That's not good enough, is it?"

Astera snorted. "It didn't really give away a whole lot."

A few moments passed, and Astera had just begun to think she had pushed too far when he spoke again. "My call-sign was earned pretty early in my career. I was in the Campaign Grinders, a merc unit that was big enough to be an army for sale. I was part of the infantry division, and my platoon was meant to ambush a supply convoy during some border skirmish. Turned out the convoy wasn't as lightly guarded as we were led to believe. A squad of mechs dispatched from their destination met the convoy just as we launched our assault. Between the extra squad, the convoy guard mechs and vehicles, it was going to be tough, even with the element of surprise."

Sitting up, the commander abandoned his sleeping bag and leaned against the cave wall as he continued. "I threw every-thing I could think of at the targets that filled my screen. I chewed through my cannon rounds. Emptied my rotary machine guns within the first few minutes. I was running so hot from using the few lasers I had and could tell the mech I was facing was on its last legs, but none of my weapons were cycling fast enough. The missile weapon he had left was nearly reloaded, so I grabbed a tree in my mech's hand. I went to swing it, but one of the vehicles blasted the top of it off. So, I punched the mech with the segment of trunk I had left in my grip. I crushed the cockpit of the mech, and the pilot inside with it."

The way the commander told the story had it playing out in Astera's mind like an action film. She smiled, amused by the resourcefulness, and imagined that his colleagues must have been telling that story for years after the fact.

"So, after that, my Sarge started calling me Knuckle Duster and the name stuck."

"Very resourceful of you," she said with a small laugh. "What about Back Breaker? Is that a name you've carried through for all of your mechs, or is this bird special?" She pointed to the mech curled over them.

He followed the gesture and smiled at the scuffed, a.k.a. "seasoned," chassis of Back Breaker. "She's special. She was the first spearhead class mech the Triple C ever bought. Back then, I still went out on a lot of the missions. Usually, our battle plan would involve the Infantry Wing engaging the target. Then, I'd join the fight from the flank or follow a path that would bring me around to an advantageous position. That much firepower from a place you don't expect tends to end a fight pretty fast. So, the OGs said my involvement was usually backbreaking for the enemy. Hence the reason she carries that nickname."

Astera let out a low whistle as she reappraised the mech above them. "Good to know I was on the money when I said a lot of time and love went into her," she said. "How long ago did you start the company?"

"As a standalone entity? We're two months from our eight-year anniversary." His voice slowed and he gazed off in the distance, his lips moving quietly as it seemed he was trying to figure something out. "Yeah, eight years."

Reaching out and running her fingers along the panel of Back Breaker's foot beside her hip, Astera smiled. The Condor might have scratches and dents on its grey and purple panels, but it was clearly well loved. "That's a good span for a mech," she said, genuinely impressed. "Growing up, my parents taught me to treat our mechs like family members. You take care of them; they take care of you. The Voidstalkers don't see it that way. A lot of mercenary companies don't seem to, either. It's nice to know you hold that level of respect for the birds."

The commander's eyes lingered on Astera's hand as she

touched his mech, and he smiled. "Like I said, they love you back if you show them love."

Some pilots were very particular about other people touching their mechs, claiming that poor luck or bad shots can rub off if someone other than the pilot and engineer touched it. Astera wouldn't have been surprised if the commander asked her to stop, but from the smile on his face he didn't mind. He seemed calm and relaxed as he watched her drum her fingers over the painted metal.

"So, you started the company almost eight years ago." Astera let out a soft sigh and let her palm rest against the machine. She turned, focusing her attention back on the commander. Something in his expression made her feel a little braver. "What were you running from?"

His smile faltered. "After a while, me, and some people I trust started working as a special detachment of the Campaign Grinders. At the time, the Grinders' aim to be an army for the highest bidder turned them into the permanent army for the Concordant Compact, basically the bank of the galaxy. Overnight, the financiers of the wars of the Core Worlds turned into their own faction and started taking over planets. That's not what I wanted to do."

His lips pursed, tightening as he reflected on his past. "One day, we went out on a mission on our jumpship and just ... never came back. By then, the Grinders had become a legit army and were making too much money to worry about where me, the OGs, and the Latagarosh had gone. We took on some jobs as part of the Grinders as our ship still carried that registry, but eventually, people started to figure us out. So, we took the money we made, officially registered as the Triple C, and became independent. Thankfully, our old bosses have cushy desk jobs somewhere near the galactic core, making way too much money to worry about us. But some nights I wonder ..."

"If your past will come back to haunt you." Astera finished the sentence. So many pieces of the puzzle fell into place. Why the company only took on good jobs, why he made sure he kept his crew safe and well compensated ... why he was willing to accept runaways like her without judgment. "I guess we're not all that different, you and I."

"Now you know why I don't care that you're a pirate. Some people would say I'm one because I stole a ship from my employer. Anyone who knows that story doesn't seem to care given my company's performance ever since, but it's why the jobs we choose matter," he explained.

Astera understood. It all seemed like a lucky, well-timed break on behalf of the commander and his friends. She was glad they had taken the opportunity. The Void needed more people like them. It was too easy to get caught up in the shadier schemes in the universe. They needed pinpricks of light like the Triple C to help balance that out.

"Even though I was under their banner for just over ten years, I never considered myself a Voidstalker, or a pirate. Sometimes, other people give us those labels, and we take them because we have to. Or because they're convenient ... but that is not how I see myself. Or you."

Astera traced the Voidstalker's infamous asymmetrical "V" in the dirt beside her before scrubbing it out with her palm. She rolled onto her side so she could see the commander properly and felt the casing she wore tucked into her tank top slip out from between her breasts and rest against the ground close to her shoulder. She noticed him track the movement, his eyes on the glint of the metal in the light of their small camp.

"Am I allowed to ask more about that?" the commander

probed tentatively, tearing his attention away from the casing and looking into her eyes with an expression that made her squirm. Not in a bad way, though. More so because it was like he was actually looking at *her*, and seeing her for who she was, rather than who she pretended to be. "The message on it sounds like a promise."

Astera wrapped her hand around the casing. Her heart beat faster at the direct question, and despite her natural urge to lie, there was a part of her that wanted to tell him the truth. Wanted him to know more about her.

"I didn't succeed but you can do it," Astera recited softly, rolling the metal around in her hand and letting out a low sigh. She looked over at him. "It's a long story, but my family knew my husband for many years before we were married. They never really saw eye to eye, and after a particularly nasty incident where my mother tried, and failed, to pull us away from his influence, she tried to shoot him, and she missed."

Letting her shaking fingers unfurl, Astera held the new cord up so the item in question hung right before her eyes.

"This is the casing of the bullet she fired. It wasn't long after the attempt that he forced me to marry him. It was just like him to do that, too. To show my mother how powerless she was to leave by holding me hostage. So, my mother gave me this as a reminder ... or an apology ... or a promise. I'm not sure which. All I knew was that, before she died, she hoped I would be able to get myself unstuck," Astera explained, looking over at the commander and wondering if this would be what changed his mind about her. "I considered it. There were so many nights where—"

Astera's voice caught in her throat and her eyes burned. She blinked away the tears and swallowed the emotion as she found a way to tell her story without the details that hurt so much.

"Where I had an opportunity to follow through. So many times I could have tried to end him and escape, but ... I couldn't do it."

Closing her eyes and taking a deep breath, Astera tucked the casing back into her tank top. She took a few moments to gather herself, and to escape the commander's watchful gaze.

"Was it because you had feelings for him?"

The idea made Astera laugh a little, but she gave the commander a reassuring smile so he would know he hadn't offended her. It was a fair assumption. Even the most toxic relationships could involve some element of love, no matter how twisted.

"No." Her denial was firm. Truthful. "I held no affection or warmth for him at all. I just ... didn't want to be that person. We don't always pick our circumstances, but we do have the power to control our reactions to them."

"So, you escaped instead," the commander said.

"So, I escaped instead," Astera confirmed, finally feeling like she could look at him. Once more, she was unable to find a single shred of judgment in his expression. "I keep the casing as a reminder that I am in control of my destiny now. That I have made a lot of difficult choices, and I can keep making them no matter how hard they are. I keep it to remind me of who I want to be, not who I was."

Silence fell between them, but they still watched each other. Despite the fact they were laying on opposite sides of the cave, the mutual disclosures made Astera feel closer to the commander than she had to anyone since she lost her mother. Three weeks earlier, the thought would have terrified her, but now? A gentle warmth grew, spreading from her fluttering heart, and out through her chest, her stomach, and her limbs.

The way the commander's eyes lingered on her made her feel less like a puzzle he was trying to put together, and more like a person he was learning to understand.

It felt good to be seen.

Before Astera could analyze the change any further, the commander let out a long breath. "Thank you for sharing that with me," he said, looking down at his hands. "Do you think you can sleep now?"

Astera didn't think so, but she had just dumped a lot of difficult information on him, and she wanted to give him some space. "Yes."

He turned off the small camp light beside his hip and scooted from the wall to lay down in his sleeping bag again. As he did, he turned away from her, putting a barrier back between them. Giving them both some privacy.

Astera tucked her arm back into the sleeping bag again and pulled it up to her chin. She didn't really think she could sleep, but she needed to try. They had a big day ahead of them. "Good night, Commander."

She closed her eyes and forced herself to slow, using the same technique she had used in the mouth of the cave. Her tired limbs stilled in her sleeping bag, and the sound of the commander's steady breathing, and the continuing storm outside, helped soothe her worries.

Just as Astera thought she might drift off, the commander's voice broke through the darkness.

"Henri. You can call me Henri," he said without rolling over. "Void, let me amend that. You should still call me Commander, or Knuckle Duster, in an official capacity, but after all we've been through, it's Henri from now on."

Astera smiled sleepily. "Then good night, Henri," she corrected, too tired to bother trying to hide the warmth in her tone.

CHAPTER 27

HENRI NEVER SLEPT TOO DEEPLY when he was on a mission. He had gotten a couple of hours of shut-eye before he woke and sat on a rock in the cave as the storm slowed down outside. As he waited for Astera to wake, his mind rolled around her final words to him before she fell asleep.

There was something in the way she wished him good night. A sweet, unguarded warmth in her tone. After sharing so much about himself with her, and hearing more about her secret past, he was not surprised, but Henri prided himself on keeping things professional between himself and his staff. Annalise was the only person he had slept with over the years, and that was because their history predated the Triple C. Somehow, he had given Astera permission to call him by his name, and he found that he did not regret it in the slightest.

Not being able to sleep gave him plenty of time to over-analyze things. As the day grew longer, he had to put it aside. He had to get his head back on the task at hand. Too many good pilots brought their baggage on missions with them and not many of those that did came back. He told himself that he would take some time to consider things when he got back to the Latagarosh.

Hearing a sudden intake of breath, Henri turned back to see Astera stretching as she roused. "Good timing. We have a few hours of daylight left to get out of here and back to Mother Hen, provided she stayed planet-side."

Astera blinked at him, dazed for a few seconds as she woke fully. Then, she nodded as she rubbed her eyes. "You don't want to wait for nightfall?" Her voice was, distractingly, husky from sleep.

Henri shook his head. "After what you told me, I want them out when the suns are up. If they run as hot as you say, the cool night air will work for them. If we go now, they will have to be more aware of their heat levels."

"That makes sense." Astera got to her feet and stretched again. She still had her flight suit overalls tied down around her waist, but the arms had come loose as she slept, so they were hanging down her legs and the zip met just below her belly button, which Henri could see because her stretching made her tank ride up just a touch. "I'm going to take a quick walk." She gestured past the protective shell of the mechs, towards the front of the cave.

"I'll join you. Don't want you grabbed, or spotted, unexpectedly before we make our daring escape." Henri hopped off his rock, eager to stretch his legs. He fell in beside her, slowing his steps to match her pace. "Just so you're aware, you're not getting extra shower time for this mission."

A laugh spluttered from her before she groaned melodramatically. "But I already stink so bad," Astera protested. "If you won't do it for me, consider it a favor to everyone who has to come within a couple of meters of me."

Henri chuckled. He was standing within a meter of her, and he wouldn't complain about how she smelled. "You just have to be economical with your water ration, that's all. Don't go getting any ideas about getting wounded again to get extra time, either."

"Void, you're ruining all my plans," Astera muttered. "Did anyone ever tell you that you're a spoilsport, Henri?"

Henri liked the way she said his name. He wondered if he could make her find a way to say it again, but quickly pushed that thought from his mind. They were on a dangerous planet; he couldn't afford any distractions.

"I've been called a lot worse. But I'm sure you could sneak in and steal some water from Eggles," he offered, bringing up the specialist's name to remind himself of the relationship he had been watching grow over the past week or so.

Astera laughed, but it sounded forced, even to Henri. "Yeah, suppose I could."

"That didn't sound too convincing." He took her hand gently and turned her to face him. That was not the way he thought someone in a new relationship would respond, and after learning what he did last night, he wanted to make sure she was okay.

She looked up into his eyes, and her own widened. "It's nothing like that," she promised earnestly. "Martin is a nice guy. He's just ...." she trailed off, as if searching for a word, before frowning and repeating, "nice."

Thinking back to what he had seen in the Mess Hall, Henri nodded. "He's trying too hard, isn't he? He wants to be his perfect self for fear that you won't like the real Martin. It seems like he's new to all of this so he probably doesn't know how to be himself in a relationship."

Astera shook her head. "No, it's not quite that." She hesitated a moment, her nose scrunching in the way he noticed it did when she was trying to figure something out. "He's doing pretty well being himself. I'm the one not being *myself*, and he doesn't seem to notice. Even if he did, I'm not sure he would care. I could replace myself with any of the other scouts, and he would probably be just as pleased."

"What makes you say that?" Henri released her hand and turned to resume walking.

Silence fell between them for a few moments. Just as Henri began to think Astera may not answer, she cleared her throat and spoke. "Well, he doesn't know anything about me. Not really. Admittedly, I've gotten good at avoiding answering questions about my past from people, but he never asks. I know all about his family, where he grew up, his favorite foods, colors, music ... but he's never really wanted to know any of that about me," she admitted. "I mean, you know more about me, and the most time we've ever spent together is one day, and most of that was sleeping. I've been talking to Martin for weeks."

Henri frowned. "Yeah, that's not healthy. He probably has a pre-packed, pre-made, version of you that he doesn't want to destroy with new information. Have you asked him about it? Maybe he doesn't realize what he's doing."

"I haven't," Astera confessed, sounding as if it was not something she really wanted to do. "But you're right. I don't think he'd do it on purpose. He is a nice guy." She glanced at him. "I suppose you've seen it before? Women flocking your way and wanting Knuckle Duster, not Henri."

"When word of some of our missions get around, people want to get close to the legend. They are so desperate to be part of something bigger than themselves, they'll take any sliver they can get. The Void is so vast that no one wants to be lost in it," he said, letting her know that she was not alone. "They chase people for all the wrong reasons, but if someone is right for you, you don't need to chase them. They'll be there by your side whenever you turn to look for them."

Astera's footsteps slowed as they approached the mouth of the cavern. The light patter of rain could still be heard outside, but it was more of a gentle drizzle by now, and weak enough to let sunshine through. With any luck, it would be over soon.

"Legends aren't what they're made out to be," Astera said, her voice softer. Whether it was because they were close to the open, or for another reason, Henri couldn't be sure. "I just want someone who looks at me and really sees *me*. I don't know if that's possible. Maybe I'm just being naive."

"If someone does see the real you, it would be impossible not to fall for you." Henri meant it to be supportive, but hearing it echo around them, he knew he'd gone a step too far as Astera's commanding officer. He could have apologized, or ended the conversation there, but he figured that having gone so far, going another step probably wouldn't hurt, especially if it helped her feel seen. By him, at least. "To make it through all you have, and to come out of it with the mentality you've got, shows strength and fortitude that anyone would value in a partner."

Astera stopped walking and looked at him, seeming to assess his comments, to see if the compliments were real. Slowly, her lips curved into the gentlest of smiles. "Thank you, Henri," she said, voice tinged with emotions. She then let out a soft breath and rolled her shoulders. "I ... I'm gonna take walk in the forest for a sec, okay? I'll be back."

"You really shouldn't leave the cave. In fact, we should get the mech start-up process underway," he reminded her, looking away to avoid having to watch her stretch again.

"Henri, surely you can let a lady use the head. If I'm gone longer than four minutes, you can send out a search party," she said, voice wry and amused.

Belatedly, Henri realized the purpose of their walk and he

cursed his short-sightedness. He chuckled somewhat nervously. "Yeah, sorry. Don't take too long, though."

After giving him a playful approximation of a salute, Astera walked down the hill from the cave mouth. Lingering near the entrance, he tried to listen for patrolling mechs, but the valley outside was quiet. Rather than wait, he turned back into the cave and went about striking the camp. As he put away the lamp, he thought back on the parts of her body his eyes had drifted over when the casing fell out of her tank. And when she stretched. And how she had looked so beautiful, so peaceful, as she slept curled up in her sleeping bag.

Given what Astera had said about Martin, he banished those thoughts from his mind. He didn't want to fall into the same trap. Also, he needed to get his mind on the task at hand again. Using the time to recall the valleys, ridges, and cliffs the crater had made, he tried to picture the best way through. Astera would need that route for the first part of his plan.

When Astera returned, her exposed skin was dewy and it was clear she had used some of the light spray of rain to freshen up her skin after sleeping so close to the dirt for the night. She walked straight over, holding Henri's duffel open wide so he could wrestle the sleeping bags and other items back in there.

After everything was neatly packed, Astera brushed the dust off her hands and put them on her hips as she peered above them. "It's going to be harder to get into them than it was to jump out," she said, nose wrinkled thoughtfully as her eyes darted between the mech limbs, as if charting her course back into the cockpit.

"Little trick, grab the handles of the breast plate of your cockpit and activate the closing mechanism. It will lift you up into place and you can slide your legs in before strapping into the harness," he advised.

"Oh, good idea. I can manage that." Astera sounded confident in her ability to follow his plan. "What about you, will you be all right to scramble into Back Breaker?"

The position of the mechs meant that it had been easy enough for Henri to climb down, but getting back in would take a little more strength and flexibility. "I think so, if you keep Calliope right where she is."

With a grunt, Henri tossed his bag up onto Calliope. He climbed up her bent legs to get on her back as well. With another toss through the open hatch on Back Breaker's head, the bag was back where it belonged. Getting himself inside was trickier than Henri figured.

Henri jumped, catching the rim of the hatch with both hands. Reversing his grip to a chin-up grip, he swung his legs back and forth. Once he had enough momentum, he kicked his legs up over his head and into the hatch, pulling himself in in after. It wasn't graceful and he wound up dragging himself along his viewport, but finally, he was in.

"Made it," he called out the hatch. "Commence start-up procedures." He pulled himself into his seat and strapped in. Using a hand to brace himself during the process, he managed to get the five-point harness locked, and the straps tightened, so he could let the chair do the work of holding him in position. With his hands free, he began the process of bringing his Condor back to life.

While he worked, he heard the hatch of the Hummingbird cycle and lock into place. A few seconds later, the auxiliary power of the scout mech hummed on, and Astera's voice sounded through the comms, "Nicely done, Knuckle Duster. Good to see that even the old pilots still have it."

"If I didn't, I'd retire, Starfall. Standby for mission update," Henri responded as the power for his comm system switched back on. They usually ran on batteries for missions like this, so it would take a few minutes for the fusion cores to build up enough energy to start the reactors.

"I'm sending you new nav info. Once I have access to our scan data, that is," Henri added as he managed to get the map open again. He didn't need the vacuum protection seals on Baldalan so he stole some power from the life support systems to get the nav and maps working. As he traveled backward along the path he made in his mind, he saw he needed to alter it slightly to give Starfall the best route out of here. Once he was satisfied, he sent it to her nav computer.

"Starfall, is your nav online yet?" he asked as he rebalanced his battery systems. Already, he could feel the magnetic rings of the fusion core building energy. He had to get this ironed out before his core came online. If patrol mechs were nearby, they'd catch the energy signature, even inside the cave.

There was a split-second delay. "Nav computer back online ... data received. Loading it up now. Want me to wait until you get moving to activate my core?" Starfall asked, most likely hoping to save him from dealing with any extra exhaust head warming Back Breaker.

"No, yours won't take as long as mine. You should engage yours in ... eighty-two seconds. That way we should come online at the same time." Checking the time on his HUD, Henri hoped he did the math right. If she came online first, she'd be powered up, but trapped under his still immobile mech. That would give her nowhere to go if someone detected her signature.

"Copy that," Astera acknowledged.

The seconds ticked by and, right on cue, Calliope and Backbreaker's reactors flared to life.

"Did you want me to see if they're using any of their usual

comms channels, Knuckle Duster?" Astera asked as Henri started to back out his bent over mech from the tight space.

"No, I don't want to tip them off. Now that we are both online, let me clear the tunnel. Follow me out as soon as you can," he explained, even as he walked his legs back, reversing his crawl out of the tunnel. It took a lot of his skill, picturing the position of his limbs and the dimensions of the tunnel. One misplaced leg and he might bring the cave down, trapping Astera and her smaller mech inside.

Closing his eyes, he tried to feel the arms and legs of the mech as extensions of his own, twisting the joysticks in his hands, and pressing the pedals under his feet, in just the right way. Each time he moved, though, a slight rain of pebbles and dust fell on him. Even with his best intentions, it seemed the terrain protested his presence. Eventually, the soft grind of stone gave way to the sound of dirt against his frame. Pushing the controls forward, he brought the Condor to its feet, stepping to the side of the cave entrance to give Astera room to exit.

"When you clear the tunnel, you need to be on the move, following those coordinates on your nav as I have them laid out. Don't stop or turn to look for me. When you hit the third turn, break radio silence, and tell Mother Hen we're on our way back. Hopefully they are still at the primary location," Henri said, as he started to see the slender legs of Calliope working their way back out of the cave. It seemed even the smaller mech had no good place to turn around.

"That's an awful lot of *you* and very little *we*, Knuckle Duster." Astera's voice was sharp as she ducked Calliope's head at an angle, which must have left her hanging in the harness. Henri could only imagine how painful that must have been on her freshly healed body.

"I'll be covering your escape. I won't be far behind. You

keep your throttle pinned, understand?" he said, reaching down to help Calliope stand. The sooner she was vertical, the faster she could move. "I'm hoping you're loud and heavy enough to set their seismic sensors off."

"Copy that. I'll do my best to make some noise, Knuckle Duster. Hope your guns stay cool." Astera's comms cut just as she backed out of the cave and got the Hummingbird to its feet. The instant she was vertical, she pushed the mech into motion, the powerful engine singing as she throttled it to full power.

Henri stood and watched the Hummingbird set off the way they came. Switching on some audio filters in his headset, he worked to minimize the hum of the core under his seat. One thing he picked up last night was the cavern walls carried sound very effectively. If he could hear footfalls, it meant that mechs were on the other side. He switched his sensors off, realizing the high ferrite content of the crater walls made them useless anyway. Reaching up, he flipped down his manual crosshairs. It had been a while since he used manual sighting, but some skills never disappear.

As he waited, he heard the mech footfalls he was waiting for. "They're in pursuit," he muttered to himself, pushing his throttle up. Back Breaker set off at a slow pace, staying on the softer soil. Moving across the valley, he followed the wall as much as he could. With the way that the crater walls and ridges formed, Astera was well beyond the curve of this valley. Though he wasn't trying to keep a visual on her. He was keeping a visual on the gap ahead that they had used previously to get to cover.

As he figured, the pirates knew the terrain well. The pair of patrol mechs that must have caught Starfall on the seismic sensors cut through the gap ahead of him. Clearly, they were trying to get onto a path that would intercept with the fleeing mech. The pilots were suffering from tunnel vision and didn't think to look the other way when coming through the gap. Two cannon rounds to the back of the one on the right were enough to send it toppling, nose first, into the turf. With all the extra weight they were packing, as Astera explained to him, the usually sturdy Falcon-class mechs were top heavy.

The second mech whirled around in a panic, shooting with the two oversized lasers it was carrying. But Henri wasn't standing where he had been a moment ago, he was already circling the remaining mech. He rotated through his four smaller class lasers, peppering the pirate with shot after shot. The pirate didn't fire back, the guns were too hot from the first rounds and hadn't been given enough coolant to cycle with any meaningful rate.

Henri stalked the inexperienced pilot and punched through his viewport. The cockpit collapsed and the frame crumpled to the ground. "You better be moving, Starfall," he muttered as he set off along her path himself. He glanced at the radio, wondering if the canyons were keeping him from hearing her on the comms with Mother Hen. Hopefully they would be responding by now.

CHAPTER 28

ASTERA WAS JUST ABOUT to call to Mother Hen when she felt the rumbling explosions from farther back down the forest path. Her body instinctively tensed, and her first thought was that she needed to keep moving. Her second was that she hoped that was Henri firing on the enemy, not the other way around. She wished she could ask, but that was not an acceptable reason to break radio silence with her mission partner.

Nudging the radio button with her chin, Astera called, "Starfall to Mother Hen, come in, Mother Hen."

"M—ther—en he—" the reply transmission stuttered and skipped through the headset, and Astera swore under her breath. She hoped that she could get away with minimal radio signals, but there was still too much distance between her and the ship.

With a flurry of flicks and twists of her fingers, Astera added more juice to her radio power and rerouted the transmissions through the Latagarosh's antennae instead. All the while, she kept Calliope on the path the commander had laid out for her.

"Starfall to Mother Hen, can we try that again please?" Astera hoped her adjustments were enough. If they weren't, then she had just made herself more visible to the Voidstalkers for nothing.

"Mother Hen here, receiving loud and clear. Can we get a sit rep, Starfall?"

Astera grinned at Captain Darlek's familiar voice. "You've got two birds incoming. We're about an hour away. I'll call again when we're closer. Just needed to let you know to prep for departure." Astera gasped as Calliope's left foot slipped on some wet moss and she landed the right more firmly to stay balanced. "Mother Hen, can you confirm which location you will be at?"

"We will be on station at the backup location. If you don't think you can reach it, we can perform a hot pick-up at the primary location. However, we may need a bit more time to reach it safely," Captain Darlek explained.

"Understandable, Captain." Astera's face set with determination. It wasn't ideal, but they had no other choice. "I'm going to check nav and see what will work. Hold the line."

Keeping Calliope up and stable was usually second nature to Astera, but it was only her training that helped her maintain equilibrium when she had to split her attention between her navigation unit and the view of the path ahead. Her hands knew the locations of her controls by instinct though, so it was only a few seconds before the ping of the backup location flashed on her screen.

The alternate landing zone was south of the crater near a lake. There was a stable shelf of solid ground that gave a flat space for Mother Hen to land, and allowed unbroken sight lines to detect any approaching enemy mechs. It was a few extra kilometers away compared to the crater, but it should be achievable by Astera's calculation.

It was a good location; the real trouble would be defending their asses while they crossed the span between the trees and the ship. Still, it was better than being picked up by the Voidstalkers.

"Mother Hen, Starfall again. How much lead time do you need before we decide on final pick-up point?" Astera wasn't sure how things were going behind her, or what they would encounter ahead. She wanted to give herself, and Henri, as much flexibility as possible.

Suddenly, another voice cut through the chatter between Starfall and Mother Hen. "Mother Hen, Knuckle Duster, proceed to secondary location. Starfall, Knuckle Duster, disregard previous navigation path. Continue at speed along your valley. When you reach the third opening in the ridge wall to your right, turn and face to the east. When you do, I want you out of cover. Make it as obvious as you can," the commander ordered.

A breath of relief escaped from Astera at the sound of the commander's voice through the comms, even if his orders were ... odd. Still, she trusted him. He wouldn't leave her like a sitting duck if there wasn't a good reason for it. "Copy that, Knuckle Duster. Third opening to the right, face east. Do I need to draw attention, or just stand there looking pretty?"

"Your mech running should draw enough attention. Be ready to move from that position when I say. Do not move until I do, though, understand?" the commander replied.

Astera thought, *he must be bouncing his signal off the ship's antennas in orbit, too. For all his talk of remaining radio silent, putting out comms of that strength must be part of his plan.*

"Copy," Astera said. Once more, she didn't truly know the point of the order, yet she intended to follow it. On another day, she might have joked about the semantics, but this wasn't one of those breezy, boring missions where that kind of thing would fly. She needed the commander to know she would do as he asked, and they both needed to concentrate.

Rather than take the turn to the left and head south to the primary landing zone nav point, Astera's new route followed the notch she was in. That path slowly turned north, following a now dry river bed. There was evidence of all the different tracks that water took through the area. Some erosion gaps were evident in the crater ridge walls. The first two she passed were too small for a mech, even a Humming-bird. The third was easily thirteen meters across. With no trees or rocks, it was a very exposed gap.

The stones to Astera's left rang with the approaching foot falls of two more patrol mechs. Like before, it was hard to tell how far away they were. There were so many echoes in the area, and she wasn't sure if the mechs would take seconds, or hours, to show.

It turned out that Astera didn't have long to wait.

An Eagle-like mech strode down the slope from the opening to the north, carrying a missile pod in place of each of its arms. Normally, a weapon system like that would be on a bigger mech like a Condor, or a Roc, and Astera could see the sway in the machine as it shifted weight from one leg to another. Behind it was a real mongrel of a mech. Nothing on it seemed to match, or fit, where it was supposed to.

The mechs didn't turn towards Calliope right away. With her standing still, her signature on the seismic sensors must have been pretty minimal. With hands hovering over her controls, all she could do was watch them linger just over eighty-nine meters away, according to her targeting screen. Then the torsos started to twist, the pilots probably making a visual scan. Sure enough, as they turned, the legs of both mechs shifted under their chassis, squaring up to face her.

That kind of move was meant to brace the mech for firing. All her instincts screamed at her to find cover. Astera's fingers drummed against her control sticks as her heart thundered in her chest.

"Starfall, on my mark, sidestep south. Disengage and move at flank speed to secondary location," the commander ordered. Then, a split second later, "Execute."

That final word meant she was to do as he said without wasting time with a radio acknowledgement. Astera yanked the controls to make Calliope shift to the right. The light of the twin suns that had been behind her now shone directly on the windshields of the two mechs in the dip below. Just before she turned to flee, Back Breaker emerged from a wooded notch to the south, firing off his cannons at the temporarily blinded pilots.

As much as Astera wanted to stay and watch the commander's plan unfold fully, she had been given an order. She followed the route to the secondary location. It was a relatively easy run for Calliope, the softer ground finally cushioning the footfalls and making the escape less physically jarring on her joints.

Off in the distance, Astera caught sight of Mother Hen. She was so glad to see the ship. Almost as glad as she was on her previous mission. "Knuckle Duster, visual contact with Mother Hen confirmed. What's your status?"

The rumbles and rapid-fire snaps of weapons still thundered behind her.

There was no response to her radio call. Even as she watched Mother Hen landing across the way, she didn't hear anything from the commander.

Astera frowned but maintained her heading. She had to count to ten out loud to stop herself from pestering the commander too soon. "Knuckle Duster, Starfall. I repeat: what's your status?"

Again, the radio was stubbornly silent.

As Astera cleared the area and entered the space between the lake and the crater, a great explosion rattled the world around her. The vibration rung through the ground and reverberated up through Calliope's feet and into her spine.

A cry burst from Astera at the sheer impact of the explosion. Calliope stumbled to a halt on the still-shaking ground as Astera whipped her mech's torso around. "Henri?" she yelled into the comms. "Void, Henri, answer me!"

"Don't use names on the comms, Starfall. Maintain operational security," Captain Darlek scolded. "Mother Hen is on station, awaiting pick up." The dropship captain was her usual calm, steady self, despite the fireworks.

"Knuckle Duster, what's your status?" Astera called again, barely restraining the urge to tell the captain to go Void herself. Every single part of Astera's body was light and shaky as she waited for Henri's response. There had to be one. He had to be okay.

"Starfall, keep moving," Darlek barked.

There was still no response from Henri.

"No. I'm going back." Astera turned Calliope's torso into position and kicked her off into a run, looping around and adjusting her heading for where she saw Henri last.

"Starfall, stand down. Your orders are to get out of the area. We will remain on station, but we are not to engage in a rescue mission," Captain Darlek reminded her.

"If we all sit on our asses, there may not be anything left to wait for," Astera argued, desperately scanning the view in front of her for any signs of life, or movement, as she retraced her steps.

"If that's the case, then all the more reason for you to get on board," the captain countered, deadpan. "He wouldn't want you throwing yourself away on a fool's errand, Starfall."

Calliope skidded to a stop before Astera even realized she'd pulled back on the controls. Dust billowed around the mech. "Fuck," Astera panted. Her eyes burned and her throat was so tight she could scarcely breathe.

"Fuck, fuck, fuck." Astera whipped Calliope back around and high-tailed it for Mother Hen. The closer she got, the more she hated herself, and the blurrier her vision became. By the time she ran the mech up the ramp and into the loading bay she was on auto-pilot.

The silence inside the bay was deafening. Nothing left for her to do as the loading frame clamped onto Calliope and held her in place.

Then, the radio crackled to life.

"...ther—Hen, ...—kle Du—er, ... —ute to L—" The signal was so weak that the radio could only pick up every other word. "—eady for —ake—off. Mul—acts inbou—." Despite how broken the transmission was, Astera knew Henri's voice when she heard it.

Relief washed over Astera, bringing her back to the present moment with all the shock of a bucket of ice water being dumped over her head. "Henri," she gasped to herself as she pushed the release on the breastplate of her mech. As the hatch lifted, she watched the horizon and sagged with relief as Back Breaker appeared in the distance.

"Knuckle Duster, Mother Hen. Transmission is spotty. Awaiting your arrival. Covering your retreat with ship's weapons. Readying for take off," Captain Darlek radioed, keeping her language simple to make it easier for Henri to understand if reception was choppy on his end, too.

Watching with bated breath, Astera tracked each and every one of Back Breaker's staggered steps towards the ship.

When the mech was halfway across the flat, two of the Voidstalker mongrel machines appeared, damaged and smoking, in the distance. Even from where she was perched in the loading bay, Astera could see the mongrel's weapons cycling into place, ready to fire some longer-range artillery at the fleeing Condor.

"Come on, Henri ... come on," Astera muttered, grasping the edges of Calliope's cockpit, her knuckles white with the strength of her anticipation.

One of the mechs fired, but Back Breaker managed to dart off to the side at the last moment. Another shot followed, and then another. The commander's ability to dance out of range diminished with each round, his Condor not quite built for such athletics. Just as one of the missiles streaked by, so close Astera swore he would be hit, Mother Hen shook as the crew opened fire with their own weapons.

Astera collapsed against the backrest as the mechs were finally in range of the dropship's artillery. It was a matter of seconds before the two pursuing crafts were blown to pieces, flaming debris flying into the sky in a sick tableau of death and destruction.

Mother Hen stopped firing when it was clear there was no current danger, and Back Breaker staggered up the ramp. The dropship engines roared as the ramp shut after the Condor alighted, and Astera's own hands flew to the straps of her harness as the battered frame of Henri's mech was clamped into place.

"Henri," Astera called out, her voice barely carrying over the cacophony of engines around them. "Henri, are you okay? Do you need medical?"

Instead of taking the time to climb out of Calliope, Astera grabbed the edge of her cockpit and flung herself over, skimming her hands down the hot panels of the mech to slow her fall. Her feet slammed onto the metal flooring with a jarring impact, but she didn't care as she ran towards Back Breaker.

The hatch popped as the clamps locked the heavy mech into place. Henri scrambled out the top of his mech. "Follow me, Astera. We gotta get out of here." He worked his way to the ladder on the side of Back Breaker's loading frame. "I think they are sending their entire remaining contingent and all the mechs from their outlying bases after us," he announced as he hit the deck. He didn't seem to notice, or care about, the bleeding cut just below his right eye. From Astera's experience, she assumed he got it from his headset getting slammed into the side of his face. He was too determined to lead the way from the hatch to the flight deck to even stop for a gauze pad.

She frowned as she fell into step beside him. "That's concerning ..."

"I'm not sure why the Latagarosh didn't inform us. Surely the Ops room could detect what was going on in the area," Henri said, sounding annoyed at the crew in orbit.

Mother Hen would be close to out of atmosphere by the time any of the Voidstalker's mechs got in place to attack the Triple C. Her main concern in that moment was making sure that Henri was okay. Back Breaker took a lot of big hits, judging by the charred damage on the frame and the coolant she saw dripping down the panels. That had to have hurt.

Henri didn't seem bothered by the shocks of those hits. Either the weight and size of the heavier Condor absorbed them better, or years of pilot abuse in the field had numbed him to it. Either way, he strode with purpose to the cockpit. "If not for that mech's core going critical and igniting all its hydrogen, I'd be able to ask them myself. Shockwave blew off my antenna, or the important bits at least," Henri grumbled as he neared the door.

The commander launched into action the moment the cockpit door cycled open. "Captain, raise the Latagarosh. I need an update from the Ops room and an explanation as to why they maintained radio silence when we broke ours," he demanded as he walked over. Even as he did, he looked out the front viewport of the dropship as it lifted off the surface of the pirate-infested planet.

Captain Darlek, who had been shocked, at first, to see Henri and Astera enter her domain, started following orders the moment they were delivered. The fingers of her left hand danced over her comms panel as she pulled over the control column with her right to get the best angle for planet exit. "Mother Hen to Nest. Exiting Baldalan's atmosphere in under five minutes. Requesting situation report, over."

As they waited for a reply, Astera stood beside Henri and caught her breath. She could already feel the aching pull in her limbs as the adrenaline fled her system. She focused on keeping her breath slow and steady to help stem the shakes that threatened to take over her limbs, and she glanced to the side, once more to confirm that Henri was all right. He seemed to be as he finally opened the medkit on the wall and held a bandage to his cheek.

"Mother Hen, apologies for the delay. We've got a situation here. A few minutes ago, a well-armed jumpship arrived via FTL drive into the sector. Currently prepping the Latagarosh to jump. Just waiting on your arrival, over," Major La Plaz said, sounding unusually harried.

Reaching for the comms console beside him, Henri cut in. "Nest, under what authority are they claiming the planet? Who do they represent?"

Astera's breath caught in her throat, and a new sense of sheer panic rocketed through her system. She reached out, grasping the back of the empty jump seat beside her to stop herself from falling.

Not him, she silently begged the Void, *please, not him.*

She had no doubt that the Voidstalkers would seek retribution for what went down on Baldalan, she just didn't think they would be moving on it this quickly.

"Knuckle Duster, Nest. It's Samson's Heavy Brigade. Claim they have a letter of marque from the Kolos Admiralty. Looks like they're here to clean up the pirate nest you just disturbed," La Plaz relayed.

Astera let out the breath she was holding. It was another mercenary outfit. Thank the Void, they still had time. "We need to get out of this system, Commander. The Voidstalkers won't let this go," she whispered. Her head was spinning from all the emotional ups and downs over the past forty-eight hours, but she was still with it enough to know that the trouble was not yet over.

CHAPTER 29

HENRI GLANCED over his shoulder at Astera's whispered warning. She ran a shaking hand over her messy, braided pink hair, and her skin was several shades paler than it had been earlier that day in the cave.

He weighed his options carefully before speaking. "Nest, have you offered to share our intelligence with them? They must know this isn't a normal pirate operation they are going to dig out of this planet. We're dealing with Voidstalkers here."

They still had about fifteen minutes before arriving back to the Latagarosh, but the captain already had the new jump-ship on Mother Hen's scanners. Henri leaned forward to see what sort of outfit they were. At first glance, it was clear they did well for themselves. Their ship was probably in the next size category up from the Latagarosh. It appeared to have more living space on board, but it was unclear how big a Mech Bay they supported. With a name like the "Heavy Brigade," it was reasonable to assume they favored the upper end of the infantry frames and the spearhead class as well.

"Knuckle Duster, we offered. They are happy to take the

information, but they insisted on handling this on their own. They said that the Admiralty wouldn't honor any assistance we provided them with. Figured we were best off prepping to depart. Would you like me to continue readying for departure?" La Plaz asked.

Henri rubbed a hand over the stubble that had grown in since they left earlier in the day. "Send them all our sensor data and nav markers. Be ready to get underway when Mother Hen returns." He didn't like it, but there was no reason for the Triple C to hang around. Another company had shown up with a legitimate contract to engage the planet below. Standard etiquette among mercenary companies dictated that it was time for the Triple C to leave the system.

"Copy that Knuckle Duster. We'll be ready to leave when Mother Hen locks down. Nest, out."

With that sorted, Henri looked over at Astera. The news of a new ship rattled her more than it should have. Even if her ex-husband was on one of those ships, it would mean little to them. They would be out of the area before the Voidstalkers had registered that there was a change of guard, and there was no way for them to know Astera had been anywhere near the drama. "Starfall, strap in." He gestured to the empty seats towards the back of the cockpit, away from the main sensors. He rested a hand on her shoulder. "We'll be out of here soon, just hang tight."

As Astera moved to comply, Henri settled himself into one of the spare seats beside Darlek and her second in command, wanting to be front and center if something changed.

Thankfully, his precaution wasn't tested. This new mercenary company didn't move to bar Mother Hen on its return trajectory to the Latagarosh. Still, something ate at him. Something about this company's arrival. Tapping the comms panel, he reconnected with the Ops Room.

"Nest, can you pass along to the commander of the other company, Samson, I'm guessing, that I want to talk with them once I'm back on board?" Henri asked, trying to remember his transport schedule of the nearest warpship hub. He made a mental note to check later, to see when this new company would have been given their orders.

There was a delay, and then a disgruntled sounding La Plaz replied, "Knuckle Duster, that's a negative from the Command of SHB. They said they are giving us five minutes grace once Mother Hen is back before they will consider us encroaching on a duly bonded contract."

Henri rolled his eyes. Only the pettiest companies would file a grievance for double booking with the Mercenary Company Arbitration Committee. They often attempted to solve disputes between companies though, but rarely had any ability to enforce their decisions. The best they could do was cap the rating on your company seal. That was sometimes enough to lower your rates or exclude you from certain jobs, but it was more an exercise of revenge and making people waste time and resources on unnecessary paperwork. With a sigh, he hit the button. "Then you better start warming the engines for our FTL jump, Nest. We are entering the corridor for our docking."

Henri sat back and buckled his own seatbelt. He turned things over to Captain Darlek to bring Mother Hen in for a landing. Soon enough, he'd feel the pull of Latagarosh's gravity as the spin took over. Shaking his head, Henri knew he wasn't going to be able to let go of his questions about what happened here for a while. Nothing ate at him more than being a pawn in a bigger game he couldn't play.

The next twenty minutes was business as usual for

Mother Hen docking with the jumpship. The engineers went to work offloading the mechs, the pilots went for a post-flight beer, and Henri led Astera towards the Command deck for their debrief with La Plaz and the other officers.

Just as they walked past the entry to the Med Bay, the doors slid open and Annalise rushed out, holding her medical scanner. She made straight for Henri, concern on her face.

"I'm fine." His voice was sharper than intended as he waved her away. She narrowed her eyes as she saw the bandage on his cheek, and then turned her attention to Astera. "Neither of us require attention. We'll check in after debriefing."

Henry stepped around Annalise and kept walking. He heard Astera's footsteps echoing after him, so he didn't need to turn around to know she was following.

On the trip to the Command Deck, Henri got lost in his own thoughts. He went right back to the moment the Kolos Admirality gave them the ill-fated contract and worked his way forward from there. Large chunks of information and threads of inconsistency fell into place slowly, and he became unshakeably certain that there was something more sinister going on. The intersection of the Kolos Admiralty and the Voidstalker's new base, stolen turret aside, was too convenient to ignore. Was the Admiralty a double-crossed victim or a silent partner in all this?

As Henri reached the Command Deck, he realized he hadn't felt the telltale lurch of the Latagrosh getting underway yet. Opening the doors to the Ops section, he looked at Major La Plaz. "Why are we still in orbit? The SHB is probably drafting their complaint as we speak."

"You didn't give us a heading, boss," the major reminded him.

Sighing and rubbing his forehead, Henri realized he'd

been too deep in his thoughts to think of that on the way back to the ship. "Right, of course," he began his answer. To be honest, he hadn't given it any thought, but there was only one place to go when a company was between jobs. "Plot course for the nearest warp hub and check their schedule for the shortest route to Grendina Station. Let's get back to civilization for a while."

The major's face lit up. "Right away, Commander. The debriefing room is ready for you; I'll join you once I've spoken with the flight crew," he said, turning to the panel behind him.

Henri thanked La Plaz and then led Astera down the hall towards the room where the officers were waiting for them.

"We're really going to Grendina Station?" Astera asked as she hustled to catch up with his longer strides.

Henri paused in the corridor and turned to face her, smiling at the relief on her face. He understood the expression. Grendina was the unofficial hub of merc life. It sat one system away from three of the biggest players in galactic politics: the Kolos Admiralty, the Regents of Posnovum, and The Eclipse. The system itself boasted three habitable planets that screamed R&R locations. It was the perfect place for pilots, engineers, and medics to unwind while the company leaders found contracts and did other business.

Henri nodded. "Yes, but only so long as it takes us to find another job and a new scout pilot." It was tough to say, but it was the truth. The Triple C was down a pilot and Henri had to get them back to full strength.

Her face grew pensive once more and she nodded as she looked away. "Makes sense." She fell silent again.

"Yeah," Henri said, cursing himself for how casually he had put that. "But, when we get there, you can finally soak in an ocean rather than a makeshift tub," he added, trying to soften the moment.

Her eyes widened and her cheeks flushed.

He liked it when she blushed.

"You ... you knew?"

Henri chuckled. "There's very little that happens among the pilots that doesn't get back to me somehow. I may not have heard it directly, but I can put two and two together when someone pulls a container that big from the storage bay and your entire bonus water ration disappears."

"Void ...." Astera's head fell into her hands and she scrubbed at her face, smearing sweat and dirt over her smooth skin. "What a mess," she whispered so softly Henri didn't think he was supposed to hear it.

Henri slid an arm around her shoulders. "Sorry, I guess I didn't realize how badly things were going for you. I know you don't want to hear this from your superior officer, but is it worth salvaging at this point?" he asked.

"Are you asking as my superior officer, or as Henri?" She peered up at him, her eyes sparkling in the harsh light of the ship.

"After our talk, I'm not sure those are different people. But let's say it's Henri talking, does that change how you'd answer?"

"If you were just asking as my CO, I'd say it doesn't matter, because it won't impact my job performance. As Henri? My answer is yes, it may be worth salvaging ... but I'm not going to try. That's not what I want anymore."

"What do you want?" Henri asked, curious about the decision she'd made since their talk.

Astera let out a soft breath, ruffling whisps of dark brown and pink hair that had fallen from her braid during their mission. Henri had the inexplicable urge to reach out and tuck them aside for her as she scanned his charred and torn flight suit. Concern tugged at her features, but it was soon replaced by something else. She swallowed, and then her lips parted, "I spent years trying to get by, to survive all by myself. Now I'm out, and I know there are people who might accept all of me … I want more. I want—"

"Knuckle Duster, Starfall, the debriefing room is ready for you." La Plaz strode towards them and Henri snapped out of the moment, his entire body frozen in anticipation of what Astera was about to say. His intelligence officer fixed him with a rather pointed glare as he passed them and entered the debriefing room.

Not for the first time, Henri wanted to smack La Plaz across the back of his smug head. Reluctantly, he dislodged his arm from around Astera's shoulders and offered her his hand. She took it with a smile. He returned it with one of his own as he felt the tell-tale calluses on her palm and fingers that all seasoned mech pilots had.

They followed La Plaz the rest of the way down the hall and Henri reached up to activate the door panel. As he did, he realized he hadn't let Astera's hand go once they started walking. He looked down at where he was still holding it, and then up into Astera's eyes. Something sizzled between them, and he had to force himself to release her before pushing through into the debriefing room.

The post-mission debriefing always felt longer than it actually took. Having to sit and recount your activities for the report that accompanied every mission was drudgery, but it had to be done. While they hadn't been planet-side for any client, they had to justify the expenses on their books. It was all part of the financial analysis that happened every year or so that would go into the company's overall rating. As much as he hated to relive what happened below, Henri put himself through it. After what happened at the door, he needed the time to think about what such an unconscious gesture meant.

He kept looking over at Astera and it wasn't to listen to her side of the report. Something about her looked different now, but he couldn't put his finger on it.

As the debrief dragged on, Henri felt the tug of the ship jumping to faster-than-light speed to exit the system. It would be a few hours to leave and then a few days to the nearest warp hub. He chuckled at the notion that this debrief would still be happening by the time they got there.

"Something you want to add, Commander?" the major asked.

"No, I just had a funny thought. I didn't mean to interrupt," he said with a subtle smile to Astera.

She raised an eyebrow at him, a small smile tugging at her own lips as La Plaz's reprimand broke the monotony. In all fairness, she had been doing an admirable job reporting the details of the mission from her perspective. She was clear, concise, and seemed to have a good memory for the finer details. However, as the briefing moved towards the discovery that they were contending with the Voidstalkers, Henri understood her mannerisms well enough now to know that the increased professionalism was just a clever mask for detachment.

After Astera got to the part where they found the cave, Henri took over, explaining to the team how they had wedged their way into the tight space, and then found their way out a few hours before nightfall. For some reason, it felt wrong skipping over the details of what happened in that cave. The close quarters and risky situation had created a level of intimacy that he hadn't shared with a copilot since ... well, Henri couldn't remember when. However, he knew those weren't the kinds of things the mission debrief was trying to capture, but he felt like he may need to note some of it down in his personal log later, to help him make sense of it all.

Henri and Astera took turns explaining their actions during the escape as La Plaz wound through the sensor data that the Ops Team was able to capture from the Latagarosh. While Henri and Astera had to be radio silent during the mission, the Ops Team wasn't idle. At each time stamp, Henri had to explain his positioning and movement, while Astera added the orders she received and the actions she took. This section seemed to go on even longer than the preceding portion even though it was shorter, and faster, when they were actually down on the planet. It was difficult as every pilot hated to have their actions torn apart by the intelligence officer.

As the debrief moved to the evacuation section, La Plaz showed the track followed by both mechs. As he did, he turned to the commander. "Now, you turned and engaged with the pirate mech designated P-five here. Why did you not proceed at flank speed to the secondary location?"

"In my estimation, it presented a threat to Mother Hen. It was carrying long-range, guided missiles that could fire indirectly on the dropship," he explained. "Luckily for me, they didn't armor the ammunition for the system very well, so it only took a couple of shots to set off the ammo and destroy the mech. Unfortunately, the subsequent explosion of so many missiles shredded my communication antenna."

Looking across, he saw Astera shift in her seat and turn away from the wireframe map La Plaz was using to mark the mission details. Her foot started tapping against the ground in that nervous tic he had seen the previous night.

La Plaz and the others didn't seem to notice, though, as he pressed further. "And that is why you attempted to raise the commander several times after seeing the explosion plume, Starfall?" he asked, leveling a look at her.

Even Henri could see that he was setting her up for something with that question. Henri frowned, not liking the way his old friend was looking at Astera, or the way he was coiled like a snake about to strike. He wasn't sure what had happened when his comms were down, but surely it couldn't be so bad.

"I tried to reestablish communication with the commander, yes," Astera said, looking at everything but La Plaz and Henri.

"And you were unsuccessful in doing so?" La Plaz asked, but he didn't bother to wait for her answer. Steamrolling right over any attempt at an explanation, he added, "Which begs the question, why did you think your attempts would be improved by breaking comms protocol?"

La Plaz tapped something on the console, and a static filled the room. A moment later, a recording of Astera's voice broke through the buzz.

"Henri? Void, Henri, answer me!"

Henri gaped across at Astera. He'd never heard her so scared, especially on a mission. Not even when she was trying to escape Baldalan the first time. Not even when she realized they were dealing with the Voidstalkers. He didn't speak for a moment, too stunned by what he was hearing to even know what to say.

The major, however, did not have the same problem. "You should know that Captain Darlek has recommended you be placed on probation for this violation, and I am inclined to agree with her assessment. After all, is it not true that you disregarded her initial order to board Mother Hen? That you ran back toward the mission area despite standing orders to the contrary?" La Plaz pushed.

"That's enough," Henri barked, rising to his feet. "We're all on the same side here, Major. Everyone is home safe. We're not doing this witch hunt over a simple mistake under fire. In fact, everybody out. You have enough to start your reports," the commander ordered, looking around the room.

Everyone froze, most likely surprised by Henri's sudden outburst. "Now," he yelled. The Ops crew jumped up and shuffled out. La Plaz strode over as Astera rose from her seat, shell-shocked.

"Commander, this isn't a witch hunt. Darlek is simply following protocol," he said in a tone that grated at Henri. The way La Plaz spoke to Henri made him think that the major believed he was being irrational.

"Then you wait, you talk to me about it, and you process the probation recommendation if I give you permission. You do not bring it up during the debrief. Dismissed, Major." Henri was sure to dismiss him formally so the major knew not to add another word before he left.

La Plaz's face set hard at the obvious dismissal, and he cast Astera a concerned glance before he turned and strode from the room. He waved an angry hand at the Command team members who were staring at the doorway to the briefing room with curiosity, and they scattered back to their stations.

"I'm sorry, I should leave," Astera stammered, making straight for the door, not looking at Henri.

"Astera, stop. Please stay," Henri said, his voice a little calmer, a little softer. "What happened out there? I've never heard you lose it like that before."

She stopped as he asked, but her back was still to him. Her shoulders shook as she let out a long, slow breath. "When you didn't make contact, I thought they'd killed you," she said, turning her face just enough so that he could see her profile, see the way her lips trembled.

"But you know what I wanted you to do if that happened. That's why we have standing orders," Henri said, coming around the table to face her. "You know how important it is to get someone back from the mission, especially with firsthand information."

"I couldn't just leave if there was a chance you were alive on the planet." Astera looked up at him, a hint of the emotion that he'd heard in the recording was still in her eyes. "I needed to see if there was something I could do to help, to get you back. I couldn't just leave you there, after— after—" She stopped, shaking her head ever so slightly.

"Hey, hey, hey ..." Henri stepped closer, taking Astera in his arms in a supportive embrace. "I know. I know losing Sleeves still hurts. But you can't let that rob you of your good sense," he said, drawing her into his chest. With the height difference, her head came up to the base of his chin. Rubbing her back, Henri added. "But it's okay, because I'm still here."

"It wasn't Sleeves I was thinking about, Henri," Astera whispered, pulling her head back just enough so that she could look up at him, her dark eyes wavering with emotion. "It was you."

Henri peered down into those eyes and a completely different woman was looking back at him. For the first time, it felt like he was meeting Astera. Not the persona put on to make it in a mercenary company or the scared woman that hoped she wasn't going to be fired. He saw the real Astera and it was not what he expected to see. It was such a change that his rational mind took a back seat for a moment and his impulsive side showed him what he actually needed. Leaning down, he brought his lips to hers in a soft, explorative kiss.

Initially, Astera tensed in his arms, and Henri worried he had read the situation wrong, but then, with a soft moan, she melted against him. She wrapped her warm arms around his shoulders and deepened the kiss.

Henri reciprocated, groaning in surprise. He slid his hands to her waist and held onto her, enjoying how his sense of touch gave him a much better understanding of her figure than the view of her in her jumpsuit had. He leaned down to make the angle easier, and her hands moved to the back of his neck, fingertips brushing the sensitive skin there before running over his hair.

Astera did not seem inclined to end the kiss, and Henri wasn't about to stop something that felt so damn good. He pushed his hands around her waist and rested them on the small of her back. Astera's breath caught in the kiss, and Henri smiled as he moved his lips from hers, over her cheek, and found her neck. He didn't want to muffle any of the sounds she was making with his own mouth anymore, especially not as he moved his hands lower and cupped her ass.

"Yes," Astera gasped.

That single word was enough to cause Henri to press her into the wall of the debriefing room. As he did, the display built into it registered the pressure and assumed it was meant to be switched on. The video feed of the company's last contract payment meeting started playing immediately. Henri's hand snapped out to stop the video. Looking down into Astera's eyes, he couldn't help a laugh at how silly the moment was. They were both breathing heavily, still swept up in the after-effects of the kiss.

"Not here," he said, shaking his head. Then, he took a risk. "My quarters?"

She licked her lips as she considered it.

Void, he didn't realize how much he wanted her. He looked at her lower lip, restraining the urge to kiss her again.

Finally, Astera whispered, "Yes, please."

Relieved and more than a little eager, Henri stole another peck before stepping back. He took her hand, about to lead her to his room, when his senses kicked in. "Shit, La Plaz is probably still out there." He glanced back at Astera. "You need to pretend like we had a long talk about your behavior," he said, figuring they needed a cover story to get off the administrative deck without arousing suspicion. "Follow my lead."

Turning to the door, he activated the pad beside it to get it to slide open. "Think about what I said. I'll deal with the Major; don't worry," Henri pointedly raised his voice and put a firm edge to it.

"Copy that, Commander." Astera's cheeks were still flushed from their kiss, but some of the hair that had fallen loose from her braid shifted to cover her face as she hung her head and stepped past him. "I'm sorry. I won't mess up like that again." She started walking away, making a beeline for the door.

"Good, see that you don't ..." Henri stepped out of the room and walked the length of the Ops wing with purpose, not making eye contact with anyone. Taking the turn near the end, he passed through the door nearest the walkway that would take him back to his quarters.

One of the benefits of rank was the short walk to the important parts of the ship. It only took a minute or two before he was back in the commander's suite. As soon as the door to his room shut behind him, he started shedding his flight suit, ready to be out of it after so long in his mech. Throwing on some casual clothes, he poured himself a drink from his bar before sinking onto his couch, waiting for the chime of his door, and wondering if Astera would change her mind.

CHAPTER 30

ASTERA KNEW, at least in theory, where the commander's quarters were. Like most top dog suites, it was right near the bridge, just in case there was an emergency at some unsavory hour. However, she had never had much of a reason to venture through the corridors surrounding the bridge before, apart from briefings and debriefings. Furthermore, she had certainly never walked the corridors surrounding the bridge with her head still spinning from kissing the commander. Although *kissing* felt like an understatement of what just occurred between them, especially when she could still vividly recall the warmth of his hands on her body from just moments ago, and the sting of the cold wall panel against her back as he pressed her to it.

When Astera reached Henri's door, she paused, hand raised and ready to knock as she realized what she was doing. The mission had shown her an entirely different side to the commander of the Triple C. One she liked. One she wanted to get to know more about. The way he had kissed her told her that he probably felt the same way. Still, there was part of her that was convinced it was too dangerous. Like she was still hiding. He knew almost everything there was to know, but those last little, tightly held pieces of truth ate at her. Henri had shown her repeatedly over the past few days that all he wanted to do was help keep her safe, but ... Astera's trust had been broken so many times, and the stakes were painfully high this time.

Stuck in a state of utter indecision, Astera frowned. Should she turn and walk away now, before it was too late? Or had she already passed that threshold? She was about to take a step back from the door when it cycled open, and Henri stood on the other side.

He smiled down at her. "Hey."

Insides returning to a nervous jelly state, Astera just smiled back. Any misgivings she had were burned away by the look in his eyes. "Hey," she replied, fingers curling back against her palm as she let her hand drop. She rubbed her arm as she looked him up and down, noting that he had changed into something more comfortable.

Henri didn't speak. He merely stepped back from the door to let her in. She walked in, and he gestured to the collection of bottles by the window in his room. "If you like, you can make yourself a drink and join me on the couch for a bit."

Once the door was shut, Henri moved to the couch and sank down, picking up a shallow glass that was set on a shelf beside it and taking a sip of the amber liquid as he got settled.

"Thanks." Astera was genuinely grateful for the chance to breathe and collect herself as she went to the bar and looked at the bottles. She noticed a carafe of water, and decided it would be safest to pour herself a glass of that. "You know, I've spent the last year and a half trying to avoid getting on your radar ... now I don't want to be anywhere else." She slowly turned to face him, cradling her glass in her hands.

Henri rose from the couch and crossed the room. He

gently took the glass from her hands and set it on the counter beside her. "You're welcome here anytime," he said softly as he slid a finger under her chin. Lifting it up, he pressed his lips to hers.

Even though ten minutes and many words had passed since their last kiss, it was easy to sink right back into where they had left off. It was a heady rush to feel Henri's arm wrap around her waist as he lifted her up into the kiss, and held her body against his. She deepened the kiss, and couldn't believe there was even a moment where she considered not knocking on his door.

Despite the intoxicating taste of him, and how good it felt to be in his arms, Astera eventually rested her palms against his chest and pulled away from the kiss. They had been on Baldalan, sweating in their mechs, for far too long for her to be comfortable with him exploring more than just her lips. She needed to remedy that. "So tell me, Henri," she whispered, "does the commander get a decent water ration? Or should I donate some of mine so we can get cleaned up together?"

Henri smiled and her heart skipped a beat. "One of the perks of command, Starfall. You get to set the rationing schedule," he teased, stealing a kiss. "I could use some help washing two days of humidity out of my back, though."

Astera chuckled softly. "Henri, I'm not sure that high-lighting how dirty you are is the best way to pick me up," she said, voice light with teasing as she scrunched her nose. "You're lucky I'm just as dirty, otherwise it might not have worked." She looked from his eyes to his lips but stepped back to stop herself from kissing him again.

Henri smiled and let her step back. Catching her hand with his, he led her through his suite to his bathroom. It was spacious, given they were on a ship, and the shower stall looked like it could comfortably fit the two of them.

Drawing her into his arms as the bathroom door shut behind them, Henri asked, "Need a hand getting out of this?"

"Yes," Astera lied.

She didn't *need* a hand, but she *wanted* one.

Without hesitation, Henri unzipped her flight suit to her hips and pushed it off her shoulders. Her skin felt like it was on fire as his palms slipped beneath her tank and skimmed over her stomach to push the top higher. Astera waited until it was up high enough to tug her arms out and let him pull it over her head.

As soon as it was off, Henri curled his frame around her, bringing his lips to her neck as his hands drifted down into the back of her pants. He kneaded her ass as he lifted her up against him, kissing and sucking softly at the curve of her neck.

Astera moaned and tilted her face to the side to give him easier access to her skin. She automatically reached up to cup the back of his head and hold him to her. With her free hand, she tugged at the hem of his shirt, desperately wanting to feel his bare skin against hers.

Henri reacted by scooping Astera up off the floor. He sat her on the counter by his sink as he stepped back. With the space that gave, he took her hands and put them on his hips. Smiling down at her, he seemed to pause, giving her time to slip his shirt off as she desired.

Astera smiled at the gesture, then grabbed his shirt and pulled it up and off between eager kisses. She dropped the t-shirt on the floor beside her tank and then rested her hands on his shoulders, pulling him back to her for a longer kiss as she let her hands slip down his chest, palms tingling at the heat of his skin. She felt the remnants of over a decade of work as a mech pilot on his skin. A few burn scars and healed abrasions were among the highlights of her hands' tour of his chest. It was also clear that time was starting to catch up with him; there was a slight pull to his skin, even over the hardness of his muscles, and despite all the work he must have done to keep in fighting shape.

Astera didn't mind the wear and tear. If anything, they were the hallmark of a life of adventure and survival. Each scar would have a story, and part of her hoped she would get to learn some of them.

"Well, this explains the acrobatics in the cave," she muttered between kisses as she moved her lips to his neck and ran her hands down his strong arms, to guide them around her waist.

"Never know when I might have to get back out there." He lifted her off the counter and set her back down on her feet. His big hands moved around her hips to find the zip at the front of her flight suit. He undid it and pulled it open with ease before sliding his hands over the curve of her ass again to help it over the swell of her hips. The loose clothing hit the deck with a thunk, as he held her hands to help step out of the clothing puddle and her boots all at once.

She squeezed Henri's hands as she regained her balance, and then reached for the waistband of his pants. She hesitated as she looked up at him, wanting to make sure it was okay.

Instead of answering with words, he nodded and stepped out of his boots. He didn't speak as she worked the catch and peeled his fly open. Henri leaned in, stealing a kiss, and slipping his hands under the back of her less than fashionable, but functional, binding bra. It might not be comfortable, but any pilot with breasts wouldn't go without one in a mech, as the shaking could be agony.

Figuring that Henri knew his way around bras well enough, Astera left him to it as she ran her hands along the lines of his back, and let her lips explore his neck. He continued to explore too, and it gave her the confidence to let her hands drift even lower to run over his ass. Instinctively, she pulled his hips closer to hers and she moaned softly against his neck.

Henri peeled her bra up and up. Astera lifted her arms as soon as she needed to for him to slip it off, but she looped them back around his shoulders as she leaned back in to kiss the other side of his neck without delay. It was a relief to be free from the bra, but it was even better to feel the hills and valleys of his chest against hers. As they kissed, his hands slipped once more into the back of her underwear and he grabbed her ass.

A small giggle escaped Astera's lips as she realized that, beyond a doubt, Henri was definitely an ass man. She wasn't going to complain, though. She liked his hands there. He used the position to slide her panties down and Astera stepped out of them when they fell to the floor. Returning the favor, Astera picked at the waistband of his underwear and started pulling them down too, eager to get into the shower so she wouldn't have to worry about turning him off with the lingering scents of their mission.

As soon as she freed him from his underwear, Henri seemed to pick up on what she wanted. He slid the shower door open before backing into the wider than normal stall. The shower head was more akin to something one might see in the Core Worlds. Ship showers minimized excess water on the body to save on wastewater. This one seemed more of a luxury than a utility. That luxury was evident when the door slid closed behind Astera and the water switched on over their heads. "Perks of the rank," Henri whispered, smiling against her lips.

Astera let out an appreciative sigh. "Damn ... I should become a commander. This is amazing," she said as the water streamed over her head and down her back. She leaned away from him just enough to let it cascade between their bodies as well.

Henri walked his gaze down her body, taking it all in. The expression of raw appreciation on his face made her breath catch in her throat. "I'd rather you didn't. Only way to be commander is to start your own company," he warned playfully. "Which means you wouldn't be around to share this particular shower with me."

He may have been teasing her, but Astera was good enough at reading people to hear the question hidden in that statement. Hearing it only made her want him more. "You're willing to share your water ration on more than one occasion?" she asked, keeping humor in her own reply, because the thought of asking if he wanted to see her again outright terrified her.

Gently pushing some wet hair back off her face, he said, "Only if you choose to come by. My door will always be open for you."

Astera's knees went weak, and she rested her palms on his chest to help keep herself steady. She pressed her cheek against his palm. "I would like that."

Henri smiled before kissing her again, this time with more tenderness and care. His held her waist, keeping her close as he walked her back and pressed her against the wall. His hands slid around to her front, gently sliding up her stomach to caress her breasts, as she traced her fingers down her side and slipped them between their bodies. "Not yet," Henri whispered, taking her hands in his and sliding them up along the shower panels behind her. "I want to concentrate on you."

If Astera wasn't already slick with need, she would have been made so immediately by the promise in his words. Henri used one of his hands to pin both of hers above her head. "Is this okay?"

"Yes." Astera knew she should have felt vulnerable, being naked and pinned to the wall like that. Even though Henri was much stronger than her, she was confident he would let her go immediately if she asked him to. But she didn't want to ask for that. She wanted nothing more than to feel his body on hers. In hers.

Pressing herself against Henri, Astera caught a quick smirk as he leaned in and nipped at her earlobe. He then peppered kisses down her neck as he trailed his free hand down her body. Slipping easily under the back of her knee, he lifted her leg up and guided it to hook around his hip. With it held up and out of the way, he traced his way down the back of her thigh until his fingers brushed her intimately. Despite all the calluses and rough skin, Henri seemed to know how to touch her gently enough to draw out her pleasure.

"Oh, Henri ..." she muttered, feeling his touch shiver all the way up her spine.

"More like this?" he asked, his hand still lazily caressing her. He seemed to enjoy the reactions he pulled from Astera as she arched off the wall of the shower stall.

"More, please." The words spilled from her as his finger-tips sent ripples of pleasure through her. Henri continued to explore, tease, and tantalize her further. He didn't seem to be rushing her to a climax. With her hands pinned above her head, Astera was unable to touch him and return the favor. The position served as a wonderful reminder that all Astera needed to focus on was luxuriating in her own pleasure.

Astera lost track of time, but somewhere in the space between moans, she felt Henri's fingers slide down her slit and press against her entrance. He pulled back, lips moist from kissing her shower-soaked neck. "May I?" he asked, fingers poised and ready to move at her request.

"Void, please," she panted, her hips bucking against his hand.

Everything he did just made Astera want more. When his fingers pushed inside her, she cried out. She instinctively pushed her hips down against him, and she leaned forward to kiss away that somewhat smug smile he wore as he knew what he was doing to her.

Henri seemed to take that kiss as a good sign and he redoubled his efforts. Not only using his fingers, but his thumb as well, to stimulate Astera more and more. His lips landed back on her neck as he upped his pace, bringing her to greater and greater heights seemingly effortlessly.

The dedication Henri showed to making Astera feel good was a rush in and of itself. In the fleeting moments where she remembered that a whole universe existed outside the sensitive strains of her own pleasure, she'd open her eyes and become enraptured by the way Henri watched her, how he seemed perfectly content to please her, even if he wasn't being pleasured himself.

He was good at it, too. It wasn't long before each thrust or stroke of his fingers added a new layer of ecstasy to the growing climb, and her hips bucked against his hands of their own accord. She writhed against the wall, wrists twisting in his grip, but not trying to escape, as she got closer and closer to her peak. "Henri ... I'm so close," she panted, warning him, giving him a chance to stop if he needed to.

"Then let it out," he said simply. His face was the picture of sensual determination as he played her body like a musician played a finely tuned instrument, and brought her to a crescendo.

Astera lost all control of herself. She didn't know what she said, or how she moved. All she knew was how she felt.

And she felt good.

Coming down was a whole other experience. Panting hard she sagged against his grip on her wrists. Her entire body sizzled with aftershocks of her orgasm, snapping along her veins like jolts of electricity. There were so many thoughts racing through her mind as she came back to herself, but there was only one that she could seem to find words for. "I want you inside me ... please."

"I will be soon, but really we haven't used the shower yet." Henri kissed her softly.

Grabbing the washcloth from the rack in the corner, he used the dispenser in the wall to pour some body wash on it. When it was thoroughly soapy, Henri spent the next half hour tenderly washing every square inch of Astera's body, stealing reverent, tender kisses along the way. As he moved, he would use the suds to clean himself, too. Even though she had caught sight of just how hard he was, he didn't use the shower as an excuse to grind up against her. It was all about letting her feel just how nice it was to have his hands caressing her body. It was the most patient, sensual string of touching Astera had ever encountered, and it made her feel so valued.

Henri finished washing Astera just moments before the water shut off, signalling that even he didn't get unlimited shower time. Astera cupped his cheek and drew him in closer for a kiss. She enjoyed the feeling of their bodies pressed together, but it wasn't long before the suction of the exhaust in the bathroom took away the steam keeping them warm.

"Let's get dried off," she murmured, still utterly aware of the fact she had not yet given him anything in return for the plethora of attention he had lavished upon her. "I think I'd like to see if being Commander gets you a better bed, too."

"Oh, it's a pretty great bed," Henri said, sliding the door open. Stepping out, he pulled two towels from the locker that served as his linen closet. They weren't very big, but more than absorbent enough. He gave one to Astera, and the pair dried off quickly. When they were done, Henri came up behind Astera and wrapped his arms around her waist. His lips found her shoulder as he kissed her neck. "I didn't expect this when we dropped onto Baldalan," he admitted as he held her.

Astera leaned into him, turning her face to brush a kiss against his jawline. "Expect what?" she asked softly, not wanting to make any assumptions with someone in such a position of power.

"That we'd be here in my room together. I try not to think of my staff like this, but I can't help it with you," he admitted, one of the hands on her hips moved around, caressing her stomach, and sliding higher, his thumb stroking the underside of her breast in the most intoxicating manner. "After we spoke in that cave, I can't help but want to get to know you better. I have a feeling, from the way you called out on the comms, that you might feel the same way."

The caress of his breath against her skin was enough to have her feeling dizzy all over again. She turned around in his embrace and kissed him. After a moment, she pulled back enough so that her lips rested against his. "Hearing that explosion, thinking something had happened to you ..." She grasped at his shoulders as she took a step back towards the door. "I couldn't bear the thought of something happening to you. Not when you were the first person who I could ever be truly honest with." She stole another kiss. "And who was honest with me."

Astera stepped back again, this time peeling her body from his as she took his hand and led him into the bedroom.

She walked all the way over to the edge of his bed before pulling him closer again and looked into his eyes as she slid her hands down his chest. Lower, and lower, until she settled one palm on his hip and wrapped the other around the hardness that had been pressed between them.

"Is it okay for us to do this?" she asked quietly. "You said that you try not to think of your staff like this. Are you sure you won't regret it?"

"That depends. Are you here with your Commander or with Henri?"

The fact that he even asked showed Astera that he, like her, was used to people being more interested in his image than in him as a person. "Henri," she replied without hesitation. "Definitely Henri." She stole a quick kiss and stroked his length, before adding with a smirk, "Don't get me wrong, I like the commander, but he can be a little bossy sometimes," she teased, wanting to ease some of the growing seriousness.

Henri's smile slipped away slowly as her hand moved. His eyes closed a blink at a time as his head tipped back. "You'll have to forgive him, the commander's been under a lot of stress lately," he answered, voice infused with a low thrum of need.

"Oh, I imagine so." She chuckled softly, kissing his neck after he bared it to her. "I'm sorry to be the cause of some of that. Hopefully you'll let me make it up to you?" She turned him around so that his back was to the bed. She kept moving her hand on him, finding every sound and movement he made encouraging.

"It might take a while, but I'm sure I'll find it within myself to forgive you," Henri kept the banter going, even as he swelled and pulsed in Astera's grip.

"I'll be sure to make the most of the opportunity," Astera promised, letting go of him for a moment so she could use both hands to gently press against his chest and get him to sit on the edge of the bed. She then resumed the slow, teasing stroke from before.

Even with what they had done in the shower, he was patient and willing to let her guide her own actions. It was not something she was used to, and the sense of control was heady. "Fuck ... you're already so hard," she whispered between kisses as she wedged her legs between his knees to stand closer to him.

"It tends to happen when I get to pleasure and wash a gorgeous naked woman in the shower." Henri leaned back to rest on his hands. He watched her stroke him before looking into her eyes. He didn't say much more, giving her time and space to do as she pleased.

"That is fair, I suppose." The compliment in his words warmed her. She slowly sank to her knees between his legs, dragging her lips from his cheek, down his neck, over his shoulders, and traveling farther down his chest. All the while, she let her hand glide up and down his length, watching him to gauge his reactions. He didn't move to rush her lower at any stage. If anything, he seemed more than content to let her explore.

Astera ran her hands over his body to better learn the shape of it, just like he had done with hers in the shower. She allowed herself time to let her lips and tongue learn the taste of his skin, and when she reached the hardness in her fist, she tasted that, too. As Astera's mouth explored, a groan slipped from Henri and his shaft throbbed against her tongue.

It was quite a novel and arousing situation for Astera, because every time she pulled a reaction from Henri, it made her own need grow. When she looked to his face, all he did was smile. He moved his arms to rest on his elbows as she took him deeper in her mouth, getting a better angle to watch.

Keeping that line of eye contact, Astera moaned around him, and rested her hands on his thighs as she started to move up and down his length, experimenting with pressure and speed, and feeling a rush of excitement every time she earned a new sound of relief, or when his fingers grasped at the sheets beside him.

"That feels amazing," Henri said between panted breaths. The huskiness in his words made Astera's core twitch, and a jolt of arousal zapped through her. She moaned, and he twitched in her mouth.

With a sudden, undeniable sense of need, Astera pulled off him and looked into his eyes. She got to her feet and stepped back, guiding his legs closed so that she could crawl onto the edge of the bed. She claimed his mouth as she straddled his hips and settled down against him, pressing his slick member between their bodies. "I'm sorry. I need to feel you," she whispered, hoping he wouldn't hold it against her as she ground her hips in slow, purposeful circles.

"Do whatever you need to do," Henri whispered, laying flat on the bed. As she moved, Henri slid his hands down her back to rest on her ass. He clutched at her, using his grip to just hold her, rather than to position, or shift, her hips.

"I think your hands have found a new favorite spot." She smiled as she leaned down, sucking and nibbling at his collarbone.

"Indeed ... it's so nice and grabbable," he teased back. He shifted up so that he could steal a deep, sensual kiss. When he finally pulled away, he looked into her eyes, "Keep going, please."

That simple request sent a thrill through Astera. It was a sign that he needed something too, that she was doing something right. She gladly obliged, sucking more intently at his skin as she moved her hips enough for Henri's tip to catch at her entrance. She looked down at him, making sure this was what he meant.

"I've had the twist." Henri jutted his chin towards the place where their bodies were nearly joined as he referred to the temporary procedure some men had to prevent accidental pregnancies. He reached up and brushed a thumb over her cheek.

Astera leaned into his touch, grateful for the knowledge. "I'm on birth control, too."

Henri moved his hand down to cup her breast, and he brushed that same thumb over her nipple. "Then don't stop until you're satisfied."

Astera didn't need to be told twice. She pushed her hips down and moaned as she took him inside her. She kept going until he was fully sheathed, and she rested her hands on his chest, catching her breath at the sudden, delicious fullness. She was drawn back into the moment as Henri toyed with her nipple. She bucked her hips, earning a grunt from him that made sure she did it again, and again, and again.

Even though he was pinned down by her hips, Henri was never still. He kept his hands busy, massaging, and teasing Astera's body in ways that heightened her own pleasure. Even as his own moans became more desperate, he let her guide the pace. There was no sense that he just wanted to take over, to finish things off for himself. He seemed to enjoy watching her as she started to bounce on him, and when she fell forward against him to get a better angle, his lips found her ear.

"That's it, Astera," he urged, nipping at her earlobe. "Keep going. Don't ever hold back around me. Feel it with your whole body."

Astera was not used to hearing that. Pleasure was never really part of sex when she was married and, more recently, it was an afterthought. This was different, though. Henri had ensured she was taken care of before he even got close to getting anything for himself. Even now, he was urging her to see to her own needs.

Words failed Astera, so she showed her gratitude with a deep, passionate kiss. She moaned into his mouth as she found just the right bounce and grind to take advantage of how sensitive she still was. She closed her eyes and rested her head on Henri's shoulder as she gave herself permission to enjoy the climb.

Astera wasn't sure how long it took, but it soon became clear that her peak was inevitable. Henri pressed his lips to her cheek and muttered words of encouragement, imploring her to let go. It was just what she needed to hear to let a second orgasm course through her.

When her own movements faltered in the peak of her pleasure, Henri gently held her hips and kept moving until her moans turned to whimpers. He kissed her flushed neck and shoulders as she caught her breath.

"Can we change position?" Henri ran his hands down her back, grasping her ass again. She nodded, her hair brushing against him. He held her hips close to his, and with a buck and a twist, he rolled her onto her back.

"You were right," Astera panted as she sank into the mattress. "This bed is amazing."

Henri chuckled as he sucked at the tight skin over her collarbone. "I'd like to think what happens in the bed is even better." Then, all amusement fled her mind as he started to move.

The motion of Henri's hips was so well controlled, so practiced. She wrapped her arms around his shoulders and relished how each movement drove them closer together. His lips found hers again, and as they kissed, he slipped his hands under her hips and moved her farther up the bed so he could shift onto his knees. The angle made Astera cry out as it hit all her sensitive parts. When she looked up, she saw a satisfied grin on his face as he hit that spot over and over again.

"Come again for me," he whispered, nipping at her neck. "The sounds you make when you come turn me on so much."

The compliment sent a thrill of desire through her, and Astera gave him what he was asked for. As her peak approached, Henri reached up, planting his hand against the wall above his bed, using the leverage to really drive into her. He grunted at the shift, and soon he joined her, pulling out and using his free hand to finish, spilling his seed over her stomach.

Astera was still in the midst of coming down as Henri collapsed onto the bed. He slid an arm under her shoulders and drew her against his side, pressing a soft kiss on her forehead as his hand floated down to caress her hip.

Astera wished she could linger there longer, but she was acutely aware that they were in Henri's room. The reality of what they had done hit her, and the last thing she wanted to do was overstay her welcome. He had said his door would open for her, but that did not mean he wanted her to hang around for prolonged periods of time. "I should clean up, let you get some rest." She sat up, hating that the moment had to come to an end.

CHAPTER 31

HENRI EYES WERE ALREADY DRIFTING SHUT in the warmth of his afterglow when he felt Astera shifting and drawing away from him. He lifted his head, incredulous of the words she was saying. It was hard to justify them against what they just shared. While it made sense on some level for her not to be spotted leaving his quarters in the morning, Henri didn't really care.

"Do you have to leave? I'd much rather you stay," he offered, sitting up and leaning on his hand as he watched Astera trying to slide out the side of the bed.

Astera paused, the sheets had fallen far enough off her body that Henri had a full view of her naked back, complete with all its bruises and scars. Reminders of their shared vocation, and perhaps more. "You don't have to say that just because of what we did," she replied, her voice soft.

"I know." He slid closer to her and wrapped his arms around her waist. He pressed his bare chest against the roadmap of trauma on her back. Her muscles were tense, even as he brought his head up beside hers. "But I want to." He kissed her shoulder.

With a soft breath, she relaxed against him. She turned her face and he caught sight of the smallest hint of a smile. "If you're sure."

"I wouldn't have asked you to join me if I was going to make you leave right after." He hugged her tighter. "Come back to bed."

"I'll clean up and be right back, I promise." She kissed his cheek before slipping from his arms. For a moment, her hand lingered on the blanket folded on the end of his bed, as if she might pluck it up and wrap it around herself, but then she stood up without it and walked to the bathroom, giving him a full view of her body from behind as she went.

Henri smiled to himself as the moment passed. It was a sign that she wasn't ashamed of her past, or herself, around him. He heard the tap turn on in his bathroom, so he fluffed the pillows and neatened the sheets to make things more comfortable for them both. He slipped under the covers and fought off the urge to sleep while he waited for Astera.

Luckily, it wasn't long before Astera emerged from the bathroom. She had the robe he kept on a hook in the bathroom wrapped tightly around her as she walked over. He liked seeing his robe on her and appreciated it even more knowing her naked skin was against the fabric.

Astera's expression was tentative as she approached, and when she got to the bed, she plucked at the tie around her waist and let the garment drop off her shoulders. She caught it before it slithered to the ground and draped it over the edge of one of his bedside tables. He lifted the sheets for her, and she slid in with him, laying close enough that he could feel the heat radiating off her skin as she laid on her side to face him. "I'm glad you got to the ship safely today," she said, tracing her fingers over his jawline and sending shivers down his spine.

The tenderness in her words warmed his heart. "Me too,"

he whispered as he drew her closer. Even in the heat of the battle, he wasn't too concerned about his own safety, but after hearing things from her point of view at the debriefing, he could understand why she was worried. "Come on, let's get some sleep," he said, hoping the intimacy would help her push aside the memories and rest. He laid on his back and guided her to lay her head on his chest. He gently kissed her hair and breathed in the sweet, fresh scent of her. He closed his eyes and relished the feeling of having a warm, naked body against his as he drifted off to sleep.

It had been years since Annalise stayed the night.

Annalise ...

Henri winced, the sleepiness lifting as his mind conjured an image of his beautiful friend. Everything had happened so fast that he hadn't thought about what this might mean for them and their relationship. It had been a mostly sexual and an intimate friendship, but they both knew it would never go further. They wanted different things. He'd never brought up the possibility of moving on to someone else because it never occurred to him that he would want anyone but her. Now, he'd done something so out of character. He did something without a plan. Without thought of the consequences. This was exactly why he avoided such impulsivity.

Even as he kicked himself for his rashness, Henri was surprised guilt didn't accompany his frustration. He'd have loved to handle the situation better, but what he shared with Astera was not about mere gratification. He knew that as he looked down at her pink hair splayed out across his chest. They had both learned enough about each other over the past few days that the interest and attraction was genuine, and the time they had just spent together was something he needed more than he had known. That kind of self indulgence wasn't something he chose for himself often, which was why his arrangement with Annalise worked so well in his mind. He didn't have to worry about entanglements that would complicate things in the company, and both he and Annalise could have their needs met safely.

He'd have to talk with Annalise at some point, preferably before she found out about he and Astera some other way... or before she dropped by for one of their regular sessions.

Even with all those thoughts roiling in his head, Henri was able to disconnect and fall asleep quickly. Pilots with any significant experience could do the same; sleep was such a precious commodity on the battlefield, they couldn't afford to spend hours trying to drift off.

Another commonality between pilots was that they were often ready to jump into action at the sound of loud noises. It was this trait that had Henri out of bed and pulling up his pants before he realized he was awake. It took a moment for the pounding on his door to filter through the haze of his rousing consciousness. The chime of the door comms panel rung intermittently with the knocks and made him groan.

"I'm up," he yelled, "I'm up, just hang on a Void-damned second." He made sure his fly was aligned and fastened his pants before he jogged over to the door, not bothering with a shirt. He slammed his hand against the panel and it opened. "What?" he snapped at whatever poor soul was waiting there. He knew he should have been less abrupt, but his head was pounding, and he wasn't sure he had even gotten more than half an hour of sleep.

Johansen froze, arm poised for another violent knock. Beside her, Zhang looked as though he was about to faint. He snapped to attention, turning to Henri and wincing.

"I'm sorry, Commander. I tried to suggest we wait until you woke–" Zhang spluttered.

Johansen waved a hand to shut him up. "Starfall is missing," she snapped, apparently not wanting to waste any time. "None of my scouts have seen her. I even checked in with that Ops kid ... what's his name? Endle?"

"Eggles, ma'am," Zhang provided, earning him a disparaging look from the leader of the scouts.

"Eggles. He hasn't seen her yet, either. I spoke to La Plaz, he said she finished up the debriefing, but no one has spotted her since. He told me to check with you." Johansen finally stopped to take a breath.

"She's on the ship, Sergeant. She made it back here. I'm sure she's fine," Henri started, manually sliding the door partially closed on himself. He wasn't sure how good of a view they had of the bed from the door, but he'd rather the crew not find out what happened this way.

"This ship is huge and, quite frankly, parts of it are dangerous." Johansen was always the type to argue against vague assurances. "She's lost a friend and colleague recently, and has just come back from an intense mission. I know Starfall. It isn't like her to disappear on us. I'm concerned, Commander."

"Did you stop to think she needed time for herself? I was on that mission with her, Sergeant, and La Plaz must have mentioned that it got emotional for her down there. Just give her some space. I'm sure she will turn up. In the meantime, I'll have the Engineering staff make sure the utility crawl spaces and hazard areas are clear. Good enough?" he asked, lying in hopes to placate her while he tried to avoid looking back into his quarters as he heard shifting.

"Henri ... what's wrong?" Astera's voice floated over, her tone somewhat dazed and still clogged with sleep. There was the whisper of sheets along the floor as she padded closer.

Henri's eyes shut as soon as he heard her. Dropping his head, he stepped back, giving the other two a chance to see who had spoken. After a defeated breath, he lifted his head and looked at Johansen. "You can probably call off that search now," he said dryly.

"Oh." The single word had to be the shortest sentence Henri had ever heard Johansen utter. Zhang, meanwhile, sounded as though he was choking.

"I trust that the two of you will keep the commander's business to yourselves?" Henri looked back and forth between the stunned visitors.

"Of course, Commander. Yes, of course," Zhang promised quickly. Thinking back, Henri realized the young man never saw women in his room before. His shock was also a good reminder that Henri was going to need some new boundaries in place with his assistant if this thing with Astera continued.

Johansen wasn't as easily distracted, and she was far too protective of her pilots to just let it go. She tilted her head so she could look right past Henri, even though she was an old colleague and one of the OGs. "Are you okay, Starfall?" Something in Johansen's posture reminded Henri of a fierce lioness, just waiting for its prey to twitch so it could pounce.

"Yes." Astera stepped forward to position herself slightly behind Henri's shoulder. "I'm good. This was my choice, Greta." The sleepiness that previously suffused her voice had dissipated.

The clarity and determination in Astera's response was enough to ease the coiled tension in Johansen. She ran a hand through her black hair and shook her head. "Void, Starfall. I thought ... actually, it doesn't matter what I thought." She shook her head and turned her attention to Henri, her dark brows shifting into a sharp "v," her lips pursed. "I know you're the commander and all Henri, but I'm telling you now ... if anything happens to my girl, I'll hold you accountable."

"That's why I put you in charge of the scouts, Greta." A

smile curling Henri's lips, despite Johansen's intense stare. "Trust me, I know there's a line of people waiting to pummel me if I screw this up, all right?"

"You're damn right there are. So, make sure you don't screw it up," Greta replied, but the bite in her words was gone. She looked past him again. "And Starfall? I still expect to see your ass in training in the morning. No slacking off, even if you are—" she stopped herself in a rare moment of showing that she actually possessed a verbal filter, and waved vaguely between Astera and Henri. "Well ... this. Now get some proper rest. You'll need it."

Johansen turned and started walking down the hall, but her steps halted as she cast Henri's assistant an annoyed, derisive glare. "For the sake of everything good in the Void, stop gawking Zhang."

"Uh, yes. Sorry, Sergeant. Sorry, Commander," he said before racing after the leader of the scouts.

Henri sighed as the pair walked back toward the Ops section, probably to tell La Plaz to stand down the search party. Pulling the door closed and locking it, he turned to her. "Not ideal, but not the worst ..."

Astera winced. "I'm sorry," she said, focusing on the ground. "I was still half asleep. I should have stayed quiet in bed. I wasn't thinking straight. I just heard the concern in Johansen's voice and reacted."

Seeing her instinctual response, Henri took her in his arms. Drawing her head to rest on his chest, he stood there with her, rubbing her back gently. "Please don't feel you need to apologize. I should have been more careful about opening the door for them. Also, I don't want you to start thinking that what we did was wrong. We just did things a little out of order." Henri couldn't help a light chuckle at the absurdity of the situation.

"You can say that again." Astera laughed, but her amusement was short lived as she sucked in a breath. "Oh, no ... poor Martin." The guilt in her voice was tangible.

Henri sighed, not enjoying that particular reminder. "Would you like me to go with you when you talk with him?" he offered, watching her reaction to make sure she felt safe having that conversation.

She shook her head. "Thanks for offering, but no. I owe it to him to speak to him in private."

"I understand. We can talk about it after—"

Henri's words were cut off by a chime from the comm screen in his room. Normally, it was muted except for urgent messages. After Zhang and Greta stopped by, however, he assumed it was someone in Ops with an update about the search for Astera. "One sec, I'd better deal with this." Henri let her go and crossed his room in a few purposeful strides.

He stood directly in front of the camera lens to shield Astera from view and activated the wall-mounted panel to see the major staring back at him. "Ah, La Plaz, I assume Johansen found you?"

"No sir, that's been settled. Some news came across the Net that I think you'll want to hear," La Plaz answered. Even on the display, Henri could tell from the set of the older man's jaw that he was concerned about whatever it was.

Closing the video feed from Ops, Henri opened the report the major had forwarded to him. He scanned the summary, wondering why it would cause the unflappable head of his Intelligence branch such distress. That was, until Henri read the location data on the missive.

Baldalan.

"What in the Void? Are people already reporting on what we did?" Henri muttered to himself as he scrolled down the page. As he did, it soon became clear that the report was about Samson's Heavy Brigade, not the Triple C. Henri's eyes widened as he read the casualty list. Between the pilots listed as killed in action and missing, it was enough to account for the entire complement of the company.

"Samson, how did you let that happen?" Henri asked rhetorically, wondering how they ran the operation in such a way that allowed for their entire company to be wiped out in less than a day. It also occurred to him that, if he and Astera had not gotten out when they did, their names might have been on a list like this, too.

Henri tried to keep reading the casualty report to figure out what had happened, but a voice call from La Plaz interrupted him again. "Commander?"

"Go ahead, Major," Henri answered, still stunned.

"Sorry, Commander, but we're getting a distress signal from the jumpship for Samson's Heavy Brigade," La Plaz reported dispassionately, probably annoyed that they had declined the offer of information that might have saved so many lives.

"Put it through." Henri grabbed a fresh shirt from a nearby drawer and pulled it on.

The screen scrambled as the feed shifted to the high distortion signal from the jumpship in distress. Henri could only make out a few words: "pursuit," "enemy," "fighters," and "pirate." Henri did his best to clean up the audio, working with the Ops division through the major. As he did, another signal broke through the distress signal, overriding it with higher power.

"This is Captain Kilgrove, commanding the jumpship Void Maker. Baldalan is under my jurisdiction. Any ships approaching, or attempting to land, will be destroyed utterly, and without hesitation. The near complete destruction of

Samson's Heavy Brigade is just a small sample of our attack capacity. This is your first and only warning."

"Regis ..."

The single horrified word tore Henri's attention away from his comms unit. He whipped around to find Astera sitting on the edge of his bed. She was as pale as the sheet she clutched to her chest, and her whole body shook enough to make the fabric ripple. Henri crossed the room in three long strides and sank down to his knees in front of her, resting his hands on her shoulders.

"Astera?"

Her wide eyes met his. "We have to run," she said, the words desperate, almost frantic. "The Latagarosh has no hope against the Void Maker. We need to hide. We have to do something, Henri, he won't—"

"Hey, hey ..." Henri pulled her against his chest. "Astera, it's fine. I don't intend to return to that quadrant."

A burst of static filled the room. Henri had seen Astera's panic and responded immediately, completely forgetting that his audio channel was open, and that he was still on a call with La Plaz.

It wasn't La Plaz who spoke, though. It was the cool, calculated voice of Captain Kilgrove that continued. "The Voidstalkers also wish to offer a final warning to the company that sought to destroy our operations. Triple C, we do not take your interference lightly. We will be seeking retribution. Captain Regis Kilgrove, out."

Astera's trembling intensified. Henri looked back over his shoulder, in the direction of his comms unit, so it would pick up his voice more clearly. "La Plaz, are you still there?"

"Yes, Commander," La Plaz replied without hesitation. Henri realized the major probably heard every word that passed between himself and Astera. Yet another person who now knew about them. Well, La Plaz had probably already figured it out, given the fact he sent Johansen directly to Henri's quarters ... but that was a problem he would deal with later.

Right now, he had more important matters to deal with.

"Maintain course for Grendina. Forward a recording of the first part of that comm message to the various warp corridor companies; they need to be aware that there is a pirate jumpship out here. Also, see if we can schedule a meeting with the reps from Armitage Limited as soon as we arrive. We need to upgrade our weapons systems as a priority. Over and out."

Those last three words were recognized by the system, and the audio channel closed. Henri sighed in resignation as he rested his chin against Astera's hair. He couldn't help but marvel at just how swiftly a supposedly simple contract had derailed the future of the Triple C.

TO BE CONTINUED...

IF YOU ENJOYED THIS BOOK...

Reader reviews are crucial for helping indie authors share their stories with the world. If you enjoyed The Voidstalker Extraction (Triple C Reports: Book One), please consider leaving a review on one of the following sites:

GOODREADS

AMAZON

If you would like more news, updates, sneak peeks, and bonus content, visit:

www.shipitpublishing.com

@ShipItPublishing on Instagram and Facebook.

@ShipItPub on Twitter.

If you wish to contact the authors, they would love to hear from you. You can email them at:

contact@shipitpublishing.com

livevans@shipitpublishing.com

jaythomas@shipitpublishing.com

CPSIA information can be obtained
at www.ICGtesting.com
Printed in the USA
BVHW051155061222
653543BV00017B/141